THE GAMES PEOPLE PLAY

The Games People Play

Gary Thacker

1889 books

Copyright © Gary Thacker 2020

All rights reserved

The moral rights of the author have been asserted.

Cover Artwork © Nathan Bennett www.nathanbennett.com

www.1889books.co.uk

ISBN: 978-1-9163622-3-9

For My Beautiful Princess Dolores

Dream

As far back as Jon Moreton could remember, he had always wanted to be a professional footballer. As with so many other aspiring hopefuls having a sprinkle of magic in their feet and stars in their eyes, it just hadn't happened for him. No one had ever approached him or his parents after any game and introduced himself as a scout for any club, big or small. Not particularly big or robust in stature, he was the wiry but sinuous athlete. He had ability, was strong enough, big enough and quick enough, but did all that add up to *enough*?

After leaving school he had joined Ridgeway FC, a local amateur club, and quickly progressed to the first team. It was a decent level of football. For Moreton however, the major attraction was their player development structure. The club both encouraged, and sponsored, players to pursue coaching qualifications. For anyone with Moreton's attitude to learning and aptitude for how the game was played, it was an ideal opportunity. He had swiftly passed through the Level One and Two courses and, shortly after his nineteenth birthday, gained his UEFA B Certificate. He was the youngest player at Ridgeway ever to have done so, and the club used his talents to coach some of the players who rarely played for the first team.

Particular among this group was Charlie Broome. Although the same age as Moreton, and friends since school days, they were very different, both with regard to character and background. Moreton was from working-class stock, whereas Charlie Broome had enjoyed a more privileged background. Charlie was the son of Bobby Broome, owner of Broome Interiors, Ridgeway's main sponsor and benefactor of the club. Broome senior had mortgaged his home to fund his enterprise, neglecting to ask, or even inform, his wife. It was one of a number of guilts that would later haunt him. It did, however, turn out to be a sound investment. With a natural aptitude for business, Bobby Broome had recognised the mistakes of his previous employers and, backing his own judgement, proved that he knew how to make a business work efficiently. In a little over 20 years, Broome Interiors had grown into a successful regional business.

Bobby Broome was the archetypical local boy made good and to many in the town he was celebrated for rescuing the local professional football club, in addition to his interests in Ridgeway FC. It was something he had felt almost obliged to do: he was from the area and had the ability to save the club. Taking control when it was in danger of dropping out of the Football League entirely, and applying his commercial acumen, rather than any substantial financial support, Broome's intervention had turned the club's fortunes around. Relegation was avoided, and two years later, as the club established financial stability, it was promoted back to the third tier, where it had pottered along, hardly causing a ripple in the larger football pool.

Relentless dedication, regular late nights and time away from home, inevitably had costs, however: his family life inevitably compromised. It was not until he was thirty-nine that his son came along. Tragically, his wife died soon afterwards and, for so many reasons, some real, some only perceived through reflective guilt, Bobby Broome always felt apologetic towards his son, salving his regrets with a constant need to make up for lost time – and the loss of the boy's mother. Financial largesse often seemed the easiest, if not perhaps best, remedy for the ills of his soul.

Perhaps inevitably, but also unfairly, Charlie Broome had become the target for antagonistic banter among many of the other players at Ridgeway. The perception of him only being at Ridgeway because of his father's financial support was an easy path to follow. Especially if someone led you there, and many were more than willing to trail along for the ride – and the laughs. The running joke became that Broome should become the team's "sweeper," not so much in the sense of the player who covers the back line and initiates forward play, but the man who stands in the dressing rooms, with a brush cleaning it out after the game. His name made the jibe easy and it was a neat, if callous, way to keep someone in their place.

The prestige of Moreton at the club, offered a shield for his friend, but the barbs persisted in clandestine ways. Charlie Broome, at least on the surface, displayed a disinterested disregard to his accusers.

One evening, following a training session at Ridgeway, John Moreton's life would change forever. Called into the manager's office, he was introduced to a scout from a Premier League club who, it transpired, had been following up on reports of this talented, albeit late-developing player at the club. The chance he had waited so long for was suddenly there to be grasped. The following few months had flown by: visits to the club, trials and discussions with the manager and coaches. A short contract was offered and signed, with the potential to be extended should he be able to prove his worth. Despite having to play catch-up with players coming through from the club's academy, his talent shone through and he became a full-time professional footballer with a two-year contract.

Graduating through the levels of the club, his chance for first team action came in a midweek, home League Cup game. Two players had gone down with injury and there was an important league game the following Saturday. The manager had been reluctant to risk too many of his regular players, especially playing against a League Two team with a bit of a roughhouse reputation. It was a chance to rest some players and promote a few promising youngsters from the U21 team to test their mettle. Moreton would be on the bench. Number 34 on his back. Not for the U21s, but for the first team.

A scrappy game, with no goals at halftime, seemed to have stymied Moreton's hopes. With the second period underway, and the opposition team's legs tiring from increasingly forlornly chasing the ball, the goals had started to go in. At 3-0, the manager had told him to go and warm up. Jumping to his feet, he jogged up and down the sidelines, stretching his muscles. A shrill whistle and a wave of the hand called him back to the dugout. The manager had spoken to him. 'Be calm, son. Play your natural game. Keep it simple.' The ball drifted behind the home goal for a goal kick and up went the board. In bright green lights, shone the number 34. There had been thirteen minutes left of the game when he entered the field. Barely more than three of those had elapsed when he left it again.

He harried and scurried around when out of possession and looked for a pass when his team had the ball. It felt like the game was passing him by. The opposition were tired, but also now frustrated at being kept at arm's length and with little prospect of getting into a game that was, by now, surely lost. Then the ball came towards him. An opponent had played it too far ahead and Moreton saw the chance to gain possession and set up a counter-attack. He nipped in to slip the ball away and was already looking up field to pass the ball when a studs-up challenge caught him across the knee of his standing leg. He felt an unnatural popping sensation inside the joint and fell to the floor.

At first, there was no pain. All he could hear were the raucous shouts of the fans enraged at the challenge. Players milled around, swearing and pushing each other as the referee brandished the red card. His assailant stood over him and patted him on the shoulder in mock apology. He had looked down at the leg, now held firmly straight in front of him, as he cupped the swelling knee joint in his hands. Still no pain. Perhaps he had been lucky. Then he tried to bend the knee. Vivid colours washed over him in diagonally sharp angles of agony. It was pain like he had never known before, and he thought his knee was going to explode. He screamed out in agony.

On came the medical team with calm words and easing the knee straight again. For the next few minutes Moreton lay on the damp grass; the pain now at least bearable. He was placed on a stretcher with his legs strapped together, and he remembered the applause of the fans as he was carried out of the light into the darkness of the tunnel. An oxygen mask offered comfort, and a strange blurring of sensation and vision. He had enjoyed a mere three minutes and twelve seconds of time on the pitch. It would cost him three operations and long, torrid months of rehabilitation.

When you're at a football club, and injured, the medical staff are your only friends. Other players shy away from you, as if the condition was contagious. That's how it felt for Moreton anyway. The road ahead was full of warning signs. Danger ahead. No through road. Reduced speed limit. Worst of all was the one that said he may never get back to full fitness and football: diversion ahead. The whole world seemed to go on without him; so did the summer and the beginning of the next season. After hardly having a chance to make his mark in the team, he hadn't become the club's *forgotten* player. He was the player no one had even got to know.

Now it was time to get the strength back into the leg. Fifteen months and painful operations had passed since that dark day and his second season with the club was well past halfway through. It began to dawn on him that any chance of a new contract may evaporate before he could even get back onto the field. He was now twenty-three, no youngster any more. For the next couple of months, he would share his recovery time with a fellow traveller. Someone with whom he would form an unlikely bond.

Billy Swan was a forward in the sense of the classic number ten, with the boyish looks that did him little harm in pursuit of the opposite sex. It was an endeavour he took to with unhealthy zeal, given his profession. On the pitch, he was a throwback to the days when footballers developed their ability by kicking a ball around in the street. This was no product of some state-of-the-art academy facility that churned out battery hen footballers who knew all of the skills but had precious little practice in deploying them when it mattered most. Swan's footballing education had been accumulated on the "Hackney Marshes" parks around the East End of London. The school of hard knocks had taught him how to look after himself. The credo taught him to silkily avoid the roughhouse challenges of opponents and push himself when fame and finance was up for grabs.

Swan had joined the club three seasons ago, moving to the North-West from his native London, where he had played for three Premier League clubs, two of which had been relegated before selling him on. Blessed with outstanding talent, it was a gift that would always be denied its full flowering by an almost total disregard for the dedication and professionalism required to play at the top level. Despite this reticence to commit placing a restraining lid on the progress in his career, he had still won two full England caps. A paltry reward, given his talent, but an overly generous one given his application.

Playing football was merely a job to Billy Swan. Both his career and the transfers between various clubs, who were at first excited by the talent, and then disillusioned by the accompanying attitude, were driven by money. He would unashamedly tell anyone and everyone prepared to listen that, 'It ain't about the football. It's about the dosh!' Very much a product of his upbringing, here was man who had come through the ranks from humble beginnings, then been entranced by the things his new-found wealth could bring him.

His previous club had been relegated. The season had been a long struggle and Billy Swan was not the player you look to if the requirement is for dedication and application. At the end of the season, to no one's surprise the club were more than happy to cash in on him, and an offer to move out of London for the first time in his career arrived. After negotiating a deal that gave him an increase in wages, he signed.

The early months of his time with the new club had been filled with the sort of extravagant skills and goals that built his reputation but, as was so often the case, such days in the sun were eventually to lapse into more shaded times as the daily routine quickly became tedious, and, without the bright lights of the capital, boredom set in. Injuries, with time out of the team often magnified by a marked reluctance to return to action, became more and more frequent; although there were times when unavailability was genuine. Swan's reputation as a skilful exponent on the field often provoked a more cynical approach from less gifted opponents. A damaged ankle caused by a defender's disguised, but wholly intentional, stamp on the joint whilst Swan lay on the ground was the latest of these. It was also the reason why he was sharing a treatment room, and the attentions of the club's medical team, with Jon Moreton.

At the turn of the year, and with returns to action on the cards for both players across the next couple of months, the passage of time was an important factor for their futures. For Moreton, there was the desire to get back into action and prove that he was worth a place in the manager's plans. Billy Swan's contract was also running down. At the end of the season he would be thirty-five years old and out of contract. The club had an option to extend it for a further twelve months but that was unlikely to happen unless Swan could convince them to do so before the season ended. Alternatively, he would be an ageing former star with no club and limited opportunities. The situation brought the young, dedicated player and the ageing renegade into an unlikely partnership and, against all the odds, they developed a friendship born of sweat, suffering and shared aspirations. Each had the qualities that the other lacked, but neither envied the other's gifts, weaknesses or attitude. Combined they would have made a world-beating footballer, opposite sides of the same footballing coin. Misery likes company, or so the old adage goes, and Moreton and Swan were drawn closer together as the time went by at ever slower rates and their individual races to recovery drew to conclusion. By March, both were officially declared fit to return to training, but that was only a milestone on the journey. Although they had put in the hours in the gym to maintain fitness as much as possible, the difference between being fit and being match fit is substantial and not swiftly resolved.

As soon as Moreton began playing again, his mind was filled with doubts. There was always going to be a little pain as the joint came under pressure again, and it wasn't too bad. That's what he had told himself anyway. He needed to drive on. March drifted away, as the recovering players worked through seemingly endless and unrewarding training sessions. Now, as April began with no great end of season pressure on the club – perhaps they would get their chances.

The first game of the new month saw Swan on the bench for a home game against the season's champions-elect. It was hardly the sort of game many would have looked for as a comeback opportunity, but Billy Swan would never consider himself to be one of the many. Sitting behind the dugout with the other injured and reserve players, Jon Moreton felt an undeniable pang of envy as he watched his erstwhile companion-in-injury on the cusp of returning to action.

The game had not gone well. With hardly anything to play for, the team had been compliant, if hardly willing, victims for their opponents' swaggering confidence. Three goals down at home and with twenty minutes to play, Swan was sent on. By this time, the fans were resigned to losing against the club that had dominated much of the season. In this game, though, Billy Swan had a point to prove. The first time he received the ball, he elegantly skipped inside his marker before a step-over deceived the fullback. Driving into the area, a desperate tackle from behind may have just made contact with the ball, but Swan plunged to the turf and the referee awarded a penalty. Picking himself up, Swan collected the ball and placed it on the spot.

Penalties and Billy Swan. The result always seemed inevitable. 'Never missed one,' he would claim. 'Never. Not as a pro, not in my youth days, not even at school. Find any kid who ever played with me on the street or any park who said anything different and I'll call him a liar. Goalkeeper on the line. Twelve yards out and no defenders. Piece of absolute piss.' It was big talk but, in training or practice games, let alone first team action, Moreton could find no fault with the assertion, and no one ever stepped forward to gainsay Swan's braggart claims.

A feint in his run-up sent the goalkeeper sprawling to the right as Swan rolled the ball into the opposite corner. He collected the ball from the net and running back to the centre circle, waved his arms in exaggerated upward sweeps, apparently to try and encourage more support from the fans. This was Billy Swan, though, and he made sure that the manager had seen him and his apparent show of passion for the cause.

There were still ten minutes to go when he scored again. Collecting a pass, he glided into the area and past a defender before dropping his shoulder to sit the goalkeeper down and walk the ball into the net. It was the sort of skill that transfixed many a manager, causing them to gamble someone else's money and their own reputations on acquiring Swan's extravagant ability. There would be no more goals, but at the end of the game with the home fans chanting his name, Billy Swan had walked from the field confident that the new extended deal was in his pocket.

Seeing Moreton on the way back to the dressing room, he wrapped an arm around the younger man. 'Sorted,' he declared. 'How about that for the perfect performance?'

'Nearly,' Moreton replied. 'We still lost.'

'Bollocks to that. Bollocks to the game and who won. I scored twice and the crowd loved me. The contract extension is in the bag, mate. Back of the net, just like the ball!' He gave a little shimmy to Moreton in the way he had scored the second goal.

Jon Moreton's chance for redemption wouldn't arrive until the final home game of the season, as entry from the bench brought a fifteen-minute cameo. He had trotted onto the pitch for his second outing for the club's first team. His debut had lasted slightly more than three minutes. This time it would be ten. A couple of easy passes with the ball received and moved on to a team-mate eased him into the game. His concerns for the pain still present in his knee were tucked away out of sight, as he settled into the game. Then, a pass came to him with a defender at his back. He knew that if he let the ball run through his legs and spun after it, he would be clear.

As he looked to turn, the defender tried to intercept the ball, inadvertently standing on Moreton's foot. Already committed to the 180-degree rotation, the rest of Moreton's body turned quickly to chase the ball, whilst the foot remained pointing in the opposite direction. Something had to give and inevitably it was his knee. In that instant, as the pain arrowed to his brain from the damaged joint, Jon Moreton knew that his career as a professional footballer was over.

A different injury to the first one, but still serious enough to mean a few months out of action. No operation was required, but when the news came to him that the club were not going to offer him a new contract, it felt like his heart had been cut out. They would honour the end of his contract and still look after him, offering medical support. He would still be contracted as a professional footballer, but that was merely the legal definition. In everyone else's eyes, he was now an ex-professional footballer.

A few weeks later, as Moreton lay in the physiotherapist's room with the medical team working on him, Billy Swan had burst through the door. Both Moreton and the masseur working on his leg looked sharply up. Moreton was drawn to the anger on his long-time treatment room companion's face. He hadn't seen Swan since the day of the game when he had been injured. Now he was standing in the doorway shaking his head with rage. 'Bastards,' he fumed.

Moreton was initially puzzled. Unlike his first injury, this had merely been a matter of ill fortune.

'Bastards,' Swan repeated.

Moreton's analysis of Swan's profanity had been awry. In typical fashion, Billy Swan had been absorbed by his own situation to the total exclusion of anyone else's.

'They've released me. Brainless bastards.'

'No way, Billy,' Moreton said, conjuring up as much sympathy as his own situation would permit.

'That dozy idiot of a manager told me that he'd been instructed to trim the age of the squad.'

'I'm sorry, Billy.' Moreton had felt genuinely sorry for the man standing in front of him, who now seemed more like a lost small boy than a thirty-five-year-old man.

'Trim the age of the squad. More like trim the ability of the squad. Ah, bollocks to the lot of them. I hope their poxy club gets relegated. Then, turning to leave, he looked back at Moreton and smiled. It was the sort of expression that few were ever privileged to see on the face of Billy Swan. There was a genuine affection between them. 'I'm off. There's plenty of clubs that want to sign me. Look after yourself, kid. Always look after number one.' He slammed the door and stormed out.

The masseur had stayed quiet throughout the conversation, paying strict and over-avid attention to the leg in front of him. He shook his head, sighing. 'What a twat.'

Moreton half-smiled. 'What a waste,' he had been thinking. Neither Moreton or Swan knew it at the time, but fate would bring the two of them together again in four years' time.

Eventually Jon Moreton returned to the Midlands. The doctors had strongly advised against any even semi-serious attempt at resurrecting a playing career. Playing football had been the major element of Moreton's life up to that point, but he was mature enough to take the advice on board and, returning to Ridgeway turned his mind to coaching.

A Door Opens and Closes

By this time, bereft of his friend, Charlie Broome had drifted away from Ridgeway to join his father's business, but news of Moreton's ill fortune and return to Ridgeway filtered through to him. A few evenings later, during training at Ridgeway, a sleek black Porsche Boxster glided into the car park next to the training pitch where Moreton, in regulation sweatshirt, shorts and rolled-down socks that betrayed the scars around his right knee, was conducting a training session. The seductive purr of the car's engine always drew attention to the Porsche and particularly its driver, and Moreton's charges were hardly exempt from the auto envy as the car drew to a halt. As the door quietly opened, out stepped Charlie Broome.

His immaculate attire was in sharp contrast to that of Jon Moreton. A white open-necked shirt and blue designer jeans were rounded off by shoes that precluded any inclination to wear socks as they would distract from the exquisitely and expensively cut leather. Seeing Broome on the sidelines, Moreton jogged eagerly over towards his old friend.

'How's it going, Chaz? Crappy set of wheels. I'd have thought you could at least stretch to a Ford Fiesta!'

'Yeah, not bad, I suppose. I think I'll throw it away and get a new one when it gets dirty, though. I'm keeping the Ferrari in the garage. It's just for Sunday best, or when that night's girl warrants a bit of extra attention.'

Moreton slapped Broome on the shoulder in the sort of comradely way he found easy.

'Anyway,' said Broome, 'enough about me. How are things with you? I heard about the injuries, mate. Really bad luck. You deserved so much better.'

Jon Moreton bowed his head slightly. Sometimes people say that it's better to have loved and lost than never to have loved at all. Jon Moreton wasn't bitter about how things had turned out, but he was hardly convinced by the old adage either. 'Yeah, it was pretty shit,' he replied.

'What's your plan then?'

'I guess I'm here for a while. Not sure for how long. It would be great to stay in the game somehow. If I could find a job that would allow me to carry on coaching, that would be ideal.'

Charlie Broome nodded, slowly, puckering his lips as if in deep contemplation.

Moreton looked at him quizzically.

'I've been talking to the old man,' Broome revealed. 'We've been friends for a long time, and you were always a good mate to me here.' Broome cocked his head around, indicating the Ridgeway set up. 'So, I thought it was about time for a bit of payback. The old man is looking for a coach for the youth section at the club. Not this dog hole, the big club, and I thought you might be interested. Having an ex-pro coaching the kids and younger players would be good for the club. You'll have a decent wage coming in, a club car and there'll be all the bloody coaching you want. What do you think then, kiddo?'

'Chaz!' Moreton eventually blurted, searching for the first words he could reach. 'Chaz, that's fantastic! Are you sure? Your dad has signed off on this, yes?'

Broome nodded, and Moreton threw his arms around him. 'Thanks, mate. You're an absolute bloody gold-plated, five-star bloody hero.'

More than a little concerned that his designer wear was now contaminated with the sweat and detritus accumulated by Moreton's training session on the pitch, Charlie Broome eased himself back a little.

'Hang on, though,' he said with a note of caution in his voice, 'before you get too carried away. There's a catch.'

Moreton looked concerned, cautiously disentangling himself from the barely tepid response to his embrace. 'What catch?'

'You've got the UEFA B qualification, haven't you?' Broome enquired, although he knew the answer.

'Yeah. I did it here, years ago.'

'Well. The old man only wants coaches who are fully qualified. He's got big ideas for the club. You know what he's like. It's one of those: "if a job's worth doing" things that he's always banging on about.'

'He wants me to get my UEFA A badge?'

'Yeah, well… Yeah, he does. He definitely does. But that's not all.'

'Well, I've got my swimming certificate for completing two widths as well,' Moreton added trying not to sound sarcastic.

Charlie Broome had hardly noticed. 'Yeah, he wants you to get that other thing as well. You know the thing that all the top coaches have, so that you can work anywhere in Europe.'

'What? The Pro Licence? That lot will take years! The UEFA A is a couple of years, add on another one at least for the PL. I'll be fifty before I can start working there.'

'Ah, I forgot to mention something, didn't I?' A mischievous grin was now playing on his features. 'You see, the old man wants you to start straight away, and he'll let you have time off to get the qualifications. Paid of course. Not only that, he'll let you use the club's facilities for whatever you need. Oh, and there's something else as well. Now what was it?' Broome looked up as if searching his memory, delighting in keeping Moreton hanging on for the denouement. 'Ah, I've got it. So long as you don't try to hug me again! He'll also sponsor you to take the badges. He'll pick up the tab for everything.'

'Chaz,' he blurted out, recovering at least part of his composure. 'Are you serious? Really? That's amazing. It's… It's…' He threw himself onto his old team-mate, knocking him to the ground.

'Jon!' spluttered Broome, climbing back to his feet and dusting himself down. 'Do you know how much this pissing shirt cost?'

Moreton just laughed. 'Charlie Broome, you are diamond. You and your dad. Two diamonds. I can't believe it.'

'Well, believe it.' Broome replied, still wiping the dust from his now far less than pristine white shirt. 'So, what shall I tell the old man?'

'Hmm, tell him OK. I suppose I can give it a go,' Moreton replied, before feigning to jump on Broome again. 'Thanks, Chaz. I owe you big time.'

'No sweat,' Broome replied. 'It's just a bit of payback.'

Arriving for the first time as a coach at a professional football club, Jon Moreton made a beeline for Bobby Broome's office to thank him for the more than generous chance he had been given.

'It was all Charlie's idea. He told me how you had been a good friend to him and how things had turned out for you up north. It's a tough old game pro football, son. Charlie wanted to give you a helping hand. He said you deserved it. Mind you, I made it clear to him that this was no charity job. I'd be expecting you to get those qualifications and develop some good young players for me. If you mess up, mate of my lad or not, you'll be out on your ear.'

It was what Moreton had been expecting and indeed hoping to hear. He wasn't looking for any kind of sinecure. This was a real job.

The following few years passed quickly as Moreton threw himself into his new role. A couple of years down the line he hit the UEFA A target and then twelve months later became one of a very select few coaches holding a Pro Licence in the country under the age of thirty.

Things at the club were looking up too. Starting off with the youth players, Moreton's coaching ability and empathy with players had reaped dividends. He was bumped up the ladder and began working with the development squad, and handed the remit to produce players for the first team.

Into his fifth year with the club, Moreton had seen two of his players graduate to the first team. The sense of pride was capped a few months later when the club won promotion to the Championship. It was a time of great rejoicing, and things seemed to be heading on up, as Moreton's reputation as a young and innovative coach began to spread. Often though, the sun seems at its brightest just the rain arrives.

A few weeks into the close season, Moreton heard rumours that a group of Far East investors wanted to buy the club. Eventually, he managed to arrange a weekend meeting with Bobby Broome, who, unusually, had been spending time away from his office. Charlie too had been away for most of the past six months, apparently pursuing a business venture in Spain.

Walking into the club on a Sunday was a strange sensation. His steps echoed around the empty building as he walked up the stairs to the Chairman's office, and knocked on the door. Bobby Broome invited the coach in and sat him down on a long couch away from the desk, before settling down beside him.

'Look,' Broome began. 'I know what you want to ask me, so let me tell you the truth.

'I took on this club all those years ago because I wanted the town to have something to be proud of. We both come from this area and the people who live and work around here have precious little else to look forward to.' The older man now seemed full of empathy for his home town and those who lived there. 'So many of the old industries have gone. Businesses that had prospered here for decades, are now derelict shells. Jobs exported away to dirt cheap economies.

Fifty, even thirty years ago, people working in some of those businesses around here had jobs for life. That's all gone now. Look at the town centre. Where there used to be big name chain stores, all you see now is shops offering crap for a pound, and next door another shop offering the same crap for ninety-nine pence. There's a glut of burger shops selling crap food that feed the overweight kids who have nothing else to do but hang around on street corners or play computer games. At least flipping burgers gives some people a job I suppose, but where's the future in that? Some say the place is in decline. I don't know if there's much more declining it can stand. That's why I wanted to save the football club. Not for me, but for the town. For the people, but most of all for the kids, to prove to them there's still hope if you have a dream and are prepared to reach out and work for it. And you, Jonny boy, have helped me to prove that. You've brought kids with talent, but no guidance, under your wing. You've polished those rough diamonds and sent them on their way. And now we've took the club up a tier as well.'

It was an emotional speech, and one that Jon Moreton knew full well was packed with sincerity. Bobby Broome picked up on the theme. 'The thing is though, I'm getting older and what with Charlie chasing this Spanish project, he isn't here to help me run the business. This promotion thing is great for the club, but it'll just mean that things are only going to get more intense. I can't really run both the business and the club any more. I've done my bit and it's time to pass on the baton. The thing is, I've had an offer to take over things from me here. An investment group wants to buy the club. They've offered me big money, but between you and me – and don't ever tell anyone else this, especially Charlie – I told them to just give me half of the offer-money, so long as they plough the rest into investment at the club. We've shaken hands on a deal, but the lawyers are going to be drumming up a massive bill going through the fine print on the contracts.'

'That all sounds great,' Moreton replied, sensing that there was still more to come that Broome had been holding back on.

'The thing is though, they want to bring in this ex-player from Italy as manager and he wants his whole bloody entourage of coaches to come with him.' Then came the bad news. 'Jon, there won't be a place for you, when I'm gone. I told them to forget it. I wouldn't let them take over if they were going to get rid of any of the staff here. We argued about it and I even told them to clear off then, and pulled the plug on the deal. The thing is though, they're right. When I'm in charge, I want my people here. You and the other guys. When they take over, how can I blame them for wanting the same?' His eyes flicked up from the downcast manner he had adopted, looking at Moreton, quietly seeking his reaction.

'Look, Boss. I understand. It's the way the game is.' Then, pointing to a light at the end of the tunnel. 'This has been a great opportunity. I've loved working here over these past few years, but my name is getting known in the game now, and it's the ideal time for me to dive into the big wide world and see what's out there.'

The two men shook hands and Jon Moreton walked out of the club.

The Pitch

Two weeks later, Jon Moreton was sitting in a bar just outside the town centre, opposite Charlie Broome. The intervening time should have been spent pursuing opportunities, but, after experiencing a number of rejections, he had felt increasingly dispirited, and sad resignation had set in. A call from his friend about a potential opportunity had therefore arrived at precisely the right time.

'It looks like things have got a bit shitty again,' Broome suggested.

'Well, it was a bit of a shock when your dad told me. You know what they say, though, when one door closes, another one opens. I've been speaking to some people and I've got a few irons in the fire. It could actually work out really well for me,' he lied.

'OK, mate,' Broome nodded. 'Keep fingers crossed, eh? Do you want me to ask the old man to make a few calls for you? He's still got some friends in the game. You never know…'

Moreton cut him off. 'No: he's done enough for me and I've got a few contacts of my own.'

Broome again nodded in compliance although knowing it was a less than totally honest assessment. 'Anyway, enough about you. Let's talk about me and why I wanted to chat to you.'

Charlie Broome leant forwards as if to let his companion in on a big secret. 'Here's the situation: I've been wanting to strike out on my own for a while now. The old man is never going to let me have control of the business until he turns his toes up and I'm a young, ambitious guy. I want to make my mark. Yes, he lets me sit in on a few meetings and introduces me as his heir apparent, but this young prince is tired of waiting for the old king to pass on the crown.'

Moreton was a little taken aback by what he heard. The terms with which Charlie Broome was referring to his father suggested a lack of respect, let alone affection.

'So, I gave the old man a proposition. Let me prove to you that I can make money and then you can hand over the business and chill out.'

Moreton looked aghast at the suggestion. The words "Bobby Broome" and "chill out" simply did not belong in the same sentence.

'Ah, don't worry, I know what you're thinking. The old man was never going to agree to that. It was just my opening pitch, though. I had a plan, you see. I told him that we'd do it properly. You might not know this, but I own equity in Broome Interiors. The old man has 59% of the shares and Mom had 39%, but she left her shares to me in her will. The business's accountant holds the other 2% in trust. They get a dividend from the profits of the business, but are mandated to vote with the majority shareholder. It was the old man's way of ensuring that no one ever took control of the business away from the family. So, I told the old man that I'd offer him half of my shares as a guarantee against a loan. I wanted him to give me enough money to buy a business that I'd been looking at in Spain. He couldn't lose, could he? I'd agree a rate of return on the loan. If all went well, he'd get money from the interest and, if it didn't, he'd get another chunk of Broome Interiors stock. Plus of course, he'd see if little old Charlie Broome was up to the mark and could hack it in the big, bad world.'

Moreton was unsure how he should respond. 'OK,' he replied, just for something to say.

Charlie Broome smiled. 'There's a bit more, though, if I paid back the loan with interest, within the agreed timescale, the old man would then have to agree to sell me 10% of his shares, at the same price as the loan, making us equal partners.

'I know what you're thinking,' he said, taking a sip of his drink. 'But it's fine. It's just to show the old man that I'm ambitious. Deep down, I'm sure he bloody loves it to be honest. He's seeing that I've got drive and an eye for opportunity. I think that's what made him agree to the deal in the first place. The papers are all set to sign, but before I can go ahead, I need to add one final piece to the jigsaw.'

At the back of Jon Moreton's mind, he knew that he wasn't going to like what was coming next.

Charlie Broome sat there for a few seconds, flicking his eyebrows up and down, inviting the inevitable question.

Eventually Moreton capitulated. 'What's the final piece, then Chaz?'

'Ah,' beamed Broome as if a long-awaited train had just drawn into the station. 'You are, my bucko! You are!'

'Me? I don't know anything about tiles or interiors. I'm not sure I'd be much help on your team.'

'That's where you're wrong, Jon boy. You're exactly what my "team" needs.' Seeing Moreton's confused demeanour, Charlie Broome decided to lay out the situation.

'As you probably know, I've been spending a lot of time in Spain over the past few months. I've had my eye on a business over there that I'd like to buy. It's in this town called Retama on the Costa Blanca. It's one of those areas on the Costas that was a bit slow to get into the building boom when lots of people from across Europe decided they wanted a bit of sun on their bones in their salad days. You with me so far?'

Moreton nodded, but still didn't see where he fitted into all of this. His puzzled demeanour betrayed the fact.

'Bear with me. Now, however, the town's jumping into that boom with both feet. Building's going wild there and people are flocking in because the prices are right. And when people build houses, what do they need?' He looked at Moreton, but received no reply. 'Interiors!' he declared triumphantly, 'and when people move up a notch on the ladder to one of the new builds, the people moving into the older place want the same. I tell you Jon, it's going to be a boom time there and I'm going to surf that wave all the way to the bank.'

It all seemed to make perfect sense to Moreton. 'Well done, Chaz, I guess you're looking to buy the business then.'

'No, mate. Not looking to. I've tied up a deal already. All I need to do is sign those papers with the old man, get the loot, do the deal, and it's mine.' Charlie Broome was in full flow now. 'It's called 'Retama Azulejos'. At least at the moment. When I get my feet under the desk, it's going to change to "Broome Cerámica." Like it? Sounds good doesn't it? You see, the best part of it was that there's this big conglomerate in Spain – Cerámica Internacional – who own outlets all over the country. They're expanding in a big way, just moving into the south of France, but looking well beyond that as well. They were well interested in buying up the business, but the way it's located made them hesitate. It sits just off a traffic roundabout, with roads on two sides. On one of the others, there's this piece of land that's about to have apartment blocks built on it. Buying that would cost mega-brass so it was never an option. On the other side, Jon boy, wait for it, you know what there is?'

Moreton hadn't got a clue, and played the one Spanish card he had in his hand. 'A bull-ring?'

Broome looked at the floor as if someone had let down a balloon at his seventh birthday party. 'No, not a bloody bull-ring. A football club!' Broome smiled noticing the sudden, if albeit slight, rise in Jon Moreton's interest level.

'It's the town's football club, Club Deportivo Retama. Let me tell you, buddy: Manchester United, it is not. It even makes the old man's club here look like a top rank organisation. There are three sides to the ground with concrete steps and a stand that the local council have condemned. You see, with the football club being there, Cerámica Internacional couldn't extend the site to make it more viable for what they wanted, otherwise it would have been worth four or five times what I agreed to pay for it. They wanted to build a factory there, as well as the outlet site, but there wasn't the space. So, while they hesitated, in rode Charlie Broome and tied up the deal. Stop Press news is that they were livid. Tough Manchego, Señors. You snooze. You lose. And Charlie Broome doesn't do siestas!'

Broome's ebullience as he revelled in the apparent business coup was revealing a side to him that Moreton had never really seen before. 'Now, Jon. Here's where you come in.' Moreton was about to be made an offer that, for so many reasons, he simply could not refuse.

'The club isn't in great shape, and when I was trying to set up the deal to buy Retama Azulejos, the local council approached me and said that it would help to lubricate the wheels a bit if I took over the club as well. It's a bit of a "community enhancement" project if you catch my drift. They love that kind of thing over there. It's like when the old man took over the club here. It was only a small-time thing, though. They were playing in what they call over there the Segunda División B when I agreed to take on the club. It's similar to the third tier over here, but it's regionalised into four groups and Retama had been pottering along there for a while.

'The old owner had just had a heart attack, and his family were looking to offload it, so it didn't cost much and it kept the council sweet. I took over the club, and the council did their thing later to push the paperwork and permissions through on setting up the deal to buy the business. Thing is, though, as the other guy had been ill for a while, he'd let things slip. He had this old man in as a manager. Local bloke, who I think was a friend of the owner and he wasn't up to the job. Results had been falling off and there was hardly anybody turning up to watch the games. Why would they? Crap team. Crap ground. Pretty much crap all round. It was just in some kind of terminal drift. So, of course the club had some money troubles as well. When I took over, I met up with the manager, this old geezer, Vicente García. He told me that we could save a bit of brass by moving on some of the first team players. He said there was a decent crop of younger players heading for the first team anyway, and he would use them to replace those leaving. I took his advice and we flogged off five players. It kept things going on the money side for a while. Problem is, with the best players gone and the club already struggling, it ended up relegated. More players shipped out, and what's left is mainly the kids that García said were going to be good enough, but weren't. To put it bluntly, the club's up shit creek without a paddle.'

Moreton thought he could see where the conversation was leading, and he didn't like the destination. 'Look, Chaz, I owe you a lot, mate. But I can't start playing again. I know it sounds like the standard's pretty low, but I'm no kid any more and my knee just wouldn't take it. I'd end up in a wheelchair.'

Although clearly a little irritated by Moreton's assumption of his intentions, Charlie Broome offered up a smile. 'Wait a bit, Jon. Hear me out. I'm not asking you if you'd turn out for a few games, mate. I wouldn't do that. I want you to come over to Retama with me and take over managing the club.'

Charlie Broome noticed the surprise on Jon Moreton's expression. 'I've sacked this García, bloke. He'd let me down. I followed his advice and he screwed up. Retama are now in the next division down. It's called the Tercera División, which sounds to me like "Third Division," but it's the fourth tier in reality, and it gets worse. It's split into eighteen regional groups. It's called the "Preferente." But I've no idea what it's supposed to be preferred to.'

After recovering from the initial shock of Broome's revelation, Jon Moreton's attention was now well and truly focused.

'I thought you might be interested, Jon. But I want to be honest with you. There's a bit of a catch. With relegation, the money problems are even worse. Owning the club has already cost me more than I planned on laying out, and playing in this little local league is only going to push things further downhill. The sponsors have bailed, so I've had to take that on as well. I've invested a lot of brass in Retama Azulejos, and having the club as another draw on my finances is stretching things beyond what I can afford without being stupid, and I'm not that.'

Charlie Broome took a sip of water, and leaned back in his chair. 'The trouble is, I can't just sell the club and cut my losses as the deal isn't signed yet. With García gone, the council have insisted on me bringing in a new manager. Someone I know and trust, who will get the job done. Otherwise, they'll play merry hell with me and I don't want to piss off important people, who could rain on my parade.'

He paused, allowing the information to settle before summing up. 'So, this is where we are. I can keep the club afloat in this league for a season. It'll cost me an arm and a leg, but it'll get the deal on the business done. The problem is, though, unless the club gets promoted at the end of the season, it'll fold. I'll have lost my brass and the town won't have a club any more. So, I need you to come over to Spain with me, take over at the club, get them promoted and everyone's happy.'

It had all got more than a little complicated for Moreton now. Like so many coaches, management had seemed like the next step on the ladder, but he'd hardly had enough time to secure his footing on his existing rung before considering the next step up. Here was the man who had opened doors for him previously, now offering another opportunity, but it seemed so distant, and not only in geographical terms. Developing the skills of a group of talented youngsters was one thing, but taking over as manager of a club – and a struggling one at that – in a foreign country, was something else entirely.

'I know what you're thinking,' Broome said interrupting Moreton's train of thought. 'But let's be honest, the only time any manager gets offered a post is when the club's in trouble. If the other guy hadn't fucked up, I wouldn't be sitting here, would I? It's the way of the world in football, Jon. You know that. Look, don't worry about handling all the boring stuff. I'll deal with wages, rent, electricity and all that financial and legal cobblers. I can get it covered by my guys at Broome Cerámica. You can have the title of manager, because that way, whatever happens it'll look good on your CV. All you'll need to do is coach the players, and let's face it Jon, that's what you want to do, isn't it?'

Moreton couldn't disagree. He choked back a few doubts and bit on the bait being dangled in front of him. 'OK, so what's involved in getting promotion?' he asked.

In that moment, Charlie Broome knew that Moreton was hooked. All he needed to do now was reel him in. 'I've been looking into it. It's all a bit complicated but the key requirement is to win the local league of eighteen clubs. That's not the end game, though. The way it's set up is that, since the 2008–09 season, the eighteen winners of the regional groups are drawn into nine two-legged ties. Win one of those and you're up. The nine losing clubs enter the play-off round for the last nine promotion spots, with clubs who had been runners-up and clubs from the league above. It all gets pretty involved from there.' Broome blew out his cheeks, leaning back in his chair, evidently relieved that all of the complicated details had been delivered.

'Cobblers to that, though. We need to get straight up. Win the league. Win the play-off tie and it's job done. Look, a few years ago, when the club was doing OK in the other league, it drew in some decent crowds and, with the area having a bit of a boom in building, more people are coming into the town and with so many of them being Brits, Germans, Dutch, Scandinavians and whatever, they're mad for football. Get the club going again, get it promoted, and it could go places.'

'I'm not sure,' Moreton said, with natural concern applying a cautionary brake on his initial interest.

Broome nodded. 'That's fair enough. I didn't expect you to jump up and down on the spot and dive in. Here's the deal as I see it. I'll pay you enough to cover your living costs and expenses. I'll find you an apartment near to the ground and I'll cover the costs. I'm flying out there next week. Come and have a look. I'll pay and if you don't fancy it, I'll fund your return flight as well. The worst that'll happen is that you'll have a week in the sun and return knowing that you looked at the opportunity and gave it the consideration it deserves. And, let's be honest, what have you got keeping you here?'

Charlie Broome was guiding his friend up the steps to the plane. Then, at precisely the right time, he delivered the coup de grace: 'Jon, I think together we can make the club deliver. Come and take a look. Don't you owe me that, at least, mate?' The line was delivered with just the right amount of pathos, enough to persuade, but not to elicit sympathy.

Jon Moreton nodded. 'Yeah. OK, Chaz. Of course. Let's go and have a look.'

Although neither would admit it to the other, both men knew that once in Spain, there was very little chance that Jon Moreton would not take up the challenge.

Reign in Spain

Forty minutes after leaving Alicante airport, Broome eased the hired, powder blue Mercedes onto the small car park in front of, what the rusting sign above the gate suggested was, the Estadio Antonio Núñez. It seemed an overly grand appellation for what was a less than impressive structure. The wall in front of the car park was painted in a deep red that seemed in sympathy with the decaying metal of the name above it. In the middle of the wall were three gates. Peering from his seat in the car, Moreton could see inside to a row of steps leading up to a blue and white painted wall, with gaps to allow access to what appeared to be the terraces on the other side. In a number of spots the paint was faded or had flaked off. There was an unmistakable air of uncaring decay.

Charlie Broome exited the car, closing the door behind him, realising that any doubts that may have been running around Moreton's mind would hardly have been assuaged by the initial impression of CD Retama's home. 'Look,' he said to Moreton. 'I know it's not too grand, but it's all about the team isn't it? I told you that the previous guy had let it all run down. There's only so much you can do in a short time, and I wanted to get the team right first. That's why you're here, mate.' Moreton half-smiled and nodded, entirely bereft of conviction.

Somewhere on the other side of the less than imposing wall, Moreton could hear the sound of footballs being kicked and the ever-accompanying shouts of players, interrupted by occasional whistles.

'Come on,' Broome called out, encouraging Moreton to follow him through the gates he had just unlocked and opened. 'Let me introduce you to a few people.'

Once through the gates, Moreton found himself standing on a narrow pathway with the concrete steps leading up to the wall in front of him. The path led off to both left and right, before curving around the steps and out of sight. To the left stood a wooden hut that looked like it would be pressed into service for drinks and food on match days. Next to it was a small and unpainted portacabin with a hand-written sign bearing the words, *Árbitro y Officiales Solamente!*

The rise in each of the steps was steep, but Broome leapt up them easily, and walked towards one of the gaps in the perimeter wall, affording a view of the playing surface. Jon Moreton followed and, arriving next to his friend, peered out through the gap, shading his eyes from the glare. If there had been any hope that the initial impression of the stadium may have been illusory, it was quickly dashed. Looking around, he saw rows of concrete steps that clearly served as seating areas, in the same dilapidated condition as the ones he had just climbed, and the wall he had passed through.

To the far left-hand corner stood a structure that had once been a stand with seating. Weeds were prominent in the rows he could see, as their green colour offered a dash of brightness in the otherwise drab and dark rows of broken and missing seats. Meshed wire netting blocked off the entrance to the stand, although no one would surely try and access it to sit there.

On the clearly synthetic pitch were around twenty players in various shirts and bibs, set up in two rondo groups. The youthfulness of the voices and appearance of the players suggested that most were teenagers. The session was being overseen by a slight figure dressed in a blue tracksuit, standing between the two groups. Despite the baggy tracksuit, Moreton saw that the figure was undoubtedly female, an assumption confirmed by the voice instructing the players. Seeing that Moreton had noticed her, Broome nudged his friend. 'That's Sophia,' he said, smiling. 'Come on. I'll introduce you.'

Seeing the two men approaching, she walked across to meet them. The baggy tracksuit gave little away but she was not much older than the players, probably in her mid-twenties. She was tanned, with sparkling eyes, her long dark hair swept back, held in place by a bright yellow headband revealing a face that should have been smiling, but her expression seemed anything but welcoming.

'*Hola!*' Broome beamed brightly, greeting her with warmth. It was an emotion clearly lacking in the reply.

Moreton sensed that the introduction would be anything but pleasant with such an apparently abrupt character. 'This is Sophia,' Broome said, turning to Moreton, before adding: 'And this is the famous English coach, Jon Moreton.' The "fame" that had been ascribed to him felt wholly inappropriate, but Moreton offered his hand in anticipation towards Sophia. A begrudging nod was all that was given in return.

'Sophia speaks perfect English,' Broome chimed in, suggesting that Moreton should say a few words at least.

'So, this is the youth squad, I assume?' he asked.

'No, Mister. This,' she said waving her arm towards the group of young footballers, 'is the first team squad. We do not have youth players any more. We cannot afford such luxuries,' she added, looking at Broome. 'We have seventeen players in our squad. We are allowed to have twenty-three, but seventeen is all we have.'

'Anyway,' Broome jumped in, 'Jon will be at the club tomorrow evening for training and he'll be taking charge of the club from there, Sophia.'

She nodded slowly in acknowledgement. Broome turned to walk away, and hooked a hand on Moreton's arm inviting him to follow.

As they walked, Moreton turned to Broome. 'What's this Mister business, Chaz?'

Broome smiled. 'It's a weird Spanish thing, Jon. Back in the day, when football was finding its way in Spain, most of the coaches were British, and were formally addressed by the players as "Mr Smith" or "Mr Jones" or whatever, and the name just became common currency from there. It caught me out as I was talking to old García. I couldn't understand why the players were calling him Mister – surely it should have been *Señor* but Sophia explained it.' Moreton nodded.

'There's a lot about Spain and this club that you don't know much about, Jon,' Broome added with smile. 'Don't worry, though, I've got it all figured out.'

Moreton returned Broome's smile, but without much conviction. With each passing minute, he was realising, how big a step this was going to be.

Back in the car, Broome smiled. 'All a bit weird for you Jon, is it?'

'Yeah... It's a new country, a new culture, a new bloody language that I don't understand and I'm really not sure I'm up to this Chaz.'

Broome turned the engine off. 'I know, Jon,' he said, looking Moreton square in the face. 'Look, don't worry about things like that. All you have to do is concentrate on the football. Of course, Spain's new but, like I told you, in this area, lots of people speak English. There's so many Ex-Pats over here now and more on the way, so it's good for their business to speak English.'

Moreton nodded a little, but without being totally convinced.

'Look, Jon. It'll be fine. Give it a couple of weeks and you'll love it here. It's new, but coaching football in the sun, eh? That's got to be good hasn't it?' Broome fired up the car again, eased it into gear and pulled off the small car park.

'Who's Sophia? She seems very aggressive.'

Broome laughed out loud. 'Ah, I was waiting for that one.'

Moreton looked across the car at Broome, confused.

'Come on, buddy,' Broome gave an overly exaggerated wink. 'She's a bit nice, isn't she?'

'I guess so. That's not what I mean. What's she doing at the club? What's her role there?'

'She came to the club with old García a while ago. I think he's her grandfather's brother or something like that. She used to play a bit herself for the club when they had a girls' team way back when, and then went to university in Madrid on some sort of Sports Science course. I'm not sure of the exact details. She coaches a group of girls, I think. It's not a team or anything, just to encourage more girls to get involved in playing. You should see her in training, mate. She could do a job for the team let me tell you, but it's not allowed of course.' He broke off the narrative and smiled. 'Hey, what a coup that would be Jon, having a girl playing for the club. That'd bring the crowds in.'

Broome turned left out of the car park. A couple of hundred yards later a commercial building loomed up on the left as they approached a traffic roundabout. 'Hey, Jon. On your left,' he said, in the manner of some tourist guide. 'You have, my own, my very own, Retama Azulejos.'

Moreton craned his neck to look across at the building. They had already passed a long high wall that seemed to be part of the property and he could see the frontage with the name above a showroom entrance.

'It looks good, doesn't it, Jon?'

'Yeah, Chaz. I guess so. Is business good at the moment?' Moreton was trying to generate a measure of enthusiasm for something that felt like an observation of the colour of seaweed as waves of uncertainty repeatedly washed over him.

'It's good, Jon. It's good. But just you wait until my plans are sorted. Nobody will recognise the place.' He laughed, as the car exited the roundabout and passed in front of a row of shops, small bars and restaurants.

'Anyway,' Broome continued, picking up the theme he had postponed to commend his enterprise, 'when I kicked García out, Sophia was going to walk as well, but promised to stay for another year to help the players with their new manager – that's you, buddy boy. I told her you would be coming and, as she speaks excellent English, she didn't want to leave the players high and dry without anyone they knew. She's not a bad kid to be fair, Jon. She loves football and the club. She'll be a big help and great to work with. She'll translate for you and understands football as well. Plus, of course, she's not bad scenery, is she?'

Moreton nodded. The barely suppressed aggression he had detected in Sophia's attitude to him now had a home. It didn't matter that it wasn't his fault. She clearly thought it was. It was family, and he was the man taking her relative's place. Broome interpreted the nod to something other than the answer to Moreton's curiosity.

'There you go, Jon,' Broome added triumphantly, 'I knew you'd think she was a bit tasty!'

'What? No,' stammered Moreton, realising what Broome had insinuated. 'I just meant that...'

Charlie Broome cut short the struggling escape attempt, as he drew the car to a halt. They had only been travelling a few minutes. After going around another roundabout and passing a few shops, bars and restaurants, they had turned left and then right, the wrong way up a one-way street, and parked.

'We're here.'

They got out the car and Moreton found himself standing in a small, quiet residential road. In front was a tall wall with a series of two-storey apartments running away along a gated pathway. Opposite was a row of houses.

'What do you think, Jon?' Broome walked towards the gate, fishing around in his pocket for a set of keys.

'I'm not, erm... sure.'

'Come and take a look.' Broome unlocked the red gate and waved his hesitant companion inside. 'It's going to be ideal. You'll love it here. It's quiet, easy to keep clean. There's a living area, two bedrooms, bathroom, a nice compact kitchen and cracking balcony.'

Broome walked a few paces forwards past low walls on either side, opening the first gate to his left. It led into a small yard area, tiled in terracotta. There was a flight of stairs and, under them, a door leading to a small storage area. Moreton looked around, trying to take it all in. The same format of building stretched away in front of him for fifty metres or so on both sides, with perhaps another dozen or so gates, before seeming to open up into another area.

Charlie Broome was already climbing the steps. 'Come on Jon. Let's get the door open and you can see inside.' Broome pointed down at his feet. 'Like the tiles, Jon?'

The steps they were walking on were the same as the ones in the yard downstairs. The raisers between them were white, patterned intricately with blue, green and red motifs. Together with the terracotta, it gave what Moreton, even in his limited experience of travel, was a Mediterranean feel.

'Where do you think the tiles came from, Jon?'

'Not sure, Chaz. Morocco?'

'Morocco? Bloody hell, Jon. Not Morocco. They're from my place. They're from Retama Azulejos, of course.'

By now, Broome had reached the top and was standing in front of the door. 'I bought this place years ago,' he explained half-turning towards Moreton. 'Only stayed here a few times, but it's how I found Retama Azulejos, you see. It was OK when I was younger, but I prefer the Caribbean to be honest. Don't come here at all any more, but I hung on to it. As I told you, prices here are booming now, so it's not a bad little investment and I rent it out occasionally to bring a bit of brass in, and keep it nice and tidy. I employ this local girl who comes in to clean and prep it up whenever anyone is staying here, so it'll be all ready for you just to move in.'

He located the key, and double-turned it. The door swung open into a dark interior Broome walked in, but Moreton hesitated outside.

'Ah.' Broome smiled. 'Don't worry, Jon. It's not that bad. It's just that all the shutters are down.' Broome reached up a hand to his left, and tugged on a strap. As he raised the shutter covering the window, light streamed in, illuminating the interior. Suddenly, everything seemed so much brighter and, as the sunshine streamed in, a pleasant heat filled the room.

Moreton followed inside. To his right, he could now see the "nice compact kitchen." It was certainly compact, with barely enough room for two people to stand side-by-side; however, he had to concede that with fridge-freezer, washing machine, cupboards, sink and cooker, all the necessary items were there.

The sound of other shutters being raised drew Moreton's attention back to what was quickly revealed as the living area. Now bathed in light as Broome had raised the shutters on the patio door leading to the balcony, Moreton could see that the entire apartment was floored in beige-patterned tiles and in front of him was a blue sofa, facing a dark wood unit with a television, DVD player and an internet hub sitting on it, next to a table with four chairs. Broome dropped a set of keys onto the table, next to a mobile phone already waiting there. He pointed at it: 'Use that over here, mate. An English one in Spain can be very expensive. This one runs through my business, so it's covered from there.'

Moreton nodded, and picked up the phone, before continuing the tour. Looking through the patio window, he had to admit that Broome hadn't oversold the balcony. It was large enough to have a table and four substantial wicker chairs around it, and was also tiled.

Broome unlocked and slid open the patio door, revealing a security grid. He unlocked it and pushed the two hinged sections apart, stepping outside. The view across the rooftops was uninterrupted to the mountains in the distance. Things were beginning to feel a whole lot better to the previously reluctant Moreton. Broome sensed his friend was warming to the whole plan. He placed a hand on Moreton's shoulder, and turning him slightly, pointed out across the rooftops. 'You probably can't see it now, Jon. But when the floodlights are on at the club, you can see them clearly from here.' Moreton strained, but in the bright sunshine, it was difficult to discern what was being pointed out to him.

Walking back inside, he followed Broome through an archway next to the table and alongside a couple of bookcases. In front of him was a bathroom.

Much like the kitchen, it was small, but had everything there. Either side of it were bedrooms. The first had a double bed and wardrobes, whilst the second had an extendable single bed and cupboards.

'What do you think then, Jon?' Broome asked with the bouncy confident tone of some estate agent anxious to close the deal.

'Yeah, it's all a bit new, but... Yeah, it's OK, Chaz. It's OK.'

'Steady on, Jon. Don't go overboard, will you.' Moreton quickly realised the impression he had given, and whilst there was still plenty of doubts in his mind, he was being anything but gracious. Here was a friend who had now twice given him opportunities, offering a hand up when he was down. He deserved better. 'I'm sorry, Chaz,' he said, smiling. 'It's just that it's all so new, mate.'

Broome smiled back and patted Moreton on the shoulder. 'I know Jon, but everything happens for a reason. Trust me. Once you settle in, you'll be fine. It's a great opportunity, and just think how impressive it'll be on your CV that you've now been a manager as well as a coach, and have worked abroad. All that, plus the Spanish sunshine, and you get to spend time with Sophia as well, eh?' He winked at Moreton.

'Yeah, you're right of course. Thanks, Chaz. It's a great opportunity. It's all new, but it won't be for long. Once I get to work, it'll be great. Thanks, buddy!' Moreton was convincing himself that it was true.

Broome passed him the keys. 'Any problems, my number's logged into that phone.' I'm at a hotel in the town, ten minutes away. Just give me a bell.' Reaching into his pocket he pulled out a wallet and handed Moreton half-a-dozen brown coloured Euro notes, together with a bank card. Moreton could see they were 50 Euro notes.

'What's this?'

'Don't get carried away, Jon. It's just an advance on your wages. There's a couple of supermarkets and shops that we passed on the way in if you want to get some things. I've already made sure you've got a few essentials in the fridge and cupboards, so you won't starve, but get out and have a stroll around. I've set up a bank account for you, and here's the card for the ATM. The piece of paper with it has the PIN number on. There are cash-points all around and they all have British flags on the display, press them and the instructions will be in English. I'll have your wages paid straight into the account.'

Moreton looked at the money and card, and then back at Broome. 'Thanks, Chaz,' he said, smiling. 'I appreciate all you're doing for me.'

'No sweat,' Broome replied, walking through the door. 'Oh,' he said, pausing and half-turning back. 'There's one other thing I forgot to mention. Most of the other apartments are often empty, people from Valencia and Madrid use them as holiday homes. There are a few occupied all year around, though. That one opposite, for example.' Broome jerked his thumb across his shoulder indicating the apartment opposite Moreton's new home. 'That one's occupied. It's where Sophia lives.' Broome beamed a smile as he turned away. 'You can thank me for that later buddy.' Reaching the gate to the road, he unlocked it and walked out, shouting back over his shoulder. 'Get settled in, Jon. I'll pick you up at five tomorrow evening.'

Moreton was still standing on the steps. He hadn't moved since his friend had delivered the news about his new neighbour. His mind had a lot of new information to digest. He walked straight through and outside onto the balcony. It was hardly dusk, but as the mountains took on a hint of grey in the distance, the floodlights of the stadium were now visible. The sight gave Moreton a sense of comfort. It may be a different country, but on a football pitch, he would always feel at home.

Unsure what to do, he gave way to the natural curiosity encouraging him to explore. He changed into his running gear of shorts and sweat shirt. Stepping out and, carefully locking the door behind him, Jon Moreton set out on a jog to discover Spain. He jogged down the almost empty street, passing shops, restaurants and a couple of bars, finally arriving at the traffic roundabout where the lights of Retama Azulejos blinked out at him from the showroom. To his left he saw a supermarket a couple of hundred metres down the road, noting that it would be an easy place to shop for things.

For a moment, he contemplated jogging across the roundabout towards the stadium to see what was going on there. He was unsure of the reception he would receive, though, and decided against it. Instead, he turned back to the complex. Opening the gate, he walked past the entrance to his apartment. Where the buildings stopped, he was delighted to see a large swimming pool, ideal for a morning swim before breakfast. The pool formed the centre of the complex with three lots of pathways leading off from each side of it.

Strolling back to his apartment, he couldn't resist looking up at the one opposite. Had Charlie Broome been joking or did Sophia really live there? Moreton climbed the stairs, opened the door of his apartment and locked it behind him. Although it was still relatively early in the evening, it had been a long and very full day. He slipped into the shower before collapsing into bed.

People

The following morning, he enjoyed a swim in the almost deserted pool, followed by a light breakfast of scrambled eggs and fruit, courtesy of the provisions Broome had left for him. The remainder of the day had dragged and been spent mainly sitting out on the balcony in the sun looking through his book of training drills. Occasionally people would walk by, deep in conversation. He envied their company, before diving back into his plans where such thoughts could be pushed to one side.

After lunch, the solitude of his apartment was becoming too much to bear and he decided to take a stroll to the supermarket he had seen the previous evening. A few minutes later, crossing the small car park, he approached the supermarket doors. Sitting on the floor, leaning against a stone pillar, an elderly man held out a cup asking for money. The doors slid open silently, inviting him inside. Unsure as to whether he was ready to engage in any kind of commercial activity, however, he hesitated as a couple walked past him. Chatting in English, they walked into the shop and, as if magnetised by the familiar tongue, he followed. The doors slid shut behind him. 'OK,' he thought. 'I'm in. Now I have to buy something!'

He walked up and down the aisles filled with all sorts of foods and other provisions, and opted to buy a pineapple and a jar of mayonnaise. It felt uncontroversial enough, and he joined the queue at the tills, before realising the only money he had were the 50 Euro notes that Broome had given him. Worrying that he would look gauche offering such a large note for a couple of cheap items, he decided to leave the queue and reconsider his options. By now, others had filed in behind him complete with baskets and trolleys. There was no backing out.

When his turn came, he placed the pineapple and mayonnaise on the checkout belt and smiled nervously at the middle-aged lady passing his items over the scanner. 'Buenos,' she said, smiling. He smiled back feeling unsure as to what to do next. With both items passed, she recognised his hesitancy and that he probably wasn't Spanish. It was hardly unusual for the area. She pointed to the electronic readout detailing that the amount required was 7.42 Euros. He handed over the 50 Euro note, and received his change.

Stepping outside into the afternoon sun, he realised the experience had made him sweat more than would have been the case after a 5k run. He smiled to himself. 'That wasn't so difficult after all,' he thought. It was then that he realised he didn't like mayonnaise. 'Why did I pick that!' he said almost out loud. Turning back to the door of the supermarket, he reached down and passed the jar to the man sitting on the floor. Then he gave him the pineapple as well. The man smiled indulgently back at him, saying something in Spanish. Moreton just hoped it was a thank you of sorts, and not that he didn't like mayonnaise – or pineapple.

Arriving back, at the apartment, he went to the fridge, and reached inside for one of the bottles of beer, and went outside to sit on the balcony. The warm sun felt good, and, as he sat down and swallowed some of the cold beer, considered that perhaps this might not be so bad after all. He leaned back in the wicker chair and put his feet up on the one opposite. He'd survived most of his first day alone in Spain, visited a shop and bought some items. Giving them away had made him feel better as well. He'd planned out his training for the evening, and now he was sitting in the sunshine with a beer awaiting the Mercedes to roll up and deliver him to the ground.

Five o'clock came and went with no sign of Charlie Broome or his Mercedes. Moreton picked up his bag, left the apartment, and once through the gate of the complex, sat down on the kerb. Twenty minutes later, he heard a familiar engine noise as Broome turned the corner, again going the wrong way down the one-way street, and pulled up in front of where Moreton was seated.

He stood up and brushed himself down before getting into the car. 'How's it going, Jon?'

'Yeah, all right, Chaz. Went for a swim. Had a walk around. Did a bit of shopping. You know how it is,' he smiled to himself, hoping it would sound impressive to Broome.

'OK, Jon,' Broome said, raising an eyebrow. 'Shall we get to work?'

'Can't see why not, Chaz.'

Five minutes or so later, they were climbing the concrete steps at the Estadio Antonio Núñez. As they breached the wall, they could see Sophia and the players going through a stretching regime. Moreton nodded in approval. He'd have been disappointed if, upon arriving late, the players had been merely sitting around. Reaching the foot of the steps, Broome stopped and placed a hand on Moreton's shoulder. 'I'm going to leave you here for a while, Jon,' he said, nodding down the road back in the direction of Retama Azulejos. 'I need to go and spend a bit of time with my boys and girls and see what they're up. Got a bit of a business meet on after, so it might be late before I can pick you up. Is that OK?'

'Don't worry about it, Chaz. When I'm done here, I can jog it back to the apartment. Be a good chance to unwind as well.'

'You sure?' Receiving nods in reply, he agreed and walked back up the steps and out of the stadium. A few seconds later, Moreton heard the Mercedes driving away.

Waking across the pitch he offered himself some unspoken reassurance. 'I've done the shopping, so I can do this,' he said to himself as he approached Sophia.

'Hi,' he said pleasantly, hoping for something similar in return. She turned and replied with a barely discernible nod.

'Mister,' she replied flatly.

'Look,' said Moreton jumping in with both feet. 'I know there's a tradition, but can we drop the "Mister" business, please? I'm Jon, and it would be great if you'd call me that. I don't mind the players calling me Mister, but if we're going to be working together, it should be on first name terms. Is that OK?'

The Spanish girl looked at him quizzically. '*Vale*,' she said. Then shortly afterwards: 'OK.'

'Great. So, what's your name?'

With hardly a pause, Sophia looked him in the eyes and said: 'My name is Dolores Sophia Isabella Medina Garrigues.'

Moreton choked back a laugh, immediately holding up his hand to apologise.

'What is funny?' Sophia questioned although she knew the answer.

'I'm sorry. I really just wanted to know what I should call you.' Moreton hesitated, then corrected himself: 'That's a bit too much to say. Aside from the fact that I'll never remember it, if I want to ask you something during in a game, it would be full time by the time I got it right.' He laughed a little nervously, and received a suppressed half smile in response.

'Look,' he went on. 'I know you probably don't like me because I'm the guy Charlie brought in to replace your grandfather's brother, but that's nothing to do with me. I'm here to do a job for the club, for the players, for the town. I'm a decent guy and I'd like us to work together.'

She paused for a while apparently weighing up her reply. 'Señor Broome said that I would be working for you, translating, a little physiotherapy duty and sometimes helping with the training. Is that correct?'

Realising that there was a possibility of progress, Moreton pressed on: 'Well, Señor Broome tells me that you used to play for this club, you have a degree in Sports Science and played for the university football team. You have a passion for football and care about the club. Let's see how things work out, but no, I don't want you to work for me.' He paused, then smiled again. 'I want you to work with me. I want you to help me make the club successful. I want us to do that together.'

Sophia looked a little unconvinced, but slowly nodded. 'If what you say is true, you need to prove this to a lot of people here, me included,' she replied slowly and deliberately. 'No one is sure about Señor Broome. He sacked a great man and brought you in. Why? What can you do that he could not? You have a lot of things to prove to a lot of people.' She hung onto the last sentence to leave no room for doubt. 'OK, let's see how it goes, but for now, you can call me Sophia.'

'Great,' Moreton said nodding in agreement as if some major peace treaty had been agreed between warring factions. 'Let's get things moving.'

Moreton counted up the players and quickly confirmed to himself that if the squad he had to work with comprised seventeen players they were all in attendance, noting that there was still enthusiasm in the squad, regardless of what had happened recently.

'I want to set up a short-sided game: a quarter of the pitch. Just mark out a couple of goals with cones. You know the players: balance it out with some of the better players being a man short. I want to see how each of them play, and perhaps you can tell me more about them.'

Sophia nodded and walked towards the players calling out a series of names and instructions in Spanish. Listening, the group looked at her, and then across at Moreton as they broke up and set out the pitch as she had instructed them. Sophia collected one of the balls and threw it among them and got the game underway, before turning back to return to Moreton who was standing a few steps back from the players.

'So,' Moreton said to her as she stood by him, watching the impromptu game. Tell me a little about the players, please... Sophia?'

The smile that played briefly across her face was difficult to hide.

'We have two goalkeepers: Paco Jiménez is at the far side.' Sophia raised her arm indicating the goalkeeper in a green top with cut-off sleeves. 'Paco is very experienced. He played for two seasons in a Primera División squad, when my grandfather's brother was coaching there. He didn't play very often, but he was an outstanding goalkeeper when he was younger. He came to Retama with my grandfather's brother, to support him. They've had a relationship as coach and player for a very long time. He's very loyal, and when my grandfather's brother was pushed out by your friend,' Sophia paused and looked at Moreton, 'Paco was all for leaving. He's an electrician, and has a business in the town that he started when he moved here a couple of years ago. He employs people, and mainly runs the office, but said that when Señor Broome removed my grandfather's brother that it would be more fun working full time than playing. He's never really changed his mind, but just hasn't moved yet.'

Jiménez looked every inch the ex-professional, although a veteran, he had a commanding authority. 'How old is he?' Moreton asked innocently. He was taken aback by the vehemence of the reply.

'He's very experienced, and has always kept himself in good shape. He looks after the younger players, especially Juan.'

'Sophia, I wasn't trying to say he was too old. I just wanted to know a little more about him – truthfully.'

Sophia looked up and smiled apologetically. 'OK. I'm sorry. We've had a lot of things to deal with over the past few months. Your friend taking over the club. Players being moved on. Relegation. Other players leaving, and then my grandfather's brother being pushed out. As a group, we look after each other now. We all fight for each other. In fact, I think that's why Paco is still here.'

Moreton smiled. 'I understand. I'm on your side. I know I have to prove that to you, and I will, but for now, please try and give me the benefit of the doubt.'

They watched the play for a while. A slightly built player with swept-back hair held in place with a band, received a pass, instantly controlled, and was through on goal with just Jiménez to beat. He feinted to shoot a couple of times trying to trick the older man into committing to a dive, but the veteran was too wise to fall for the ruse. Then he drew the goalkeeper onto his left side, before flicking the ball past him with the outside of his foot. '*Guapo!*' he shouted as the ball bounced behind the goalkeeper and rolled over the line, turning towards the rest of his team with his arms aloft. Ignoring the ball, Jiménez walked up behind him and grabbed him by the shoulder, turning him around to face the older man.

The conversation lasted mere seconds, and was very much one way. The younger man stood with head slightly bowed. It had the appearance of a teacher reprimanding a child, and broadly that's what it was. When they separated, the younger man trotted off the pitch retrieved the ball, and returned to the game, handing it to Jiménez as he passed. The older man patted him on the back and the game resumed. Moreton looked at Sophia questioningly.

'Revi.' She smiled, identifying the young player for Moreton's benefit. 'He's such a good player but sometimes he forgets himself and lets his ability get the better of his personality.'

'What did he say to Paco when he scored?'

'Ah: *Guapo!*' she replied. 'It means "beautiful" but sometimes, occasionally, it can mean a little more than that.' Sophia hesitated, flushing slightly.

'More than that?'

'Well, it also means perhaps a little sexy as well sometimes. It's all about the situation. You know…' She laughed, nervously. 'You know: hot?'

They both laughed, feeling equally embarrassed to mention such things after merely breaking the ice a few minutes earlier. There's nothing like a little heat to ease the thawing process.

Sophia regained her composure. 'Paco, was reminding Revi about respect. He probably told him that if he had saved the shot, he wouldn't have been boastful about it and that Revi should remember that to celebrate a goal is fine, but he must always maintain dignity.'

Moreton turned to look at the young woman next to him. 'How do you know what he said.'

'Because I know Paco'

Moreton turned back to watch the game. 'And who is Juan?'

'Juan?' Sophia questioned in reply.

'You said that the reason Paco is still here is because he looked after the younger players, and you mentioned someone called Juan.'

Sophia nodded and pointed to the other end of the pitch. Wearing gloves and a yellow top in the other goal was a much younger man.

'That's Juan. He's only young – like so many of these kids. Nineteen, and he looks up to Paco like a father. A lot of them do to be honest.'

Juan Torres was slim and looked nervous when the ball came near him. Whereas, at the other end, Jiménez would call out instructions all the time, Torres was almost silent in comparison.

'He's only played for the team a few times. Usually when Paco wasn't available. We were fighting relegation for so long last season that every game was important and we couldn't risk leaving Paco out just to give Juan some experience, but it didn't really help his confidence. He never complains, but you can just tell. Paco says he's got real talent and with a little more confidence, he could become an outstanding goalkeeper.'

As Moreton watched the younger goalkeeper, it was difficult to discern any latent talent there, but he could certainly see that there was not so much a lack of confidence, but perhaps a little deficiency in self-belief. His experience with younger players had taught him to identify these things, and he was impressed that Jiménez was keen to develop his younger, potential, rival.

'I think that Paco could be very useful to us, Sophia.'

She smiled a little, but looked unconvinced. 'I'm not so sure,' she replied shaking her head gently. 'He hates you,' she explained.

'What? Why? What have I done to him?' he added, half-realising the answer as the words left his mouth.

'Your friend sacked his mentor, his friend. Here was a man who had coached at the highest level in Spain. He'd returned to his home town and volunteered to help the club out. He was managing the club for nothing, no payment. He brought so many years of experience to the club, and he brought Paco with him as well. Then your friend arrives, saying how things had to change. Change is acceptable, but your friend ripped the squad apart, forced transfers to save money, and perhaps for other ways to gain money as well. Then he blamed Paco's friend and kicked him out to bring you in. A *famous* English coach. Paco then discovers that you've never even coached a first team squad in any division in England. Your friend stops the youth team saying anyone who wanted to stay at the club should be in the first team squad. He wanted to stop the girls' squad as well – my players, that I coach – but I told him if he did, I would leave as well. It's not as if he pays me anything other than a few expenses, so he gave in and I stayed. Paco thinks there's something underhand going on – lots of us do – and whatever it is, he thinks that you're involved.'

Moreton was disappointed to have his suspicions confirmed, but hardly surprised. 'I understand, I guess I'll just have to work hard to convince him that it's not true.' Moreton paused briefly before adding: 'Can you do something for me, please? Can you stop calling Charlie *your friend*. It feels as if a wall has been built between him and everyone at the club, and that can't help things. He can come over a bit strange with people, I know that. But he's spent money on the club and has plans for it. I know he has. He's told me about them. A bit later, you might get to him know him well enough to call him Charlie, but until then, let's try calling him Señor Broome. Is that OK?'

Sophia seemed unconvinced, but nodded in slow acknowledgement.

'Who knows, as time goes on, he might become your friend, as well.'

Sophia hardly looked convinced.

They stood watching for a while, without further conversation, and the first hints of warmth slowly drifted away. 'Who's the guy with the beard at the back, in front of Juan?' Moreton asked, trying to get things moving in a positive direction again. This bearded defender was calling for the ball and organising his team-mates. The silence had felt so pervasive that when Sophia replied, Moreton was a little surprised.

'Alejandro is our captain. He has been with the club a long time. As you can see, he defends well and organises others. Everyone at the club, even Paco respects him as our leader.'

Moreton noticed that even in the short-sided game they were playing, Sanz hardly ventured away from his defensive post. Moreton asked about another defender, a fair-haired player, with boyish looks and unkempt demeanour.

'That's Guido, but he's no Alejandro.'

It wasn't difficult for Moreton to understand what Sophia meant. The bearded Sanz was constantly talking to his team-mate about staying in position and how to react when the opposition had the ball.

'I'm guessing he didn't play over much last season?'

'No. He was mainly with the youth team. He's only eighteen now, and when your fr… I mean when Señor Broome disbanded the team, he moved into the first team squad. He is fast though.'

Both pairs of eyes concentrated on the mop of fair hair as he responded to calls from his skipper. 'Why is he playing as a defender? It's not his best position surely. Wouldn't he be better playing further forwards?'

'I don't know. He hardly ever played in the team at all, and always seemed to panic when the ball came near him. See how Alejandro controls him.'

Moreton could indeed see, but though Guido was being told nothing wrong, he wasn't learning much, and hardly progressing.

'The other defender is Adrián.' He was black, short and muscular. The sort of player who had little fear in a challenge and always came out on top physically. 'Even in these games no one tries to go around Adrián. He does not like to get beaten at anything, and tackles very firmly.' It wasn't difficult to see the description fitted the player. 'And yet, in other ways, he is so gentle.'

Moreton looked a little perplexed. Watching the squat muscular defender on the field like some bulldog in search of someone to bite, "gentle" hardly seemed to fit the player. 'What do you mean?'

Sophia looked down at the floor. 'It's a sad story, but you should know. Everyone does. It's better that way.' She paused before speaking again. 'About two years ago, Adrián and his wife lost their baby.' She stopped again. The memories were difficult to recall, and required tears as payment for their arrival. 'He was born very early, and was so small. He fought so hard, but in the end, it was too much. He was just two weeks old. The whole thing tore Adrián apart for months. He and his wife went to live with her parents for a while. He spent all of his time looking after his wife. They tell me that he was away for about three months. I was still in Madrid at the time, but Alvaro heard about it all from Paco, and he told me. It was a bad time for everyone. Some of the other players who were here at the time said that after training, they'd often find him sitting alone in the dressing room, crying – until someone saw him – then he'd change and say everything was all right. To his wife, he was the strong one, who carried her and her parents through the grief. He cried his tears alone.'

Jon Moreton felt like an intruder blundering into a family tragedy talking about football, when it was surely the least important thing in the world, by comparison. 'Please, there's no need to say any more.'

Sophia looked up at him. 'No. It was a very difficult time, but then a few months ago, just as the club was getting relegated, Adrián announced that Ana, his wife, was pregnant again, with the baby due around Christmas time. We were all so happy for them.'

It was clearly something that Sophia thought he should know, but it all felt uncomfortable. He wanted to move things on.

'Please tell me about the players defending on the other team, Sophia.'

She also seemed relieved to have unburdened herself of what she considered a duty, albeit an unpleasant one. 'Firstly, there is Kiko and Victor.' They are both very young, but García – that's my grandfather's brother – believed they would become an outstanding pair of centre backs. Last season was too early for them, but when so many of the players left, he was forced to play them and they suffered a lot at first. Towards the end, you could tell they had matured. Kiko is the strong one, tall and athletic. Victor is the calm one, nothing ruffles him. Both are very bright, quick and eager to learn. Now they have played together for a season, although Kiko is still only seventeen and Victor a little older, they have some playing time behind them and will be strong for us.'

It was good to hear what Sophia was saying, but even better to hear her say that the players would be strong "for us" not "for you."

'So Kiko is the stopper? He nodded towards the tall black teenager standing head and shoulders above so many of the other players and looking a decade older than his relatively tender years. 'And Victor is the sweeper. Yes?' Some English idioms can be lost in translation, but football is a universal language.

Sophia nodded in firm agreement. 'They are so good that Felipe isn't really needed in this sort of game, as the space is restricted.' Felipe Blanco was the other defender alongside the dominant Kiko and the elegant Victor. Whilst the other two went about their business, Felipe was chatting away constantly, not imparting tactical information, but offering up quips and laughs.

'He has problems concentrating on his game.'

'Felipe, *Concentración!*' she yelled out in a sharp voice that startled Moreton.

The short blond defender, smiled and waved in acknowledgement. Alongside him, Victor and Kiko shook their heads in unison, having never really understood how their team-mate could play football and not give it his full attention.

'Felipe isn't a bad person and he'll fit in anywhere the team needs him to be. It's not that he doesn't care, he really does. It's just his way. He enjoys himself playing, but he lets it show too much.'

It was hardly a bad character trait, but Moreton could also appreciate how it failed to sit well with the diligent Kiko and Victor.

'We have six defenders in the squad. That is if you include Felipe. We have the same number in midfield, but they are very different.'

Moreton was listening, but also thinking ahead. If they were going to talk about the players further forwards, he wanted to change things in the game that would expose their skills and weaknesses more acutely.

'Sophia, can you tell the players that they're only allowed two touches on the ball please? Just two, no more. Otherwise they lose possession.'

Sophia nodded and walked over to the players. She stopped the game and spoke to them, before returning.

'In midfield…'

'Wait a moment please?' Moreton cut across her. He was watching how the players reacted to the restriction and how they adjusted their play when they had the ball. More important to him, though, was how a player's team-mates reacted to him being in possession. With the requirement to move the ball on quickly, it was increasingly important that players helped each other and offered passing opportunities. Otherwise, the ball would inevitably be cleared long and possession lost.

After a while he turned back to Sophia. 'I'm sorry. I wanted to see how they adapted, and also how quickly. It's like putting that Rondo exercise into a game but with a direction to play in as well. So, tell me about our midfielders.'

Sophia nodded appreciatively, quietly impressed by what Moreton had said.

'We have Samuel,' she began. 'His family moved here some years ago from Morocco and opened a restaurant in the town selling African food. I've been there quite a few times. The food is very good. Samuel joined them last year and came to the club shortly afterwards.'

Moreton watched as Samuel filled the space ahead of Kiko and Victor, receiving short passes and finding space, busying himself in the middle of the pitch, often simply being available. 'What's he like?'

'As a player?'

'No, as a person.'

'I don't know him very well to be honest. I don't think anybody here does. He's very quiet. Not in a bad way, you understand. He's just a naturally quiet person. Then there's Revi,' she added, smiling. 'He's probably our best footballer. No, not the best player, but the most gifted footballer. Do you understand what I mean?'

Moreton nodded. He understood perfectly.

'On the other team, Antonio Vasquez is our wide player. He's really good with the ball at his feet and can go past defenders comfortably on either side.'

Moreton turned from the game and looked at Sophia. She was describing a rare and valuable talent. 'Really?'

'Yes,' she replied, nodding enthusiastically. 'One thing, however. He doesn't like getting kicked too much.'

Moreton laughed. 'Nobody does, Sophia,' he replied, but he knew what she meant. 'I'll bet he doesn't try to go around Adrián too often in these sorts of games then, does he?'

There was no need for any spoken reply. The smile sufficed.

'Matías is a bit like Samuel. He's twenty-three now, and has played that pivot role for most of the time he has been with the club. Some of the other players think he is very limited, but he knows what he's good at. It's a bit the same as with Alejandro. He'll get the ball and pass it on. Often people don't notice such players in a game, but García always liked him playing there.'

Sophia had started to describe her grandfather's brother as García, rather than by the familial relationship. It felt like another step forward.

'And there's Juan Palermo.' She nodded towards the large muscular figure playing on the flank nearest to them. Whereas Felipe seemed to take everything too lightly, Palermo looked the sort of player who in contrast, took everything too seriously. A misplaced pass would incur his wrath and at one stage a rant at Adrián for such a perceived misdemeanour threatened to boil over, until Sanz stepped in to calm things. 'He comes from a not very pleasant part of the town,' Sophia explained. 'It's better there now than it was, but when Juan was growing up, you needed to be tough to survive. He's never really changed. He's still friendly with the same people from his days as a teenager. Most of them are OK really, but a few others…' She hesitated a little, searching for appropriate words, but the message had been delivered.

Moreton nodded.

'He is brave and committed, however,' she added. 'And he scores goals for us.'

'There's also Sebastián. He's still only sixteen and someone else who came out of the youth team, like Guido. He's left-footed, so often gets pushed out there when he gets a game, which hasn't been very often.'

Looking across the pitch Moreton discerned the player in question. Small, wearing a shirt that appeared to be three sizes too big for him, Moreton could easily have believed that Sebastián was four years younger than that.

'He's so different to Palermo,' Sophia went on. 'His family is wealthy. He's bright and speaks perfect English. He hasn't played a first-team game yet, so I don't know that much about him, but he was always in the team for the youth set up and García thought that he may grow into a good player, but perhaps not yet. I'm not sure – he seems such a child.'

Sebastián certainly looked like the junior member of the squad. His childlike features fitted well in his short and thin frame. He had the look of an infant that had wandered into an adult's game. It wasn't far from the truth.

'I'm not sure that he'll be with us long anyway,' Sophia picked up again as Moreton was musing. 'He'll either be going to university or into the family business. They own a large and very expensive hotel in the town. It's where your... It's where Señor Broome is staying.' She smiled sheepishly.

It was returned by Moreton with a wry smile of admonishment.

'What about our forwards then? Who scores the goals for us?'

Imperceptibly, Sophia slowly shook her head, looking down at the floor.

'Ah, who scores the goals for us... ? If you ask García, he'll tell that this was the main problem.'

Moreton realised that a sensitive subject was being opened up.

Sophia sighed. 'You remember that we lost a number of players when... Señor Broome took control of the club?'

Moreton nodded.

'Well, Fouad was one of the players that left. We lost five players. Four of them were good; that's why moving them out brought in money. But Fouad, was very good. Very good. He scored the goals for us.' There was a wistful tone in Sophia's voice that portrayed the feeling of loss as much as the words she spoke. 'Fouad came to us from García's old La Liga club. He joined their youth team after moving from Morocco. Things didn't work out for him. He was young, and in a strange place with no friends, and no one to help him. An old friend of García who was working at the club got in touch and told him about Fouad. He was very young, at the time, seventeen, I think, and wanted to leave and go back home. He was unhappy and deliberately started playing badly, so that he would be sent back to Morocco. Whether the club believed he wasn't good enough, or for other reasons he wasn't going to make it, they released him. García's contact told him that although he probably wouldn't have ever made the first-team anyway, he could still score goals at a lower level – especially if he was happy. He said that although he wasn't very big or fast, there was something about him that meant he could score goals. He was always in the right place to score, and when a chance came, he would fight to score. García trusted his friend's opinion. He went and spoke to Fouad and asked him to come to Retama. He said the club would pay for his living costs and promised him that if things didn't work out, he would pay for him to go back to Morocco out of his own pocket. So, Fouad started with us last season.' She paused and looked up at Moreton, before glancing downwards once more. 'He scored the goals for us.' Moreton returned the glance, expecting Sophia to continue, but she didn't.

'What happened?'

Looking up again, she continued: 'It went well. García was very good with the players, he knew how to work with them, and how they were all different. Fouad liked him and trusted him. The problem was, that he was too good. Other clubs saw him and the goals he was scoring. He was with us for about half of the season when we heard that he was moving. There's a club in another region of the Preferente called Atlético Santa Kristina. Two years ago, the club was taken over by a very big corporation called Cerámica Internacional. Do you know them? They're very famous.'

Moreton nodded slowly. The name rang a bell.

'Well, anyway, Fouad had scored twelve goals in his first eight games for us. Things were going well, but half way through the season, just as Señor Broome took over here, Atlético approached Fouad. They told him that they would pay him lots of money and that they would also pay for his family to join him in Spain. García was really upset. He had looked after Fouad so well. He was scoring goals and everything looked good. Señor Broome spoke to him and said it would be unfair to stop Fouad moving, as having his family together again was what he wanted. He told him that Fouad had spoken to him and said that he wanted to go. García wanted to speak to Fouad himself, but Señor Broome told him it would be unfair to put pressure on a young player like that. García said that he understood, and Fouad left. He never even said goodbye.'

Moreton shook his head. 'These things happen in football.'

'I know, but leaving without saying goodbye wasn't like Fouad. He wasn't like that.'

Moreton felt obliged to try and commiserate. 'Perhaps he felt a little embarrassed to be leaving?'

'Perhaps. Though, later we heard that Atlético had paid more money than we had been told, and that Señor Broome had kept it for himself. All part of an agreement of some kind.'

It was Moreton's turn to be less than convinced. 'That's not really fair, Sophia, is it? Charlie has put money into this club and if Fouad wanted to move to be with his family, he did the decent thing by letting him go. If he'd made him stay, Fouad would just have been unhappy again, wouldn't he?'

'Perhaps you're right. But it was such a loss. From there we hardly scored many goals for the rest of the season. Bendonces scored most of them, he scored twelve for the whole season; Fouad had got that many in his first eight games! Losing five players so quickly killed the squad, but losing Fouad was like a dagger into the club's heart. Relegation was always going to be a real problem from then, but Señor Broome insisted. García reluctantly agreed. We were relegated and then García was asked to leave.' There was rising anger in her voice. It spoke of frustration, but also a sense of betrayal.

Moreton thought it best to move things on: 'You mentioned Bendonces.'

'Yes, Tomás. Before Fouad came, and after he left, Tomás was our main striker.' She pointed towards a tall, muscular, bearded figure on the pitch. 'I can understand that he didn't like Fouad taking his place, but it was clearly the right thing to do for the club. García always said that Tomás had everything he needed to be a good goal scorer, but that he hardly used any of it.'

'Lazy?' Moreton asked, hoping that he had understood the inference.

'Yes. García always said he was lazy. Whenever he scored, he would go mad in celebration. Even easy goals, a goal when we were losing 6-0 was like scoring in a cup final to him. García once told him that if he enjoyed scoring so much, he should work harder, as he would score more goals that way. Tomás was a little different in character. He always said that if the team was better, he would try harder. He wasn't García's favourite player. He often joked that the reason Tomás had a beard was that he was probably too lazy to shave.'

Moreton laughed, but appreciated his fellow coach's frustration. 'Didn't García have any other options? Are there other forwards he could have put into the team?'

Sophia smiled. 'Not really. Tomás isn't a bad person. It's just who he is. It's just how he sees things. The other two forwards are both very young and García thought they were not ready for the first-team.'

Moreton thought he knew what was coming. 'As well as Fouad, some of the other players who left were forwards?'

Sophia nodded. 'All we had left was Santi and José. They are only eighteen and seventeen now and, remember, this all happened last season, when they were even younger. José would play occasionally when Bendonces was injured or couldn't play. He's Palermo's younger brother, but so different from him. He's tall but doesn't look very strong. When he played, he was often just knocked about by defenders, before Juan came across to sort things out for him. Some say that he's different to Palermo because he's always had his big brother to protect him and has never had to fight his own battles. I don't know. Although Juan isn't much taller than him, the way he plays he just looks a lot smaller and needs protection. I think he'd be lost without his brother to look after him.'

Moreton watched for a while and considered that perhaps, despite what Sophia was suggesting, the opposite might well be the truth.

'Is that Santi?' Moreton asked, looking towards the only player on the pitch that Sophia hadn't spoken of. Whilst Bendonces was playing as a forward on one team, José and another tall, but still clearly young, player were paired for the other.

'Yes. García said that Santi could be a very good forward in time, but needed to learn a lot. García always said it was about potential for Santi. He thought he could be as good as Fouad. Potential, you see? It's just that in the race to become accomplished, Fouad got there first, and Santi still had a bit of course to run.'

Throughout, Moreton had been making mental notes of what he had been told, what he had seen and thought. 'Thanks, Sophia,' he said, smiling warmly. 'That was really helpful.'

Sophia nodded. 'So, what do you think? What can the *famous* English coach do with these players?'

Moreton felt the barbs in the comment. His look probably betrayed his wounded feelings.

'I'm sorry. That didn't sound very nice did it?'

'No,' Moreton said, trying not to sound too abrupt or defensive. 'It didn't really.'

Sophia blushed. 'I'm sorry. I didn't mean it to sound like that,' she looked at Moreton smiling, almost asking for forgiveness.

He smiled back. 'OK. Anyway, I don't really know what I think yet. Can you call them in and run through a cool down while I write up some notes?'

'Sure.' Sophia nodded. 'OK.'

Moreton walked towards the bag he had left by the side of the pitch, taking out a notepad and pen and began scribbling. Occasionally, he'd glance up, looking at the players as if confirming the identities and characteristics of each of them. Some of the looks were at Sophia, as she ran through a short regime of exercises and stretches to rid aching muscles of lactic acid.

Ten minutes later, Sophia strolled over to where Moreton was sitting, still engrossed in his note taking. She looked over his shoulder. Rather than writing, all she could see was a series of sketches and diagrams, annotated with words and symbols. Moreton looked up. He hadn't noticed her walking towards him and smiled with slight embarrassment at her seeing his work. 'It's just my own kind of shorthand.'

'What does it all mean?'

'Well, it just tells me who did what. What they didn't do, and what I think they could and should do, I guess,' he replied, being unintentionally cryptic. 'It'll help me to remember when I go over things later tonight.'

She nodded slowly. 'Is that what you do? Note things down and then go over it again?'

Moreton felt a little as if he was being quizzed, but only in a gentle way. 'Pretty much. Usually it's with players that I know, but this is a bit more difficult as all the guys are new to me. I'm probably going to have missed a lot of stuff, but it's a start.' He stood up, and packed the notepad back into his bag.

'Would it help,' Sophia asked quietly. 'If I was with you?'

Already half-turned to walk off the pitch, Moreton stopped and turned back. Suddenly they weren't two coaches standing in the middle of a football pitch. They were just two people, standing together. Moreton felt uncomfortably vulnerable. He found himself truly looking at Sophia for the first time and noticing things about her. Despite her baggy clothing, she was clearly athletic, toned, with pleasingly round features and high cheekbones that emphasised her tanned face.

Moreton hesitated, thinking too much about how to reply without feeling awkward about it. He failed. 'Erm, I'm not sure,' he said, knowing it was the wrong answer.

'It might help you to remember things,' she said, opening the door for him to remedy the error.

'Well… I guess so… Yes, of course, it would.'

'Look, I don't know if Señor Broome mentioned this to you, but at the moment, I'm living in the apartment opposite you on the complex.'

'No, I didn't know,' he lied.

'Well, I do: directly opposite. I'm going to go and see the old guy who looks after the ground and make sure everyone has left before he locks up. Then, I'm heading back to the apartment to change. How about if I knock at your door at about eight? We can go down to the bar to talk about the players, and I'll buy you a glass of wine to make up for what I said earlier. Is that OK?'

It sounded perfect to Moreton, but he didn't want to let it be too obvious. 'Yeah, OK,' he replied, immediately realising his affected tone had been far too casual. 'That would be great. I'll see you later.'

He flung the bag across one shoulder and set off for the half mile or so back to the apartment as a smile flicked over his face.

Wine

After jogging from the ground, Moreton arrived back at the apartment, showered, changed and eaten – and waited. He'd put on some music, but had hardly been listening. Normally, he could look at his notes for hours. In his mind, he'd picture players that he'd worked with. What they did well, and what needed to be improved. How could he make the changes that would progress a player's development? What about this session? – concentrate on retaining possession. Or that one? – moving the ball quickly. Limited touches. Following passes. Drills on shooting or finding spaces. Forward runs, and pressure, support and cover drills. This time, though, the pictures just washed over him. It was 7.02 p.m. and he had waited.

Walking into the small kitchen, the window afforded a view across the pathway towards Sophia's apartment. In the steadily darkening sky, he could discern a light in the apartment, but the blinds were closed. He made a cup of tea. It was 7.14 p.m.

He sat on the sofa in jeans and freshly ironed T-shirt. It was 7.40 p.m. 'It's too early,' he told himself, but he didn't want to be late. What had Sophia said? Did she say 8 p.m. or *around* 8 p.m? He wasn't sure, but wanted to be ready. He'd looked at his notes and added a few more scribbles, crossed them out and added some more. He'd put the book down, picked it up, and put it down again. He moved it from the sofa to the table, and put his pen next to it. It was 7.47 p.m.

Now he was sitting on the sofa again and it was 7.49 p.m. He sighed and stretched, trying to convince himself to be casual. She was just being friendly and helpful. She cared about the club and wanted them to do well. She wanted him to do well. She liked him. Wait! Where did that come from? 'Hang on,' he said out loud. 'Hang on,' then back inside his own thoughts. Where did that come from? He told himself that they were just going to talk about football over a glass of wine, and he felt a little easier. It could be anybody. A man, a woman, it didn't matter. They were just going to talk about football. It was 7.51 p.m. He hadn't convinced himself. Must try harder! He did. It was still hardly convincing. 'Just keep things in perspective,' he said out loud again, as if the spoken word would inject more certainty to the thought process. 'Just concentrate on football things. That's what you're good at,' again out loud. 'Christ, what am I doing?' he laughed, mocking himself. It was 7.54 p.m.

He was still considering his whole attitude to be worthy of comic rebuke when a gentle tap at the door roused him from self-contemplation. 'Jeez. Here we go,' he said quietly. Then increasing the volume: 'Yeah, just a minute.' Grabbing the book and pen, he hurried to the door, fumbling the key in the lock. Eventually discovering the required dexterity, he opened the door. Without the headband she had worn earlier, Sophia's dark hair was free to cascade down and over shoulders. Dressed in a patterned shirt and denim jeans, she smiled. 'All ready to go?'

As they strolled across the road in front of the complex and then down towards the crossroads, Moreton wanted to say something, but could think of nothing that wouldn't sound crass. Eventually, it was Sophia who spoke. 'What do you think of our town then, Jon?' It felt strange to hear her say his name. Had she not done that when they were at the ground? He couldn't remember, but perhaps it was a "different time, different place, different situation" sort of thing. He was still contemplating when he replied, stumbling over his words.

'Yeah, well, yeah,' he babbled before regaining a semblance of composure. 'To be honest, I haven't seen that much of it,' before adding: 'It seems nice' and wishing he hadn't. It sounded forced, because it was. Rapidly following up with: 'I went to the shop,' before realising it was another mistake.

Sophia smiled, 'The shop?'

'Yeah, I bought a pineapple and some mayonnaise,' he said, instantly regretting the unnecessary verbosity involved. He chastised himself quietly. 'I bought a pineapple and some mayonnaise!' His inner critical voice mocked him mercilessly. It was the sort of statement that hardly prompted a casual response, and Sophia failed to find an appropriate one.

'Oh, do you like mayonnaise then?'

'No, not really.' He smiled gently; tumbles, stumbles and self-criticism were then cast aside as he laughed. 'I gave it to the guy who was sitting outside asking for spare change.'

Sophia joined in the laughter.

'I gave him the pineapple too,' Moreton added and they both laughed again as frozen waters melted and chunks of broken ice floated away down the warming river.

By the time they arrived at the bar by the first traffic roundabout, both felt easier in the other's company.

'Here we are. This is Carlito's bar. There are others nearby, but I wanted to bring you to a Spanish bar, rather than one where tourists usually go.'

The bar felt unlike anything Moreton had been used to in England. Two rows of five dark wooden tables, each with four chairs surrounding them filled the room, with four high stools at the bar. At far side of the room was a large television, but it was playing only music. Sophia walked to the third table in the row alongside the large window facing back outside across a covered seating area and, beyond that, towards the road. Sitting down, Moreton took one of the seats opposite her.

A waitress came across to the table and said something to Sophia in Spanish. She replied, before they both laughed gently. Moreton smiled, feeling it was the right thing to do, but having no real idea whether it was appropriate or not.

Sophia leaned forward conspiratorially, and Moreton responded in kind.

'She asked me if you were my new boyfriend,' she whispered.

Moreton was unsure what to say, but Sophia picked up the theme again.

'I told her no, you were my boss. But we both know that's not true, don't we?'

Moreton was unsure what she was meant. Was she alluding to the conversation about working *with* him, rather than *for* him, or implying something else. The waitress returned with two glasses of white wine and placed them on the table.

'I hope white wine is OK,' Sophia asked slightly nervously. 'I wasn't sure.'

'Yeah, no problems. Sophia,' he replied. He thought it best not to mention that he hardly drank alcohol at all, not due to any commitment to temperance, but merely because it wasn't something he enjoyed, aside from an occasional beer or two. And wine was something that he only ever had at the Christmas dinner table with his parents. He picked up the glass and took a sip, deciding that it was not all that unpleasant.

'Good?' Sophia asked.

'Perfect,' Moreton replied.

They both eased into the comfort of the chairs, the evening, and each other's company.

'So, you told me earlier that you would work hard to convince me that we were wrong about Señor Broome… and wrong about you also.' It was hardly the start to the conversation Moreton was hoping for. Something about football or anything remotely pleasant would have been much more welcome. Now he felt on the defensive again.

'So,' she continued, perhaps sensing his unease. 'Tell me about you, who you are, where you come from and why you are here in Retama.'

On a different day, in other circumstances, Moreton may have responded differently, but he was consumed by a need for the woman sitting opposite to like him. This was his chance to convince her of his intentions. Well, those that he was prepared to admit to himself, anyway.

He took another sip of wine and told his story. For the next fifteen minutes or so, he took Sophia through his life and football career, always being careful not to sound self-aggrandising, or wrapped up in self-pity. From school, through the time at Ridgeway, how he'd become involved in coaching and the chance to become a professional footballer, avoiding too much detail about the injuries that had compelled him to abandon those dreams. The mental wound was still raw. Even if the physical one on his right knee had healed, the scars of both remained.

He then explained how Charlie Broome had persuaded his father to give him such a big break into professional coaching. How he'd earned his badges, his work with young players there, the success he had enjoyed and then how things had ended with the club being sold.

Moreton could tell that Sophia was surprised at how helpful Charlie Broome had been to him. Modesty had prevented him describing how he had helped the young Broome when they were both playing at Ridgeway, and how he had protected him from the harsh banter of some of the other players.

'Señor Broome does not give people the impression that he is nice,' Sophia explained after hearing the story. 'No one at Retama is convinced by him. They feel that they don't know him very well, and that he doesn't want that to change. I think that is why people do not trust him.' She half-smiled. 'And why I think people here do not trust you – or perhaps did not, at least.' The smile broadened, and Moreton responded in full measure.

'I understand. Charlie can be a bit funny sometimes. Well, not funny, but difficult to appreciate, difficult to like, I suppose. Sometimes he doesn't try hard enough to convince people.' Moreton struggled to articulate what he meant, but Sophia seemed to understand, and nodded slowly.

'And he is why you are here?'

Moreton nodded and explained how difficult it had been after the club had been sold and how he had felt so down. He looked down at the table, picking up his wine glass up, gently tilting it and moving the liquid inside around in gentle swirls as the thoughts swum in his mind. He was quiet for a moment.

'And what happened, then?' Sophia asked, gently lowering a ladder for him to climb up, and clear of the sad introspection. Moreton raised his gaze, and the sight of Sophia sitting opposite him caused an involuntary burst of happiness to push the sad memories to the back of his mind once more.

'And then,' he said, suddenly feeling positive again. 'And then, along came the cavalry again, in the familiar shape of Charlie Broome.' He explained how his friend had contacted him and described the business he had bought in Spain, the football club and the chance to resurrect it. He left out the part about how Broome had described García as some old friend of the previous owner who didn't know what he was doing. Surely, that had been a misunderstanding. He knew that Sophia would not appreciate the less than flattering description of her grandfather's brother. 'That's the story of my life,' he concluded. 'That's how I came to be here in Spain. In Retama,' he paused. 'How I come to be sitting here, with you.'

He smiled.

Sophia did too.

Feeling unburdened, he sat back in his chair and took another sip of wine. Perhaps it was the atmosphere, or more likely the company, but he was getting to appreciate the taste. A comforting relaxation spread over him and before he had chance to think what he was saying, the words had tumbled from his lips. 'So, do you have a boyfriend?' he asked.

Sophia put her hand to her mouth to stifle a laugh, but failed.

'I'm sorry,' Moreton stumbled. 'Sorry, sorry. That's none of my business. I don't even know where that came from.'

Sophia laughed again with gentle empathy. 'No,' she replied, half-laughing. 'No, I don't have a boyfriend at the moment. Were you asking because of what Elena said earlier?'

Initially puzzled, Moreton realised that Elena must be the waitress. Like a man drowning in a sea of embarrassment, he grasped for the rope that may have been inadvertently thrown to him.

'Yes,' he replied all too quickly. 'I was asking because of what Elena had said to you.' Then adding: 'I didn't want to cause any problems,' and wishing he hadn't.

Sophia smiled indulgently. 'There are no problems. I explained things to Elena. She's a good friend. I've known her since we were at school together.'

It opened a door for Moreton, and he walked quickly through it.

'I guess if you've known her a long time, you must come from here as well then?'

'Yes, I've always lived in Retama.' Then she corrected herself: 'Apart from when I was at university in Madrid, when I lived there… with my boyfriend.'

Moreton had just picked up his glass to take another sip, but the added comment made him hesitate, before realising that he had done so. He swiftly raised the glass and took a drink, swallowing quickly and coughing, as air and liquid combined argumentatively in his throat.

'Sorry,' he said, spluttering and coughing again. It gave him a moment to recover his composure. 'I don't normally drink wine.'

Sophia was laughing a little, but trying to suppress it. 'Are you OK?'

'Yeah, yeah. I'm fine. You went to university in Madrid, then? What were you studying there? When was that?'

Sophia decided it was time to reciprocate, and tell Moreton a little more. 'Retama is my home. I was born here, and stayed until university. I fell in love with football and joined the girls' team at the club. It seems so long ago now. I would have been nine or ten at the time, and I played there for a few years. The club was much bigger in those days. They had lots of teams: boys and girls of different age groups, a youth team and a first team that was playing in Segunda División B and doing well. Not always near the top, but very safe in that league and they attracted three or four thousand people to watch the games at home. The Estadio Antonio Núñez was a really bright and alive place then. So much was going on and it was the centre of the community. Look at it now,' she paused with clear sadness in her eyes. 'It's such a mess now. No one has loved it for such a long time.'

'Well, they do now,' Moreton chimed in. It was his turn to rescue her from melancholy memories. 'Charlie and me. We're here to help get it back on its feet again. Bring back the good times. He can sort all the business stuff out, and I – with you – can get things right on the field.'

She smiled and looked up. 'Yes, we can.' She raised her glass in salute, and then continued. 'My father was an accountant in the town. He had a successful business. I was lucky. We were quite wealthy. He invested in a number of projects in Retama. One of them was the complex where you are staying. He bought four of the apartments there. I'm living in one of them at the moment. My father thought it would give me somewhere to go to after university. A place where I could be independent, but also where he knew I was safe, before I decided what I wanted to do.'

'Do your parents still live here then?'

'Oh, no. They always wanted to live in a quiet village in the mountains where we used to go on holidays when I was young. It's called Árboles Altos. It's not far away, perhaps a couple of hours in a car, but they were always happy there – I was too when we were on holiday. So tranquil. When I went to university, my father decided to sell the business and most of his investments in Retama, and bought a nice house in the village. They still live there now.'

Sophia paused for a moment smiling to herself, then added: 'Actually, they have a football club there as well. It's only a small club, but they'll be playing in the same league as Retama next season, so you'll get to see the village. My parents might even come to watch the game. You could meet them.'

The final four words dropped into the conversation like a boulder plunged into a shallow pool, and the resulting wave of embarrassment washed over them both. 'They may not be there, however,' Sophia hurriedly added. 'They spend a lot of time in Madrid and go on holiday frequently as well. They like Italy. We went there on holiday as well. Have you been to Italy?' Staccato words flew out of her mouth as she tried to dampen down the unease with a blanket of random sentences.

'Err, no. I've never been to Italy. Is it nice?' He too was feeling less than composed.

'Is it nice where?' Sophia asked, a little lost in her own maze of words.

'Italy.'

'Italy? What?'

It was time to try and move things back onto a more comfortable plane, and Moreton pointed the way. 'So, your parents left Retama when you went to university, then?'

'Yes, I studied Sports Science there. It was how I met Alvaro.'

Moreton looked up inquisitively. 'Alvaro? Who's Alvaro?'

Sophia blushed a little. 'He was my boyfriend.'

'Ah.'

'When you go to university in a new, strange, big city, it's really difficult. Some people knew lots of the other students that were on the same courses, but I knew no one. I was just me, from Retama, and I would have been alone, knowing no one, if it wasn't for Paco.'

Moreton looked confused. 'Paco? The goalkeeper from this afternoon? He was at the university?'

Sophia laughed, not at the logic Moreton had applied, but the concept of Paco Jiménez at a university.

'No,' she replied laughing. 'Of course not.'

Moreton felt a little chastened.

Sophia quickly moved to explain. 'Paco was at the same club as García at the time. He's been at three different clubs with him. García always trusted Paco, not only as a goalkeeper, but also as a man. Someone he could rely on to be strong and do the right things in the right way. So, whenever García moved to a new club, he tried to take Paco with him.'

Realising that more details were required, Sophia continued. 'You see, García and Paco talked a lot. They were more like friends than coach and player. García told him that I was going to university in Madrid, and how he was concerned because I wouldn't know anyone. Paco told him that he had a nephew who was in his last year at the same university, and said that he would ask him to look out for me, and at least be a friendly face there. He grew into being more than that.'

'Alvaro?'

Sophia nodded, and they both sipped their wine, knowing the next few minutes would be a little uncomfortable, and delaying the inevitable.

'Alvaro was so nice. He showed me around and, at first, was just someone to talk to, but, as time went on, we became closer and for the last four months of his time there we pretty much lived together.'

For the first time in her life when she had told someone about the relationship, it felt a little like a confession.

To Moreton, despite any affected air of indifference, it was something that he wanted to have the conversation swiftly moved beyond, but there was a morbid fascination about knowing more; a need to understand what it meant for Sophia.

'It didn't last that long,' she said, almost as if trying to draw a veil over the subject.

'Why?'

'It was his final year. He was studying the same subject, but being older than me, we were only there, together, for a few short months. We had agreed that there would be no regrets or sadness. That we would enjoy our time together and remain friends afterwards. He was going to work at a naval training academy in Galicia after university. It's a long way away from Retama. The opposite side of the country. So after he had to leave, we would be happy. We had agreed.' Sophia looked sad.

'I see,' said Moreton.

'Then he left…'

They both sat there quietly for a moment. Then she looked up. 'You see,' she said. 'That's why I know Paco: because of Alvaro. No, not how I *know* Paco, but how I *know about* Paco. How he is. Paco feels he has to look after me. With my father in Árboles Altos, he's like my special uncle, my guardian.' She smiled. 'I think it's the real reason he stays at the club, you know? I told you he was there to look after us. Me, especially,' she added. 'I think he's sworn a blood oath to García. I quite like it actually. It makes me feel like a princess with a knight in armour to make sure I'm OK, and protected from anything – or anyone – bad.'

Recovered, from the sadness, she seemed herself again. 'You're not *bad*, are you?' She smiled.

'No, I'm not bad.' He smiled back. 'Your English is very good. I'm afraid that I can hardly speak a word of Spanish.'

Sophia nodded slowly. 'I went to a very good school, and learning English was an important subject there. In a town like Retama with so many people from other countries coming to live here, especially from the United Kingdom, it is important. Retama is becoming a very cosmopolitan town. Plus, when I was in Madrid, there were some students from England and Scotland there. It helped to keep my language skills going.' She hesitated for a second. 'And, Alvaro spoke English as well.'

'So, you graduated from Madrid, and then what?' He felt it was time to put Alvaro back under cover. What Sophia had told him about Jiménez resonated with him. He better understood why he mistrusted Charlie Broome becoming part of the set up at Retama. Jiménez would probably be the last member of the team he would be able to convince of his intentions, but also the most important one.

'I came back here. García had now retired, and he had also come back to Retama. The club was in trouble and he volunteered to help out. There was very little money, but he agreed to take on the work for free.' She looked Moreton directly in the eyes, emphasising the sincerity of her words, and almost challenging him to dispute it. 'He's an amazing person. Not just a great football coach, but a great man as well. No other club at this level would have a coach who has worked in the Primera División. Do you know how special that is?' It was something she spoke of which such passion that even if he had harboured thoughts of making a comment, he would have been quickly dissuaded.

'And you decided to go and help him?'

She nodded. 'I came back to Retama, unsure of what I wanted to do. I had qualified in Sports Science, and wanted to work in football somehow, somewhere. I moved into the apartment and decided to go and help out García, at least for a while. It was the best thing I ever did. I learnt more from him in one season than in all my time in university. It wasn't only how to develop and improve players, it was about understanding why knowing each one of them is so important. They are not machines. They are people. Working with García and the players was so good, and yet, in the end, so sad. I learnt to love the players. They are like my family. They were García's family, and they became my family too. Then your… then Señor Broome comes along and tells García he has to release so many good players, especially Fouad. We tried to bring in players from the youth team to fill in the gaps, but they were too young. It was too soon. Looking back, we were always going to get relegated, and then García is removed. I was so angry.' It felt like the end of the story, but it wasn't. 'And I also kept my girls' squad as well,' she added with more than a hint of triumph.

This time it was Moreton who raised his glass in salute, reflecting on how Sophia describing the club as being a family was so reminiscent of the way Bobby Broome looked at things.

They both smiled. Sophia waved to Elena and said something in Spanish that Moreton didn't understand. Elena appeared at the table with a bottle of wine and poured some into their glasses. Casting a quick glance at Moreton, she hastily turned to Sophia and spoke quietly to her. The two women laughed as if they were on the inside of a secret that no one else was party to. Elena patted Sophia on the shoulder as she walked away, and added something as she left.

'What did she say?' Moreton asked, picking up his full glass.

'Oh, nothing really. Just some girl talk.' She picked up her glass and took a sip, looking out of the window.

He wasn't going to be invited to join the girl talk.

As the evening ticked on towards night, the conversation becomes less personal and more concerned with the fates and fortunes of Club Deportivo Retama. They spoke about the players and Moreton added more notes to his book. The bar had filled and started to emptying again, and by ten o'clock he was comfortable with the information he had. Sophia told him that the players normally trained three times a week on Tuesdays, Wednesdays and Friday for two hours from 8 p.m. The training had been brought forward today, at the request of Charlie Broome, to give Moreton a chance to meet the players.

For most of the time, whilst they were talking about the team, their drinks remained untouched. It was far more comfortable territory than what had preceded it. When they rose to leave the bar, both glasses were still half full – or half empty. The verdict would be delivered later. There was a new understanding between them, a few barriers had been broken down, but an odd one or two had been erected in their places.

Leaving the bar, they walked back to the complex, chatting about the sort of non-descript things that two people talk about when comfortable in each other's company. Unlocking and passing through the gate, they said goodnight. Sophia patted Moreton on the arm, before turning away to climb the stairs to her apartment. He paused for a moment watching her enter and close the door without looking back. He had hoped she would. He turned and climbed towards his own door, opened it and went in.

As he closed the door behind him, Sophia watched him from her window, before closing the blinds.

Opening

Wednesday passed slowly for Moreton. He swam for a while, enjoying the pool. With just a few others there it was pleasantly quiet and he had plenty of clear water to himself. Much of the rest of the time was spent catching up on news from home via the internet, reflecting on the previous evening and thinking about the training session that would take place later in the day.

After lunch, he had taken a call from Charlie Broome enquiring about how he thought things were looking. He'd explained that it was early days really, and he'd like to have a few sessions training first before he could make any real comment, saying nothing about his meeting with Sophia.

By 7.30 p.m. he was out of the apartment and ready to jog down to the ground. He thought about knocking on Sophia's door, but decided not to. He unlocked the gate to the complex, threw his keys into his bag and set off. He was surprised to see so many of the small shops still working and, as he reached the roundabout by Retama Azulejos, that the showroom was still open with customers walking in and out. Putting his thoughts to one side, he carried on until he arrived at the gates of the ground. They were closed, but unlocked. He pushed them open, walked in, and eased them closed again behind him. Jumping up the steep concrete steps, he noticed how quiet it was and reaching the top, the view out onto the pitch revealed why. There was no one there.

He flicked back the sleeve of his sweatshirt to look at his watch. It was 7.55. Still a little early, but only by a few minutes. He walked down the concrete steps and vaulted over the wall onto the playing surface. Walking to the centre-circle, he set his bag on the floor and looked around for a sight of anyone, but he was alone. He sat down, opened his bag and pulled out his notebook.

He wasn't sure how long he'd been sitting there going over his notes again, refreshing his mind but, sometime later, off to his left, he heard voices. Looking up and, shading his eyes, saw a stream of players heading towards him. Alongside them was Sophia. As they walked towards him, she said something to them, and the group trotted towards the edge of the pitch before jogging around its edges for a couple of circuits. Sophia walked over to him.

Dressed in baggy tracksuit bottoms, and the red, white and black hooped football shirt of her university team, with a pink headband, she looked so different, and yet so pleasingly similar.

'Hi,' she said.

'Hi,' he replied, incapable of not smiling. 'What's going on? I expected people to be here and ready to start at eight, not rolling in as a group ten minutes later… with you alongside them.'

Sophia shook her head. 'They were here and ready to go before you arrived. I wanted to talk to them first, so I took them off the pitch into the dressing room. I wanted to talk to them while you weren't there.'

'Why? What did you want to talk to them about?' He felt more than a little betrayed.

'I wanted to talk to them about you. I wanted to tell them about last night. Well, some of it anyway. I listened to what you said and thought it through. I wanted to tell them that they should give you a chance; that I thought you may genuinely be here to try and help them – and the club – no matter how you came to be here, and what went before. I told them that I thought you were, you know, well – not bad.' Her smile broadened at the last two words. Moreton hoped he had understood what Sophia meant by them.

'Thanks, I won't let you down.'

Sophia nodded. 'You had better not let anyone down. Paco still doesn't trust you and the others aren't really convinced. You still have a lot of work to do. By the way, I told them that we talked on the way back, not that we went out last evening together. I didn't want to put Paco on alert about something that was as innocent as that, otherwise he'd have been watching you like a hawk. You know that he's my guardian.'

Moreton, half-smiled, putting considerations for anything but football out of his mind, at least for a while. It was work time. Having finished their circuits jogging, the players assembled in front of Moreton and Sophia, and began stretches. 'What do you want to do?' Sophia asked, turning towards Moreton.

'You take the session, I just want to watch.'

'OK. What do you want me to work on?'

'Right. Set up some passing drills with 3 v 2 overloads in 5 by 5 metre grids. Lose possession and you go into the two. Then, condition it to just two touches. Ten minutes of each. After that, we'll have some shooting drills, passes cut back from the line and first-time shots, rotate the keepers. I want to see both Jiménez and Juan in action. Then I want to see how you work corners at the moment, both attacking and defending.' It was nothing too involved, but would allow him to watch the players at work, and also evaluate how Sophia ran things. All he needed to do now, was to get the word *innocent* out of his head.

Sophia walked away and spoke to the players, separating them into grids for the passing drill. Moreton's gaze followed her as she started the practices and set the players into action, cajoling and criticising, but also laughing with them when they made mistakes. In her football shirt and tracksuit trousers, with her dark hair swept back, he could tell that she was now *at work* with any other thoughts put to one side.

The 3 v 2 drill was always popular, fairly basic, but with a competitive edge. Sophia had included both goalkeepers in the drill. It was something Moreton hadn't expected her to do, but he knew the logic was sound. The last man in defence was also the first man in attack. In the modern game, even for goalkeepers, ability on the ball was viewed as being of increasing importance. He was impressed that she had done it.

Moreton walked around watching each of the groups in turn, paying particular attention to the forwards, Bendonces, Santi and José. He had learnt from experience with younger players that forwards often considered these sorts of things unnecessary and irrelevant to their game. Many of them were passive and often content to be in the "two" chasing possession, although chasing would hardly be an apt description for the sort of wandering round they often did.

Reaching the group with Revi, Adrián and Santi as the three and Bendonces and Felipe Blanco as the defenders, he could quickly discern that the former of the pair fitted into that pattern. Lunges and half-hearted stretches were less than convincing displays of simulated effort. The only time that Bendonces appeared to become energised was when the ball was with Santi. It was as if he felt he could impose himself on someone he considered to be both his understudy and easily dominated. At other times, it would just be Felipe chasing around. He called Sophia over to him.

'Ask them to stop please? And then start them again. Count how many passes are completed with those two defending.' Sophia did so and they both watched as the ball was passed around by the three. Each time possession was lost, Sophia started them again with the same two in the middle. After a couple of minutes play, Moreton walked into the grid and, holding his arms out, asked them to stop.

He walked back towards Sophia. 'I got eight, four, eight and six,' he called out.

She nodded.

'And the only time they lost the ball was when Bendonces hassled Santi out of possession. Yes?'

She nodded again.

'Right.' He walked to the next grid. All of the players had stopped as they watched Moreton. He beckoned to Victor to join the group and pointed to Santi to replace him. 'OK. Same thing. Let's go.' They watched, as this time, Bendonces was even more passive, with his perceived victim now removed, there was no easy prey. He trotted around covering half the ground that the energetic and enthusiastic Felipe did. Again, after a couple of minutes, Moreton called a halt.

'OK,' he said to Sophia, 'let's set up the shooting drill. Ball laid back from the corner of goal line and penalty area, rotating in turn from the left and the right flanks, shots from the edge of the box, first time only, rotate the passers every dozen passes or so. Let's have six shots at each keeper.'

As Sophia passed on the instructions, Moreton walked to his bag and took out the notebook, scribbling down some brief notes as he walked back towards the penalty area where the drill was being set up. Balls were being played in and shots on goal followed. It was the sort of drill forwards enjoyed, and now Bendonces was in his element. First in the queue to shoot, he drilled home his first attempt as Jiménez vainly stretched to the corner. As the line of players each moved forwards again in rotation, he also scored the second, smiling confidently as he peeled away fist pumping at his side. As the third attempt came to him from the right, the pass was slightly long from Vasquez. The forward coolly controlled with his left foot before hammering home again with his right. He then waved angrily and shouted towards Vasquez, clearly annoyed at the inaccuracy of the pass.

Without hesitation, Moreton strode forward, waving his hands to stop the drill. He walked to the edge of the penalty area shaking his head and crossing his arms in front of him as if wiping out the goal. '*Uno*,' he called out stridently, raising one finger into the air. '*Uno. Si?* He nodded with exaggeration. '*Duo?* No,' he confirmed shaking his head to emphasise the point. He then swept both arms forwards at his side indicating that the drill should begin again. As he walked back to Sophia, he cast a sideways glance towards Bendonces who was talking quietly to Revi. It took little command of the Spanish language to understand his attitude and reaction to Moreton's intervention.

Sophia looked to him quizzically. He had expected it. 'In a game, there's never going to be the perfect pass to you. This drill isn't about how many goals you can score. It's about testing your technique, challenging your technique. It's about looking at where you can improve, where you need to improve. He could have hit the ball with his left foot. He might have missed, but if he's weak on that foot, it's where he needs to improve and you only do that by working on the weakness. He just wanted to score, though.'

The shooting continued. 'In that passing drill, after the change, what was the pass count?'

Sophia scanned her memory for a moment. 'Ten, eight, and nine, I think.'

He smiled. 'The exact number doesn't matter. The point is that it was more than before, wasn't it?'

She nodded.

'Why was that do you think?'

'Because Victor is better in possession than Santi?'

'That's true. But it's more than that. Footballers are people.' He paused, shaking his head a little and laughed at his own remark. 'Do you remember when you told me that García knew the players as people as well as footballers? How he thought that was important?'

Sophia nodded.

It sounded strange when spoken out loud, but it was something that he had always found important when he was coaching, be it at Ridgeway, or with the professionals as his career had progressed. He had been delighted that García had a similar approach. Despite what Charlie Broome had said about him, this man clearly knew the game and how to develop players.

'They're all different. Bendonces,' he said, nodding at the player as he scored from another shot, and pointedly looked at Moreton as if in defiance, 'he sees himself as the main goal scorer here, and perhaps he is. The problem is that if he believes that, he'll never be anything more than that, and over time, that will go as well. He dominates Santi. He probably does the same with José as well. He thinks he's top dog and wants things to stay that way.'

Moreton could tell that Sophia wasn't totally convinced.

'Look, do you remember when you told me about Paco? About how he looked after the younger players. I think you said that he thought Juan had got real talent as a goalkeeper, but lacked confidence, and could become a great goalkeeper. How Paco worked with him?'

Sophia nodded slowly, and Moreton could tell she was picking up on his thoughts.

'Does Bendonces do the same with Santi or José? Has he ever said how good they could be? Has he ever encouraged them, helped them, or did he ever suggest to García that one of them should play in front of him?' Moreton was watching the drill continue. He knew the answer without even looking at Sophia for confirmation. 'Good players know they need to learn. Great players know they need to never stop learning. When you think you know all the answers, it's time to realise that you don't know all of the questions. Bendonces has closed his school book.'

He smiled at Sophia, and was pleased to see her nod in agreement.

'It would be really useful, though, if we had someone with decent experience to help the younger forwards,' he lamented. 'Bendonces, just isn't that guy.'

The affirmation encouraged him to go on. 'I'm going to take a guess at how García had the team line up last season. Is that OK?'

Sophia didn't reply, but looked at him with a less than fully convinced expression.

'Paco in goal, of course. Alejandro, Kiko, Victor and Adrián at the back with Vasquez on one flank and Palermo on the other. Samuel and Matías in the centre. Revi and Bendonces as the forwards. Is that correct?'

Sophia appeared less than happy with the opinion ventured. 'Yes,' she said hardly disguising the irritation in her voice. 'García had no choice. Fouad had gone. So had many others. We were left with just a few players and these kids. What could he do? So many of them were just too young to play and when they did, they were hardly a match for the other team.'

Moreton quickly realised how his words had caused offence. 'No, I wasn't criticising anything that García did. The point I was making is that it was precisely the team that I would have picked as well. What other choice did he have?'

Sophia was clearly still annoyed, but her ire had eased a little.

'The thing is, that now, some of these players are a little older and, thanks to García, having played and trained under him, a lot wiser about the game. We have a few options that García didn't have. And that's thanks to him and the work he did.' The words, entirely sincere as they were, had the desired effect. Balm had soothed away the anger and understandable defence of her great uncle.

They stood in silence for a minute or so, although it felt like much longer as more shots went in. Eventually, Moreton decided to move things on. 'Let's set up a few corners. We'll have Torres in goal. We can change to Paco after five minutes or so, but I want him to feel he's part of things, rather than being just someone who watches.'

Sophia smiled and nodded.

'We'll have Alejandro, Kiko, Victor, Adrián, Matías and Samuel defending. The others in attack. I want to see how we set up. Let's just have ten minutes – five with Torres and five with Paco between the sticks, and then we can have a warm down and call it a day.'

Moreton was scribbling notes as Sophia set things in place, and was still engrossed in his thoughts when the first corner came in. Vasquez crossed from the right and the first ball was over hit. Bendonces spoke to José, and pointed towards Kiko. The young man trotted over obediently towards the teenage defender. The next corner was crossed in more accurately, and as Kiko moved towards it, José blocked his run and Bendonces filled the space to head home. Sophia looked towards Moreton, but his head was still buried in his notebook. The next one was too close to the goalkeeper and Torres came out to catch. A shout from Jiménez standing beside the goal and applause for the young goalkeeper snatched Moreton's attention back to the action in front of him. Sophia looked across from where she was standing, smiled and nodded to Moreton. He smiled back. Ten minutes later, the session ended and, after a warm down, Sophia sent the players to the dressing room before walking over to Moreton.

'What did you think?'

'Well, I'm getting to know the players better. It would be good if we could arrange a couple of practice games before the season starts. That would be much more helpful.'

'I know a few people. Leave it with me.'

They walked over to where Moreton had left his bag. As he was putting his notebook away, Sophia had an idea. 'There's a club not far from here. They only run a youth team. It's a small club, and not very serious but the coach there is a good person and he looks after his players. He might bring a team to play us in a practice game.'

Raising his attention from the newly stowed and organised bag, Moreton stood up again. 'That sounds good. Tell them it's just a practice game. No one's going to be keeping score, and playing against a youth team will mean our younger guys aren't going to feel intimidated.'

'OK, I'll speak to him,' she said, walking away, before stopping. 'I thought you didn't speak Spanish?' she said playfully, and with a wide smile.

'Sorry?'

'*Uno. Dos. Si. No!* What other words do you need?' She laughed.

Moreton had been so wrapped up in getting the message across to the players that he hadn't realised what he had done. 'Oh, yes. I'm a pretty quick learner.' He laughed as well.

'*Uno*,' repeated Sophia, pointing to herself. '*Dos*,' she continued, pointing to both of them in turn. '*Si?*' It was almost a question, but not quite. So nearly, but still not quite. Then '*No.*' She shook her head and then shrugged her shoulders with a smile.

'I need to go and speak to the guys and make sure everything is locked up,' she said, before turning and jogging away.

Moreton picked up his bag, walked across the pitch, up the concrete steps and down the other side, through the gate and into the street outside. It had been an interesting session, and already Moreton was getting a better idea of the players at the club, and forming some ideas of what he could do with them. He slung the bag over his shoulder and walked rather than jogged back towards the apartment.

As he approached the roundabout by Retama Azulejos, he could see some workmen with scaffolding at the front of the showroom. The façade had been painted from its previous red colours to an entirely new livery, green and white. They had also just replaced the sign there. What had once been a business named after its location, was now one that carried its new owner's name. In bright white letters on a green background, the name Broome Cerámica announced its arrival in Retama. Moreton walked on, lost in his thoughts about the session, but despite a concentration to the contrary, the words *innocent*, *uno*, *dos*, *si* and *no* kept elbowing their way into his consciousness. He tried to bat them away but they were insistent.

Back in the apartment, he had just come out of the shower when there was a knock at the door. As far as he knew, there were only two people in the town who knew he was there – Charlie Broome and Sophia. Hurriedly, he threw on a T-shirt and a clean pair of jogging bottoms, before heading towards the door.

Opening it, he smiled to see Sophia there, still in her football top and tracksuit bottoms, clearly having just returned from the stadium. Unsure of the motive for the call, Moreton fumbled his words. 'Hi,' he said. 'How are you?'

She laughed pleasantly without mocking his awkwardness.

'I'm still fine. Nothing much has changed in the last hour or so'

'Yeah, sorry.' He laughed. 'I just got out of the shower.'

She looked at his hair, still wet. 'Yes, I can see. Look, I've spoken with Nicolás.'

'Nicolás?'.

'Nicolás. The man who coaches the youth team we were speaking about.'

'Oh, yes.'

'I spoke with him about organising a game and he wasn't too sure as his players are young to be going into a game against a full age team.'

Moreton suddenly realised how awkward it felt to be talking to Sophia, keeping her outside as if she was some kind of door-to-door double-glazing salesperson.

'Do you want to come in?'

'I really need to shower,' she replied, brushing dust from her tracksuit trousers before wiping her forehead with the shirt sleeve.

'That's fine,' he said innocently, stepping to one side to invite her inside.

'Are you inviting me into your apartment to take a shower here?' she asked smirking.

'N-n-no. No. No. I just meant that it was OK. Not to shower here. But to come in as you were. As you are. It's fine.' He laughed. 'Sorry.'

They both laughed.

'Probably best not to. Anyway, I've spoken with Nicolás and he said he could arrange it, but he'd like him and a couple of the other coaches to play as well, to keep things more even. I told him that was OK. Is it?'

Moreton thought for a second before agreeing. 'Yeah, that's fine.'

'OK, a week on Sunday, they'll be over in the afternoon for a four o'clock start.'

Moreton nodded again. 'That's great.'

Sophia turned to walk back down the steps and, as she did so, a flood of confidence washed over Moreton. 'You don't want that shower then?' he laughed, before all composure drained away and he blanched slightly at what he had said.

Sophia smiled back up at him from the bottom of the steps. 'Probably best not to'.

He nodded and smiled back, watching her cross the narrow pathway, through the gate and up the steps to her own apartment opposite. Unlocking the door, she turned and saw him still standing there.

'Not yet, anyway.' She opened the door, entered and closed it behind her.

Moreton stood there for a few seconds searching for the right words in reply, before discovering that none existed and even if the forlorn quest had found any bon mots, there was no one there to hear them. He turned and closed the door behind him.

Link

The next few days passed fairly uneventfully. Moreton was becoming more used to the flow of life in Retama. He had even mastered the art of shopping at the supermarket without suggesting a strange menu of foods to the man who always sat outside. As was becoming a habit, however, he dropped a few coins into the old man's battered cup instead, receiving a smile as a receipt. Other than when reviewing notes, working on adaptations of training drills or potential tactical formations, his time was spent mainly reading, and looking at news – usually pertaining to football at home – on his phone or iPad. Visits to the pool became an increasing and pleasant pastime as the Spanish summer grew in intensity.

Occasionally, when preparing a meal, he would find himself looking out from his kitchen window towards the door opposite, before his consciousness shook him from such wanton caprice. Sometimes when reading, he'd hear a door close and assume it was Sophia, arriving or departing – he couldn't be sure – and, resisting the temptation to jump up and check, would merely sit and try to dismiss any such thoughts from his mind.

It was on such a Thursday evening that a news item on the iPad caught his attention: *Former Premier League Star arrested after Nightclub brawl* blared the headline. Below it was a picture of a weary, and somewhat the worse-for-wear man who looked very much like Billy Swan used to. Attention piqued, by his former team-mate's plight, he eagerly scrolled down to see the details.

Having returned to London, the report related that Swan had been working on local radio talk shows provoking controversy with the required amount of outlandish comment and offering punditry during games as well as featuring on the sort of after dinner speaking circuit, often glibly described as being applicable primarily to "Gentlemen's Clubs."

With radio exposure limited in the off season, Swan had been undertaking a hectic schedule of speaking engagements and, after completing one of them in the capital, a group of men from a local football club had offered to take him out on the town, eagerly grasping the opportunity to be seen with a celebrity. Swan needed little encouragement for such soirees, and after the regular copious drinking at the event, they had ended up at a nightclub in the West End. More drinks had followed, after which, on his way across the dance floor for a call of nature, Swan had been inevitably jostled, stumbling into a girl, and knocking her to the floor. Her partner had taken aggressive exception to what he thought had been a deliberate push and had immediately lunged for Swan who, in his inebriated state, had hardly been able to defend himself or avoid the contact.

After the confrontation had attracted more participants on either side, the intervention of the club's bouncers, and a management call to the police – plus a tip-off to the local paparazzi – had brought matters to a conclusion. The story ended with the statement that the authorities were looking into the matter with a view to prosecuting Swan for assault on the girl who had sustained a fracture to the leg. Whether that had occurred with the initial contact, or as part of the collateral action during the all-in brawl that followed was unclear.

The report also related that Swan's contract with the publicity company that arranged his radio slots and appearances was being reviewed "…in light of changed circumstances."

Whilst many others reading the article – especially those inside the game who had experienced the frustration of working with Billy Swan – would have felt that it was some kind of inevitable outcome, a kind of rough justice for someone who had been gifted so much ability only to squander it on the fripperies of celebrity, Moreton felt only sympathy. Whatever the weaknesses of Billy Swan, Moreton was firmly of the conviction that none of them were driven by malevolence. He placed the iPad down on the sofa by his side, shaking his head slowly in sad reflection at the fate that had befallen the man who he had formed an unlikely bond with whilst sharing a road to recovery from injury.

Then, a thought struck him. He stood up, hesitated for a second, took the couple of steps towards the table where his phone was sitting. He stopped again, looking back at the iPad that bore an insistent reminder, a call of caution, that his thought was surely folly. He picked up the phone and, finding the contacts listings searched out "Chaz." There was another moment of doubt before he pressed the call button. Once done, there was no turning back. The fates, that would shape so many events in the coming months, were set in motion.

'Billy Swan!' Charlie Broome looked at Moreton with a surprise bordering on incredulity. 'Are you kidding, Jon?' It was hardly a question. Moreton sat across the desk from Broome in his office at Broome Cerámica. The meeting had been prompted by that telephone call the previous evening, when Moreton had asked his friend if he had ten minutes to chat over an idea he had come up with. By now, the owner of Broome Cerámica was regretting taking the call at all.

'Look, I know what you're thinking…' Moreton protested.

'Really, Jon? Do you?'

'Chaz. Listen to me. Just give me five minutes to explain.'

Broome eased back into the large black leather chair. It wasn't what anyone – especially Charlie Broome at that moment – would describe as a relaxed pose, but even so, the sigh of resigned acceptance that accompanied it, suggested to Moreton that it was an invitation to make his pitch. He seized the opportunity.

'I know the guy's got a bad reputation,' he said, trying to dispel the all-pervading air of negativity in the room. 'And, to be honest, some of it was fair. Billy's always been a bit of a rebel, but so much of that is down to his background; the environment he grew up in, and how he had to learn to look after himself.'

The expression on Broome's face had hardly been changed by Moreton's opening gambit. 'This isn't helping, Jon. You know that don't you? Are you suggesting that I should apologise for being born into my family, and then do this clown some kind of favour just because his upbringing was something akin to East Enders?'

Moreton realised that his reasoning had been misinterpreted. 'Of course not, Chaz.' He held his arms out wide inviting acceptance. 'I wasn't relating his situation to you at all. All I'm saying is that he had a rough time as a kid, and that shaped his outlook on life. I'm not sure this is going to make my plan more amenable to you, but here's an example of what I mean. There's something Billy always used to say that, to be honest, always pissed me off. "It ain't about football. It's about the dosh!" He'd grown up with no money in a deprived area of London. He valued money because, when he was growing up, he'd never had any. Oh yeah. And one other thing. He'd also tell anyone who'd listen to him that it's all about looking after number one.'

Moreton laid out his plan. 'When I was injured and trying to get back to fitness at the club, Billy was out of action at the same time and we shared some gruelling hours in the gym, on the physio's table and working through painful exercises. You know how committed I am Chaz. Well, Billy worked every bit as hard as I did. He drove me on as well. He knew that he had to get fit to get a new contract and earn the money he wanted. Some people called him lazy and said that his attitude hacked coaches and team-mates off. It probably did, but, if he saw something in it for himself, he'd work his bollocks off to get it. On top of that, he's probably the most gifted player I've ever seen.'

Was he getting anywhere? Moreton wasn't sure, but at least Broome hadn't cut him off. He pressed on. 'Look, Chaz. There's a lot of young players down there,' he continued nodding in the vague direction of the nearby home of CD Retama. 'Some are pretty talented, but they're just kids and need someone with experience to set them up and guide them in games. Paco's good, but he's a goalkeeper and stuck at one end of the pitch…'

Moreton stopped for a second, noticing that the mention of Paco's name had brought a reaction from Broome. Not exactly a wince, but an almost imperceptible raising of the eyebrows. A memory of Jiménez's reaction after he had been told that García was being removed was hardly a pleasant recollection. He continued. 'I can't do it. I'd love to be playing again, but it would be a crazy thing to do. I could end up in a wheelchair, and Bendonces isn't going to do it. He's too wrapped up in himself.'

'The guy with the beard?' Broome enquired.

Moreton nodded.

'Yeah, he's a miserable sod,' Broome confirmed, inducing a wry smile of understanding from Moreton. 'And, no Jon. You can't play.'

'But Billy could be that man.'

'Isn't he about fifty now, though?'

'I think he's thirty-five or thirty-six now.' His research ahead of the meeting had suggested otherwise, but he had resolved that so long as he only declared it as an opinion rather than a fact, it didn't count as being misleading. 'Besides, I don't want him doing too much running. He can play just off the striker and ahead of the midfield. At this level, he could probably play in his fifties anyway. He'll just need to get the ball, pass it on, look for the opportunities to create openings and stick his goals away when the chances come. He can do that Chaz. At this level, at his age, he can do that. No problem!'

Broome had recovered his composure. He leant forward, elbows on the desk and chin resting on interlocked fingers. Moreton thought he was making progress. It soon became clear that he was.

'OK, Jon,' Broome said slowly and in carefully measured tones. 'Let's suppose, just for a minute, that I think this crazy idea has some hidden merit that I can't see. Why would someone like Billy Swan consider coming out to here? This is Retama, Jon. It's not Madrid or Barcelona. I'm not sure this is the sort of place he'd think was attractive.'

Ahead of the meeting, Moreton had planned the conversation with the same meticulous attention to detail that he applied to his training sessions. There's always the unexpected, requiring a bit of thinking on your feet, but the question that the man behind the desk had just posed was always going to be asked.

'That's a fair question, Chaz,' he said, as if musing on the conundrum. 'Here's how I see it, though: you probably saw the news about the nightclub incident.'

Broome nodded slowly, as if his argument was now being made for him.

'Yeah, well. Not great I give you,' Moreton said, before playing his cards. 'That all meant that he's now going to lose his radio work and the public appearances, and speaking options will dry up. Basically, he'll be out of work, with no income. Plus, I've made a couple of calls to some old team-mates, and rumour has it that Billy's in debt to some of the sort of people you don't want to be in debt to, gambling debts apparently. So, getting out of the country for a while, might just be what the doctor ordered. You're good at financial negotiations. You could offer to pay him enough to live on for the months he's here. Plus, I know how you like business deals – tell him there's a decent bonus in it for him, if he helps to get the right outcome for the club. Give him the right incentive and, as I said, he'll work like a demon to get it. If he gets the club promoted, you'll be quids in and he'll get the brass he needs. Everyone's a winner.'

With his pitch delivered, Moreton sat back in his chair. Broome's expression was inscrutable, but Moreton knew that the idea had been established as having at least some merit. The financial aspect was always going to be key. Had he delivered the pitch well? A small portion of flattery, served with delicacy can taste so sweet. Too much, though, clumsily posited, and the palate will react with bitterness, provoking disdain and anger. The next few moments would decide.

Broome raised his chin from where it had rested on his hands. He pursed his lips in thought, and then rubbed his forefinger across them, temporarily lost in perusal and seemingly oblivious to the presence of the other person in the room.

'Tell you what, Chaz,' Moreton said, to break the silence. 'I'll even speak to him myself. You don't need to do anything yet. I'll make the suggestion, and if he blows me off, we can forget it. Nothing lost.'

He was expecting a response. None came. Broome was clearly still considering the suggestion. Eventually he spoke. Initially, it wasn't the response that Moreton had been hoping for.

'No,' Broome said slowly, but with a tone that suggested he would brook no argument to his conclusion. 'No, Jon.'

Moreton felt more than a little disappointed, but his mood would be lifted.

'Leave it to me,' Broome added, with a smile now spreading across those lips. 'I'll speak to him. I know a few people who can put me in touch with your

Mr Swan. I'll make a few calls today. I'm flying back to England tomorrow for a few days, to meet with the old man and the accountants. If he's interested, I can arrange a meeting with him and let's see how it pans out.'

The uplift in Moreton's mood was obvious, but Broome quickly stepped in to temper any overly optimistic assumptions.

'Jon,' he declared with a firmness that illustrated his perception of the power relationship between them. 'No promises, OK? There are five hundred reasons why this isn't going to happen, and only one that says it might. If I don't get the vibe that your friend is going to guarantee me the return on investment that I require, then it's a non-starter. The door's closed on it. You understand, Jon?'

The tone of voice and demeanour of the declaration felt uncomfortable to Moreton, but at least he'd got the most part of what he had gone into the meeting for.

'Sure, Chaz,' he replied. 'That's fair enough.'

With that, and after exchanging a few pleasantries, wishing Broome a safe journey and asking to be remembered to his father, Moreton left the office, closing the door behind him. He smiled at the receptionist '*Hasta luego*,' she called after him. He turned, smiled and nodded at her – hoping it was the correct response.

Old and the New

Training sessions were well attended and as he deployed more of the drills he had used so successfully when working at Bobby Broome's club, Moreton felt he was achieving a better understanding of the squad, both as players and people. There also seemed to be an easing of tension between the players and him; something he was happy to ascribe to the persuasions of Sophia. Drills became more developed: when and how to change the direction of attack, transition at the change of possession, pressing in the final third, were all well received.

Initially, Moreton had thought that it was merely a general acceptance that the sessions were useful. He asked Sophia what the players had thought of the recent training sessions.

'Ah,' she said with a knowing smile, adding: 'They like them.'

'That's great.'

'Do you know why?'

'I guess because they work,' he said hesitantly, and immediately realising that there was much more to the matter than he had realised.

Sophia smiled again. 'Well, yes. But that's not the main reason.'

His confidence shaken; Moreton awaited the completion of the explanation.

'It's because they are very similar to what García did. Not the same of course, but they can see the similarities in approach. And if García was doing the same things, they know that they are right.' She nodded slowly in confirmation of her own comments.

'OK,' Moreton replied.

'And, they know that perhaps you may be a little like the "great coach" that Señor Broome said you were.' She laughed happily. He did too.

Inevitably, given their regular conversations at training, the relationship with Sophia had become much less awkward, the common language of football made for easy conversations.

On the day before the practice game, Moreton had asked for the players to come to the Estadio Antonio Núñez for an extra session. He was quick to add, that it wasn't for training, but to discuss the game. He was both delighted, and a little pleasantly surprised when he arrived at the ground to find the entire squad already there. He'd planned to take them into the changing-room to hold the session indoors, having always found that conversations in a closed environment helped to concentrate minds on the matter at hand. Sophia told him however that perhaps it might be a little crowded in there. With all of the players, plus the two of them, there wouldn't be much room. It felt like the right place to be, though, so he had gone ahead.

Once inside, the reasons for Sophia's concern were clear. What had seemed a somewhat cold and uninvitingly dark room when Moreton had first visited it, was now over full with bodies, each fully dressed rather than in football strip. Benches wrapped along three sides of the room, with an open entrance to a small shower area off to one side. The floor was tiled, but cracked in a number of places and the blue paint was flaking away, revealing the yellowing plaster beneath it. It seemed to fit in with the atmosphere of decay prevalent throughout the stadium. The stifling atmosphere precluded any long debate, so Moreton got to work.

Through Sophia's translation, he related how important it was to treat the following day's game as a training session. The score didn't matter. He was looking for how the team combined. How they worked. Who was best fitted to which position. What combinations worked best. He also told them that he would make any number of changes throughout the game, and move players around into different positions. He asked Sophia to make it clear that, when he made changes, the players should always take it seriously, but never take it personally. He wasn't sure if there was a similar phrase in Spanish, but trusted her to get the message across effectively. Nothing would be about criticism. It would all be about learning for the players, for him, and for Sophia.

The team was read out. Jiménez would start in goal, but he asked Sophia to say that Torres would take over after halftime. He wanted both goalkeepers to be fully involved. The back four would be Alejandro, Kiko, Victor and Adrián. The two wide players were to be Vasquez and Palermo, with Samuel and Matías in the centre. Revi would play as the number ten with Bendonces leading the line. There were nods of acknowledgement from all around as starting players, as well as those left out, felt comfortable with the selection – if for opposing reasons. Moreton sensed this, and had plans to change both emotions.

After arranging the time to turn up on the following day, the players left. Sophia and Moreton were alone in the dressing room as he tidied up his notes and packed them into the bag.

'I will get the old man to lock up,' she said, walking out of the door. Moreton sat down on bench and looked around him. The room hardly gave off the sort of atmosphere required for an invigorating team-talk before a game. He sighed, and then an idea struck him.

A couple of moments later, Sophia appeared back at the door accompanied by an old man whose appearance suggested a great, but indeterminate, age. Wearing a blue cardigan over a shirt that was probably once white, rather than the greyish hue of its present condition, brown trousers and heavy boots, it was topped off with a blue cap carrying a faded crest on its front.

'Jon, this is Esteban. He's looks after the stadium, and does all the odd jobs to keep the place running.'

'Hi,' said Moreton. Then correcting himself: '*Hola.*' The response from Esteban was gruff, indiscernible and unaccompanied by any change to the grizzled facial expression.

'He's going to lock up if you're ready to leave,' she added. Moreton jumped to his feet in reply.

'Are you in any hurry to go? Are you doing anything tonight?'

Sophia looked a little confused. 'What? Are you asking me out?'

He hesitated briefly. 'No. No… Well, perhaps in a way. Well how about *no*, and then *yes*?' The answer had hardly resolved the query.

Esteban, not understanding any of the exchange merely stood implacably by.

'I've got an idea. And Esteban might be just the man to make it happen.'
They both looked at the old man, who stared blankly at them in reply.

Two hours later, the three of them left the dressing room and Esteban locked the door. Both Sophia and Moreton were splattered with flecks of blue, as some Dalmatian designed with an inappropriate colour palette. As they walked across the pitch, climbed the concrete steps and descended the other side towards the gates, with Esteban trailing a way behind them, they laughed at the state each of them had got into. Had either ever decided to pursue an alternative career, it seemed certain that interior decorating would not be a wise choice.

A further hour had passed when, with showers and change of clothes completed, they were sitting in Carlito's bar with a glass of wine in front of them. Sophia explained more to Moreton about Esteban. He had played for the club many years ago, then stayed on to help train the younger players, eventually becoming a permanent fixture at the club. Having CD Retama without Esteban was unthinkable, and the club could hardly function without him. He lived just a few minutes away from the Estadio Antonio Núñez, and was there most days doing odd jobs, as other more strenuous tasks were now beyond him due to his age and the long-term effects on his knees of playing football for so long. Moreton listened carefully.

'That's amazing,' he said, at last. 'Every club should have an Esteban, and they should be looked after and honoured by their clubs.'

Sophia smiled tolerantly. 'In Spain, a lot of small clubs do have such people. I sometimes wish that there was more we could do for Esteban, but there's not much in life that he wants. His wife died about ten years ago, his daughter is married and now lives in Valencia. She visits and has asked him to go to live with her family in the city, but Esteban would never leave Retama. It's his town, and the club is his life. I suppose it's all he has left really.'

Moreton could see that Sophia had great affection for the old man.

They both sat in silence for a few seconds, as a melancholy cloud descended on them. Eventually, it was Sophia who lifted the mood. 'So,' she said raising her glass with a smile. 'This is what you mean by taking a girl out?'

They both laughed.

'Well, not really. It's not like painting the town red, is it? In fact, it's a bit like painting the town blue.'

Behind the bar Elena tapped a colleague on the shoulder, whispered something and nodded towards the couple sitting at the table, enjoying each other's company.

Homecoming

Arriving at the ground the following day, Moreton found Sophia in conversation with Esteban, standing by a large package on the floor at the foot of the concrete steps.

'Hi,' he called as he walked across to them. 'How are you?' he asked Sophia. 'And what's in the package?'

'I'm fine. And I was going to ask you about the package. It has your name on it.'

'Really?'

'Apparently, Esteban received a call from a courier service saying they had a delivery for you and it was to come to here. And… And well, here it is. So, what is it?'

'I have no idea. Honestly, no one knows me here except you and Charlie.'

'Well, it's not from me.'

A metre or so square, the box was secured with copious amounts of tape. Moreton tried to pull at a loose edge to gain access, but it was well wrapped. Esteban reached into the pocket of his cardigan and pulled out a pen knife. Flipping open one of the blades, he passed it to Moreton. The sharp blade proved a worthy ally in convincing the package to offer up its contents. Moreton reached in and pulled out something in a cellophane bag. At first the contents were unclear, but seemed to be just one of a number of similar items in the box. Tearing open the bag though, out came a blue football shirt. Moreton unfolded the shirt, revealing a large white number four on the back, and turning it around he saw the Retama club badge on the left breast and in bold green letters placed on a white patch, the legend: Broome Cerámica.

'Wow!' He reached back into the box and it quickly became clear that it contained a complete set of dark blue shirts and shorts together with white socks. Towards the bottom of the box Sophia noticed a piece of paper. As Moreton was checking all of the numbers and shirts, repeating 'Wow,' every few seconds, she reached into the box and picked out the paper. On it, handwritten, were five words and a scribbled signature. It read "Thought these might be useful." It was signed: "Charlie."

Sophia tried to hand the note to Moreton, but his attention was elsewhere. By now twenty-two sets of kit had been revealed, the first and last numbers being all green, and allocated to the goalkeepers, but the box still wasn't empty. At the bottom lay two more bags in the same blue colour, but these were zipped tracksuit tops. Reaching in Moreton, pulled out the first one. With the same club badge emblazoned on the left, on the right, the initials in bright white lettering read "JM." He opened the top revealing the lettering and showed it to Sophia. She smiled. 'Wait,' he said, before dipping into the box for the final item. He lifted the second tracksuit top clear of its package, opening it out as he did. Much the same as the first one, it too carried a series of lettering. This one read "SG" and he handed it Sophia beaming broadly. 'Wow,' she exclaimed. Apparently, it was her turn to do so.

'Charlie Broome you bloody diamond,' Moreton said out loud. Sophia smiled at him and nodded approvingly. 'Quick,' he said. 'We've got to do something. He gathered as many of the kits as he could carry, asking Sophia to do the same, then ran up the steps, down the other side and across the pitch towards the dressing room. Esteban had already unlocked the door. Moreton threw it open and strode purposefully inside, closely followed by Sophia. The change from yesterday was immediately noticeable. Instead of the old blue flaking paint and plaster providing a backdrop, the walls were now painted afresh in bright blue. The tiles were still cracked, but the room looked brighter and so much more inviting.

'Sophia,' he said. 'Help me lay out the kits on the benches.'

They set to work, with laughs bordering on the giggles of excited schoolchildren. It was almost done when they came to a sudden halt. The number eight shirt was missing.

'Oh no,' Moreton exclaimed. 'Oh no.'

Just at that moment Esteban appeared at the door holding a shirt. He mumbled something to Sophia who laughed, and patted him on the shoulder playfully. She took the number eight shirt from the old man, folded it, and placed it neatly in its allotted position completing the set.

She looked at Moreton. 'Esteban was holding the shirt when we ran over here. It used to be his number when he played for Retama.'

Moreton smiled at the old man.

'*Lo siento*,' the old man muttered quietly.

'He said he was sorry.'

'I know,' Moreton replied. He walked over to Esteban and shook his hand. '*Gracias*,' he said, smiling. This time, there was definitely a movement in the old man's features. An oft-disregarded smile played across the features, making an irregular appearance. Still shaking Esteban's hand, he patted the old man on the shoulder with his free hand.

Suddenly, all three started as they heard voices from outside. The players were arriving. Grabbing Sophia by the arm, snatching up each of their new tracksuit tops and some other kit, he pulled her outside, leaving Esteban in the dressing room on his own. He guided Sophia a little way onto the pitch, and then stood there greeting the players as they arrived.

'Tell them,' he whispered to Sophia, 'that Esteban has a surprise for each of them in the dressing room as they pass.'

As the players entered in small groups, they could hear the excited talk coming from the dressing room as the decorating and new kits were discovered. Moreton understood hardly any of what was being said, but it wasn't difficult to discern that it was having a positive effect. Bendonces was the last to arrive, on his own, strolling across the pitch. In an exaggerated gesture to indicate that the forward was late, Moreton looked towards his watch. Any difference in the cadence of Bendonces stride was marginal, if noticeable at all. Sophia passed on the message to him as he passed, as she had with all of the other players, but received barely any hint of acknowledgement.

At that moment, another group of people began to descend the steps towards the pitch. Sophia waved at them. 'It's Nicolás,' she explained walking away from Moreton and towards the new arrivals. She chatted to them for a few moments, before pointing towards the visitors' dressing rooms and returning to Moreton. 'They've asked if one of their people can referee. A lot of the players are young, and it will help them to feel a little more secure.'

'That's fine,' Moreton agreed. They turned to walk back to the dressing room, stopping on the way to pick up and put on their tracksuit tops, zipping them up with a flourish and a smile. Then, as Esteban walked out of the dressing room, they walked in. As they entered, the players burst into applause and cheers. Moreton looked a little abashed. 'Didn't you tell them Esteban did the painting?'.

'Yes,' she replied, before speaking to Paco Jiménez who was sitting near to her. He replied and then she nodded.

'They all tried to thank Esteban,' she explained. 'But he told them that it was us. All he had done was find a couple of half-empty pots of paint, and then cleaned up afterwards.' Moreton turned around to see the figure of Esteban shuffling slowly away. He smiled at him. 'He didn't tell them about the kits. He didn't understand what the note had said. They don't know where they have come from.'

'Tell them,' Moreton replied. 'Tell them, it was Charlie.'

Sophia spoke to the players and, at first, they seemed unconvinced of the information given. Slowly though, as Sophia explained that neither she nor Moreton had known anything about it, an acceptance swept around the room.

It fell to Paco Jiménez to speak for the team. 'Mister,' he said. 'From all of us thank you, and please thank Señor Broome as well.' For the first time Moreton discovered that Jiménez could speak perfect English. His immediate reaction was to think whether he had ever said anything injudicious whilst in the goalkeeper's earshot, but the contemplation was disturbed by another round of applause. Moreton was now feeling quite uncomfortable, albeit also very happy. He crossed his arms in front of himself in a motion calling for the applause to stop. He opened the door of the dressing room, and threw out an arm inviting the players to leave.

'*Arriba Retama!*' he shouted. The players returned the call and filed out onto the pitch. For the first time at a game as a manager of a football club, Moreton walked to the trainers' dugout and sat down.

Very much as Moreton had intended, the game was much more of a training session than anything akin to an official game, although for some that didn't seem to be the case. With twenty minutes played, Retama were leading 2-0, with both goals coming from Bendonces. The first a simple header after a cross from Vasquez had eluded the young goalkeeper. The second, a tap in after Revi had pulled a ball back from the goal-line. The next time the ball rolled out of play, Moreton decided to make his first changes. The goal scorer was not impressed.

The first change was to remove him and send on Santi in his place. The young replacement looked more than a little doubtfully at Moreton as he motioned for him to go on in place of Bendonces. He held out a hand to shake with the bearded forward leaving the field, but it was almost ignored. Head down and muttering audibly as he passed the dugout, Bendonces went across to where the other members of the squad were gathered, just off the pitch, and sat down. From the dugout, Moreton watched the sullen performance, and shook his head slowly, before returning his attention to the game. By halftime, other changes had been made. Samuel was replaced and Revi moved back into the centre of midfield allowing Jose Palermo to take up his position.

As the referee ended the first period, rather than go back to the dressing room, Moreton called the group together to sit out on the pitch, and using Sophia to translate mentioned about the other changes he would make for the second-half. Torres replaced Jiménez. Felipe would play instead of Revi and Sebastián replaced Matías. Moreton asked Sophia to tell Felipe that he was playing alongside the youngster and had to be the senior partner. He must concentrate. Sophia nodded and passed on the message. He watched the player's reaction, as Felipe's blond head slowly nodded up and down in acknowledgment. The final change was to introduce Guido, not as a defender, but in place of Juan Palermo.

'There'll be more changes in the second-half,' Moreton concluded as the referee called the teams together again. Bendonces climbed to his feet, and as Moreton walked back to the dugout, he saw Bendonces call to Sophia, speaking to her before turning and strolling back to the dressing room.

'What's going on?' he asked her when she joined him.

'He said that he has a problem with his ankle and can't play any more today,' she replied, with a slight sigh.

The fact that she had related news of the apparent injury by stating that the player had told her that he had an injury, rather than relating it as fact, carried an obvious implication.

'Did he not let you check the injury? You're the club physio and the person who deals with those sorts of things.'

Sophia shook her head slowly. 'No, he told me it was an old injury and it just needed rest. He's gone to get changed and will then go home.'

'How much trouble did he have with this old injury, last season?'

Sophia looked at him without reply. It told the complete story.

'OK,' Moreton conceded. 'OK.'

Initially, the second half of the game was a little disjointed for Retama as the new players settled into their roles. The other team came into the game more and, ten minutes in, they scored. A pass through caused hesitation between Torres and Victor. The defender expected the goalkeeper to come and claim the ball but, short of confidence, inexperience set in and, in the moment of hesitation, an opponent nipped in between them and rolled the ball into the net with the goalkeeper out of position.

Jiménez stood up from the group of players sitting by the dugout, and walked around towards the goal where Torres was standing. Before he could get there, though, Felipe Blanco had beaten him to it. Clearly having similar thoughts, he trotted up to Torres and put a consoling arm around his shoulder, patting him on the back, before walking back into position and clapping his hands to encourage the team on. Moreton nodded subconsciously, and Sophia smiled. Different reactions to the same shared emotion.

As the game progressed, things began to gel for Retama. With the speedy Guido on one flank and the tricky Vasquez on the other, the forward line threatened with increased regularity. A ball from Victor saw Guido galloping into space, leaving his marker trailing. Driving into the penalty area, he drew the goalkeeper before squaring the ball for Santi to score. Five minutes later, another ball out of defence saw Guido clear again, this time he chose to shoot, but the ball struck the far post before bouncing clear. The young player had created more chances in his short time on the pitch than Palermo had in the entire first half.

'His pace is going to be valuable to us.' Moreton said, smiling.

It was clear from her smile that Sophia agreed.

A few minutes later, Vasquez scored after beating two men and going around the goalkeeper. It was a goal full of skill and promise. Moreton stood up from the bench and applauded the virtuosity. Almost from the restart, Felipe and Sebastián exchanged passes moving forwards, before the latter found Santi running clear. A clipped shot found the net and Retama were purring. Moreton called Palermo across and asked Sophia to tell him that he was going back on, but to play as a front man. At the next break in play, Santi was called off and Palermo sent on. Clearly delighted with his two goals, he walked across to Moreton before joining his team-mates. 'Thanks Mister,' he said with a beaming smile.

Moreton slapped him on the arm in congratulation. 'Are there more where those two came from?' he asked. The young forward looked a little embarrassed and hesitated. Moreton answered his own question. 'There are many more where those two came from,' he asserted. Santi nodded. Moreton sat down again. Santi walked back to receive the acclaim of his team-mates.

Looking on, Moreton asked Sophia. 'He speaks English?'

She nodded. 'Some of them do. I told you it's not that unusual here.'

'Paco, Santi, who else?'

'Most of them speak a little, but who speaks it well?' She questioned herself. 'Well, Revi does and Matías. Sebastián of course. He's very bright as well. I suppose it's the younger ones mainly.'

Moreton made his final change. Revi was restored to the midfield alongside Sebastián, and Felipe was sent into the back line to replace Sanz. Shortly before the end of the game, the two Palermo brothers linked up and Juan added another goal. Laughing, he walked over to his sibling, and picked him up into the air, before putting him down again and patting him on the head with exaggerated fraternal affection. It was the final action of the game. It had been a hugely beneficial exercise for Moreton. The only downside had been the attitude of Bendonces.

Sophia spoke with Nicolás for a short while before walking over to Moreton. 'He wants to know if you want to play another game next week?'

'Really?'

'Yes,' she confirmed. 'He said it had been good for his players to play against a team with so many outstanding young players. He told me that they will have learnt a lot from the game.'

It was a clear compliment, but Moreton shied away from it a little.

'Yeah, well. Yeah, tell him OK, and thank him and his players, will you?'

Sophia nodded and walked back towards where Nicolás was gathered with his coaches and players.

She spoke to them for a while, and as she turned back towards Moreton, Nicolás waved towards him, and the others in the group clapped. Sophia returned to Moreton's side, and he waved back and raised his arms in exaggerated applause towards them as well.

Back in the dressing room, Moreton asked all of the players to sit down for a short time before showering. With Sophia translating, he thanked them all for their efforts and for accepting the changes he had made with a good attitude. As Sophia had finished the final part of that phrase, a few of the players laughed a little, whilst others bowed and shook their heads. The references to Bendonces were clear to all.

Then, Moreton asked if anyone wanted to say anything.

Jiménez raised a hand.

Moreton nodded, inviting him to continue.

'Why change the forwards so much, but not the defence?' he asked in Spanish. Sophia translated.

'Good question,' Moreton replied. 'Why do you think?'

Jiménez shrugged.

'I think you have a good idea of why.' He smiled at the vastly experienced goalkeeper. 'Yes?'

Jiménez nodded slowly, understanding the English, as Sophia translated for most of the others.

'Defences flourish on understanding. The goal wasn't Juan's fault,' Moreton said. 'It wasn't Kiko's either. A goalkeeper and his defence are one unit, not two. They need to understand each other.' He looked across to where Torres was sitting quietly. 'Juan needs to play more with our back line. We will be playing Nicolás's team again next week. Juan will play in goal for the whole game.'

Jiménez nodded without a hint of dispute.

'Anyone else?' Moreton asked.

Revi spoke in broken but understandable English. 'Where was eight?'

The other players looked at him, and he repeated the question in Spanish, adding an explanation.

Sophia translated. 'He said that he didn't see anyone wearing the number eight shirt during the game.'

She looked at Moreton quizzically. 'Did we lose it again?'

Moreton shook his head. 'I don't think so,' he said, smiling. 'I think Esteban is around somewhere outside, could you call him over please?'

With a questioning look, Sophia hesitated for a moment. 'I'm sure he hasn't got it,' she said.

'I'm sure you're right. But would you call him over anyway.'

Still unconvinced of Moreton's motive, Sophia walked out of the dressing room, returning a few seconds later with Esteban trailing behind her. As the old man entered, some of the players who had understood the conversation were explaining it to their team-mates.

Esteban stood in the doorway, unsure why he had been asked to join the players there. Moreton beckoned him forward, until he was standing in the middle of the dressing room. Moreton reached into his bag and took out something blue wrapped in cellophane. He spoke quietly to Sophia before placing an arm round Esteban's shoulder, placing the bag in the old man's hand as she spoke.

In a voice, quivering with obvious emotion, she looked at the old man. '*De CD Retama a Esteban. Por siempre nuestro número ocho!*'

Esteban opened the bag and removed the blue Retama shirt he had been holding an hour or so ago. The harsh spell of old was dispelled by a smile as wide as his face could manage. He clutched the shirt to his heart as everyone in the room burst into applause. He doffed his cap and waved it in the air. The faded badge of CD Retama on the front of his headwear seemed to glisten.

The room was still full of applause as Sophia spoke. 'That was a wonderful thing to do,' she said to Moreton with beaming admiration and a tear running gently down her face.

'I'm retiring the number eight shirt. No one else will ever wear it. It will be Esteban's for ever.'

Sophia leant across to the old man and whispered into his ear. The old man choked back his emotion with difficulty. With Moreton's arm still around his shoulders, he reached for the younger man's free hand and shook it warmly, before embracing the Englishman. The room cheered again, as Esteban separated from Moreton. Sophia reached up and planted a gentle kiss on Moreton's cheek. '*Bienvenido a Retama,*' she said softly. More cheers rang out, and only Jiménez looked slightly less than totally wrapped up in the moment. Sophia wiped the tear away with the back of her hand, before kissing Moreton's other cheek, adding 'Welcome to Retama.'

New Arrival

The next week passed quickly. Moreton used the training sessions on Tuesday and Wednesday to look at the game and how to improve the things that required particular attention. There was a determined move to work with the back line and goalkeeper, building confidence and understanding. The man between the posts though, wasn't Jiménez. Given that Torres would be starting in the next friendly game, all of the focus was on him. Jiménez stood by the side of the goal offering encouragement to his young counterpart, but as the sessions continued, he felt less and less required to offer advice. The session had ended, with Jiménez draping an arm around Torres as they walked from the pitch.

At the end of the ground nearest to the gate, two figures stood at the top of the concrete steps, watching as the players filed back to the dressing-room. Charlie Broome called out to Moreton. Raising a hand to shield his eyes from the setting sun, he looked towards the location of the voice, and waved to his friend. The pair descended the steps towards the pitch and hopped over the wall, walking towards Moreton and Sophia. As they did so, Jon Moreton smiled. Next to the sharply dressed figure of Charlie Broome, he instantly recognised, the shabby and shuffling gate of a former team-mate. It was Billy Swan.

Although he had never particularly had the looks of a finely-tuned athlete, his naturally slim and trim bearing had been lost somewhat. The reduction in training and increased amounts of alcohol had brought with it a few extra pounds. At thirty-nine years old, Billy Swan looked every inch the ex-professional footballer, latterly given to excesses, that he was.

'Who's that with Señor Broome?' Sophia asked.

'That – is Billy Swan. I think he's our new player.'

'Our new player? That's Billy Swan?' Sophia looked at the figure drawing closer across the pitch and turned to Moreton. 'Are you sure that's Billy Swan. Or is it just someone who has eaten Billy Swan?'

Moreton didn't answer.

Appropriately, the four met in the centre circle and, after greeting Broome, and a brief embrace with his old team-mate, Moreton introduced Swan to Sophia. Holding out his arm in Swan's direction, he spoke. 'Sophia, this is probably the most skilful footballer that I've ever had the privilege to play with. This is Billy Swan.' And then: 'Billy, this is Sophia.' She offered her hand to the newcomer.

With the sort of over grandiose approach that went down well with girls in nightclubs who had overindulged on over expensive drinks, ready and willing to be bowled over, Swan bowed slightly, bringing Sophia's hand towards his face and kissed it.

'Enchanté Sophie,' he said.

Standing next to him, Broome clearly a little embarrassed at Swan's gauche manner, raised his eyebrows to Moreton, who offered a wry smile in return.

'Hola, Señor Swan,' she replied. 'But it's Sophia, not Sophie, and this is Spain not France.' She took her hand back, subconsciously wiping it on her tracksuit trousers.

'Oh, sorry love,' Swan chirped, his Cockney accent dropping into place. 'My bad.'

Deciding that discretion was the better part of valour, Moreton decided to postpone any further interaction between Sophia and Billy Swan, asking her to check that Esteban was going to lock up. She nodded, and walked away. A few seconds later she looked back and Swan offered up a wave.

'See you later, Sophie,' he said.

'Bloody hell, Billy. It's Sophia!' Moreton almost hissed.

'Sorry love. See you later Sophia,' Swan shouted, hanging on to the last letter of the name with an undue amount of emphasis.

'That was very nice thing to say, Jon,' Swan said, turning to his erstwhile team-mate. 'True, of course. But very nice.'

Moreton was a little confused. 'What? Billy?'

'Saying I was the most amazingly talented player you'd ever seen in your whole life,' Swan replied. 'Very nice. And true of course. In fairness, you weren't bad yourself. Who knows what would have happened if you hadn't got crocked? How is the knee by the way?'

'The knee's fine. Well, as fine as it's ever going to be. And I'm not really sure that is what I said, Billy.'

Charlie Broome decided it was time to get things moving along.

'Look, gents. I don't want to break up this little mutual appreciation society, but I've got things to do. Come back to the office and we can have a chat about how things are going to work out.'

The three men left the pitch, climbed up and down the concrete steps, went through the gate and arrived at Broome's Mercedes parked outside.

Moreton grabbed Swan's arm and moved him away from the car. 'You drive, Chaz. Billy and me will walk. It'll only take ten minutes, and we can have a quick catch up on the way.'

'OK, see you there. Just come right up.' Broome jumped into the car and drove back to Broome Cerámica.

'So, walking, eh? Are you trying to make out that I need the exercise, Jon?' Swan joked, prodding Moreton in the ribs.

'Well, there's a few extra pounds in there, Billy,' Moreton replied laughing with, rather than at, his old friend. 'It's great to have you here, mate. When I approached Charlie about trying to get you to come out, I wasn't really sure how I was going to sell it to you, but Charlie took that one off my hands and, whatever he said, it seems to have worked.'

'Yeah,' Swan replied, but the chirpiness in his voice had disappeared.

Moreton waited to see if anything else was going to be added. It wasn't.

'How did he convince you then?'

Swan sighed a little. 'It's all about timing, as the bishop said to the barmaid,' he replied with an exaggerated attempt to lift his tone again.

'The nightclub thing?'

Swan nodded.

'I saw it on the news. It didn't look good, Billy.'

'It didn't feel bloody good either, Jon. I'd been to one of those dinners, given it a bit of the patter, and a few of the blokes there asked me if I fancied a trip to the West End. Of course, I did. Why wouldn't I? They wanted to be seen out with the famous Billy Swan and were happy to pick up the tab on the drinks, so everyone was happy. One of them, Dave, Derek, Don, something like that, had rung his mate, a photographer with a local rag to come out and get some pictures so he could get his ugly mug on page one as being a friend of the stars. Fair enough, he was paying and it kept him happy. Trouble is, I was going for a leak and this drunken geezer lurches across and pushed me into this girl who fell over and hurt herself. Her fella takes a swing at me and the next thing I know, it's bloody chaos with everyone throwing punches, chairs and glasses flying around, and I'm being shoved out of the door by the bouncers, straight into the hands of plod. And who's outside with his Box Brownie, but this bloody photographer. He's lapping it up and before I knew what was what, he'd sold the pictures and I'm front page news in the tabloids.'

'Christ, Billy. What a mess. I heard the girl had a broken leg,' Moreton said, mustering as much sympathy as he could.

'Did she cobblers,' Swan snorted. 'The papers made that up. She's fine. The coppers gave me a bit of a nagging about not being a naughty boy, and all that sort of stuff, but a couple of them were football fans, so we got to talking and, as no one was really hurt, they said if I paid for the damage, they'd let me off with warning. In the end, for what that cost me, I could have gone out on the lash five weeks on the trot, partied and pulled every bird in the place.'

'So, it was all blown up out of proportion then?'

Swan sighed and looked down at the floor.

'Problem is Jon. It doesn't matter what's true. It matters what the papers say. The radio station said that they were cancelling my contract because my image wasn't in-keeping with their profile. What a load of bollocks. What profile do they have? Poxy little radio station. About as professional as two kids down the garden shed with tin cans and a bit of string. And then, the PR company that gets me the after dinner speaking things hears about me being ditched and says–' Swan adopted an affected, upper-class speaking voice, '"–that without the air time you're lacking the oxygen of public recognition." What kind of crap is that? I'm Billy Swan. I'm famous for playing football, not chatting to two morons on the radio while some plonkers ring in with daft questions just so I can argue with them. With all that of course, my agent gets in touch saying he might have to ditch me as well, because he can't help me any more. Help me? Who was he trying to kid? He's been lapping at my bowl of money for long enough, so I told him to sod off.'

'Charlie's approach came at the right time then?' Moreton added thinking that Swan's tale of woe was completed, but there was more to come.

'And then some, Jon. With no brass coming in a couple of blokes from my old patch got in touch and offered to lend me some dosh. I owed a bit of brass to a couple of dodgy geezers, and needed to get them off my back, so I took it. It was going to cost a bit to repay, but I thought all the crap would blow over soon, and I could pay it back easy when I was back on the wireless and doing some gigs. Trouble is though, that it didn't blow over. Jon, I owed money to the sort of people you do not want to owe money to, mate. They can do the sort of damage that would make your knee injury look like a little scratch. I had to find a way to pay them.'

'And that's when you heard from Charlie?'

'Yeah, pretty much. He got in touch. Told me a friend had given him my details and could we meet up for something that would be to my advantage. I asked him if that meant dosh and when he said yes, I went for it. So, he tells me about you and this little club out in Spain. Tells me that if I come out here and play for the club, he'll pay off the debt as part of the deal, and fund my living in Spain.'

'I guess that solved the big problem, but is that it? Is that all he offered you?'

Swan glanced at Moreton, questioningly. He hesitated before speaking, and stopped walking. 'He also said that if I helped him to make things work out right, there'd be a bonus in it for me.' He paused, looking directly at Moreton, as if having his former team-mate fully understand his plight was a demanding necessity. 'Jon, he was talking proper dosh. Real money.' He looked back at the ground as they resumed walking with the showroom now in sight.

'Well, that's great mate. With you on board, we can get this club promoted and everybody wins.'

'Yeah,' Swan replied apparently unconvinced. 'Everybody wins.' A moment passed before he added: 'I really need the money, Jon.'

'I know Billy. I understand.'

A few minutes later, they entered the showroom of Broome Cerámica. Neither had spoken for a while, but as they started to climb the stairs, Swan perked up again. 'Hey, that Sophie's a bit fit. She yours, Jon?' Barely audible, Moreton whispered under his breath, 'Christ, Billy!' The receptionist smiled as she waved them to go straight in.

Charlie Broome was seated behind his desk with a telephone trapped precariously between shoulder and the side of his head. Without breaking the flow of his conversation, he motioned them to come in and sit down, before bringing the telephone conversation to a close. 'Yeah, that's right. It's what I said isn't it?' A hint of irritation had slipped into his discourse. 'Yes, it will. Yes, it will.' He repeated with an increasing tone to emphasise that the point wasn't up for discussion. 'You do what you need to do, and I'll make sure my end is delivered. Simple as.' He put the receiver down.

'Christ, guys. Some people...' Broome picked his hands up from the desk and opened his arms towards the two men sitting opposite him. 'So, where are we?'

Moreton spoke first. 'First things first, Chaz. Thanks for getting Billy here. He's going to make all the difference in the end. I know he is.'

Broome smiled. 'He'd better,' he replied, turning towards the ageing footballer. 'Yeah?' he asked of Swan.

'Yeah, sure,' Swan nodded slowly.

'So, what's the plan, Jon?' The enquiry was business like, rather than polite.

'I've got your pieces all in place now. What's the opening gambit? Where are you moving your pawn?'

'Well, we've got this second friendly game coming up on Sunday, and the league starts the following week, so there isn't much time to get young Billy up to speed and fit to play.'

Broome nodded slowly. 'OK,' he said.

'Yeah. We'll need to bring him in easily, though. If we just plunge him in from the off, it's easy to get injuries when you haven't played for a while. Plus,' he continued with a nod towards Swan, 'This boy is no spring chicken any more!'

Broome smiled a little.

Swan didn't. 'Cheeky git,' he said, before offering Moreton a mock clip around the back of his head.

'Can he play in the friendly?' Broome enquired.

'I don't think so,' Moreton replied. 'It may be best just to have him on the sidelines with me and Sophia. Perhaps I can put him on the bench for the opening league game the following week. He won't be ready to start, but if we need something late on, it might be possible to throw him on to pull something out of the bag, but let's see how it goes, eh?'

Broome nodded. 'Your call, Jon.'

'Are you staying on the complex, Billy?' Moreton asked, turning to Swan.

'Complex? What you on about, mate?'

'No, Jon,' Broome interceded. 'Billy's staying at the same hotel as me.'

'It's a bit of all right, Jon.' Swan jumped into the conversation. 'Very posh. Right up my street.'

'OK,' Moreton said, unconvinced.

'Don't worry about it, Jon. I've got it all sorted,' Broome replied, rising from his chair. 'Anyway, you two had better clear off. I've got work to do.'

Swan walked towards the office door ahead of his two companions. Broome took the opportunity for a quiet word with Moreton. 'He's costing me money, Jon. And I know his reputation. Let's just say I want to keep an eye on him. I can trust you, but Mr Swan's a bit different. You understand, don't you?'

Outside of the office, Broome spoke quietly to the receptionist, who picked up the telephone, pressed a couple of buttons and spoke a few words in Spanish before hanging up, and nodding to Broome. 'Gonzalo's downstairs, Billy,' he said to Swan. 'He'll run you back to the hotel.'

'See you later, Billy,' Moreton called out as his old team-mate trotted down the stairs towards the door. Swan raised an arm to wave as he walked through the showroom and towards the building's exit.

'Training on Friday at eight o'clock.' Another wave.

Broome put his hand on Moreton's shoulder. 'Don't worry, Jon,' he said. 'He'll be there. Having him at the hotel – nowhere near my room, of course. He's got one of the tourist ones – means that I can keep an eye on the investment. I've told him that the hotel has everything he wants, food, drink, television from back home, DVDs in his room, whatever. I've told him he can have whatever he wants and it's on me.'

Moreton looked at Broome, but received the answer to his query before asking it.

'I'm not daft, Jon,' he half-laughed. 'I made it clear to him. Alcohol is banned, or the deal's off. It's all so I can make sure he's on the straight and narrow. I've allocated one of the guys from here to drive him around. Also, to keep an eye on him whenever he leaves the hotel at all. Got to watch my investment.'

'Nice,' Moreton replied without conviction. It sounded almost like a period of house arrest, but he had to concede that there was a logic to the regime from Broome's perspective.

Misunderstanding Moreton's implication, Broome responded. 'Look, Jon. I really couldn't afford to put you both up in the hotel. As I said, it's just that I need to be comfortable that your mate isn't going off the rails. Anyway, you're happy where you are, aren't you? It has its attractions there.' He smiled at Moreton, inviting him to reciprocate.

'Yeah,' came the reply, but Moreton's consciousness was drifting away. 'Yeah, no… Yeah, I know. Of course, I am. It's all good, buddy.'

Reading his companion's thoughts, Broome nudged Moreton slightly with a knowing smile. 'I meant the pool Jon, and that it was near to the ground, mate.'

'Yeah. Yeah, Chaz,' came the unconvincing reply. 'That's what I meant too.'

Numbers Game

When Moreton arrived for the Friday training, he was both delighted and a little surprised to find Swan already kitted out for the session and standing in the middle of the pitch with Sophia as the other players assembled. He hadn't been sure how successful Broome's attempts at inserting a little order into Billy Swan's life would be. It was an encouraging start. The van parked in the car-park in its pristine, new Broome Cerámica livery and the driver he passed, wearing a T-shirt to match, his head buried in a newspaper, was an indication that the plan was going well, at least so far.

'Hi Sophia.' Moreton smiled, as he reached the group.

'All right, Jon,' Swan cut in. 'Like the gear?' He moved his arms up and down to invite Moreton's opinion of his clothing. Even with the extra poundage gained since he last played, Billy Swan still had the appearance of a footballer, and wearing what was clearly a new top, shorts and socks, he looked ready for work.

'Nice, Billy.' Moreton smiled with genuine affection.

'Your mate Charlie sorted it all out. Gonzo brought it to my room this morning when he picked me up.'

'I think it's Gonzalo,' Moreton corrected.

'Yeah, Gonzalo. That's what I said isn't it. Gonzo, it's all the same. I call him Gonzo. He likes it.' Then, looking up he shouted across to the driver sitting on the concrete steps. 'Hey, Gonzo!' Swan held up his arms with thumbs raised. 'Yo,' he bellowed.

Shielding their eyes, Moreton, Sophia and the players all looked towards the figure semi-hidden behind the newspaper. A slight movement to look up from his reading material was barely noticeable.

'See,' Swan announced triumphantly. 'He loves it.'

Sophia and Moreton looked at each other. One apologetically, the other empathetically.

'What?' Swan asked. 'He loves it. He does. Well, he's a bit quiet, but we get on well. He'll soon get to know me.'

He was about to repeat his shout, but Moreton quickly reached across and prevented him from raising his arms. 'That's fine, Billy. That's fine. Let's get to work.'

The session was deliberately low-key. Moreton was keen to ease Swan back into the training routine again with as little fuss as possible and avoid any possible injuries. As soon as all the players were assembled, Sophia ran through a gentle warm-up routine followed by a couple of drills; firstly, concentrating on passes and finding space against a pressing defender, before then moving on to changing the point of attack with passes to the flanks. It was all at a gentle pace and designed specifically to give Swan a chance to get involved and, Moreton hoped, begin to impress the other players with his ability.

There was little indication that Billy Swan had lost much of the swagger that had defined his career. With the ball at his feet, he still had the ability to find team-mates unerringly and when presented a chance on goal the years rolled away. A pass inside from Vasquez found him closely marked by Kiko. Dropping his shoulder, he pivoted with a Cruyff turn, that eluded the young defender. The move put him clear on goal. A neat feint and dance around Jiménez deceived the veteran, before checking back, rolling the ball under his foot as Sanz raced back to cover, causing the defender to overshoot the challenge. Swan walked the ball over the line before placing his foot on it in triumph.

Recalling how Revi's ebullience led to a rebuke from Jiménez, Moreton winced at the thought of how things would play out if Swan had postured after the show of skill, but the moment passed. Swan picked up the ball and walked back towards Jiménez, handing it to him as he climbed to his feet. A sigh signified the relief Moreton felt.

'Guapo,' Sophia said quietly to herself.

For the last thirty minutes or so of the session, Moreton asked Sophia to set up a small-sided game, but called Swan across to him. 'Take a blow, Billy,' he said. 'Sit with me and watch.'

There was genuine disappointment in Swan's reply. 'Bloody hell, Jon. You make me work through the drills and then pull me out of the fun part.'

Moreton smiled, glancing for a second at his companion. 'Sit down, Billy. I want you to watch the players and get to know how they play.'

Swan slumped down next to Moreton.

Sophia returned, and the trio watched as the game was gently played out. Sophia and Swan sat either side of Moreton and, five minutes or so afterwards, a gentle leg nudge to Sophia alerted her.

'What do you think, Billy?' Moreton asked.

'Me? I'm no coach, Jon. What do I know? I just play. That's my job.'

'Come on, Billy. You've played top level football for a long time. You can tell who has talent and what's needed.' Playing to his old team-mate's vanity, Moreton was both looking for Swan's opinion, and encouraging him to become more involved with the players.

'Well, seeing as you ask,' Swan said at last, taking the bait. 'That big guy at the back,' he began, pointing to Kiko. 'He's a big unit. Not bad, but a bit green around the gills.'

Sophia looked confused not understanding the idiom. Moreton shook his head slightly, suggesting he would explain. 'He's only a kid, Billy. Still seventeen or eighteen, I think. So, he's got time to learn.' Sophia nodded slightly indicating she had understood.

'Bloody hell,' Swan remarked, turning to Moreton. 'Really? He's gonna be a big lad when he grows up, ain't he! Got suckered into the old "Dutchman" when I turned past him, but OK. He's just a kid then. Plenty of learning time to come.'

'A lot of them are kids, Billy. That's why someone like you, with loads of experience, will be so valuable. Especially in the forward line.'

'Yeah,' Swan replied, absently. 'There's one out there who runs like an electric eel. Is his name Giddy, or something like that?'

Moreton suppressed a gentle chuckle. 'Guido?'

Billy Swan hardly noticed the correction. 'Yeah, Giddy. Yeah, that's him. If he had a paper round, you'd get the news from him quicker than watching it on the telly.'

Another suppressed laugh.

'*He's* got a trick or two,' Swan added, pointing across the field.

'Who's that, Billy?'

'The little kid on the far side with the long black hair.'

Moreton recognised that Swan was talking about Vasquez. 'He can beat a man Billy. On either side. But he hardly ever seems to have the confidence to score.'

'Never had that trouble, myself,' Swan replied, laughing. Then, noticing that Sophia was also listening, he extended the conversation: 'I said, never had that trouble myself, Sophie.'

Clearly less than impressed, Sophia frowned, ensuring that her feelings had been clearly expressed.

'Billy!' Moreton dragged the conversation back to the field of play as Revi slid a pass through to Bendonces to fire past Torres.

'*He's* not bad, Jon.' Swan ventured, attention now back on the action in front of him.

'Who?' Moreton asked, thinking Swan was referring to the man who was now trotting back for the restart with a self-satisfied grin. '*Him?*' Moreton asked, pointing towards the bearded forward.

'No!' Swan said firmly. 'He's a knob.'

Sophia struggled to suppress a snigger. The meaning of that phrase had clearly not escaped her.

'The one with the headband.' Swan was referring to Revi. 'He's got a bit about him.' Swan looked up towards the sky in mock reflection. 'Reminds me a bit of a young Billy Swan.'

Moreton smiled, and nudged the speaker playfully.

'Well, not really. He's a long way off that, ain't he, Jon? Eh, mate? There's only one Billy Swan, and here he is buddy. But you've got a football field and a ball and here am I stuck sitting next to you being Andy bloody Gray.'

Swan laughed, despite himself.

Moreton joined in, but Sophia wasn't sure. 'Who is 'Andy bloody Gray'?' she asked. Both men laughed again.

Two days later, they played the second practice game against the youth team. Other than Torres now being in goal instead of Jiménez, the team that started was the same. There was something else. Moreton asked Sophia to explain that the club would be running a fixed squad numbering system for the season.

'We are a squad, not a team,' he said. Holding out a list, he read out the numbers he was allocating. 'Each player will have that shirt for the rest of the season. They should take it home with them. They should wash it themselves. They should bring it with them to the game. It was the number that belonged to them, and they belonged to it, and the squad it represented.' Sophia translated each part in turn, and an increasing number of the players nodded in agreement as the sentences were repeated.

Number one went to Jiménez with Torres taking the other green shirt with twenty-two on the back.

Next came the defence with number two going to Alejandro Sanz, along with the captain's armband. Adrián received number three with Kiko and Victor given five and six respectively. The two first choice wide men were next. Antonio Vasquez was seven and Juan Palermo eleven. Samuel was given number four and Revi ten. As Moreton handed the shirt to the young player with the perpetual headband, he could feel the eyes of Billy Swan burning a hole into the side of his head. Bendonces was delighted to have the number nine.

With the number eight shirt not available, the remainder of one to eleven had now gone. As he progressed, Moreton added a little explanation of his thinking to some of the numbers. Guido was given twelve. And Felipe Blanco sixteen. When it came to Matías, he asked Sophia to explain that he would normally have been given the number eight shirt, but as this wasn't possible, he hoped that eighteen would be acceptable. The quiet midfielder, nodded and smiled, without a shade of dissent. Sebastián took the number fifteen with the same good humour. There were then just three players remaining.

For José, Moreton asked Sophia to explain that, with his elder brother having number eleven, that is one and one, the younger sibling should have twenty-one, that is two and one. Both brothers smiled as Sophia explained the thought. A similar logic applied with Santi being given number nineteen, being the next in line for the number nine shirt. It just left Billy Swan.

Moreton took a deep breath and asked Sophia to explain that Swan had often worn the number ten shirt when he played, but that shirt was Revi's and he was going to tell a little story about why he was allocating a particular number to Swan. A player who had always worn the number nine shirt had been out injured for a while and, in his absence, the shirt had obviously gone to another player. When he returned to fitness and the team, although he was still selected to play alongside the returning forward, the player who had been wearing the number nine offered the shirt back to him. The gesture was refused by the returnee, however, saying that as he was still in the team, he should keep the number and it would be wrong for someone else coming in to take that from him. The player then dipped his hand into a pile of unallocated shirts and pulled one out. He took that number as his own and, as his fame increased, he would always be associated with that number.

It was a long tale, but Sophia repeated it faithfully as the players listened in. She nodded to him when she had finished. Moreton dipped his hand into the remaining bag of shirts and pulled one out, handing it to his old team-mate. Swan opened it up, revealing the number.

Moreton nodded to Sophia and completed the tale. 'That shirt was number fourteen, and the player was Johan Cruyff.' Swan beamed at the compliment, and reaching up, shook Moreton's hand.

The team that Nicolás had brought along to the first game had been overwhelmingly made up of youth players with a few coaches filling in the spaces. That had changed now. There was still the same number of younger players, but more of them started on the bench with almost half of the starting team apparently comprising Nicolás and his fellow coaches. It suggested that this would be a more competitive game, at least physically anyway.

From the start, Moreton's team were put under pressure with crosses being fired into the box, testing out Torres. The young goalkeeper coped well, though, collecting the over-hit ones and allowing his defenders to deal with others as the communication flowed well between them. Further forward it was a battle in midfield and, not long in, Samuel got tangled up in a tackle, twisting his ankle. Sophia went on to the pitch to check him out. Although the damage wasn't too serious, she signalled to Moreton that it was best for him to come off rather than risk it getting worse. Shuffling the players slightly, Moreton moved Revi back into the middle of the midfield alongside Matías, told Palermo to play behind Bendonces and sent Guido on to play on the flank.

Samuel limped back to the sidelines and Esteban, wearing his usual blue cardigan and brown trousers brought some ice for Sophia to apply to the player's ankle. Seeing the old man walk towards them with the ice, Moreton asked Sophia: 'Why is he not wearing the shirt we gave him. It's to wear, not put in a drawer.'

Sophia smiled, gently rebuking the questioner. 'Shirts are for match days. He will wear it when we are playing real games.'

Halftime came without any scoring, and again Moreton shuffled the players around.

Palermo was withdrawn in favour of his younger brother. Felipe Blanco went on instead of Sanz and Sebastián replaced Vasquez.

'What about Santi?' Sophia asked. Are you sending him on instead of Bendonces?' The striker had clearly felt that the change was likely. Other than Billy Swan, who sat forlornly as the others moved in and out of the game, Santi was the only one not given a chance so far, and the logical move was to replace him as the striker.

Moreton shook his head. 'Not yet. He nodded at Bendonces and waved him and the other players back onto the pitch to resume the game.

'Billy,' Moreton said turning to the player sitting on the ground by the dugout. 'I'm leaving you out today. It's not worth the risk after just one training session.' There was obvious disappointment on Swan's face. Recognising that a little ego massaging was required, Moreton added. 'You don't need to prove anything to me, Billy.'

It worked.

'Yeah, Jon. That's true.'

The game continued to be goalless and, with Torres increasingly confident, and the changed Retama team out-muscled by the older opposition players kept on the pitch as their younger team-mates switched on and off around them, the game seemed destined to end that way. With fifteen minutes or so left to play, Moreton called Santi across to him. Remembering that he was one of the players that could speak English, he whispered a single word in the teenager's ear, receiving a nod in return. At the next break of play, he waved to the referee about the change.

On the field, Bendonces looked across and seeing Santi about to come on, realised that he would be leaving the game. He trotted towards the dugout, but Moreton waved his arms at him, telling him to stay on. Instead, it was Revi that was called off.

Sophia was confused. 'Why not Bendonces?'

Moreton smiled. 'I'm trying something. Sometimes, when you want to open a door, you need to turn a knob.'

He patted her on the shoulder. 'If I'm right, you'll see.'

Eight minutes later, his plan bore fruit. A cross into the box was collected by Torres. He rolled the ball out to Victor who played it quickly into midfield where the newly arrived Santi received and turned, full of running against the older players whose legs were now tiring. Driving forward, he then fed the ball into space ahead of the speedy Guido on the flank. Outpacing his marker, he reached the ball just before it ran over the dead ball line and squared it into the box. Aware of the blond youngster's pace, Bendonces had anticipated the ball being reached before it ran out of play. It gave him an edge as he drove forward ahead of his marker. As the ball came in, he stretched out a leg and diverted it into the goal. It was hardly the most perfect goal he had scored, but, having been trusted to stay on the field throughout the game when the obvious move was to replace him, it felt good. Regaining his feet, he jumped and punched the air.

As his team-mates joined in the celebration, walking back to restart the game, the bearded forward saw Moreton on the sidelines calling him over. Believing that he would now be substituted as he had scored, Bendonces walked slowly across towards the dugout. As he reached Moreton however, the coach lifted both arms in the air, offering up his palms for a double high-five celebration. Bendonces grinned and slapped Moreton's palms. As he turned to return to the field Moreton slapped him on the back, before walking back to Sophia. 'Knob turned. Door opened.' He smiled.

The rest of the game was played out without further scoring and after shaking hands, the players returned to the sidelines. Sophia went across to talk with Nicolás, as the players and Moreton retired to the dressing room to shower and change. Fifteen minutes or so later they filed out of the building to find Sophia talking with Esteban outside. Moreton stopped to talk with the two of them as the players walked past and left the ground. A few patted Moreton as they walked by, but Bendonces stopped and shook his hand before leaving. Sophia nodded to Moreton. 'Open door?' No reply was required.

There were now no more practice games to prepare for the league. There would be training on the following Tuesday, Wednesday and Friday, but then, the season would begin. Moreton, Sophia and the players left with a feeling of confidence after the game. The first few weeks of the new season would test that confidence to the extreme.

Opposition

After training on Tuesday, Moreton could detect a growing enthusiasm for the season. A couple of days rest appeared to have been all that was required for Samuel's ankle to recover. The following day brought an unpleasant surprise, though. Arriving at the ground, the look of concern on Sophia's face suggested something was wrong.

'I've just had a call from Revi,' she explained. 'He cannot attend this evening, and may not be available for Sunday either.'

'What?' His tone revealed more than a noticeable trace of irritation.

'It is unavoidable,' Sophia quickly replied. 'His grandmother is seriously ill and the family need to travel to Sevilla to be with her.'

Moreton didn't respond.

Sophia went on, clearly unhappy at the apparent lack of empathy. 'Jon, these are not full-time professional footballers. They have lives outside of CD Retama, and sometimes other matters are more important than football.'

Moreton slowly nodded. 'I'm sorry. Of course, I understand. I guess I was just a little disappointed, that's all. He's a key player in the team.'

'I know, but Retama is our family too, and when one of us is in trouble, we help each other. We understand. We care.'

'You're right. I was being a prat. Sorry, again. Please don't tell the players how I reacted.'

'Of course not.'

As they assembled, the players quickly became aware of the news. Revi had already told some of them that they were likely to be starting the game without one of their best players. Throughout the training Moreton paid particular attention to Billy Swan. He would have been the ideal replacement to slide into the gap left by Revi's absence. With just a couple of light training sessions under his belt, after a few years of hardly playing at all, throwing him into the first game of the season hardly seemed sensible. Should he risk it? There's little doubt that, if asked, Swan would have said he could play. In his professional days, he would have happily sat on the bench every day so long as his money wasn't affected. Now, however, Moreton knew that the success of the team, or otherwise, would very much affect Swan's financial rewards, and as such he would surely be committed. The session ended without Moreton reaching a decision.

For the following Friday, he was planning the final preparation ahead of Sunday's game with a light session, revealing his line-up for the game and explaining how he wanted the team to play. One piece of information was missing, though. He knew nothing about any of the teams Retama would be facing: who was good, who was less so and, more urgently, what sort of game it would be on Sunday. Sophia had given him a copy of the fixture list, but the opposition clubs were merely names that meant very little to him. He had decided, however, to try and change all that.

Over recent days, Moreton had spent so much of his time around the apartment working on his plans, reading, watching TV, swimming or jogging around the local area. The days seemed to slip by and aside from training sessions, he had seen very little of Sophia. It was something that he wanted to change but, until now, there hadn't seemed an easy way to achieve that. After the session had finished, and the players had showered and left, he decided that the time was right.

'Do you have plans for this evening, Sophia?' he asked, falteringly.

'Why do you ask?'

'I was thinking, that perhaps we could meet up later, maybe go for a glass of wine. I need to ask you about the teams that we're going to be facing. And understand more about what we need to do if we're going to be successful.' It sounded far less convincing when said out loud than it had in his mind when rehearsing the line.

Sophia's gaze met his. Her eyes were deep and dark and Moreton felt like he could drown in them. The answer that came back, however, was hardly what he had hoped for.

'No, I have to study tonight for an hour or so.'

His heart sank, but the smile that followed her reply, lifted him again.

'Let me cook dinner for you tomorrow instead, and we can talk over coffee.'

She smiled knowing both that her playful tease had been successful and that Moreton had now been rewarded with more than he had hoped for.

'Knock on my door at eight tomorrow evening.'

'Sure. That'll be great.' It was precisely what he meant, but felt more than a little overstated when he said it. 'I'll look forward to it.'

'Oh, not too much, I hope. Cooking is not the best thing that I do.'

Her comment felt a little strained to Moreton, but he reminded himself that English wasn't Sophia's first language. There was a temptation to ask what it was that she was better at, but wisely he managed to suppress the urge. His polite laughter was both a safety valve and a way to exit the desert island of awkward moments upon which he had been temporarily marooned.

'Will you check with Esteban to see everything is all locked up,' he asked, swimming frantically towards a distant shore.

'Of course.'

Picking up his bag, he turned and walked across the pitch towards the concrete steps.

'Eight. Don't forget,' she called after him.

His turn and smile didn't exactly say that there was no chance whatsoever of that happening, but it was true nonetheless.

The following evening, at precisely eight o'clock, Jon Moreton, dressed in his best pair of jeans and a blue shirt, knocked on the door of the apartment opposite his own. Sophia greeted him with a warm smile, and as she stepped back, to invite him inside, she was partially hidden by the door.

The layout of the apartment was very similar to his own, but the atmosphere was much more traditionally Spanish. A long sofa faced a wall unit with a small television on it and a collection of photographs. There was a small table with two chairs and placemats set for dinner. A small desk was set against the opposite wall, covered with pages of written paper and two folders, leaning against three books. Moreton looked at the title of the one nearest to him, but it was beyond his knowledge of Spanish. The third word out of the four in the title was easier to translate: 'Fútbol' was recognisable in a lot of languages.

'This is nice,' he said, referring to the apartment as he turned back to look at Sophia, and only now seeing her fully. She was wearing a sleeveless yellow dress with blue designs of birds in flight. It was loosely tied at the low neckline with lace and the narrow waist accentuated the delicate curves of her body. Running down to knee-length, it also had a slit in the side that gently exposed a tanned and toned thigh when she walked. Jon Moreton was more than a little stunned.

'Very nice,' he repeated absently.

Offering a gentle mock courtesy, Sophia smiled. 'Thank you,' she said impishly.

'No, sorry. I meant the apartment was very nice. Not you,' Headlights on, full speed ahead, straight into the brick wall. On he sped. 'Well, you're nice as well, of course. I mean they're both nice.' Brakes failed. Accelerator stuck. 'Not them both. I mean you both. You and the apartment.' The wall came crashing down upon him, broken masonry and dust covering him, but still leaving nowhere to hide.

Sophia laughed. 'I think there's a compliment in there somewhere. You have a think and try and work it out, while I get us both a glass of wine. Dinner in about twenty minutes, if that's OK?'

Reverse gear engaged. Moreton tried to disentangle himself from the conversational carnage.

'That's great.' He sighed. 'Thanks.'

Sophia disappeared into the small kitchen area, returning with two glasses of white wine.

'Sit down, Jon.' She motioned to the sofa, which was long enough for them both to sit without it feeling too intimate, but when Sophia also sat down after passing him one of the glasses, the side of the dress drifted down again and the exposed part of Sophia's leg snared his attention mercilessly. He took a quick gulp of his wine, coughing it back slightly as it flooded down his throat.

'It's a nice apartment isn't it?' he said, reaching out for a subject to concentrate on.

'I think so. I'm afraid the desk is a little messy, but I know where everything is when it's like that, and it's easier for me to work that way when I'm studying.'

'What are you studying, then? Is it something continuing from your university?'

Sophia hesitated before answering. 'Yes, I suppose so. Yes, it is really.'

Moreton nodded expecting more to follow.

'I'm studying for an exam that will allow me to work in some of the Spanish government's organisations, running sports clinics for the people there. It's quite involved as there are lots of different elements to it, not just coaching, but also health promotion, well-being, pastoral care. I'm not sure what I want to do with it, but while I'm here in Retama with the time I have, I wanted to use it to further my qualifications. Who knows, it may get me a job somewhere.'

Moreton smiled. 'Good for you. You know, until I started on my coaching courses, I never really did much studying. I was always OK at school, but I guess that wasn't because I tried very hard. I look back and think that I could have done so much better if I'd have tried, but all I really wanted to do was play football and, strangely, that's what got me into studying again. I do sometimes wonder where I'd have been if I had given education a bigger swing rather than running away to play football at every opportunity.'

'Well, doing what you did, brought you here, didn't it? So, perhaps playing football was the right decision for you.'

He smiled. 'True enough,' he said, and they clinked glasses before sipping the wine.

'I hope you like Italian food. I got so used to cooking pasta at university that it's a bit of a speciality of mine now. We have spaghetti in a sauce. A bit like Spaghetti Bolognese, but not quite.'

'Yeah, that sounds great.'

'I'm just going to check on the food,' Sophia said walking into the small kitchen area.

Moreton looked around at the room and his eye alighted on the photographs surrounding the television. A number of them featured Sophia and an older couple that he assumed were her parents. To the right one photograph frame was lying face down. Assuming it had been knocked over, Moreton set it right again. Immediately, he wished he hadn't. The picture was of Sophia and a man. He appeared to be in his mid-twenties, dark-haired with a closely trimmed beard. He was taller and standing behind her with his arms around her waist, and his head resting on her shoulder. It took very little imagination for Moreton to realise that the man in the picture was Alvaro. He set the picture frame back down as he had found it, and quickly returned to his seat, as Sophia entered the room.

'A couple of minutes, and we're ready.' She smiled, but Moreton's thoughts were elsewhere. 'Would you like another glass of wine?' she added, realising that her guest's attention was not fully on what she had said.

'Sorry... Sorry, I was thinking about something I need to do. A phone call to my parents,' he lied. 'I haven't spoken to them for a few days,' he added, digging the pit of dishonestly a little deeper by adding a truth.

'I know. I should speak to my parents every day, but with the studying and the football, I often forget as well. Do you miss them?'

'Yeah. I do really. Spain is very nice, but I don't really know anybody here. Chaz and Billy are in a hotel on the other side of town, and it's just easier to go for a jog, swim, read or watch some old DVDs than go out and catch a bus or walk to meet up with them. Chaz is often at Broome Cerámica of course, but he's got a business to run, and doesn't want me popping in for a chat if I'm bored. To be honest, we never really mixed socially very much when we were in England anyway, and I guess we have even less in common now than we did in those days. Same with Billy. Actually, even more so with Billy. I've never socialised with Billy.' He laughed, before continuing. 'I spend most of the evenings sitting on the balcony and reading, watching videos or working on training drills.' He laughed a little self-deprecatingly. 'Wow, that sounds boring, doesn't it?'

'You know me. And there's not much travelling required to come and visit me.' She marched out steps with her fingers. 'Twenty paces? Perhaps fifteen for you?' She smiled. 'I also spend evenings on the balcony, mostly studying, but sometimes reading. It's a little strange isn't it? Our apartments are mirrored so we're on the far-side of each other when we're on our balconies. Perhaps we should share each other's balcony occasionally, and be lonely together.'

She smiled pleasantly before speaking again. 'Is it a little awkward for you? A little difficult?'

Moreton knew exactly what Sophia was alluding to, but that same difficulty barred him from confirming it. 'Difficult? I'm not sure what you mean?' he said, plunging himself into the pit of dishonesty for a second time in a few minutes. The deceit was hardly convincing.

'Jon,' she said, sitting down next to him on the sofa. 'You're a man and I'm a woman. I think we like each other, don't we?'

She placed her hand on his knee and looked at him intently. It was no time for evasive tactics. Confession time beckoned insistently.

'Yes,' he replied softly. 'Well, I like you, anyway.'

'And I like you as well. So, let's like each other. Accept that and see where we go. Yes?'

'Yes,' Moreton replied, as their faces moved closer together.

The emotionally-charged moment hung in the air, before a noise of overflowing boiling water from the kitchen dragged them back to more mundane matters. Sophia jumped to her feet. Any impulsive action was now placed onto the back burner. The front burner – with boiling water spilling over it – demanded immediate attention. A few minutes later, two people sat across a dinner-table chatting, composure restored.

'So, how is my cooking?' Sophia asked, partway through the meal.

'It's very good. I'm a pasta fan myself,' he added, without realising the consequences.

'Really? Then next time, you can cook for me.' The implications now front and centre, Moreton blanched at the thought of his fairly basic culinary ability being exposed, but the prospect of another evening spent with Sophia overcame it in an instant.

'Sure. It's a date. I mean, not a date… well, not a date as such. But, you know, yeah… let's do it. Erm, well, yeah. I mean I'd be delighted.'

'That would be great.'

He sighed deeply, then laughed, peering over the rim of the rapidly deepening hole in the ground that he seemed to be firmly intent on digging for himself.

Sophia laughed too, placing the back of a hand to her mouth, and reaching out to plant the other on top of one of Moreton's.

'Relax, Jon,' she said through the laughter.

The rest of the meal passed without any further complications, and over coffee the conversation moved onto the much more comfortable issue of football. Sophia reached over to her desk and picked up a piece of paper. 'This is the fixture list for the season that I showed you earlier,' she said, indicating the paper. 'Señor Broome passed it to me a couple of weeks before you arrived. I know a little about most of the clubs, but not much about some of them, as they were in a different division to Retama last year.'

'That's OK. I just want to get a feeling for who's who, especially for the first few games. Just so that I have an idea what to expect. I'm planning to announce the starting team after training on Friday, but want to know a little about who we're playing. Also,' he added, now in the realms of football, where any relationship issues were within his comfort zone, 'I want to discuss my ideas on selection with you. We'll pick the team together.'

Sophia's smile widened. 'OK,' she said, picking up the paper. 'I know it sometimes works out differently in England, but the normal way here is to play all of the other clubs in the first half of the season and then you play the return fixtures in the second half in the same order. So, here's who the clubs are that we have to beat.'

She shook the paper a little in an exaggerated fashion, indicating it was business time. The smile as she did so, still reflected a less than overly sober tone to the proceedings. 'Shall we go through the list in the order that we play them?'

'Yes, please. That would be ideal.'

'I'll tell you what I know, and, if there's anything you want to ask, I'll try and answer, but remember, some of the clubs are just names to me too. Especially the newer ones.' She drained the last of her coffee. 'Our first game is on Sunday.'

'Yes,' Moreton smiled indulgently. 'I know that!'

'All right then.' Sophia shook the paper again. 'Here we go.'

'Politanio are a big club. Their premier team play Segunda División. They don't often threaten to achieve promotion to the Primera, but are rarely in trouble either. We will be facing their B team. Some clubs use their second teams to give younger players experience in competitive football, or maybe when a player has a had a long injury lay-off. It means they will be competing against other club's best players and can be a good way of testing abilities or fitness. This is what Politanio do. Most of the players we will be facing on Sunday will be young, but this doesn't mean it will be an easy game. The players will be the best of their youth team and they'll be out to impress.'

'Sounds like it will be a tough start for us. Anything else on them?'

'Yes. They were relegated along with us last season. League position isn't that important to them. The whole idea is to use the team to develop players, but they would still expect to be in a higher league where the teams they are competing against would be a better test for their players. Also, they have just appointed a new coach to the team. Francisco played for many years with Politanio, but after retiring, he joined a different club to make his name as a coach. He did very well, and almost achieved promotion, but just missed out. It was an easy decision to bring him back. All the young players there know him as a club hero, and also now as a successful coach. They will expect to get promotion.'

Moreton listened intently. It was clear that Retama's opening fixture would be difficult.

'It is a difficult way to start our season,' Sophia confirmed. 'But at least we are at home, so we have that advantage.'

'You mentioned that they were relegated along with Retama last season. How did we get on against them?'

'When we played them away, early in the season, it was a good game. Fouad scored twice, I think, and we won. When the home game came around, he had left, and we lost to them. It was not a nice game, as García had needed to put in so many younger players to replace those who had left. It was young players against young players mainly, but their young players were so much better. We may have lost by five or six goals. I'm not sure. It was the sort of game you try and forget.'

Moreton nodded. He'd experienced similar things when he was coaching. Write it off, learn what you can, and move on.

'After that, we visit the university club. Universidad San Juan is a team made up of students, but that doesn't mean they are weak. A lot of them are studying Sports Sciences or similar, so are very much into sports, and being a university, they have a lot of players to choose from.'

She paused, glancing at Moreton as he looked down, concentrating and taking in the information.

'And they have a former professional player coaching them. He went into education after retiring.'

'Another easy game then?'

'There aren't many easy games, Jon. Then we play Independiente Lacitana, I don't know that much about them, but they've been in this division for quite a while, and are always around the middle of the table. CD Mostodra are local rivals. The town is about ten kilometres away and is the nearest other football club to Retama. Being so local, a lot of the players in each club know each other. Sometimes that is good, if they are friends. Sometimes, it is bad if they aren't, and any kind of arguments can end up involving everyone. They are not one of the better clubs. As they are local rivals, there will be lots of pride amongst the players. They will want be able to show off as the winners to everyone.'

'Bragging rights,' mumbled Moreton.

'Sorry? What's right?'

'Sorry, I mean it's about "bragging rights" then. It's a phrase that people use in England if they can go to work the day after a game and their team has beaten local rivals, who may have fans in the same place. It works for players too.'

'OK. Jon, can you remember all of this? There are nineteen clubs, and already there may be too much to remember from knowing nothing about them. Shall we stop there? We can discuss the others nearer the time we play them.'

'No, it's fine. I might not remember all the details, but it's good to get a feel for the type of opposition we're going to face.'

'OK, then. I'll keep most of the rest fairly short, then. Yes?'

'Sure,' Moreton agreed, a little disappointed but hiding it successfully. It was an ideal way to spend an evening, and once back in his apartment, he knew he would be missing spending time with Sophia.

'UD Callosa a part of a bigger sports club. They have a successful basketball team, and that is their main thing. Football is not their priority. San Esteban is a club based in a small village so may not be very good. We are playing away against them first and the facilities will be small and probably quite old.'

'A bit like Retama's?' Moreton suggested, rapidly wishing he hadn't.

'Not really,' she said, barely disguising her irritation at the perceived slight.

Moreton tried to redeem the situation. 'But their dressing room may not have been so newly painted.'

'Perhaps' came the almost curt reply, before Sophia moved on. 'Anyway, Sobrolepeña Industrial CF are probably just the opposite to San Esteban's situation. The club is operated by the major company in the town. They own it and supply all of the facilities. They have a rule that only people who work for the company can play for them. There used to be rumours going around that they sometimes offered jobs to good players merely to get them into the team, but they haven't really been very successful, so it may not be true. Costa Locos were promoted last season, so I don't know much about them. It would be unusual for a junior team to achieve promotion, however, and then be successful the following year, so they may not be that much of a threat.

'We played Parque del Rey a couple of seasons ago,' Sophia continued, as the names and information became increasingly muddled in Moreton's mind. 'They were relegated the season before we were. For many years they had been in the same division as Retama, but when they were relegated a lot of players left. Last season, I think they were near the bottom of the league. Torre del Olmos are another small club, but they are well organised and have always had reasonably good teams. Desorio is a coastal town, a little like Retama, so there are lots of foreign residents living there and the club has been mainly taken over by them. It's more of a social club now than a sporting one, but you'll probably hear a few English voices there.'

The comment provoked a thought in Moreton's mind. 'As there are a lot of foreign people living in Retama, why are there none involved with the club?'

Sophia lowered the paper and thought for a second.

'Perhaps because Retama is still relatively new as a town for people from different countries to come and live in. Desorio became a holiday destination in the early days when Spain was promoting tourism. One of the very first. It's probably true that the foreign, often English, community there is more established and has become involved in the society there. Perhaps that will happen here too, but it hasn't yet.'

'Yeah guess so.' The conversation with Charlie Broome about how Retama was racing to catch up with other towns on the coast came back to Moreton's mind.

'UD Palancio are an interesting club. Well, perhaps it's better to say they were, anyway.' Sophia picked up the list again. 'This is the club that Francisco was with before he returned to Politanio. They came close to promotion last season, but when he left, a lot of their best players saw it as a signal to leave too. Many of them moved to a relatively new club nearby called Estrella Azul. I don't know much about them, but if they picked up some of Palancio's better players, they will have a good team.'

A smile spread over Sophia's face as she reached the next name on the list. 'Ah', she said. 'Árboles Altos. But you know something about this place already, don't you?'

Moreton's mind entered panic mode. There had been so many names flooding over him during the last fifteen minutes or so, that they had become a haze, incoherent, scrambled and barely remembered. His expression betrayed the situation. Sophia waited, with increasing impatience.

'Jon?' she asked, accusingly.

The fog cleared. 'Ah, Árboles Altos,' he recalled with relief. 'That's where your parents live, isn't it? A quiet village in the mountains. You went on holidays there when you were younger. Of course, I remember, Sophia.' The affected nonchalance was unconvincing, even to himself.

'That's right,' she looked at him with a playful accusation before returning to the list.

'UD Araganza are not very good, and will probably struggle this season. They usually do, but end up above the relegation places. And that just leaves two more.'

Moreton was relieved. Even with the attraction of Sophia, upon which to focus his attention, the details of so much she had said were drifting away.

'San Vicente are a very old club, owned by an old aristocratic family. The club is always very polite and the players well-mannered. It is very much the sort of club where friendship and enjoying the game comes before any big desire to win games. But they are always decent teams and will be in the middle of the table at the end of the season, as they always are.'

Sophia put the paper down on the table in front of her. 'And then there is Torreaño CF. They're not named after a town, Torreaño is a small part of a town, and the club is very much of that area, rather than the town. They are probably the best club in the division. You remember that I mentioned earlier that Costa Locos had been promoted last season, and it's unusual for a junior team to get promotion again, the following term. Well, it's unusual, but not impossible.'

She leant back in her chair. 'You may have heard of the story about Torreaño CF. It was big news here in Spain. Especially in this region.'

Moreton shook his head. 'I don't think so. Why? What about them?'

'San Julio del Rio is a town a few kilometres inland from the coast about fifty kilometres away. It was always a fairly quiet town, a little into the hills, but one area of it was built onto the side of a hill overlooking a beautiful valley and out towards the sea. It became very popular with wealthy people, business owners and even a few musicians and actors are said to own houses there. That area is called Torreaño. A few years ago, a local businessman – a very wealthy local businessman – moved there and decided to buy the football club. It was a very small junior club, a couple of divisions down from the league we are in now, but he spent a lot of money. The ground was refurbished and modernised, new players arrived, and the club took off. It has gained promotion twice in two years, and last season they signed a striker from the Segunda, Montero. He was never going to play in the Primera, but why would someone playing well and scoring goals in that division, drop down to go and play for Torreaño?'

Moreton's gesture of rubbing his thumb and forefinger together illustrated that he knew the answer.

Sophia nodded. 'I think he scored something like thirty-eight goals last season. The other clubs had no answer and they will be the one of the big teams to beat this year. If anyone can.'

She reached across the room, and slid the paper back onto her desk. 'So, Jon. How much of that do you remember?'

He pursed his lips. 'Not that much, I guess. Can you go through it again?'

For a moment Sophia thought him serious, before his laughter dismissed the thought.

'OK,' he said. 'So, Sunday is Politanio. Let's talk team selection.' He leant forward on the table. 'I think that changing anything much for the first game would be a mistake, so my thought is to go with what García would have done. We don't want to give the players a sense that we're going to come in and rip everything up.'

Sophia nodded slowly in agreement.

'So, Paco in goal. Alejandro, Kiko, Victor and Adrián. Vasquez and Palermo on the flanks with Samuel and Matías in the middle. Now comes the tricky bit. And I want to hear what you think about this.'

The invitation was instantly accepted and Sophia listened intently.

'I think we have to start with Bendonces up front. After the last game he's in a good frame of mind, plus with Politanio having a lot of younger players, he may feel pretty confident. The problem is who do we replace Revi with? What do you think?'

Sophia was clearly pleased to be so clearly involved in the process.

'Politanio's team may be young, but they will be good, so we must not get overrun in midfield.'

She invited Moreton's acquiescence. It came with a nod.

'We could play Palermo behind Bendonces. And fill out the flank position with Guido. Playing in front of Alejandro, he'll have lots of advice to keep him on his game, and Palermo will get involved in the middle as well as having the height and muscle to support Bendonces. The other thing is, we could just put Felipe in the middle and detail him to play in the middle of a three and leave Bendonces on his own. But, what about Billy Swan. Isn't that where you wanted to play him anyway?'

Moreton was impressed with Sophia's thoughts. They were precisely the options he had considered himself.

'To be honest,' he said. 'If it was four or five games into the season, I'd slot Billy in, no problem. But he hasn't played for so long, and a few training sessions isn't going to get rid of the physical rust. Plus, he's no youngster any more. The last thing I want is to put him in now, see him pull one of those old muscles and miss the next three or four games. I'm just not sure.'

Sophia looked at the table, and then back up at Moreton. 'Is he just too old. Can he still play?'

'Definitely. Billy's the sort of player that never ran too much anyway. His ability does the running for him. No offence, but at this level, he could be fifty and still be able to boss a game. Honestly, Sophia, he's really that good if he's up for it, and as I understand things, he's got a lot riding on the outcome of this season with Chaz.'

'Then, I think you should play him. Anything else is second choice. Yes?'

'I guess so. OK, then. That's what we'll do. I'll tell him to take it easy and let the younger legs do the running for him. We're sorted then.'

'Yes.'

Moreton stood up. 'I should be going,' he said somewhat reluctantly.

'I suppose so. I need to do a little reading before sleep tonight.' She nodded towards the books on the desk.

'Oh, I'm sorry.' Moreton felt suddenly guilty and selfish. 'You should have said.'

'No, don't worry. There's not much to do, but I like to lie in bed and read before sleep. It helps me to remember things better.'

The image of Sophia lying in bed lodged briefly in Moreton's mind, but the weight of it was too much to bear. He quickly chased it away, as he walked to the door. Opening it, he turned back to Sophia who was following him.

'Thanks for dinner. And thanks for the information and letting me talk through the team issues with you.'

'My pleasure,' she replied, reaching up and kissing him on the cheek.

He smiled and started down the steps.

'Don't forget,' she called after him. 'It's your turn to cook next time. It's a date!' The last word made him look back up at the doorway where Sophia stood, her body silhouetted and the yellow dress bright in the gathering dusk.

Words. Deeds

The following evening, a very gentle session was concluded early and Moreton relayed the team selection, including Billy Swan. He then went on to explain how it would be important against a team such as Politanio to be sure that everyone worked very hard. The defence must be compact and disciplined. The midfield players would be important, to ensure that the control of the game isn't gifted to the opposition. Even the wide players must work back to support Samuel and Matías.

'If we do this,' he explained. 'And can gain possession in midfield, we can hurt them. Look to play to Billy. Don't worry if he's marked. He can beat a player and find space for a pass to open up chances.'

Then, turning his attention to Bendonces: 'You are our warrior,' he said. 'Billy will find you with passes and you will score.'

He paused while Sophia translated, then spoke again.

'I know you will score.'

Another pause.

'You know you will score.'

One more pause.

'I trust you.'

A final pause.

'We all trust you, Tomás.'

As the Sophia related the final words, using his name, Bendonces seemed to grow inches in stature.

It was precisely what Moreton had intended. If someone has an ego, tap into it. Fuel it. Use it.

He allowed the words to hang in the air for a while as they seeped into the players, filling them with confidence, as water engorges a sponge. Then, he picked up the theme again. He told them he believed they had come a long way in the short time that they had been working together, but that Sunday was the start of the real journey, and that, as with most journeys, unexpected things would happen. They would face many problems, but he was convinced that this team, this squad, this family was full of strong players and strong people, and if they believed in themselves and each other, that strength would double. As Sophia stopped talking, spontaneous applause broke out among the group.

Moreton joined in, and as shouts from the group rose and then fell, he held his arms out in front of him to indicate a required return to concentrated silence. He paused for a moment, allowing time to ensure their attention was focused on him. Then, in an entirely unrehearsed motion, he slowly raised his arms in front of him, slowly but purposefully curling each hand into a clenched fist, shouting, '*Somos Retama!*' Back came the echoing call, and everyone applauded, again. Scanning the players, he noticed even Billy Swan had joined in. It was an emotion tingling moment. Despite any doubts Moreton had, the encouraging signs over the past few weeks meant he now felt the squad was ready.

As the group broke up and headed towards the dressing room, Moreton walked back towards his bag and inevitably pulled out his notebook and pen, scribbling away for a couple of moments before looking back up again. The players were trailing from the pitch in groups of two or three, but he particularly noticed that Swan was with Kiko and Victor. They looked an odd group. Victor, neat and impeccable, Kiko, muscular and tall, every inch the athlete, and Billy Swan, like some ageing entertainer who had seen better days – precisely because that's what he was. The arms of Kiko and Victor draped over Swan's shoulders suggested that despite their differences, they were forming a solid friendship. Moreton thought to himself that if he could bring such disparate characters together, this whole thing may just work out.

As he stood there, lost temporarily in his thoughts, Sophia walked back, and stood beside him.

'Jon,' she said, drawing his attention back to the here and now. 'That was wonderful. It made me want to play as well!'

Moreton smiled with warmth. 'To be honest,' he said. 'Me too!'

'Can I ask you something?'

'Sure.'

'Where did the Spanish come from? "*Somos?*" Are you keeping something from me?'

'I told you that I spend a lot of time reading, didn't I? There are a few Spanish-English Dictionaries in the apartment. I guess Chaz has put them there for the people who rented it, so I took a flip through and thought it would be useful to learn a few phrases at least.'

'Ah. That's good. You should learn more of the language so that you feel more a part of Spain, and less like a visitor.'

'Yeah, that's what I was thinking too.'

'Pretty soon. You won't need me at all.'

The words struck Moreton like a dart.

'No. I will always need you.'

The words were delivered with a sincerity bordering on fierce conviction, but once spoken, doubt and insecurity washed over him again.

'For the team, for the club, I mean. My Spanish will never be good enough. I will always need you to be here.'

He felt an almost irresistible urge to hold Sophia. To place an arm around her, and draw her close to him.

Her warm smile reassured him.

'And I will always need you, Jon,' she replied, placing a hand on his arm. 'For the team.'

He wanted to reach out. Just a hand on her arm, but then what?

The dilemma was removed as Esteban shuffled across the pitch towards them. Seeing him approaching, and clearly feeling the moment just as poignantly as Moreton had, Sophia raised an arm to greet the old man. They both turned towards the approaching figure, in studied silence, mentally encouraging him to hurry so that his presence would break the tension. Arriving, eventually, Esteban reached out a hand and shook with Moreton, before talking to Sophia. Moreton took the opportunity to divert his attention to his bag, unnecessarily rearranging the contents before closing and throwing it over his shoulder.

Esteban turned away and Sophia returned to Moreton. 'He will check everything is secure and lock up,' she said, focusing all attention on the mundane matters of the moment.

'That's great. So, I'll see you on Sunday afternoon.

She nodded.

'OK. I'll see you then.' He turned to walk away. Then stopped. Jon Moreton had spent so much of his adult life analysing things. What to do in this or that situation. Reviewing the events of the day. What went well. What didn't. How can this be made better? How can that be changed? Strategise, plan, organise. But none of that applied to this moment. This brief passing moment that, if not seized, may forever be something lamented upon during cold, dark, lonely nights, when sleep doesn't easily come. "Act!" His instincts screamed at him. Cold logic preached caution, but it lost the battle. Emotional demands were assuaged.

'Sophia,' he said.

She looked up in surprise.

'Do you also study on weekends?'

'No.'

There was no going back now.

'Do you have a favourite restaurant in Retama?'

'Of course. Are you looking for a recommendation?'

'Well, I guess a little bit. Yes, I am.'

With the need to analyse things temporarily at least locked away, he was actually enjoying the spontaneous freedom of the moment.

'If you don't have other plans tomorrow evening, how about you come with me to the restaurant and show me how good it is?'

'I have no other plans. Do you need to talk more about the team, or the game? Is this about football?'

'No. It's not about football. It's about you and me. I can't really cook pasta very well. To be honest, I can't really cook anything particularly well. So, you know that "date" we spoke about? We could do this instead.'

The smile that spread across Sophia's face negated any requirement for words.

'Shall we say, seven tomorrow evening then?' Moreton ventured. 'I assume, we'll need to go into town.'

'Not really. I know a nice little restaurant very near to us. And Jon... they serve pasta as well. You might pick up a few hints. Call at my door at eight. Seven is much too early to eat dinner in Spain. We can have a glass of wine before we go out. I'll reserve a table for us.'

'OK.' He smiled. 'I'll see you then.'

He turned, threw the bag over his shoulder again, and started to stride away. He hadn't gone five more paces however, when Sophia called out to him. He turned.

'Jon. It's a date!' Then she turned and headed in the opposite direction.

Moreton smiled to himself. 'Yes, it is,' he said aloud to himself, before breaking into a jog that didn't end until he reached his apartment. The smile remained in place for just as long.

Evening Match

For a number of hours of the following day, Jon Moreton was repeatedly amazed at the boldness that had gripped him. The day was as long as any other but felt doubly so to Moreton. Eventually, the clock dragged its unforgivingly tardy hands around to five to eight. Wearing jeans and a bright green shirt, that he had changed three times in the fifteen minutes before leaving, he walked out of the apartment. The last couple of hours had been spent alternating between what he should wear, and musing about what Sophia would decide on. He'd come to the conclusion that, as this was now officially a date, there would be no need for her to dress down, and at the same time realising that his limited wardrobe meant there was little capacity to dress to impress himself. He felt more than a little inadequate, but anticipation quelled such thoughts.

He quickly crossed the distance between the two apartments and tapped gently on the door. A few moments later it opened, with Sophia's head popping around it, leaving the rest of her unseen behind it.

'Come in,' she said. 'I have a bottle of wine open.'

Moreton entered with a smile, while Sophia disappeared into the kitchen area. He could hear the sound of liquid being poured into a glass, and, as he waited, he inevitably looked ahead to where the small television was surrounded by photographs. Instantly, he noticed that the picture that had been lying face down during his previous visit was no longer there. Had it been repositioned? He looked around at all of the other pictures on the unit, but could not see it. He was about to contemplate what this may mean when Sophia came back into the room. Holding a glass of wine in each hand, she stood framed in the doorway. For Jon Moreton, all other pictures in the room were instantly downgraded to utter unimportance by the vision.

'Wine?' she asked.

Her hair fell around the side of her face, wonderfully defining the beauty of her smile, dark eyes, high cheekbones and red lips. Unconsciously, he looked her up and down. A short-sleeved, sky-blue Indian cotton shirt, with the top three buttons unfastened and sheer at the shoulders, illustrated the bronzed tan of her arms and torso in vivid contrast. It hung in delicate pleats emphasising her pert and rounded breasts. Beneath was a black pencil thin skirt, cut just above the knee, that wrapped seductively around her lower body, with the possessive embrace of a jealous lover. Heeled black shoes that raised her height by a couple of inches, calling attention to the smooth and delicate, elongated curve of her legs, completed the ensemble.

Moreton was temporarily transfixed. Sophia stood still for a moment, with the glasses held out, awaiting an answer to her question, but also realising that her efforts and decisions of the past couple of hours had been vindicated.

'Jon? Wine?' she repeated, tilting her head to one side slightly. The movement snatched the hypnotised Moreton from his trance.

'Yes,' he replied. 'Yes, please. Thanks.'

Sophia walked across and passed him a glass.

'You look fabulous.'

'Thank you,' Sophia replied, offering a mock curtsey, before sitting down alongside him on the sofa.

All afternoon, he had been telling himself to talk about anything other than football. Going down that path had blighted so many of his relationships before and, although perhaps it would not have been the death knell of this particular one, he didn't want to risk it. 'So, where are we going to eat then?' he asked.

'It's not far. In fact, you'll have passed it any number of times on the way to the stadium and coming back. It's in the row of shops just past Carlito's, before the roundabout by Broome Cerámica. It's called Bella Cucina.'

Moreton scanned his memory but he couldn't recall seeing it.

Sophia came to the rescue. 'It's quite small, at least from the outside,' but inside it's really very nice. I go there quite often with my friends. It's not expensive and the food is really nice. The kitchen is open to see from the tables, so you can watch your food being cooked as you wait.'

'Sounds, nice. You do like your Italian food, don't you?'

'I do. In fact, I like most Mediterranean food. French, Italian, Greek, Moroccan, and of course, Spanish.'

'What about British food?' Moreton asked mischievously, feeling wonderfully relaxed now, but almost giddy with senses heightened. 'I guess you may not be too much into the sort of things we eat over there. I don't think British cooking has too great a reputation.'

'That's not really fair,' Sophia protested lightly. 'My favourite chef's book to follow recipes on is Keith Floyd. I have two of his books, look.'

She reached over to a pile of books by the side of her desk and picked two out, waving them at Moreton.

'See,' she declared, triumphantly. 'British chef!'

Moreton smiled, indulgently. 'Yeah, British chef, but I think most of his recipes aren't.'

'Ah,' Sophia conceded, taking a sip of wine while looking over the top of the glass at Moreton and smiling stealthily.

Moreton smiled back.

'Tell you what,' he said. 'For our second date, I'll cook you a Keith Floyd dish. How about that? I'll look for something really different on the internet and I'll cook it. It'll probably be a disaster, but we can always bin it and go out instead.'

Immediately he could tell that something wasn't right. It had hardly been a hysterically funny comment, but an indulgent smile would have been expected. What had he said? Sophia's smile had disappeared, replaced with a look of uncertainty.

'I'm sorry,' he said quickly, trying to repair whatever damage he had inadvertently caused. 'Is that a bad idea? My cooking isn't really that bad, honestly.'

Sophia reached out a hand and placed it on his.

'No, Jon? It's nothing to do with your cooking, but can we just see how things go? Let's see if we both enjoy this evening and take it from there. Let's not talk about second dates or anything like that. One step at a time, please. It's difficult... I'm not sure... It's just that I... Is that all right?'

'Of course. I'm sorry. I didn't mean anything by it. I wasn't trying to rush you or anything. I wasn't trying to do anything really. I was just talking.'

Words piled on words.

'I know. Anyway, we must be going now. I've reserved our table for 8.30, and the restaurant gets busy on a Saturday evening.'

Moreton glanced at his watch. It was barely ten minutes past eight and the restaurant could be no more than five minutes away, but he recognised that this wasn't the time to say anything that may have complicated things.

'Sure,' he said. 'Let's go.'

Sophia picked up a brightly coloured shawl from the back of her chair and Moreton held it for her as she slipped it over her shoulders. They placed the still amply full glasses of wine on the table and left the apartment. A few minutes later, they opened the door of a narrowly fronted restaurant and walked inside. A waiter guided them to a table, and after staring at the menu for a few minutes they placed their orders. The evening passed pleasantly as they exchanged stories of their childhoods, schooldays and how their lives had moved in so many different ways, but seemed to have preselected paths that, no matter the number of happy or sad diversions on the way, seemed to have guided them inevitably to this place and time, together.

Finding out more about each other appeared to carry no outward signs of complication and, by the time the coffee arrived, Moreton realised that they hadn't spoken about football, Retama or the game the following day. He hadn't missed it at all. Their conversation had even flowed as the coffee sat on the table, ignored and now cold, as the restaurant staff began to tidy up around them, indicating wordlessly that, perhaps, it was time to leave.

Eventually, the ever increasingly strident but polite message was acknowledged and they stood to leave. Moreton insisted on paying the bill, and they left the restaurant walking out together into the still pleasantly warm temperature of a late Spanish evening.

Arriving back at the complex, opening the exterior gate, Moreton held it ajar as Sophia passed inside before gently letting it close. Standing at their individual gates, with the steps and the doors of their apartments watching over them like some disapproving observers, Moreton asked if she had enjoyed the evening.

'Yes,' she replied, and the smile returned to her face. 'Yes, I have. Thank you so much, Jon. It was really nice.'

'OK, goodnight then. Big game tomorrow,' he confirmed, draping the comfort blanket of football around him. 'Start of the season. Start of something big for us.'

'Yes. The start of something big.'

She reached up again and kissed him on the cheek once more. They then both hesitated for a moment, enraptured by each other's eyes, before Sophia turned and hurried through the gate. At the top of the stairs, she blew him a kiss.

'See you tomorrow,' she said. And then she was gone.

In Sophia's apartment, with the light still off, she walked across to the unit with the television and photographs. Opening a drawer to one side, she reached in and took out a framed photograph. It was a picture of two lovers. A tall man with a trimmed beard, standing behind a girl with his head on her shoulder and his arms around her waist. She smiled at the picture as a tear rolled down her cheek, and then put it back in the drawer.

Noticing the two glasses of wine, she picked up the first one, and drained it quickly. Placing the empty glass down, she then picked up the second, holding it into front of her face, rubbing her finger around the rim, as other tears tracked the path of the first ones. She drank a small amount of the wine as if it would help to ease an impossible decision, now made. The glass was placed back down next to the other. One now empty, the other so nearly full.

She sighed, then smiled, then cried a little. She sat down on the sofa and sniffed back the tears, reaching for her mobile phone and tapping on the required contact. The tone rang out a couple of times before a man's voice answered softly.

'*Sophia?*' It asked gently.

She sighed. '*Si, Alvaro,*' she said with all the kindness she could find. '*Si, soy yo. Podemos hablar un momento, por favor? Lo siento mucho, pero necesito decirte algo.*'

Kick-Off

Arriving at the Estadio Antonio Núñez the following afternoon felt different for Moreton. Outside were two large coaches. One emblazoned with the name Politanio in bright red lettering clearly belonging to the visiting club, the other perhaps bringing a group of their fans along. Alongside the Politanio coach, dwarfed by the size of the visitors' transport was a small van, liveried in the colours and name of Broome Cerámica. That Billy Swan had arrived before him brought him up a little. He then realised that the timing of the journey was more Broome-inspired than Swan-orchestrated.

Moreton crested the rise of the concrete steps and descended the other side, the sight of the playing surface filling him with an excited anticipation. It was like an empty piece of paper, a canvas awaiting the brush strokes that would paint the picture of a football match. It was a time when anything was possible. Especially when it heralded the start of a new season. Hopping over the wall, he could see Sophia sitting on the bench by the side of the pitch. She looked small and forlorn, lonely, looking out into the middle distance of the far side of the ground. He walked across, but she didn't seem to notice his approach.

'Hi,' he said when just a few yards away.

Shaken from her contemplation, Sophia glanced up and smiled. 'Hi, Jon.'

He was nervous, but asked the question anyway. 'Are you OK?'

She didn't answer immediately.

He pressed on. 'It's just that you seemed a little distracted last night. I didn't want to pry, so I didn't ask, but if you need someone to talk to about something, I'm always here for you.'

She smiled and sighed in acknowledgement.

'So long as it's in English, though,' he added. 'My Spanish is still very poor!'

They both laughed, but only briefly and politely, and Moreton felt pleased that his rehearsed quip had broken the ice.

He waited, and eventually Sophia spoke. 'There was just something that I needed to do. It had been on my mind for some time, but it's done now. All sorted and finished.'

It sounded less than totally convincing.

'You sure? If your mind is somewhere else...'

'No, my mind is totally here, with you. No distractions.'

She reached out and squeezed his hand tenderly.

'If we win today, we need to arrange when you are going to cook me that Keith Floyd meal in celebration.'

It was all the confirmation he needed to hear, and any doubts about culinary expertise were put to one side.

Fifteen minutes later, they were standing outside of the dressing room in their initialled blue Retama tracksuit tops, awaiting the call from inside that all was ready for them to enter.

'I love this time of the season,' Moreton confided to Sophia. 'Everything is about to start. Anything can happen, and we can shape it as we want. It's up to us to create something special.'

The door to the dressing room opened to the serious faces of the players waiting inside.

Moreton spoke of the things he wanted the players to concentrate on in the upcoming game. He went around the room talking to each in turn, emphasising how they all had an important role to play, how each could influence the outcome of the game, but how if they worked together, with each other and for each other, there was no limit to what they could achieve.

There was a special mention to Billy Swan. 'Don't run, Billy,' Moreton counselled earnestly. 'Just play. Let these guys run.' It brought laughter and nudges to Swan as Sophia translated. In exaggerated fashion, Swan raised his thumbs in the air, then cupped his ears to indicate to the others that they should listen, moving his fingers in a running motion, before putting his feet up across Kiko's thighs and placing his hands behind his head on Victor's lap. Everyone laughed, and Swan winked at Moreton.

When it was time to go out onto the pitch, it felt like the team was ready. As they exited the dressing room, Moreton called after them, '*Somos Retama!*' The echoing call came back.

Walking from the dressing room, into the bright sunshine, Moreton wasn't sure how many spectators would be in the ground. He had hoped for a few hundred at least, but it was questionable whether there were a hundred in total. To one side was a collection of fans decked in the red and white colours of the visiting club. Passengers from the coach he had seen outside, and others that must have arrived by car. It would be difficult estimate their number, but it was certain that the visiting fans would comfortably outnumber those supporting Retama. It was clear that the team would need to convince the local people that the club was worth following again.

Entering the pitch to head towards the bench, Sophia and Moreton passed Esteban. In place of his normal greying shirt was the bright blue number eight Retama top that Moreton had given to him. Moreton patted him on the shoulder, and the old man smiled, reaching up to touch the badge on his shirt, grasping it. Neither could speak each other's language, but the action spoke louder than any numbers of words.

Reaching the bench, Moreton and Sophia were approached by a group of officials wearing red tracksuits with white piping and the badge of Politanio emblazoned on the front and the name on the back. Shaking hands cordially, before returning to their own bench, Sophia pointed out a man in his early forties, with prematurely greying hair. 'That's Francisco,' she said. Moreton nodded in acknowledgement as the ex-player shouted final instructions to his team lining up for kick-off. Moreton looked across to his players, and those sitting alongside him and Sophia on the bench. Wearing their new strip for the first time in an official game, they lost nothing in comparison to the red shirts and white shorts of the visitors, it was time to go to work. The referee blew the whistle and Jon Moreton's time as manager of CD Retama was under way.

Despite Retama harrying and scurrying around to try and disrupt their opponents studied possession, the first few minutes passed without a blue-shirted player coming into any meaningful contact with the ball. The phase ended with a cross, hit from a tight angle, that Jiménez comfortably held, before bowling the ball out towards the waiting Victor. The visitors' team dropped back into their own half following the drilled instructions of their coach as the elegant defender and Kiko exchanged passes, steadily advancing towards the halfway line.

Ahead of them, Billy Swan had caught the eye of Victor as he moved away from the penalty area, dutifully followed by his marking defender. Acknowledging the move, Victor fed the ball to Swan's feet. Effortlessly controlling the ball, Swan pivoted to face his opponent before dragging the ball to one side. The defender leaned across to block the movement, slightly unbalancing himself. At the same instant, Swan whipped the ball back through the defender's legs and accelerated clear for a few yards. Drawn to the danger like a moth to a candle, the player marking Bendonces was magnetically attracted to the ball, and the pass to the Retama number nine burnt him in the same way that the moth is destroyed by the hypnotising deadly beauty of the flame. The bearded striker was through on goal. He advanced to the edge of the area before coolly firing home. With less than five minutes on the clock, incredibly, Retama had the lead.

On the bench, Moreton, Sophia and the substitutes jumped around hugging in unrestrained celebration. Out on the pitch, a gathering crowd of players did the same, piling on top of the celebrating striker in unrestrained joy. Just outside the penalty area a small knot of Retama players were in less celebratory mood. Billy Swan was standing, head bowed, with Kiko and Victor. The two younger men had arms around the older man's shoulder as he reached down and rubbed the back of his right thigh.

As things calmed, Moreton noticed the three players, and instantly knew what had happened. 'Crap,' he said to Sophia. 'I think he's pulled a hamstring.' As the other players walked back from their celebrations, the realisation also seemed to dawn on them. Celebration turned to concern, and after a few seconds it became clear that Billy Swan's debut in Spanish football was done.

Moreton indicated to Guido that he would be going on to replace Swan, and the young Spaniard jumped to his feet. With Kiko and Victor supporting him, the stricken veteran limped to the sidelines shaking his head. 'Hammy,' he mouthed towards Moreton as he approached. Signalling to the referee, Moreton sent on Guido to replace Swan. He asked Sophia to tell Palermo to go into the ten position and that Guido would replace him on the flank. Retama had started their season on a high, but the rest of this opening game would quickly tumble into disaster.

By halftime, Retama had been run ragged by the young and ebulliently skilled Politanio players. The defence had battled defiantly, but lacking any way of forcing play in the opposite direction, apart from a couple of sorties along the flank by an outnumbered Vasquez, the pressure had increased until the defence cracked. The equaliser had come fifteen minutes before the break and by the time the referee had ended the first period, Retama had conceded twice more.

The half-time break was quiet and the players sat in the dressing room with heads down and spirits moving in the same direction. Kiko and Victor sat either side of Swan, offering quiet words of consolation. He spoke no Spanish and neither Kiko or Victor knew much English, but the messages were clearly being delivered with empathy, and received in the same vein, as Swan's wry smile illustrated. Rousing belief in players clearly being outplayed by a more able team was new to Moreton. Last season had become a sorry tale of defeat after defeat, and the habit of losing was like a comfortable pair of slippers, easy to slip into, but difficult to cast off again. Confidence can be the most fragile of flowers and the reserves built up over the previous few weeks, were now leaking away in front of Moreton's eyes.

With Sophia relating his words, Moreton tried to re-energise his team. 'The next goal is big! We get it and the game's open again,' he insisted. Support came from Paco Jiménez. The old professional had been in similar circumstances enough times in his long career to know that it was fight or suffer humiliation. When Moreton had finished, the goalkeeper stood up and clapped his hands aggressively at each of the players walking around to face each of them as he did so. 'Arriba!' he shouted out several times. Alejandro Sanz, so often the quiet but always inspiring captain, echoed the call, and almost out of duty, rather than belief, a few of the players responded and repeated. Moreton did not understand what the word meant, but was clear of its intent. He joined in as well, before opening the dressing room door to send his players out for the second half.

For the next twenty minutes of the game, Retama battled against the waves of attacks, but through sheer determination and a stubborn refusal to bend the knee, they held out. On the bench, Moreton's hopes began to rise again. Turning to Sophia he betrayed how hope had got the better of logic and expectation. 'Just one break,' he said. 'We just need one break to score and we can turn this around.' As the game progressed, though, with legs, minds and emotional fervour running virtually on empty, the inevitable happened. Two more quick goals inside the last fifteen minutes extinguished any forlorn hopes of redemption.

With ten minutes remaining, he called Santi and José Palermo across to him and asked Sophia to tell them they would be going on. At the next break in play, he signalled Juan Palermo and Bendonces to come off, sending on the two young forwards. On his way off, the older of Palermo brothers patted his younger sibling on the head and slapped him on the back as they exchanged places. Bendonces left the field without such grace.

Politanio were seemingly sated by the five goals they had scored and began to ease down. With just a couple of minutes to go, a long clearance from Kiko, hammering the ball away from a corner, found Guido breaking into space. Outpacing his marker, he drove on deep into the Politanio half and then the penalty area. The goalkeeper came out to narrow the angle, but Guido rolled the ball across the box to where a supporting Santi had sprinted up in support to stroke the ball into the empty net. Moreton jumped to his feet to celebrate as the remainder of the bench, merely applauded the seemingly meaningless goal. In contrast to the celebrations that greeted the first goal, the handshakes between players were markedly low key.

When he sat down again, Sophia turned to Moreton. 'It's too late,' she said, sadly.

'It's never too late to score a goal. It won't change this game, but it shows that the players hadn't given up. There's still fight in them, and two of the younger players combined for the goal. It will make the other young ones think they can do it too, and the older ones will realise that there's still a bright future to be gained here.'

Sophia appeared less than convinced. 'Do you think so, Jon? Really, do you think so?'

Moreton shook his head in mock sadness, before smiling. 'No, Sophia,' he replied. 'I don't *think* so.' He paused. 'I *know* so. The next few games are going to be difficult, but we will improve as we play more games. You can improve on technique and awareness, but you need players to have heart and desire. You can't teach that. It's either there or it isn't. Paco has it. Alejandro has it, and for the first part of the second half, almost all of the players out there had it.'

Sophia had clearly been lifted by his words. 'Almost,' she said, as the referee brought the game to a close. 'Who…?'

Moreton cut her off her question, pointing towards the player trudging towards the dressing room as the others, including the unused substitutes, walked around shaking hands with the opposition players. The scorer of Retama's first goal slammed the dressing room door behind him. Moreton shook his head in sad resignation.

Their attention was then drawn to the man in the red tracksuit with prematurely greying hair. He held his hand out to shake with Moreton, a gesture the Retama manager returned cordially. Francisco spoke a few words in Spanish, but Moreton didn't understand. He turned to Sophia who quickly explained that he didn't speak very much Spanish. Francisco nodded and smiled.

'Your players…' Francisco said to Moreton in hesitant English. 'Your players…' He was clearly searching for the right word. Eventually he found a way of conveying the intended message. He closed his right fist and tapped it against the left side of his chest.

Moreton smiled at the clear compliment.

'Heart!' he said.

'*Si*,' Francisco replied, nodding. 'Heart! *Corazon!*'

Moreton smiled back, deploying one of the few words in Spanish he was comfortable with. 'Gracias,' he said.

The manager of the victorious team then spoke to Sophia. Moreton understood very few of the words, but recognised Billy Swan being mentioned. Eventually, Francisco reached out his hand once more to sake with Moreton again. '*Buena suerte!*' offered the man in the red tracksuit before turning and walking away towards the visitors' dressing room.

After collecting various items from the bench, Moreton and Sophia followed towards the Retama dressing room.

'What were you talking about?'

'He asked me if the player who had been injured was Billy Swan,' Sophia revealed with a smile. 'When I told him that it was, he was very impressed. He told me that he remembered watching him play many years ago and that he was very talented, very skilful.'

Moreton was pleased by the information.

'That was nice of him.'

'Yes, it was. He also said that I should tell you that your team has great spirit about them. He was confident that his team would be near the top at the end of the season and that your team would be near to it as well.'

Moreton held out a hand to stop Sophia.

'No,' he said firmly, causing Sophia look surprised at the interjection. 'Not my team, Sophia. It's our team.'

Sophia nodded in agreement and smiled despite herself.

'Yes, Jon. He said that he could see that the team had great potential, and once the younger players had a little more experience they would progress. He said that when Billy had beaten their defender so easily to create the goal, the young lad had learnt more in that second than in a week of coaching on a training pitch. All of his players thought they were destined for the first team, but Billy had shown them that they still had a lot to learn, and that they still needed to work hard. He also said that your… our young players had learnt a lot too.'

Moreton was enthused by the comments that Sophia had passed on and felt almost elated, despite the result of the game. They entered the dressing room with renewed confidence, only to be met by a group of players clearly lacking in the same emotion. Seizing the moment, and fearing that anything else he had to say may not be sufficient, he asked Sophia to tell the players what Francisco had said. As he watched the reactions to her words, he noticed that, when Swan's name was mentioned, how the veteran player looked up from his downcast demeanour and smiled. Here was someone who fed on such praise, and his confidence levels were immediately topped up to the mark designated as "brash," and the muscular right arm of Kiko wrapped itself around Swan's shoulder hugging the smiling Englishman towards him with a warmth and affection that made the remainder of the group smile, as Victor patted Swan's thigh. The two centre backs operating as a team off the pitch as well as on it.

The smiles spread around the group as Sophia continued to repeat Francisco's complimentary words, lifting the gloom like a glimpse of the sun, warming a chilly day. Then Moreton noticed that someone was missing. Where was Bendonces? For a moment he felt like stopping Sophia to ask the question, but thought better of it. The mood of the players was lifting, and he wanted nothing to spoil that. So he waited. As she finished, Jiménez began the applause for them all. It was quickly joined by the others. Moreton and Sophia turned to leave so that the players could shower and change. As he opened the door to leave, Sanz called after him. 'Mister,' he said in that soft but powerful tone that always demanded respect from the other players. '*Somos Retama.*' Moreton smiled and nodded agreement. '*Si, Alejandro*' he agreed. '*Somos Retama.*'

Ups and Downs

Standing outside of the dressing room, Moreton asked Sophia about Bendonces and why he wasn't there. She had no idea.

'Leave it with me,' she told Moreton. 'I'm going to find Esteban, and when some of the players come out, I'll speak with them. Are you going straight home?'

'Yeah, I'm going to have to do some thinking as to how we work with Billy not available.'

'OK, when I get back, I'll knock on your door and tell you what I've found out.'

An hour or so later, Moreton was sat on the balcony of his apartment, the ever-present notepad bearing the marks of his musings. All being well, Revi would be back for the next game, and could slot into the number ten role, but ideally, he wanted to play him further back so that he could have more of the ball as it came out of the defence, and use his ability to feed Swan and Bendonces. Such thoughts had to be shelved for now though. Until Swan was fit again, he'd need to place Revi behind the striker, with Samuel and Matías in the midfield. But Bendonces? What was the situation with him? Just as he was considering different options, a gentle knock came on his door.

Showered and wearing fresh jogging bottoms and a vest top, he walked through the apartment towards the door. The smile betrayed his delight to see Sophia standing outside. 'Come in,' he said, stepping back so that she could enter. She did so and, seeing his papers spread out on the balcony table, walked through the patio doors back out into the sunshine of the balcony. She stood there for a moment looking out across the rooftops to the mountains in the distance. Moreton followed her and watched as she stood silhouetted against the setting sun.

'I always think that the apartments on your side are better than mine,' she said, turning to face an embarrassed Moreton who felt like he had been caught doing something wrong.

'Why is that?' he enquired, recovering composure.

'Well, just look at the view,' she said, waving her hand out, indicating the scenery. 'All I can see from my balcony is the apartment opposite across the walkway. Hardly entrancing. Well, not as entrancing as your view.'

'Yes. It's not bad, is it.' Although neither his words nor his attentions were exclusively focused on the view afforded from the balcony. 'Would you like a coffee, or a glass of wine?'

'No, thank you. I need to go and shower. I just wanted to tell you what happened with Bendonces.'

Waking out onto the balcony, Moreton sat down in one of the four large wicker chairs around the table, indicating to Sophia to sit opposite him. She sat down with a sigh that suggested it wasn't going to be good news.

'Apparently, when the rest of the players returned to the dressing room, he had already changed and left. None of them knew what had happened but, while we were talking with Francisco, Alejandro telephoned him to find out where he was.'

A frown was forming on Moreton's face. 'I'm not going to like this am I?'

Sophia shook her head. 'I don't think so. But perhaps it solves a problem.'

'Perhaps?' Moreton leaned back in his chair.

'When Alejandro spoke to him, Bendonces was very short. People do not normally speak to Alejandro like that. No matter what the situation is. He is the man we all turn to when we have problems. Well, perhaps not all. Not Bendonces. He told Alejandro that he was finished with the club. He said it was going nowhere and that you had no idea about how to coach players and manage a team. Alejandro was very calm. He does not lose his temper. He simply asked if Bendonces wanted to think things over for a few days. It was pointless, though. Bendonces wouldn't listen and kept saying he was finished with it all, with all of us. He told him that he would return his kit to Esteban, but other than that, did not want to enter the ground again. Alejandro then simply thanked him for his efforts with the team in the past, said goodbye and hung up.'

Moreton brought his hands together, interlocking his fingers and resting his chin on the platform they created.

'OK... OK, he's gone now. We need to concentrate on the players who are part of our family, not the ones who have left us.'

Sophia put her hand to her mouth trying to stifle a gentle laugh.

'I'm not sure it's funny, Sophia,'

Sophia held her hand up in exaggerated apology, before resting both hands down on the table and leaning slightly forwards to explain.

'I know it's not, Jon. It's just that what you said is exactly what Alejandro said to the others, and to me.'

An impish smile, threatening to develop into a laugh, broke out over her face again. 'I'm sorry,' she said, adding: 'It's also what Alejandro suggested García would have said if he had been there.' She leaned further forward, reaching out and placing her hand on his arm. 'And, it's what he thought you would say as well.'

It was Moreton's turn to laugh a little now.

'He's a wise man, Alejandro, isn't he?'

Now Sophia had no pretence about laughing. 'He said that about you, too.'

Moreton joined in the laughter, and dropped his hands to the table as he laughed, until both of them were resting on hers.

It felt both natural and comforting but strange and uncomfortable at the same time. Without making it too obvious he drew them back and, placing them on either side of his head, leant forwards in quiet concentration.

'Are you studying tonight?' For both, it felt like a loaded question.

'No. I wasn't planning to. I don't usually study at weekends, unless there's nothing better to do.'

It felt like a loaded answer, but as with his question, it was one that couldn't be ignored.

'Look, I know you said that you didn't want to talk about second dates, but it's quite late now. How about if you go and shower and I'll rustle up some pasta and we can sit here and discuss how we're going to play things without Bendonces?'

Moreton allowed no time for hesitation before adding: 'Look, I'm not going to cook a complicated Keith Floyd recipe, so it's not the official second date anyway. It's a coaches' meeting. It's a Retama meeting. Let's call it a Retama family dinner. Is that OK?'

Sophia's smile suggested that it very much was OK. 'That sounds good. But so long as Mr Floyd doesn't mind, let's call it our second date, shall we?'

'Sure. Let's do that.'

Sophia stood to leave and Moreton followed, walking behind her through the patio door and into the living area. He was already planning what he would cook, and how he could produce something that was at least vaguely edible. Reaching the door, Sophia turned to face Moreton. Momentarily lost in culinary considerations, the sudden halt almost caused him to walk into her, and for a moment their faces were mere inches apart. This time there was no hesitation. Sophia reached up and, placing one hand on his shoulder, kissed him gently on the lips. In that moment, the line had been crossed and there was no going back.

Barely without thinking, the breathlessness of the moment swept Moreton along.

'I have a shower here as well, you know.' He smiled, adding a little brevity to allay the fears in his mind.

Sophia smiled back, placing her index figure on his lips to suggest he shouldn't say anything further. 'I'll see you later,' she said before turning and lightly skipping down the steps through the gate, across the narrow walkway, and up the steps to her apartment. Reaching her door, she turned and said, 'When do you want me?'

Moreton was tempted to shout out: 'From the first time we met, and always ever since,' but thought better of it.

'Around 8.30,' seemed more appropriate if not a little prosaic.

'OK,' she replied, before turning and closing the door.

Once back inside the realisation dawned that he was now committed to cooking something that would at least convince Sophia not to make their second date also their last one. Reaching for his iPad, he tapped the words into Google. 'How to cook pasta.' Hastily reading the results, he changed his vest for a T-shirt and headed out of the apartment, hurrying out of the complex, towards the supermarket. Pineapple and mayonnaise were not on the shopping list.

Thirty minutes later he returned, laden with two shopping bags. The first contained a packet of multi-coloured farfalle pasta, mushrooms, garlic, onions, olives and a tin of chopped tomatoes. The second had two bottles of red wine. He laid out the various ingredients on the small kitchen surface and walked to the living area to retrieve his iPad, opening the saved page on how to cook pasta. Despite having already showered once, he thought it best to do so again, changing into a fresh pair of jeans and a black short-sleeved shirt.

At 8.00 he began. Fifteen minutes would be sufficient to get the sauce bubbling away nicely, allowing it time to thicken. He could then put the pasta to boil just before Sophia arrived so that everything would be ready for ten minutes or so later.

He studiously followed the recipe, chopping onions and garlic and softening them in a pan with olive oil, before adding tomatoes, mushrooms and a handful of olives and seasoning. He continued stirring until it started to produce a pleasant smell, opened some wine, and poured a glassful into the pot, turning down the heat.

On the balcony table, he laid out mats, plates, cutlery, wine glasses and the opened the bottle of wine. With the sun dipping towards the horizon above the mountains, in measured pursuit of its daily resting place among the distant uplands, it looked a perfect setting.

Placing a pan of water on the hob to boil, a movement outside caught his eye through the kitchen window. Sophia was just leaving her apartment. He watched as she turned to lock her door, before walking down the steps and towards his door. Her black hair contrasted with the pure white dress she was wearing. Sleeveless and low at the front, it fell to a couple of inches above the knee. If there was a more effective way to emphasise her attractiveness, it would be difficult to find. The water began to bubble as a gentle knock came at his door. It was getting hot in the kitchen.

'Just a moment,' he called out, as he tipped the pasta into the boiling pan, and then gave the thickening sauce a stir as well.

Opening the door, he smiled at his guest. 'You look great,' he said without realising it was in any way gauche, quickly adding: 'I hope you're hungry.'

Sophia kissed him gently and, passing the kitchen, nodded approvingly. 'That smells good. Perhaps you're not that bad a cook after all.'

'Ah, it's just a little something I threw together,' he said in an affected voice, before quickly picking up his iPad, and clicking to clear the screen that would have betrayed his assertion. 'Let's go and sit on the balcony.'

Together they stepped into the warm evening air. The sun was still above the horizon, but a few distant clouds digested its rays, replying with a cobalt and orange tinge. The colours were vivid, and when Moreton poured them each a glass of wine, the red liquid seemed to sparkle in the light.

'*Salud!*' Sophia offered, raising her glass. Moreton responded as they settled down into the comfortable wicker chairs facing each other. The words of Billy Swan came unannounced and uninvited into Jon Moreton's consciousness. 'Hey, that Sophie's a bit fit. She yours, Jon?' He couldn't help but smile to himself as the thought wrapped itself around his mind, offering a warm glow of contentment and happiness.

'What, Jon?' Sophia asked, noticing the expression on his face.

Emotions betrayed by his demeanour, Moreton opted for evasion, then confession. 'It's nothing,' he said before correcting himself. 'No, it's not nothing. It's just that I'm happy. How weird does that sound?'

Sophia, her face looking even more beautiful in the slowly fading light, smiled at him.

'It doesn't sound weird at all. I'm happy too!'

Moreton jumped to his feet and walked around the table towards Sophia, bending down to her, as she looked up. He brushed the hair from the side of her face with the back of his hand and kissed her. Her lips felt warm and soft. For a few seconds, the world around them ceased to exist, nothing outside of their two consciousnesses, now intimately joined, had any meaning or relevance. Then, agonisingly and reluctantly Moreton separated his lips from hers and raised his head. 'I have to check the pasta,' he said, realising it was the least romantic thing he had ever said in his life.

He touched Sophia gently on the cheek and then turned away, returning to the kitchen. By this time, the sauce had thickened in a pleasing way. Picking up a wooden spoon he carefully rotated the bows of pasta in the steaming water.

'I have to check the pasta,' he repeated out loud, but softly, in self-mocking tones. 'Christ, Jon. Smooth or what.'

Moreton leant around the corner of the archway leading back into the living area so that he could see across it and out onto the balcony. He had intended to tell Sophia that dinner would be ready in a few minutes, but as he caught sight of her, now standing by the table leaning on the balcony rail looking out at the view, he hesitated briefly. Increasingly conscious of his beating heart he felt an almost irresistible urge to hold her close to him and feel her heart beating as well. As much to unchain himself from the moment as anything else, he conjured up the words he had been looking for. 'Dinner in a few minutes,' he called out with exaggerated cheerfulness. Sophia turned from her contemplations and, looking over her shoulder, smiled in reply. It melted him internally, and he quickly turned his attention back to the cooker, fearing he would surely lose consciousness had he not done so.

He strained the pasta, placed it into a shallow serving bowl, and then poured the sauce into another one, before turning off the cooker and placing the pans into the sink. Feeling that, whatever it tasted like, the food looked pretty much like the picture on his iPad, Moreton nodded to himself with quiet satisfaction. He picked up the two serving dishes and walked back to the balcony, placing them down on one of the mats with a slightly exaggerated flourish that invited the gentle round of applause that a smiling Sophia offered in congratulation.

They both sat down again and served the food. Moreton topped up the wine glasses, asking: 'What shall we drink to?'

Sophia closed one eye as if lost in thought, then replied. 'We should drink two toasts, Jon.'

Moreton cocked his head to one side, inviting an explanation.

'The first one is to Retama. The second one is to us,' she continued, raising her glass.

Moreton smiled happily and complied as they clinked glasses a couple of times, before sipping the wine. Putting his glass down on the table Moreton, quickly picked it up again.

'Actually, it should only be one toast.'

'Why only one?'

'Because it was Retama that brought us together,' he answered triumphantly, raising his glass once more. Sophia nodded softly and smiled. They toasted and began the meal. The next thirty minutes or so passed quickly with talk of football and non-football matters passing without crossing streams. It was quickly concluded that Santi should start in place of Bendonces. There would still be an opportunity to give José some game time as well, and Revi should play the number ten role, until Billy Swan was fit again.

'What about the number nine shirt?' Sophia asked. 'Should Santi have it?'

After a moment's thought, Moreton concluded that it wasn't a good idea.

'I don't think so,' he suggested. 'He has nineteen now and has scored with that number. Probably best not to. He'll quickly learn he's our main man now. We'll keep the number nine shirt in case someone else joins the club.'

Sophia smiled a little mischievously.

'What?' Moreton asked.

It was clear that the woman sitting opposite had something in mind.

'I was just wondering if there was someone in particular you were thinking of.'

She paused, allowing the thought to lie there for a while, before continuing.

'You know. Someone else from your past in England. Perhaps Alan Shearer or Wayne Rooney. Harry Kane would be good as well. So long as he didn't mind sitting on the bench to wait for his chance to play.'

She had laughed, putting down her fork for a moment to wipe her mouth with a napkin as she did so.

'Actually, I spoke to Harry, but Chaz wouldn't stump up the wages.'

'Surely, he'd take a pay cut to come here and play? And we have a nice number nine shirt he can have. What more could any man want.'

'You...' Moreton secretly whispered to himself in the lock-up of his mind.

They chatted about families and friends. They talked about the weather and Sophia explained that it was not always sunny and warm in Retama. Sometimes it rained, and in the winter the temperatures could go down to nine or ten degrees. Moreton had laughed and told her how cold it got in England, and how temperatures would often fall below zero, and about ice and snow.

'Ah, snow,' Sophia replied with concentrated seriousness. 'We have snow here in Retama as well.'

'Really?'

'Yes, I remember it well. It was about fifteen years ago.'

The empty plates and dishes suggested that Moreton's cooking had reached the required standard. He stood up to clear them away.

'That was very nice,' she said. 'You can cook for me again.'

'No problem. I still have that Keith Floyd dish that I promised you. Perhaps on the third date?'

'Or the fourth, or the fifth.'

She rose from her chair to help him, but he declined

'I'll do it. You just sit there and chill out.'

She smiled in agreement, and as Moreton carried the plates, dishes and cutlery back to the kitchen, she turned to watch the dying embers of the sun finally take shelter behind the grey, blue mountains in the distance.

In the kitchen, Moreton placed the dishes down, before returning to collect the rest of the items from the table. He poured the last drops of wine into the glasses before taking away the empty bottle. Sophia was sitting in the chair, her bare arms resting on the rail around the top of the balcony wall, the side of her head resting on her arms. Moreton thought she looked like an oil painting, a moment caught in time and to be treasured.

'More wine?' he asked. Sophia raised her head, turned and looked at him for a moment without speaking. Moreton casually waved the empty wine bottle.

'Are you trying to get me drunk?'

'No,' he replied. 'Should I be?'

The only answer was a period of silence.

'OK, yes, then,' she replied eventually, with a smile.

Moreton wasn't sure which of the questions were being answered, but took away the empty bottle returning to the kitchen to wash up. A few minutes later, he walked back to the table with the second bottle of wine. Sophia was now leaning on the table, with her head resting on hands cupped either side of her face. He placed the bottle down and picked up his glass, draining the last of the wine, noticing that Sophia had already emptied hers. He reached for the bottle and topped them up again. All the time, Sophia merely watched him, looking intently at his face as if trying to unravel a puzzle. Moreton raised the newly filled glass to toast, but Sophia reached out a hand, and gently eased his arm back to the table, causing him to return the glass to its coaster. She took his hand in hers and stared at him intently. Eventually, in soft, vulnerable tones, she invited him into her thoughts.

'Jon. Are we going to hold each other's hearts in our hands? If we are, we must be gentle with them. We must be careful. We must be honest and kind because they are precious and so fragile. Don't ever deceive me. I will never deceive you. Make me happy and consider me important. You are very important to me, Jon. I always want you to be happy. I don't need money. I need commitment. I have no money to give, but you'll always have my commitment.'

A pause.

'Are we going to try to love each other, Jon?'

There's an old saying along the lines of 'If you fail to prepare, then prepare to fail!' It's something that Jon Moreton had always adhered to, in his work, in his life. He had always thought ahead and planned for situations and how he would deal with them. This was no different. He'd spent many hours thinking about how his relationship with Sophia was developing and where he wanted it to go. He'd even practised the words to say at particular times depending on how things felt, what had been said, what hadn't been said. Now was the time to bring all of those thoughts into action. He'd found the exact words, and committed them to memory, but as the person opposite him bared her soul and offered him her heart to hold he first stumbled, then found them. Reaching out his other hand to hold hers, he spoke with a calmness, built on conviction. 'Sophia,' he said. '*Te quiero.*'

A tiny drop of water ran silently down Sophia's cheek, followed by another, and then one more, but any possibility that even a flood of tears could wash away the smile on her face was forlorn at best.

'*Te quiero mucho,*' she said, between the tears.

'*Te quiero por siempre*,' he countered, invoking infinity, reaching the limit of the few Spanish words he had practised time and again, precisely for this occasion.

'*Te quiero más*,' Sophia raised the bar. Infinity plus one. Checkmate!

She laughed, and cried a little more.

He smiled and laughed.

Then, standing up, they held each other closely as the sun dipped out of sight.

The night belongs to lovers.

'I can feel your heart beating,' Moreton whispered into Sophia's ear.

'That's because I've given it to you, Jon. *Mi corazón es tuyo para siempre*. It's yours forever.'

'Can you feel mine?'

'I hold it in my hands. I'll never break it, Jon. Don't break mine.'

'I won't.'

They kissed now as lovers.

The morning broke bright and clear, shining through the blinds in Jon Moreton's bedroom. His eyes blinked open and, as often had been the case ever since arriving in Spain, for a brief a second, it all seemed like a dream that he had now awoken from, and he was back home in England. Reality quickly slotted back into place, though. He started to yawn, then suddenly paused. Had it really happened? He turned, and as he did so, a stream of long black hair fell into his view across the pillows on the other side of the bed. It slightly hid the shape of slender tanned female shoulders trailing away under the duvet. Cautiously, he reached out a hand and moved the hair to one side, revealing more of the soft skin that carried a fragrance only known to those who have woken up next to the person they loved.

Unable to resist the temptation to touch the still quietly sleeping Sophia, Moreton gently brushed the back of his hand against the delicate flesh of her back, prompting memories of the previous night when they had passionately celebrated their newly acknowledged love. The contact caused her to stir and Moreton both rejoiced at the response and, at the same time, regretted that he had disturbed her slumber. He wanted to hold her, though, and was jealous of Morpheus's embrace as she slept. She turned to face him and they smiled at each other, before kissing. '*Hola*,' he mouthed silently.

Moreton heard a gentle sigh from Sophia. 'You OK?' he asked.

She turned her head to face him as he mirrored her action.

'Yes. I'm OK. I more than OK.'

'I just thought you were…'

Sophia cut Moreton's thought short. 'Jon, let's not tell anyone.'

'What? About us, you mean?'

'Yes.'

Seeing her naked in the daylight was an intoxicatingly new revelation for Moreton. His eyes were drawn down towards her breasts that pointed at him with firm brown nipples. His thoughts were scrambled.

'I'm sorry, what?' he said.

Sophia laughed gently. 'Jon. Pay attention. Up here, please.'

Moreton laughed guiltily, and looked up again at Sophia's face. It bore an expression defined by intent.

'Sorry, Sophia. But it's not my fault,' he pleaded in helpless mitigation. 'I mean just…'

'Jon!' Sophia insisted, pulling the covers up to her neck in mock modesty.

'Yes, right. I'm with you.'

'I don't think we should tell anyone about us.'

'OK. I don't mind, but why?'

'Well, it's none of their business really is it.'

'I thought we were going to be honest with each other.'

Sophia bowed her slightly, and sighed.

'I'm sorry. That's not the real reason. It's mainly because a lot of the team are just getting to know you, to like you, and we need to be careful not to spoil that. We all look after each other, and if they know about us, they would all – especially Paco – be very suspicious of you. They would look to protect me, and that could cause friction.'

Moreton was less than convinced that he was being given the whole story, but what she said rang true and he didn't want to push her any further.

'OK, but when we're sitting on the bench holding hands, people are going to put two and two together.'

He paused as Sophia looked doubtfully at him.

'I'm only joking, Sophia. It's fine. If that's what you think is best, let's keep it as our little secret for the time being.'

'I do think it's best.' She leaned over to kiss him. '*Yo te quiera, mi precioso chico Ingles.*'

'I don't understand that one. I hope it was a nice thing to say.'

'It was. It was.'

With that, Sophia rolled away from him and, throwing back the light duvet stepped out of the bed. At first disappointed to be losing the closeness of contact with his new lover, Moreton took instant compensation from the sight of Sophia's nakedness as she walked from the bedroom towards the bathroom. Shortly after disappearing out of his sight, her smiling face reappeared leaning back into the bedroom.

'Jon. You remember that shower you kept inviting me to take here? I'll take it now!'

Relationships Hidden and Relationships Revealed

The remainder of the morning had been spent enjoying a breakfast of fruit and croissants on the balcony as the people of Retama began their Monday in the street below. With the dress from the previous evening being less than ideal for a morning, and having little else to wear, Moreton had given Sophia one of his training tops. Baggy, and both long in the sleeve and length on the relatively slight Sophia, Moreton couldn't help but think how attractive she looked wearing it. Ill-fitting perhaps, but with sleeves rolled up and the length covering what would have been the socially acceptable limits of her legs, the casual beauty entranced him.

The following day they arrived for training, separately. Sophia first, Moreton a few minutes later. Reaching the pitch, he noticed that Revi had returned, and went to speak to him.

'*Tu abuela? Ella es buena?*'

The youngster nodded. '*Si, Mister. Gracias.*'

Sophia smiled at them both.

Looking across to the bench, Moreton noticed a forlorn and lonely Billy Swan, looking thoroughly bored. He sat down next to his old team-mate.

'How's it going, Billy?' Moreton asked.

'Absolutely cosmic.'

'I know it's a pain, mate, but from what Sophia told me, it only looks like a slight pull, so you should recover quickly enough.'

A nod was the only reply.

Undeterred, Moreton pressed on.

'Are you doing what she advised? Rest, ice, elevate the leg when resting. Those anti-inflammatories should help as well.'

He was trying to sound buoyant, but failing.

'Yeah,' I'm doing all that. Look,' he said, pointing at his leg.

Moreton now noticed that Swan's right leg was resting on a couple of folded towels on top of an upturned bucket.

'Soon as I got here, Sophie was all over it, Jon.'

'Great.'

'She ain't a bad kid, you know. Tell you what, Jon. You could do worse, eh?'

'I know.' Moreton replied smiling inside.

Just then Sophia came across to the bench.

'Hi,' she said to Moreton in particular. 'Are you checking up on our invalid?'

Moreton wanted to hold her, to tell the world that she was his lover, but knew that he couldn't and restrained himself.

'Yeah,' he replied casually. 'I think a light session today. We'll do something a bit more intense tomorrow and then another light one on Friday to prep up for the game on Sunday. San Juan Uni, isn't it?' he asked, even though it had been a subject that he and Sophia had spoken about at length an hour or so ago.

'Yes, the university team there,' she replied, maintaining the pretence. 'How about a Rondo to get things moving, a couple of possession drills and then a short-sided easy paced game to finish off?'

'Perfect.'

Inside his brain was adding, 'and that's what you are,' as she walked back towards the players.

Walking in the opposite direction, Victor headed towards the pile of water bottles, using the break to take on some liquid lost in the heat of the early evening. Taking a couple of swallows before replacing the bottle, he took a circuitous route back to the other players, passing by the bench first, patting Swan on the head as he passed.

'*Vale?*' he asked.

Swan lifted his head, and patted Victor's held out hand as he walked away.

'Yeah,' he called after the younger man. '*Vale*, Meldrew.'

Victor raised his hand in acknowledgement as he trotted away.

Moreton was confused. 'Meldrew?'

'Yeah,' Swan replied. 'Meldrew. You know, Meldrew. Victor Meldrew,' then adopting an exaggeratedly exasperated tone. 'I don't believe it!' Moreton laughed, and patted Swan on the back.

'I'm teaching him to say it,' the injured player explained. 'You know, to say "I don't believe it." Apparently, he never scores goals, because he's always at the back. Even for corners and free kicks, it's Kiki Dee who goes forward, and he's left to mind the shop at the back. So, I've told him that if he ever scores, he has to come to me and say "I don't believe it!" all in the proper voice and everything.'

'You're priceless, Billy. You really are.' Swan's mood had lifted.

'That's bloody true mate. I am priceless.'

'You know, though, don't you, that he'll have no idea who Victor Meldrew is.'

'Course he does,' Swan insisted. 'I told him all about that actor bloke.'

Moreton's confusion was increasing by the minute.

'What? When? I didn't know Victor even spoke English.'

Swan turned to face Moreton. 'Course he does. Well, not great English like Sophie, but enough. Him and Kiki Dee can understand plenty when you talk to them.'

'What? Who the hell's Kiki Dee?' He was losing track of the conversation.

'He is, of course,' Swan insisted pointing to the figure, as always, playing alongside Victor.

'His name's Kiko, Billy.'

'Kiko? Kiki? Kiki Dee, it's the same thing ain't it? Well, near enough anyway.' He paused. 'Look, Jon. I wasn't supposed to tell you this, but it doesn't matter really. Do you remember when I first joined in a game and beat him, Kiko, with a Cruyff turn?'

'Yeah, and...'

'Well, afterwards, they collared me.'

'Who collared you?'

'Meldrew and Kiki Dee,' replied Swan, irritated, feeling his companion wasn't paying sufficient attention. 'I'd spun one on Kiki Dee and they wanted me to show them the move again, so they could be prepared to spot it and stop it. So, the following day, they came to the hotel. I had to get Gonzo to tell them where it was, and we did a bit of a run through in the hotel bar for fifteen minutes. You should have seen the faces of some of the punters in there, Jon. They didn't know what to make of it. There was me, Meldrew and Kiki Dee using a lemon from the bar as the ball. They're nice lads, Jon. We got on all right you know. I reckon we're like the Three Musketeers now. I'm that Darting bloke obviously, and they're the other two.'

Moreton was surprised and pleased in equal measure. Not only was it encouraging that Billy Swan was feeling part of the team, but also two players had sought him out to learn something outside of the normal training. He was unsure about something, though.

'Why weren't you supposed to tell me, Billy?'

'Ah, you see they didn't want you to think they were going behind your back about it. They thought you'd tell them off or something.'

'Jeez, Billy,' Moreton replied, somewhat disappointed. 'Really?'

'Yeah, I told them they were being daft, but they didn't know you that well then? So, you know…'

'I guess so.' He was about to tell his companion that the tale of the Musketeers involved three of them, plus D'Artagnan, but decided against it. There was something he had to say, though.

'Billy, you know Kiki Dee is a woman, don't you?'

Swan turned around in mock shock, face aghast with comic horror.

'Jon! Don't let him ever hear you say that. Look at him,' he pointed to the young defender out on the pitch. 'He'll bloody kill you.'

Moreton offered a wry smile in response.

'Don't be a prat, Billy. You know what I mean.'

Swan smiled and patted Moreton on the back.

'Yeah, I know just kidding. But Kiki Dee don't know that does he? I just told him Kiki Dee was a great English singer. He loves music, so he lapped it up. You should hear him sing, Jon. What a voice mate. It's that happy, "rappy" stuff, big bass drums in the garage or something like that. Think I'll teach him some Rick Astley or George Michael, you know. Proper music, eh? We can have a singsong on the coach for away games then.'

Moreton shook his head. 'Christ, Billy. You're unbelievable. Bloody unbelievable.'

'Too true mate. Too bloody true.'

The rest of the session passed, with Sophia and Moreton leaving separately, before meeting up an hour or so later in his apartment to eat and share the hours of darkness.

At the following day's session Moreton worked on integrating Revi into a deeper midfield role as a trial for when Swan could return to the number ten position, and on Friday he called out the team that would face the students of San Juan. The only changes were Revi starting in place of Swan and the young Santi playing ahead of him.

The journey to the university was a little over seventy-five minutes. On the way, despite the disappointment of losing the season's opening game, confidence had seemed to be reasonably high. However, the hope that had been engendered by the words of the opposition coach quickly felt hollow when the students of San Juan scored early on. A quickly taken free kick on the edge of the Retama box saw the ball laid across square for a player to run in and fire on goal. In typically brave manner, Adrián hurled himself in front of the ball to block the attempt. The shot struck the defender and ballooned into the air, completely wrong-footing Jiménez, before falling into the net. As quickly as they had been ahead in the opening game, this time Retama had fallen behind.

For the remainder of the game, Retama attacked and dominated, but the forward line looked lightweight and broadly ineffective. The only time they were on the cusp of breaking through was when Revi slid an intricate pass inside of the opposing right-back for Palermo to run onto, but his shot struck the far post and bounced clear. On the bench, Moreton and Sophia were becoming increasingly frustrated as halftime came and went without any tangible reward for their team's domination of the game.

José was sent on to join his brother, with fifteen minutes to play, replacing Santi. It was easy to discern that the young striker felt he had let the team down as he trudged from the pitch head down. Sophia wrapped an arm around him as he reached the bench, whispering consoling words that would have little real effect. At the full-time whistle, Retama were still trailing to the unfortunate early goal. Two games gone. Two defeats.

The mood on the return journey was subdued. The team had not played badly, but so many of the problems from last season were still there. Young players who needed more experience. Confidence was sinking, and a failure to offer any sustained threat on goal suggested that Jon Moreton still had plenty of work to do. Twenty minutes or so into the journey, Moreton's phone rang. The name on the screen revealed the caller's identity – "Chaz." He hesitated, but convinced himself, reluctantly, that his friend deserved better than to be ignored. 'Hi Chaz,' he said accepting the call. Sophia sat next to him watching sympathetically. She couldn't hear the other side of the conversation, but from Moreton's words, it was fairly easy to appreciate how things were going.

'Not great, I'm afraid.'

'No, we lost.'

'I know it's early days, mate.'

'Yeah, I know. I appreciate that.'

'Well, we actually played pretty well. Conceded a deflected goal early, but from there were on top. Hit the post, but just couldn't score.'

'Yeah, that's right, Chaz. So many of them are just kids. It would have made a world of difference to have had Billy out there. A bit of know-how, a bit of guile.'

'Not sure.'

'No, I'm not sure. Perhaps next week, but I really don't want to push him back in too early and have another problem.'

'I know, mate. You're paying him and he isn't playing. Yeah, I know, but we need to get him right first. Get the leg better and a couple more training sessions and he'll be up for it.'

'Is he?'

'Well, better him sit around there with his leg up until he's better.'

'Yeah, all right, Chaz. Cheers, mate.'

'Bye.'

Moreton ended the call and looked at Sophia. 'He's being good about it, you know. No pressure. Just kept saying that it will be all right in the end. Things will work out how they're supposed to. Although he's not happy about paying Billy to literally "have his feet up" while the games are going on. What do you think? Will he be OK for next week?'

Sophia shook her head slowly. 'I doubt it, Jon. If he was 15 years younger it would help, but given his age and he's been out of the game for a while, it's just going to take the time it takes.'

Moreton had known the answer, but was hoping to be given hope of something unexpected. 'Yeah, you're right, of course. Anything else would be stupid. Anyway, as Chaz said, there's plenty of time, and each game we play the younger lads will be getting more experience and hardened to the game.'

Sophia quickly glanced to the left and behind them to see where the others' attentions were focused. Feeling it was safe, she reached across and squeezed his thigh, smiling.

'And we have each other, as well,' she said, softly.

Moreton smiled in spite of himself. The world suddenly felt full of opportunity and positivity again.

'Yeah, that's right. And there's someone else important who's going to be joining us tonight as well, if you'd do the honour of dining with me, Señorita Garrigues.'

Sophia looked a little surprised. 'Really, Jon? Who is joining us?'

A pause.

'I thought we would be alone.'

Moreton leaned back in his chair as a smile played mischievously across his face.

'Well, it's like this. Not so much a friend of mine, but more a friend of yours. Well, not so much a friend, as perhaps a teacher.'

Sophia slapped his arm. The frustration increasing as he dangled veiled hints.

'OK,' he confessed with a smile. 'I've found a Keith Floyd recipe that you may like. I think it's about time we progressed past the pasta, don't you?'

He laughed a little, but Sophia didn't understand why.

'Past the pasta? That's pretty lame isn't it. It's a bit like "forgety the spaghetti" or "refusili the fusilli." '

He laughed out loud at the absurdity of his words.

'Anyway,' he picked up the thread again. 'If you'd like to come around about 8.30, we'll see what we can do.'

Sophia readily agreed, and any concerns about losing a football match were pushed aside for a while.

Right Recipe

In his usually meticulously prepared way, Moreton had already ensured all of the required ingredients were stocked and ready for the evening. Lardons, onion, celery, rice, cooked chicken and stock, a green pepper, a tin of chopped tomatoes and some seafood. Looking at the collection of items ranged out on the work surface of his little kitchen, he mused to himself how such a range of different things can be brought together to create something that works. A few short months ago, he would have had worried about cooking anything much beyond beans on toast, but now he was cooking a Jambalaya. Before finding the recipe online, he didn't know what such a thing was, let alone how to spell it.

He heated olive oil and got to work. As 8.30 approached and it was all cooking nicely he dashed into the bedroom and donned fresh denim jeans and a blue T-shirt. Returning to the kitchen, he noticed Sophia leave her apartment and opened the door. With the door closed, and the world excluded, they embraced and kissed as if they hadn't seen each other in days, rather than a couple of hours.

'I missed being able to hold you.'

She smiled and they hugged again.

'Wow,' broke in Sophia, peering over his shoulder into the kitchen. 'That smells nice. What is it?'

It was precisely what Moreton had hoped to hear. Confidence boosted even further, he playfully denied Sophia access to the kitchen.

'Wait and see. Come and sit at the table and I'll be with you shortly.'

Content to comply with Sophia's desire to keep their relationship secret, the table in Moreton's living area had become the default place for them to eat, and he had prepared it ready for Sophia's arrival. A bottle of chilled white wine was sitting in a cooler and two glasses waited alongside, simply asking to be filled. It was a request he quickly addressed, and as Sophia sat down at one side of the table, he raised his glass. 'Salud,' he toasted, receiving the same in reply, before returning to the kitchen. He stirred the gently bubbling pan and added the final ingredients. The steaming seafood offered up a pleasant aroma, conjuring up images of the beach that lay not more than fifteen minutes' walk away from them.

'Jon, how long will it be? It smells delightful and I'm very hungry.'

He smiled to himself. 'Have a little patience, woman.'

When it was done he sprinkled some chopped parsley on top, then ceremoniously carried it into the living area. 'There you are,' he declared triumphantly. 'One Jambalaya, courtesy of the maestro himself, Mr Keith Floyd.'

'Jambalaya. I'm not sure that I've ever tried that before, but it looks and smells wonderful. He did you manage to do all that yourself?'

It would have been easy for Moreton to claim he had cooked such things on a regular basis, but he was fairly sure that it wouldn't have been in any way convincing, and he had little intention of lying to Sophia anyway.

'I guess it's all about getting the right recipe and having someone point you in the right direction. To be honest, when I looked at all the ingredients, I wasn't sure about it. It just looked like a load of different items that were a mess, but when you have a good teacher and put things together correctly, sometimes it all works out. Anyway, I hope this has.'

Unbeknown to Moreton at the time, a similar conclusion would solve another issue for him in the not too distant future.

Sophia picked up a fork and took a small portion from the pan, placing it into her mouth. She closed her eyes with the pleasure of the food on her tongue. It was enough to make Moreton's heart skip a beat, as much for the ecstasy of the moment being displayed as the indication that indeed, "sometimes it all works out."

'That's really good, Jon.'

'Why, thank you,' he replied with growing pride, as he reached for the serving spoon.

Lying in bed the following morning, Sophia leant across to Moreton, placing her head on his shoulder. 'Jon,' she said. 'We need to be careful.'

Moreton was unsure of her intention.

Sophia sensed that he may not have understood.

'Two nights ago, my friend – you remember Elena, from Carlito's bar?'

Moreton mumbled in agreement.

'Well, she turned up at my door to talk to me. She had argued with her boyfriend and needed someone to talk to, but I wasn't there, Jon. I was here with you. I had to lie to her later when she asked me where I had been. I feel like I let her down. She's such a good friend and I really hated lying to her.'

Moreton pulled her closer to him and kissed the top of her head.

'I understand. If she's such a good friend, could you not just tell her the truth?'

Sophia sighed. 'I don't know, Jon. It's just too soon, I think.'

She paused and then tilted her head to look at his face. 'We've only been together for a few days. Do you think it's too soon, even for a close friend?'

Moreton thought for a brief moment. 'Sophia,' he said softly. 'I love you. I would have told the world the minute we decided to be together if it was up to me. I'm so happy with you, I want everyone to know what a special person you are, and how lucky I am. I know it's not that simple for you, though. This is your town. They're your people and the relationship you have with each of them is important. Only you can decide if it's too soon or not but, if you think it's important that we spend some nights in our own apartments, then that's fine with me.'

Another moment of thought. 'Well, not fine. I'll miss you, but I understand.'

Sophia pressed her head into his chest and breathed deeply.

'Thank you, Jon,' she whispered. 'Thank you for understanding. Shall we just see how things go over the next few days and take it from there?'

'That's fine. Now be quiet, I want to drift back to sleep holding you.'

'Yo te quiero,' she whispered softly.

'Yo te quiero,' he replied as sleep enveloped them together.

The following Sunday the team assembled for the game at home to Independiente Lacitana. Around Retama, news of successive defeats had hardly reignited interest in the local football club. Walking out of the dressing room and across to his place on the bench, Moreton guessed there were no more than fifty people scattered around the yawning gaps on the concrete terracing. It was understandable. But for the brief moments of ecstasy at the early goal against Politanio, there had been precious little evidence of progress.

The attendance however had been increased by two. At the far side of the ground sat a figure with his head buried in a newspaper, and Billy Swan was sitting on the bench, with his leg propped up on a bucket. Sitting down beside his friend, along with Sophia, Moreton was clearly pleased that he had decided to come to the game.

'Good to see you, Billy,' he said as things settled down for the kick-off.

'Couldn't stand another sodding day stuck in that hotel, Jon, to be honest. I had to get the girl on reception to drag Gonzo out on a Sunday, but cobblers to that. He'll be sitting reading the newspaper here, instead of at home, anyway.'

Moreton smiled briefly, hardly doubting the summary of the situation.

'This shower any good?' Swan asked, pointing to the team in red and white striped shirts.

'Not sure. Sophia tells me that they're pretty stable mid-table sort of outfit. Not pulling up any trees, but decent enough.'

He turned to look at his secret lover.

'Is that right?'

She nodded in agreement.

The previous days had been a little difficult. The two nights they had spent together felt like stolen moments, precious but brief. The nights had been worse. Moreton's bed felt uncomfortably cold and empty. After the giddy heights of their first few days as lovers, things felt much less secure. He understood, but being so close to Sophia, and yet so far away had been difficult. They had planned to be together this coming evening, though.

Perhaps driven by the unhappy hiatus Moreton had decided to change the team around hoping for a positive reaction. Bringing the young José Palermo onto the right flank instead of Vasquez, and dropping Guido into midfield in place of Samuel gave the Retama midfield an unbalanced look, but he hoped the enthusiasm of youth might bring a dividend. As the game began, it seemed possible. Sophia had been less than convinced of the changes, suggesting that it could unsettle the team that had performed well in the previous game, despite the result. Moreton was adamant, though, convinced that things needed to change. Whether that conviction was driven more by a desire to improve things on the football pitch, or in his personal life, was less clear.

The early exchanges seemed to favour the home team, as Retama pressed forward with Guido's pace a potent threat. Leaving Matías as the sole guardian ahead of the back four, however, opened up channels for a counterattack should possession be squandered. Twenty minutes passed without a goal, but as Revi tried to thread a pass through to the advancing Guido, the ball was intercepted.

Retama were exposed and a swift exchange of passes saw Jiménez beaten by a firm shot. Moreton bowed his head. The game resumed its earlier pattern but by the break there had been no further score. At halftime, he conceded to Sophia's counsel. Removing the younger of the Palermo brothers, he moved Guido to the flank, and reinstated Samuel alongside Matías. It would make the midfield more solid, but Retama also needed a goal.

As the second period began, the visitors had settled into a pattern designed merely to deny space further forward, maintain a low block, and look to strike on the break once more. It meant a frustrating time for the players in blue. Attacks were mounted again and again, but each time, the visitors' numbers snuffed out any threat. Time was ticking away, and the deeper defensive set up had blunted Guido's threat by denying him the oxygen of space to exploit his pace. With fifteen minutes remaining Moreton withdrew him and sent on Vasquez. Immediately, things got worse. An infrequent Lacitana foray up field drew rare confusion between Kiko and Victor. A Lacitana forward nipped in between them, and rifled home the second goal. The visiting team piled up in a heap, as the Retama players contemplated inevitable defeat. Sanz put arms around the shoulders of the dejected centre back partnership drawing them together with consoling words.

To all intents and purposes, the contest was over, the Lacitana players, though, reaching the end of their physical tether by the demands of chasing and harrying, drew renewed energy from the second goal. A corner floated in by Vasquez in injury time, saw Santi force the ball over the line offering a brief glimpse of what turned out to be false hope. Immediately after the restart, the referee ended the game. Retama's first three games had ended in defeat. His new recipe had ended in failure. The players shook hands and left the field. Sophia and Billy Swan followed. Jon Moreton sat on the bench as everyone else moved away.

Despite the injuries he had endured, the hard days of rehabilitation and being told his professional days were finished, he had never felt lower. He wanted to tell Sophia that he needed to leave the ground, go back to his apartment and close the blinds. He reached into his pocket for the mobile phone he had been given. He should call Charlie Broome now and tell him that this had all been a crazy idea. The job was beyond him. He should quit now while there was still time for someone else to come in and revitalise the team. He should quit. What about Sophia, though? Suddenly he was unsure about everything.

He rose from the bench slowly, and shook hands with the opposition officials, before walking slowly back to the dressing room. On the way, he passed Esteban, in his Retama shirt. The old man looked sad, but unbowed. He clenched his right hand into a fist, and hit it three times against the Retama badge over his heart. It was also the punch that Moreton needed. He shouldn't feel sorry for himself. He should feel sorry for his players and the club. His job was to solve the problem, not run away and hide from it.

Reaching the dressing room, he saw the players seated on the benches, with Sophia standing by the door, and Billy Swan leaning up against the wall next to her. He had a choice. He could sympathise or inspire. After speaking quietly and briefly to Sophia, she turned and left the dressing room. Seconds of silence passed as the players waited for their manager to speak. He was waiting for something else, though. Then the door opened again, and Sophia returned, with Esteban alongside her. Moreton took a deep breath, and spoke, asking Sophia to translate for him.

'Three games,' he said slowly. 'Three games. Three defeats.'

He paused as the players shifted uncomfortably in their seats.

'Three games. Three defeats. Defeat tests belief. It tests my belief. It tests your belief. These are tests we must not fail.'

'Three games. Three defeats. There are thirty-one more games in this season.'

Moreton placed an arm around Esteban's shoulder.

'Defeat tests his belief as well. But he does not fail that test.'

When he heard the translated words, Esteban nodded slowly. He clenched his fist and repeated the gesture he had given to Moreton outside.

'He is Retama.'

'I am Retama,' he said, the passion in his voice rising, as he too punched the badge on his chest.

He paused and looked around the room, landing his glance on Alejandro Sanz, Retama's captain, rock of the team, and acknowledged leader picked up the baton, his muscular fist punching the badge on his sweat-drenched shirt. Others followed. Sophia followed, even Billy Swan was caught up in the emotion, although his T-shirt had no badge to punch.

Moreton held his hands up to calm the clamour he had sought to create.

'Somos Retama?' he asked. 'Somos Retama!' he insisted.

'Somos Retama!' they all shouted. Alejandro Sanz jumped to his feet and gripped the club badge. The others followed, bellowing out the shout. 'Somos Retama!'

Moreton let the emotion ride for a few seconds, then raised both hands to bring it to a halt, requesting silence for his words.

'Three is a small number. Very small. Thirty-one is a larger number. Thirty-one games,' he said. 'Thirty-one games. We will lose some, but we will win more. We will triumph.'

He paused again.

'Por qué?' he asked quietly, looking around the room.

The answer came from the old man. 'Porque somos Retama!' he said in soft but definitive tones.

Moreton nodded slowly. 'Si, Esteban, mi hermano.'

The players broke into cheers again, and in those few minutes, what had felt like the end of a road had turned out to be something else entirely.

That night, with Sophia in his arms, Jon Moreton's world felt so much brighter. As she slept, he lay awake, reflecting on the moments after the game that afternoon. What would have happened had he made the call to Charlie Broome. Would he have lost the club? Would he have lost Sophia? It was something he didn't want to dwell on. He turned towards Sophia and drew her close to him. The warmth and scent of her body leant him a serenity. He drifted to sleep.

Training the following week was buoyed by the appearance of Billy Swan dressed and ready to take part. After consulting with Sophia, however, Moreton decided not to risk having him involved in a full session. Instead, he was sent to the other side of the pitch to go through some jogging and stretching exercises, with Sophia overseeing. One more week, she had assured Moreton. He was more than willing to accept her advice.

Following training on Friday, Moreton announced the team for the next game and the short visit, a mere ten kilometres or so, to CD Mostodra. Paco Jiménez would be in goal, with the settled back line of Sanz, Kiko, Víctor and Adrián. The centre of the midfield was occupied by Samuel and Matías, with Juan Palermo and Vasquez on the flanks. Revi would be in the number ten role, with Santi as the striker. As the meeting broke up, Sophia called Moreton over towards the bench, motioning him to sit down next to her. She spoke in a hushed voice.

'I'm concerned about Sunday. About the game and what might happen there.'

Moreton was less than clear about her meaning. 'The game? It won't be easy. Local matches are always a bit different. It almost doesn't matter how good the teams are. There's always a lot of local pride at stake. I'm not sure we will win, but I think we'll go close.'

Sophia looked down at her feet. 'That's not what I mean, Jon. I think there may be some trouble.'

'Can we talk about this later? Or tomorrow? We are seeing each other, aren't we?'

The sad shake of her head indicated to the contrary. 'I'm sorry, Jon. But no, not tonight or tomorrow. My parents are coming to Retama for a couple of days. They'll be staying at the hotel owned by Sebastián's parents. I will need to be with them. You understand, don't you?'

'Of course,' he said, trying to hide any disappointment.

'I wanted to tell you earlier, but didn't, because I wasn't sure.'

'Wasn't sure about what? About whether they were coming or not?'

'No Jon. About whether to tell them about you or not.'

'Ah. And you decided not to?'

'Yes. Am I a coward? Do I disappoint you?'

Moreton looked into her deep dark eyes. He wanted to hold her close and dismiss such folly with an embrace. The line of players drifting past them as they left the dressing room eliminated such a possibility, so he opted for words instead of actions. 'You could never disappoint me, Sophia. Of course, I shall miss you, but I understand. When it's time, you'll know. Now what's the trouble about the game?'

Sophia asked Moreton if had remembered what she had said about Mostodra when they had talked about the other clubs. Unsure, he asked her to remind him. She explained that a number of the players across both teams were friends, but others were very much not.

'The thing is Jon, I think it could get very nasty.'

'Do you know any of them?'

'Not really. One of the coaches there, Diego, used to live in Retama. He wasn't very well liked.'

There was more in what Sophia wasn't saying than what she was, but Moreton understood the intention.

'OK,' he said, beginning to appreciate the situation.

'You also remember how I told you that Juan Palermo was still friends with a lot of the boys he grew up with?'

Moreton nodded.

'I've heard that some of them will be at the game,' she continued. 'A lot of them are just talk. A few, however, can be trouble, often having problems with the police. They'll be expecting Palermo to be the same during the game. You understand? To be very physical.'

'I understand. Should we leave him out of the team?'

'No, I don't think so. If he's not playing, and turns up at the game with his friends – and he will – it could be worse. At least with him on the pitch, there'll be some control.'

'That makes sense. So, what can we do, then?'

'I'm not really sure there is anything we can do, other than be aware of the problem and do whatever we can if anything happens.'

Sophia stood up. 'I'll go and see Esteban,' she said, walking away. 'I'll see you for the coach on Sunday.'

'OK, and thanks for telling me. Say hello to your parents for me as well.'

Sophia stopped and turned back to face Moreton.

'I'm only kidding. Smile.'

She did, silently mouthing: 'Yo te quiero.'

Moreton smiled and put his forefinger to his lips as if some kind of zealous librarian.

The coach journey to the game was quieter than usual, with many of the players clearly aware of the tension, and how it could be ignited. Arriving at the compact ground, Moreton quickly ushered his squad into the dressing room to avoid any unnecessary contact with the opposing players or fans. Whilst rousing team talks ahead of games can often be advantageous, in circumstances such as this, he was aware that oil on troubled waters would be more sensible than petrol onto flames. He sent his team out in a determined but hopefully fully controlled mood.

Finding his way to the bench as the blue-clad players filed onto the field faced by the Mostodra team all in white, he sat down next to Sophia, but quickly noticed how unusually subdued she seemed. Seeing the opposition bench a few metres away, he walked over to shake hands with the coaches sat there. A swift and less than courteous response suggested that any animosity may not be limited to the players. One man in particular, thick set with a shaven head and sunglasses perched on the top of his gleaming pate, hardly motioned at all, ignoring Moreton's outstretched hand, offering a barely noticeable nod in exchange.

The game started at a furious pace with heavy tackles flying in from both sides. Whilst Moreton sought to calm his players, the coach with the shaven head on the other bench merely stood and raucously applauded every fiery intervention from his players; the less legitimate ones eliciting the most vigorous acclaim.

'That's Diego,' Sophia said, nodding towards the bellicose bellowing figure.

'Someone's going to get hurt here,' he replied with evident concern.

For the first twenty minutes or so, it seemed that the ball was largely irrelevant, other than to indicate where the next thunderous challenge would land. Whilst some of the Retama players were clearly more than capable of looking after themselves, particularly Sanz, Kiko and especially the teak tough Adrián, it was the less burly visiting players experiencing the more robust attention of the home players. Santi in particular was knocked to the floor several times, often when the ball was nowhere near him, but the young striker kept getting to his feet, and with the half hour mark approaching delivered the perfect riposte.

Out on the right flank, a lunging tackle aimed at Vasquez missed its target as the nippy wide man danced around his opponent. Driving towards the goal line, he looked up to see Santi heading for the near post. The cross found its target and Retama were ahead as Santi delivered his own kind of retribution. The Retama bench jumped to its feet to celebrate, with the substitutes hugging Moreton. Out of Moreton's view, as Sophia stood with her arms in the air, the clearly fuming Diego turned his attention to her.

There was no further score before the break, but as the Retama players walked back to the dressing room to count their bruises, Sebastián took hold of Moreton's arm, encouraging him to wait as he spoke softly into his ear. Stepping back from words that had clearly affected him, Moreton nodded and told Sebastián to go back to the dressing room and tell the others that he would be along shortly.

A few minutes later, Moreton entered the Retama dressing room to a series of questioning looks. 'Just something I needed to check on,' he said. 'Everything's fine.' A brief nod to Sebastián was missed by all except its intended recipient. Using the remaining time of the break, Moreton emphasised the importance of keeping control of emotions, and how a mistake, in the heat of the moment, could cost so much. He walked over to Santi and patted him on the shoulder. '¡Guapo!' he said. The young striker smiled warmly.

As the players and coaches returned to the pitch, the Mostodra bench was already waiting. Sitting down Moreton saw the shaven headed man rise and walk across. He stood in front of Sophia, and bowed his head slightly to move closer, a pair of broken sunglasses hanging from the breast pocket of his shirt. Speaking in soft tones that seemed ill-fitting given the exclamations of the first forty-five minutes, Moreton heard the words: 'Lo siento.' The gaze was then transferred to Moreton who nodded slightly. He then turned away to return to his seat. Sitting two seats from Moreton, Sebastián reached across and patted him on the shoulder. Others followed. Sophia turned to look at her secret lover quizzically.

'What did you do?' she asked.

'We just had a few words.'

'But Diego does not know any English words.'

'He knows a few now.'

Sophia smiled both with love and pride, each emotion battling to be the most intense. The former won. She reached across and planted a kiss on his cheek. 'My knight in armour.'

Back on the pitch, Santi's goal had further stoked the fires burning in the Mostodra defenders. Five minutes after the restart, as he chased a through-ball played by Revi, the home centre back crashed an elbow into the young striker's face. Santi fell to the floor holding his nose as a melee of players gathered around him, pushing and pulling at shirts. The referee waved to the Retama bench. Sophia grabbed her bag and trotted onto the pitch. Even an initial examination made it clear he could take no further part on the game. Sophia wasn't sure if his nose had been broken, but with blood oozing down his face, breathing was becoming difficult. She signalled to the bench for a substitute. Moreton waved to José to go on.

It wasn't clear whether the Mostodra players knew that the new arrival was Juan Palermo's younger brother. It seemed likely to be the case, however, as while they sought distance from the muscular elder sibling, the replacement forward suffered even more vigilant attention than that applied to Santi. Ten minutes later, another foul on the slight forward was followed up by an all-too-clear stamp on the back of his leg by the same player who had felled Santi. Fraternal anger overflowing, the elder Palermo ran over and struck the offender a blow on the jaw, knocking him to the ground. The spark ignited an inevitable explosion. A general ruckus ensued with almost all of the players involved. When things settled down, the red card waved at Palermo was predictable. The stricken Mostodra defender recovered, but as the dismissed Retama player trudged from the field, other home players shouted at him promising revenge and retribution. The still fuming Palermo wasn't slow in returning their good wishes.

Retama would now play the remaining time with just ten players. It would require the resolve of their defensive players to ensure they didn't concede, but just a couple of minutes later, one of them was removed from the play. An attempted through ball was intercepted by Samuel but, as he stretched, a Mostodra boot cut across his shin, twisting his knee. It was a reckless challenge at best, a callous one at worst and, given the threats that followed Palermo from the pitch, the latter appeared the more likely. Samuel was out of the game, and Moreton was forced into another change, sending Felipe Blanco on to cover.

The enforced changes disturbed Retama's rhythm, and ill-gained advantage brought its reward with twenty minutes remaining. A home corner was headed powerfully home to bring the scores level. Five minutes later, the turnaround looked complete. A neat turn on the edge of the visitor's penalty area eluded Adrián's challenge, and although Jiménez parried the resultant shot out, the rebound was turned into the net. Playing with ten men, a goal behind, and with José little more than a limping passenger, a fourth defeat appeared inevitable.

Gambling, Moreton pushed Sanz forward to fill the space left by Palermo's departure, leaving just three at the back. Few robust challenges would worry the powerful skipper of Retama. With two minutes remaining, Sanz drove forward with the ball at his feet. A challenge dislodged the ball, but it ran free, dropping conveniently towards Revi, some twenty yards from goal. The young playmaker looked up and curled an arcing shot into the far corner of the net, leaving the goalkeeper a mere bemused and impotent spectator. Retama's spirit had seemingly plucked a draw from the jaws of defeat. A harsh reality would follow.

As the extended injury time from the damage inflicted by the Mostodra intimidation ebbed away, the home side forced a late corner. When the ball was flighted in, the commanding Kiko seemed certain to head clear. Hidden from the referee however a hand, tugging at his shirt, compromised his jump. The ball sailed over him towards the far post, where it was nodded home for a winning goal. The final whistle followed shortly afterwards. Retama had lost their fourth game in a row.

Back in the dressing room, there was little need for any rallying cry from Moreton. The game had been a lesson, a harsh one, but a lesson nonetheless, and the young players in Moreton's squad had been compelled to grow up as footballers very quickly. Leaving the home ground of Mostodra, few members of the Retama party would feel anything but resentment for what had happened. In the months to come, the events of that day would serve the club, and its manager, well.

Four defeats in their first four games had hardly been the dream start to the season for Jon Moreton and Retama but, conversely, he thought that things were heading in the right direction. The defence looked solid enough and the emerging talents of Victor and Kiko would only further blossom with the games played, and he had little doubt about the positive influences of Sanz and Adrián.

Midfield still remained an issue. Both Samuel and Matías were hard-working and solid enough, but lacked an abundance of creative flair. The plan to play Revi in a deeper role looked the ideal solution, with the opportunity to rotate partners around him, or solidify by pairing Samuel and Matías as a more defensive block when the situation was called for. All of that depended on having Billy Swan available to play in the number ten role.

On the flanks, Antonio Vasquez was still a first choice. His assist for Santi's goal against Mostodra had shown he could create openings. On the other side, Palermo's imminent suspension opened up the opportunity for Moreton to deploy the pacey Guido. It was a decision now compelled by circumstance, but one he had contemplated anyway. At the sharp end of the team Santi was becoming a reliable source of goals, despite only being offered limited opportunities. Three strikes in four games for a team that had lost each one of those encounters was encouraging, and others remained on the bench, eager for a chance. All the ingredients were there, Moreton was sure, only the right recipe was missing. The following Wednesday evening, with Swan taking a full part in training, Sophia made a surprising suggestion.

'Jon,' she said softly. 'Would you like to meet García?'

Moreton was initially unsure.

'Why,' he asked. Then a feeling of doubt spread over him as perception and uncertainty washed away logic and trust. 'Don't you think I'm up to the job here?'

Sophia stared at him with defiance flaring in her dark eyes. 'Jon, you know that's not true. I have faith in you. The players have faith in you.' Then she smiled warmly. 'Even Esteban has faith in you.'

'I'm sorry, Sophia. That wasn't very fair, was it.'

'No Jon, it wasn't.' She gently placed a hand on his arm.

He placed his hand on top of hers and squeezed it softly. Had any of the players been playing attention to the two coaches standing by the side of the pitch, the secret they held close may have been betrayed but, for the moment at least, it remained hidden.

'I have thought about it for a few days, but was reluctant to say anything, in case you may react badly.' She looked at him again, but this time with clear sympathy. 'And you did.'

Moreton smiled with contrition.

'I think you're doing so many things correctly,' she added.

He stopped her, raising his hand slightly. 'Not me. We are doings so many things correctly.'

It was Sophia's turn to smile and acquiesce.

'Yes, so, there you are. Even if there was some criticism, and there wasn't, it would be of both of us, not just you.'

For a few seconds, the words felt like a closing of the subject, but Sophia pressed on. 'I was going to suggest that perhaps tomorrow, the three of us could meet up for dinner. Nothing special just perhaps go to Bella Cucina have some pasta and talk about football. I think it would be nice.'

Yeah, OK. That sounds good, and I'd like to meet him.'

'Good. I'll set things up.'

The following evening, after spending the previous night and much of the day with Moreton, Sophia returned to her own apartment to change before leaving to meet her great-uncle at the restaurant. An hour later, as arranged, he watched from his balcony as Sophia left the complex. A few minutes later, as arranged, Moreton followed. Exaggerated discretion still informed their movements.

It took a mere five minutes or so to reach the restaurant where they had previously eaten. The waiter smiled at Moreton as he entered, and pointed towards a table in the corner where they were sitting. García stood, offering his hand. He was tall and solid, with the appearance of a former athlete, a face that betrayed his years, somewhat puffy and wrinkled, balding with grey hair and a bushy moustache of a similar hue. His appearance suggested quiet wisdom and experience painfully gained by years of work and dogged application. The handshake was predictably firm, and immediately Moreton felt a comfortable and reassuring kinship with his new acquaintance. Sophia made the formal introduction.

Firstly, towards García: 'Este es Jon Moreton,' she said in the sort of reverential tones reserved for respected members of family. Then, to Moreton: 'Jon, this is Señor Vicente García.'

After exchanging smiles, they all sat down again. García poured a little wine into Moreton's glass, and, after ordering their food, the talk inevitably centred on football, and in particular, the fortunes of CD Retama.

García spoke English confidently, but Sophia translated as required. The two men exchanged the stories of how life had taken them to Retama, with Moreton again relating the tale – with the same emphasis and minimising of injury and ill fortune – he had told to Sophia. In turn, García spoke of his time as a journeyman player, a defender who had spent an unspectacular peripatetic career around a string of lower league clubs before turning to coaching. It was something that he quickly found was far more suited to his talents than spending time on the other side of the sharply demarcating white line. It had brought far more success, plus a not inconsiderable financial return, allowing him, after his official retirement, to spend some time back at home helping out with Retama.

The part of the story concerning Retama seemed to cause a slight sadness in the older man. He told Moreton of Fouad, how he had been a revelation for the club, someone who could have made a massive difference to their season, and the regret at losing him. The mention of Charlie Broome visibly moved sadness into a restrained, but no less obvious, resentment. Sophia spoke softly to him, though, and the moment passed as García nodded to her.

'Let's move to the future, shall we?' García suggested.

Sophia readily offered encouragement and his mood brightened.

'Sophia tells me about the games so far,' García said, haltingly. 'It has not been easy.'

Moreton felt a little defensive, but tried not to let it show.

'I don't judge you badly,' García said, sensing Moreton's unease. 'Let me be honest. I also lost so many games. We were relegated. And now you have no longer Tomás Bendonces to score his few goals.'

Moreton nodded, appreciating the empathy.

'But,' García added, with a conspiratorial wink. 'I think that is not a big loss, is it?'

He laughed, and Moreton felt himself joining in.

'Ah, but Santi,' García began again. 'Now he is free from the shadow. He is scoring goals. He could be your Fouad. He needs many games, many, many games to become a full player, a better goal scorer. Like a young racehorse, he still has some running to do, but you are doing well with him.'

Moreton smiled in agreement.

'Now,' said García, topping up Moreton's wine as the now empty food plates were removed. 'Tell me about Billy Swan.'

The next fifteen minutes or so was spent with Jon Moreton explaining about his experiences going through recovery from injury at the same time as Swan had been, how they had formed an unlikely bond, contrasting personalities glued together by mutual aspirations. He judiciously omitted the part about the alleged nightclub incident, but explained how he believed that, even at his current age, Swan could be a key element in the future of Retama and getting them to the promotion that Charlie Broome had explained was so vital. García listened patiently and intently as Moreton spoke. He paused briefly before speaking.

'You must please forgive me. But I hear so many stories about such players from England.' The old man shook his head sadly. 'I have seen him play so many times. We have English football on television over here, you understand?'

Moreton nodded.

'What talent. What ability. Such skill.'

Moreton was pleased that his companion shared his own opinions.

Then García shook his head again, slowly. 'But what a waste.'

Moreton felt compelled to defend his friend, but there was no need to do so, as García continued.

'If such a player was here, in Spain. We would rejoice in his skill and ability at football. No one is perfect. We all have faults. Coaches, well a lot of those who are often described as coaches these days, they forget that footballers are also people, young people. If you want to make a good footballer, you need to coach the man as well. You need to understand them. They are not machines.'

It was difficult for Moreton not to glance at Sophia across the table, as the old man eulogised. It was as he and García were unacquainted kindred spirits, both with a belief in how to develop footballers, and broadly in train. Moreton stole a quick glance at Sophia and her beaming smile only underscored his thoughts.

'I would have liked to have a player like Billy Swan when I was coaching,' García added. 'A few passed my way with talent, with ability, but at the time they were still young, and on the way. They had a distance to run. Billy Swan had run his race, won his race. He had the skill, and,' García raised his hand forming it into a fist in front of him. 'He had the anger. Now, Coach,' he almost growled, 'make him a footballer!'

There was clear passion in García's admiration, and frustration at an opportunity he saw as arrantly squandered.

'How many times did he play for your country?' He asked looking at Moreton.

It was almost an accusation, but the younger man fully understood the implication and empathised.

'I'm not sure. Two or three, I think.' He knew what was coming next from García. 'I know, I know,' he said agreeing in advance.

His companion would not be dissuaded from his theme. He still delivered the condemnation.

'*Un escándalo*!' he said firmly, before correcting himself for Moreton's benefit. 'I'm sorry, but such things are very bad. A big mistake.'

'It is a scandal,' Moreton conceded.

'A player like that should have played fifty times, a hundred times. He should have played at Copas Mundiales. He should be lauded. Coaches, those who call themselves coaches, how did they fail?' He stopped for a moment. 'Do you *have* him?' García asked.

Moreton was unsure of the question.

'Do you really *have* him?' García repeated. 'Is he giving everything to you, to Retama? If you *have* him, you have a chance. But you must have all of him. Not just his skill. His anger. His hunger.'

Moreton mused for a moment. 'I think you're asking me if he's fully committed.'

García nodded in reply.

'I believe so,' Moreton replied. 'With someone like Billy there are lots of things... No one ever really gets to know Billy. No one gets close to him. Certainly, no one I've known anyway. None of the players we were with, the coaches, the manager, no one really. He has a defence mechanism around him, like some kind of force field to keep people from getting too close to him, too near to him. So, if I'm being honest, I believe so. I hope so, but do I know that?' He paused. 'I hope so.' Anything else would have been hubris.

García clearly understood and appreciated Moreton's honesty.

'Help him to feel part of our family,' the old man advised. 'Sophia tells me that he's friendly with Victor and Kiko. Two wonderful boys. They can be wonderful players, and they can help you'

Moreton began to smile. 'I understand. I have an idea that may work.'

The coffees arrived to break the flow of the discussion, and Sophia excused herself, leaving the two men alone for a couple of minutes.

García spoke first. 'Sophia tells me that you enjoy cooking.'

It sounded like inconsequential small talk, but was anything but.

Moreton laughed a little. 'I try,' he admitted, cheerfully.

The old man smiled. 'Getting the ingredients sorted is fine, Jon. But sometimes, it feels like the recipe isn't right, doesn't it? Even just before everything is finished, it often looks like it won't turn out right. Yes? Do you understand what I mean? Sometimes it makes you doubt yourself. Whether you know what you're doing. Are you as good as you thought you were?' García smiled again. 'I like cooking, as well. I'm not very good, but I'm better than I was when I was younger.'

Moreton was unsure where the conversation was going, but García continued.

'When I was younger, I expected things to come out correctly.'

His speech quickened as he emphasised in staccato tones.

'Quickly, first time, every time.' He paused.' Sometimes though, you need to be a little patient. You can have the correct ingredients and the correct recipe, but if you don't also have a little patience, things may not look correct, even when they are. Do you understand what I am saying?'

'I think I do,' he said. 'Gracias. Muchas gracias.'

García smiled.

'It's a little as with you and Sophia,' the older man, seemingly mused to himself. 'You are good together.'

Moreton felt a little cornered. Was there an implication in the remark?

'You mean at Retama, as a coaching team?'

'Yes,' García smiled and narrowed his eyes. 'Yes, that too. That too.'

Singer and Song

Ahead of Sunday's game two issues occupied Jon Moreton's mind. What had García meant by his remark at the restaurant? Did he know about Sophia and him? Had Sophia told him? Surely not; she wouldn't have been so insistent on keeping their relationship quiet, then tell someone else. Had he just guessed? He considered telling Sophia about the conversation, but thought better of it. If she had told García, she would already have known, and there would be little point. If she hadn't, why worry her with it?

The other issue was Billy Swan. Sophia confirmed that Swan was probably fit to play without much danger of a recurrence, but Moreton was unsure. Would it be better to leave it another week, and perhaps put Swan on the bench in case he was needed? In the end, he decided that the latter option presented the least danger. Some changes were inevitable. Samuel wasn't fit to play and Palermo wouldn't be available for three games after his red card. Sometimes adversity offers up opportunity, though, and Moreton placed Guido on the left flank, with Sebastián alongside Mathias in midfield.

Arriving at the ground a couple of hours or so ahead of kick-off, Moreton passed underneath the rusting sign declaring Estadio Antonio Núñez, to see Paco Jiménez sitting on the concrete steps in front of him. One of the most dedicated members of the squad, the veteran was usually one of the first to arrive, but this was early, even for him. Headed bowed as Moreton entered, he hardly seemed to notice the other's approach.

'Paco?'

At the sound of the voice, Jiménez slowly raised his gaze from the floor to fix it intently on the face of Jon Moreton.

'Paco. What's the matter? Are you OK?'

The veteran goalkeeper, walked menacingly towards Moreton, grabbing the coach by the arm and guided him firmly towards the corner of the ground where the portacabin that served as the officials' changing rooms stood.

Moreton managed to shake his arm free, but could only repeat his words, but this time more insistently. 'Paco. What's the matter?'

The older man looked at Moreton with blazing eyes. 'I know,' he said, the words full of rage.

'What do you mean? You know what?'

Moreton was hoping that his fears were not about to be realised, but they were.

'Don't play with me, Mister. I know about Sophia. About Sophia and you.'

For a moment, Moreton considered denying everything, but Jiménez's undisguised anger suggested that such action would only make things worse.

'OK,' he said, trying not to make it sound like a confession, and feeling he had nothing to apologise for.

His relationship with Sophia was nothing to be ashamed of. It wasn't any kind of brief fling. He loved her. He had never been more certain of anything in his life. Why should he feel ashamed? Sophia had told him that Jiménez had sworn "a blood oath" to protect her, but he was no threat. Why was Jiménez so angry? As the shock of the moment passed, a feeling of anger also began to fill Moreton. He took a breath, then stood straight and tall in front of the shorter, but muscular Spaniard.

'OK, Paco. It's true. Sophia and I are together. We love each other. I know you think you have to look after her, but I want to do that too. Do you understand?'

Jiménez looked directly into Moreton's eyes for a second or two, before spitting out a reply.

'Love her? How can you love her? You hardly know her. A few weeks and everything changes. Her plans. Everything. You are destroying her life. Her career.'

Moreton was confused. 'What do you mean? What plans? What career? I just want to make her happy. We're happy together. What have you been told?'

'How do you think I know? Do you think someone like Sophia would just take up with you without telling Alvaro? You are destroying his life as well.'

'Alvaro? What has all this to do with Alvaro? That was over a long time ago. Well before I arrived in Spain.'

'Really? Do you think so? Then why do you think Sophia was studying for that qualification? Why was she looking to take a job at the same naval training academy in Galicia where Alvaro is? Why do you think they were looking to get back together again?' He was almost shouting now. 'Why! Why!'

'Paco,' Moreton began softly but sure of his ground. 'I promise you that I know anything about that. Well, I know she was taking some sort of qualification, but nothing about the rest of it. If you don't believe me, that's up to you, but it's true.'

Jiménez's anger was now flaring off in all directions and, as it did so, there was less of it to focus at Moreton.

'They were happy,' he said, now calmer. 'Things were good. Then Alvaro gets a call from Sophia saying that it was over, that she'd met someone else. She didn't want to hurt Alvaro, but couldn't lie to him. It took him all this time to tell me. Only now, this morning, when I spoke with Alvaro on the telephone, the truth come out. He cried.'

Jiménez looked down at the ground, and turned away from Moreton for a moment. 'He cried.' Then, looking back at Moreton: 'He was hurt, so much. They had made plans together, and now it was gone. He didn't want to tell me, but I made him. Two young people, so happy with each other. Now everything is destroyed.'

In spite of himself and the situation, Moreton felt genuine sympathy for Jiménez.

'Paco. I understand. I really do. I'm sorry for Alvaro, but I love Sophia and I think she loves me. What she said to Alvaro proves that. She wouldn't want to hurt him, but we love each other.'

Sophia's words about the "blood oath" came to mind again. 'I'm not bad,' he insisted. 'I would never hurt her.'

Jiménez looked into Moreton's eyes with renewed vigour, refocusing his anger.

'You had better not. And say nothing to Sophia about this. I have betrayed Alvaro by telling you. Do not do the same. You say that you would not hurt her, then say nothing.'

Moreton nodded slowly.

Paco Jiménez turned and walked away towards the dressing room to prepare for the game. Jon Moreton stood alone for a few minutes.

Still quietly reflecting, he hardly noticed Sophia arrive. Strolling casually through the gates, and seeing Moreton standing quietly in the corner, Sophia walked across to join him. Furtively glancing around to check for unwanted witnesses, she reached up and kissed him tenderly on the lips. 'Hola,' she whispered softly. 'Are you OK?'

The kiss drew Moreton back to the reality of the moment.

'Oh, hello. Sorry, I was miles away.'

He hadn't been, but for the first time in a while since arriving in Spain, he thought how much simpler his life would have been had he stayed in England, but Spain, Retama and Dolores Sophia Isabella Medina Garrigues was now in his blood, in his soul, and there was no turning back. He wrapped an arm around her shoulder and whispered into her ear.

'Shall we go and try and win a football match?'

She nodded and they headed off together towards the dressing room where the other players would shortly assemble.

Later, as both sets of players trotted onto the pitch, Moreton, Sophia and the substitutes took their places on the bench. The bright yellow shirts of the Callosa players, set against the blue ones of the home team were as metaphors for the bright sun and blue sky above them. It seemed a perfect setting for football and, casting the earlier confrontation with his team's goalkeeper to the back of his mind, albeit temporarily, Jon Moreton felt enthusiastic about the outcome of the game. A tap on his arm from Sophia, and the words that followed, would change all that, as confidence evaporated like early morning mist. The contact drew Moreton's attention, as Sophia spoke.

'What's wrong with Paco?'

Unsure how to react. Moreton opted for caution.

'Paco? I'm not sure. What do you mean?'

Sophia hadn't taken her gaze away from the green-shirted goalkeeper, even as Moreton replied to her. She pointed to Jiménez.

'Look, he's just standing there looking at the floor. Normally he would be shouting to his players. He looks like his mind isn't there. What's wrong with him, Jon?'

Moreton was certain that he knew the answer, but for so many reasons he couldn't acknowledge the fact. He covered the concern with misdirection.

'I don't know. Perhaps he's just not feeling well. He'll be fine. I'm sure.'

He was anything but sure and, a mere ten minutes into the game, the consequences were played out. A tame cross into the Retama box was wildly over hit and sailed harmlessly towards Jiménez's waiting arms. For reasons known only to the goalkeeper and his coach, the ball slipped between the usually firm grip of Jiménez's gloves, and trickled away behind him, before rolling apologetically over the line. The veteran turned to chase the ball down but it was forlorn. He put his hands to his head – a move echoed by Moreton and Sophia on the bench – before kicking and punching the post in frustration. Retama were a goal down, and Sophia was convinced that her concerns had proved to be valid.

'Jon, what's wrong with him?'

For a brief moment, Moreton was on the verge of telling her the truth. He raised his hand to his forehead, rubbing it slowly and intently, playing for time. This wasn't the place, this wasn't time, and this wasn't the way he should tell her. Instead, he just shook his head slowly. 'It's just a mistake. Don't be too hard on him. We all make mistakes.' It was a confession of kinds. 'He'll be OK.'

He wouldn't be.

The early part of the game had seen Retama in fairly comfortable control. As Moreton had hoped, Guido's pace was causing problems for the visitors' defence, but there was insufficient guile in the home midfield to get the ball to him in dangerous situations. Sebastián was energetic and enthusiastic, and Mathias was quietly efficient in front of the defence, but neither had the vision to pick out the penetrating pass that would cause danger. It was the role Moreton envisaged for Revi. Without a fit Billy Swan to play in the number ten role, the club's most creative player was needed there. Despite increasing amounts of possession, his team resembled something of a blunt instrument.

A rare breakout from the visitors saw them attack down their left flank. The ball was squared to an advancing midfielder some thirty yards or so from goal. With the defence well set, there seemed little danger as the Callosa player decided to shoot. Even if struck correctly it would have needed a huge slice of good fortune to find the net, but this effort was mishit, and the ball bounced scruffily three times before reaching the goal where Jiménez moved across to collect. Shuffling across goal he fell onto the ball to smoother the shot, but his timing was slightly out. Instead of gathering the ball, its fourth bounce hopped over the prostrate goalkeeper and into the net. In a game where the opposition had hardly been able to generate an attempt on the home goal worthy of the name, Retama were now two goals behind.

A few minutes later, as the referee blew for halftime, it was a disillusioned party of Retama players and staff heading back to the dressing room. Lagging somewhat behind the others was Paco Jiménez, head bowed, with Sophia's arm around his waist. The dressing room fell silent as the pair entered. Jiménez slumped down on the bench. Sophia took Moreton by the arm and guided him outside.

'He's not well,' she said, quietly. 'He feels nauseous, and says he was vomiting in the night and before the game.'

Moreton knew the real reason for Jiménez's lapses. He felt compromised by what had happened, and angry that he was being compelled to live a lie.

'Why didn't he say something then. It's cost us two goals, and now we're struggling to save a game where we should be winning.' Frustration coursed through his words.

Sophia was both angry and disappointed by the reaction.

'Jon! Do not talk to me like that.'

It wasn't a physical slap in the face, but the emotional one stung even more.

Moreton took the rebuke and knew he was lashing out at the last person in the world who deserved it. He bowed his head, before raising it again, looking at Sophia's angry expression. 'I'm sorry, Sophia. Truly. Please forgive me.'

Sophia puffed out her cheeks, before exhaling loudly. She reached her hand down and held his, squeezing it slightly.

'OK, Jon. Let's forget it. But we must also forgive Paco. He didn't want to let anyone down.'

She paused for a moment.

'Listen,' she said, pointing towards the door of the dressing room. 'Can you hear anything?'

There was only silence.

'The other players have forgiven him. There's no anger. There's no shouting. You must forgive him too, Jon. We are a family.'

Compromised by his agreement with Jiménez to tell Sophia nothing on their conversation, Moreton merely nodded, and they returned to the dressing room.

With Sophia translating, Moreton laid out his plans to turn the game round.

'Billy. Get out there and warm those muscles up. You're going on.'

Then turning to the team's other goalkeeper. 'You too, Juan.'

Both players headed out to the pitch.

'OK, things will need to change if we're going to rescue this game. We've had so much of the ball, and we'll have even more of it in the second half. They'll just sit back and defend. We can strip a bit from our defensive play to get more impetus in attack. Mathias, you can take a rest for now. Billy will play behind Santi. Revi, drop back into the middle with Sebastián. Seb, be busy, run and get active, get the ball, feed Revi.'

He walked towards the young playmaker with the long dark hair held back by the ever-present headband.

'You,' he said to Revi. 'Are the key. There's a lock on their defence, but we have the key. Turn the key.'

Enthused the player nodded enthusiastically.

'Alejandro, Adrián, push forward and support our attacks from the wide positions. Kiko and Victor can deal with any rare attacks.'

Then he turned to the goalkeeper who still sat gazing at the floor in front of him.

'Paco,' he said softly. 'This is not your fault. Sometimes things happen that we cannot control. The situation can affect us badly. It's not because you don't care. It's because you care so much. No one blames you for what happened. We are a family and we care about each other. Sometimes caring so much, hurts, but that hurt is only love expressing itself. The love we have for each other.'

Moreton paused for a moment, and looked across to Sophia, then back at Jiménez.

'I understand,' he said.

The goalkeeper raised his head and almost unperceptively nodded slowly, accepting both the message about the game, and the wider one implied within it.

Moreton clapped his hands together to lift the tempo and the players jumped to their feet, each patting the saddened goalkeeper as they left, following Sophia back to the pitch. Only Moreton and Jiménez remained.

The latter broke the silence. 'Do you understand?' he asked quietly and without malice.

'Yes, Paco. I do understand. I meant what I said. Sometimes, if you care about people so much, it can hurt. I understand about Alvaro, and I'm sorry for him, but I love Sophia. I can't apologise about that. I understand how you feel. Do you understand about me?'

It was quiet for a few seconds, then Jiménez spoke again. 'Yes. I understand.'

Moreton walked across and offered his hand. The goalkeeper stood up and accepted the proffered handshake. Moreton turned and headed towards the door, but there was one more thing to say.

Calling after the Englishman, Jiménez implored: 'Don't hurt her.'

'I won't.'

As the game restarted, Moreton's assessment was borne out. Hardly worrying about raising an attack, the visitors sat back with a packed defence. The first twenty-five minutes passed without any breakthrough. Swan's absence had done little to improve his match fitness. A couple of minutes had been the extent of his time playing in a competitive situation. It would take a while for any kind of sharpness to return. Revi was having more of the ball in his deeper role but was finding it difficult to find the opportunity to use it. Time ticked by, and as the belief began to drain away from the blue-shirted players, the confidence of their opponents grew. Entering the final ten minutes, Moreton played his final card, removing the exhausted Sebastián and throwing José on to play alongside Santi. When the breakthrough came however, it was from an altogether unexpected source.

Inside the final ten minutes, Adrián collected possession on the left flank, just inside his own half of the field, driving forward as the Callosa players funnelled back to defend their penalty area. Shouting for the ball loud enough for all to hear, Billy Swan made a diagonal run from the centre to the left side of the penalty area, magnetically attracting two defenders as he did so. Quickly grasping the opportunity, Adrián cut infield, away from Swan, exploiting the gap created and fired in a ferocious shot from the edge of the area. The ball screamed past a despairing Callosa goalkeeper and into the net.

The home bench erupted as the defender celebrated under a mass of teammates, but Moreton screamed at his players to get back into position, pointing at his watch. Now clearly rattled, the visitors' defence that had looked so solid, suddenly seemed vulnerable. A cross from Vasquez saw the younger Palermo brother crash a header against the crossbar, before a plunging save from the goalkeeper denied a long-range effort from Revi. Ninety minutes came, and passed. Still the equaliser eluded Retama. Vasquez had the ball on the right and neatly sidestepped the first defender. Another approached and fell to the same fate. Now in the area, the winger feigned to shoot, before instead cutting back inside. The third defender was beaten by the trick and, as he threw himself forward in an attempt to block the shot that never came, his momentum took the winger's standing foot from under him. It was the clearest of penalties.

The shrill whistle of the referee acknowledging the award of the spot-kick was still in the air, as Moreton jumped to his feet, bellowing a single word, again and again. 'Billy! Billy! Billy! Billy!' There was little need, however. The veteran player had already collected the ball and had it tucked under his arm, standing on the penalty spot. While a few opposition players offered unconvincing disputes against the decision, Swan waited, with the ball under his arm, oblivious to the arguments, almost bored. Eventually, the referee cleared the area. Swan placed the ball and took a few paces back. The whistle sounded and the veteran dropped into muscle memory as he jogged forward, paused, causing the goalkeeper to commit, before coolly rolling the ball into the opposite corner of the net.

Swan slowly turned towards his team-mates with arms outstretched in a pose akin to Christ the Redeemer overlooking Rio de Janeiro. His assured ability to deliver from twelve yards certainly had a Brazilian touch about it. The pose was quickly dropped as he was mobbed by relieved and celebrating team-mates. Breaking off from their celebrations, Kiko and Victor walked back to the halfway line with Swan. Reaching the centre spot, they turned to face each other and, drawing imaginary swords from their sides, they wisped the air slicing it with rapid rapier actions, before returning them to their scabbards, and patting each other on the back, laughing. Musketeers of Retama. It may have merely been a draw, but it felt like a victory, and Retama had their first point of the season. The recipe had been completed.

Despite Jiménez being absent and ruled out of playing the following Sunday due to his illness, the following week's training felt particularly upbeat. Then on Friday evening an irritated Billy Swan arrived ten minutes later than anyone else, complaining that Gonzalo had apparently been late in collecting him from the hotel; occasionally, some things that seem like unfortunate events aren't.

With only one goalkeeper, there was difficulty in arranging the normal short-sided game at the end of training, and Moreton asked Sophia to organise an attack v defence drill using the selected players in their positions, with others filling in the gaps. Ahead of this final drill Billy Swan walked towards where Moreton was sitting on the bench, inevitably, jotting notes into his book. Eventually Moreton looked up. 'All right, Billy?' he asked.

'Yeah, well... no... you know. Yeah. Do you mind if I sit this one out?'

'What's up, mate,' Moreton asked, now exhibiting a little concern. 'Is it the hamstring again?'

'No, Jon. The leg's fine. It's just that, you know, well...'

'What, Billy?'

Moreton appeared to be as much confused as he was concerned, but it was clear that something was troubling Swan. Eventually, he decided to come clean.

'Look, Jon. It's like this. Have you noticed that there was something a bit strange about Kiko tonight?'

The name that Swan used, suggested to Moreton that his time ahead of training hadn't been wasted.

'No. Why?'

'Christ, Jon. I think I'm in trouble,' Swan confided, glancing two or three times over his shoulder at the other players receiving instructions from Sophia.

'Trouble? What kind of trouble?'

'He bloody knows, don't he?' Swan whispered although there was no one within earshot.

'Who knows what, Billy?'

'Kiko knows that Kiki Dee is a woman,' came the whispered, but urgent, reply. 'Meldrew told me while we were going through that passing drill.'

He paused, taking a deep breath.

'He ain't happy, Jon. Meldrew said that he thinks I've been playing him for a fool. Taking the Mick, you know. Jon, you know me. It was only a laugh. Just a bit of fun. I really like the kid, I do. I think he's great, but Meldrew said he's going to sort me out. Jon, he's a bloody brute. Look at him. He could maim me.'

'Well, Billy. I did warn you, didn't I?'

'Thanks, Jon. Thanks a sodding bundle, mate.'

Moreton flicked his eyebrows in mock admonishment. 'What do you want me to do about it?'

'First thing: I don't want him marking me in this practice. If I'm attacking, and he's defending, he can easily drop a heavy one on or give me a dig. You know, Jon. You've been round the block, mate. You know how it works.'

'Tell you what, Billy. You sit here by me, where you'll be safe and we'll just say we wanted to rest your leg. How's that?'

'Grand, mate.' The relief in Swan's voice was palpable. He sat down beside Moreton, but as he did so, the younger man found it difficult to suppress a snigger.

Thirty minutes later, the players were sitting in the dressing room, as Moreton confirmed the starting line-up for Sunday's visit to San Esteban. With Jiménez still missing, Torres would stay in goal, behind the usual back four. Guido and Vasquez would have the flanks and with Matías and Revi in the centre. Swan would play behind Santi. Moreton paused and looked around the room. 'Anyone have any questions or anything to say?'

All was quiet, except in the far corner, a hand was raised. It was Kiko. Billy Swan had intentionally positioned himself in a seat as far away from the defender as he could. Normally he would be sat between Kiko and Victor. This time it was different, and the space between him and the big defender offered some comfort. It was only temporary though. Slowly, the defender stood up, brushing aside the hand of Victor, apparently trying to dissuade him from his intent. Swan squirmed in his seat and, as Kiko approached him, rose to his feet in the faint hope of executing a rapid exit.

'Come on now, mate. It was just a bit of fun.'

He glanced around nervously, but no one seemed keen to come to his aid as Kiko drew closer. Eventually there were mere inches between the worried face of Billy Swan and Kiko. Glaring intently into the eyes of the elder man, Kiko spoke: '*Sabes lo que tengo?*'

Not understanding the language, Billy Swan looked at Sophia for a translation. She was standing next to Moreton, both with looks of concern on their faces.

'He's asking if you know what he has got.'

Swan looked back into Kiko's face, barely inches from his own. The defender tilted his head to one side, inviting an answer; insisting on one.

Billy Swan hesitated. His brain scrambled by the imminent threat.

'I dunno, mate. I dunno.'

Kiko waited. Each passing second seemed like an hour to Swan.

'Is it the proper hump? Look, I understand if you have, but it was just a joke. You know?'

Kiko shook his head. It wasn't the correct answer. He waited for another.

'Christ. It ain't a 'ammer of a right hand is it, mate?'

Again, a shake of the head.

'Is it toothache? That can make anybody angry at someone, even when you shouldn't be.'

He looked around at the other players, Moreton and Sophia, but no one seemed likely to step in.

Again, Kiko shook his head. But now his patience appeared to be spent. He raised his right hand and pointed his index finger at Swan.

'No,' he said calmly.

Then he spoke again, aggression bristling,

'I've!' he snarled.

Swan shrank back.

'Got,' came the second word.

Swan winced.

'The.'

What was coming next? He thought an assault was on the way, but he was wrong.

In that moment, as fear gripped the veteran footballer who had accepted being kicked as part of his career, a huge smile spread across Kiko's face. Snarling turned seamlessly into singing.

'Music in me!' he serenaded Swan, lyrically.

A moment of incredulity washed over Billy Swan before the rest of the players, Moreton and Sophia joined in, picking up the tune.

'I've got the music in me. I've got the music in meeee!' they harmonised unimpressively. 'Yeah, yeah. I've got the music in me. I've got the music in meeee!'

Soon everyone in the dressing room, was singing and dancing – aside from the disbelieving Billy Swan.

Then they stopped and collapsed into laughter.

Kiko wrapped his arm around Swan, hugging him with undoubted affection.

Composure restored, swamped with floods of relief and a rapidly growing understanding, Swan pointed across the room at Victor.

'You, Meldrew,' he accused, pointing at the grinning fair-haired figure of

Victor on the other side of the room, lost in fits of laughter. 'You set me up.'

Victor nodded unapologetically.

The truth of why Gonzalo had been late, and how the plan had been conspired in his absence, now dropped into place for Billy Swan.

'Bloody Gonzo. He was in on it as well. I'll stick his bloody newspaper where the sun don't shine!'

'And you, Jon Moreton,' he pointed at the ringleader of the plan.

'And you,' now swinging his finger around the room.

'And you, and you. All of you.'

Despite himself, Billy Swan could no longer exclude himself from laughing.

Kiko walked back to the middle of the dressing room, gesturing Victor to join him there. As everyone watched, they each drew their imaginary rapiers, and stood there awaiting the missing Musketeer. Exaggerating a reluctance that wasn't really there, Billy Swan sighed deeply as much in relief as anything, rose and made it a trio. He too drew his sword and they waved the imaginary weapon in the air, before returning them to their sides, and laughing loudly.

'Family,' thought Jon Moreton to himself.

Cut of the Cloth

The game at San Esteban involved a coach journey into the foothills of the mountains just visible from Moreton's balcony. Following the draw against Callosa there was a new air of confidence among the group, and a few choruses of "I've got the music in me" were even heard to drift around from time to time. Arriving in the small village, Moreton quickly appreciated the difference to Retama. The higher altitude meant that it was cooler, and consequentially greener than in the sun-baked area he had quickly become accustomed to. It felt like a small, English West Country village, albeit with a temperature at least ten degrees higher than perhaps would be expected on an early autumnal day in Devon – and without the inevitable rain.

In keeping with the size of the village, the location for the game was also of modest proportions. There was no stand and no terracing. This was a small village club in many ways and Moreton was concerned in case that very characteristic may diminish his team's desire to win. Stepping into the portacabin that served as the dressing room, his immediate task was to drive from his players' heads any thoughts of this being a friendly encounter in the countryside. He wanted a fast start.

As the whistle started the game, however, the urgency he had been so keen to inject into his players was all too evident. Kicking-off, the home team worked the ball back through their defence. Chasing enthusiastically to harass and pressurise, Santi closed on one of the San Esteban centre backs. He played the ball back to his goalkeeper, before turning to move up field. Unaware that the Retama forward was charging in pursuit, however, as he turned, they collided, with the defender's knee inadvertently driving into Santi's thigh. Both players fell to the floor in an untidy heap.

Initially, it merely looked like an unfortunate tangle, but as the following few minutes ticked by, it became clear that Santi was struggling to run. The next time the ball ran out of play, he sat on the floor, calling to the bench for assistance. Sophia ran on to assess the damage, and five seconds later signalled to Moreton with rotating forefingers that Santi's game was done. A dead leg – a deep bruise – had resulted when the defender's knee caused the quadricep muscle to be crushed against the femur. It would not only mean he could take no further part in this game, but would also take him out of the picture for at least the next couple of games.

Seeing Sophia's signal that a substitution was necessary, Moreton first looked down at his feet, cursing his luck, knowing that his main source of goals was now going to be out of action for a while, before calling to José Palermo to take his place. As Santi limped off and slumped down among the remaining substitutes, the young forward trotted on to take his place. Returning to the coach for an ice pack, Sophia strapped it to Santi's leg, and sat down next to Moreton.

'How bad?' he asked, fearing the worst.

'It's difficult to say at this time. Probably two or three weeks.'

Moreton sighed deeply. With all the things that had happened since the start of the season, his ability to get his preferred eleven on the pitch for any length of time had been thwarted for so many different reasons. If that blow had not been sufficiently bad, however, worse was to follow.

As the game settled into a pattern, Retama were clearly the better side. Whereas Santi had grown into the team over the last few games as the team's main striker, in contrast the younger of the Palermo brothers still seemed a less than imposing figure, both physically and psychologically. Consequently, the visitors' attack was somewhat blunted. What he lacked in experience, however, José Palermo sought to make up for with enthusiasm. Such spirited endeavour would be his downfall.

A rare corner for the home team, saw José back to help his defence out. As the ball was arrowed in, he leapt to head clear. At the same time, behind him, the burly figure of Alejandro Sanz judged that the ball was going to clear the young forward's head, and jumped to challenge a San Esteban forward. The ball glanced from the home player's forehead and flew over the bar, but the momentum of the two Retama players caused them to clash heads in mid-air. Both fell to the ground, as the forehead of Sanz collided with the back of José Palermo's head, and both sustained cuts.

Five minutes later, with heads swathed in bandages, both players walked from the pitch. The forward would take no further part in the game. He had been involved in the action for just a dozen minutes. Sanz was made of sterner stuff, hewn from the hardiest of the Triassic rock of the Costa Blanca, such a minor inconvenience as a cut to his head would not deter the case-hardened captain of CD Retama. As Moreton sent Samuel into a midfield role and moved Revi forward to play alongside Swan, Sanz walked back onto the pitch. His return would not last long.

A further fifteen minutes had elapsed, still well inside the first period when the blood, seeping from the cut on the defender's head wound, graphically illustrated that the bandages swaddling his forehead were incapable of stemming the flow. Now with patches of red staining the white dressing, mere dogged attitude and commitment were insufficient.

'We have to take him off,' Sophia counselled.

It was a conclusion that Moreton had inevitably come to himself, but Sophia's words emphasised that any further delay would be unwise: 'If he stays on, and heads the ball two or three times, it will cause more damage to the injury and he could be out for weeks. Take him off now, and he can be healed and ready for the next game.'

Moreton nodded slowly. He knew it was the right decision, but it would leave the team struggling to cope.

There was little reason for further debate. As the ball ran out of play for a throw in, Moreton stood and shouted over to Sanz, motioning him to leave the field. Alongside the coach stood the young Felipe Blanco, with Sophia whispering urgently into his ear. '*Disciplina! Concentración!*' Initially, Sanz tried to ignore the blandishments of the coach, signalling to Adrián, ball in hand, to restart the game. Wisely his fellow defender shook his head, and pointed over to the bench. Sanz bowed his head, before turning and walking from the pitch. Reaching the sidelines, Sophia wrapped her arm around his wide shoulders, leading him off towards the dressing room to apply more attention to the injury.

When the referee brought the first half to a close, Moreton sighed to himself in resignation, rising slowly to his feet. As he watched the players walking back to the dressing room, he saw the latest of the Retama replacements to take to the field talking to each of his team-mates and patting the badge on his shirt. Felipe Blanco, the player who everyone thought could hardly take anything seriously was doing his job for him. Back in the dressing room, Jon Moreton knew that his first words would be the most important.

'So strong! You are so strong. You are heroes!'

He paused.

'Now we must stay heroes. They will not score. At worst we will take a draw from this game. They will not score. Not in this game. They will not score.'

He looked around at his players. Was the message getting through?

He decided to play his card. 'Why will they not score against us in this game?'

It was a demand for a response rather than a question. Sanz, his armband now passed to Adrián as he left the field, was still the leader of the team. He raised his newly bandaged head and spoke with quiet authority.

'*Porque somos Retama!*'

Both relieved and delighted, Moreton nodded.

'*Si, nuestro Capitán.*'

The second-half would inevitably be a battle to hold out with a weakened side and playing without a true striker to lead the line. It would need resolution and commitment. Revi was dropped back into midfield leaving Swan as a lone, broadly forlorn, striker to try and occupy the home defence and keep the ball as far away from the Retama goal as possible whenever that infrequent opportunity arrived.

Seeing the chance of a win, the San Esteban players pushed forward eagerly in pursuit of what would surely be an unanswered goal. Samuel and Matías harassed and hurried into challenges in the middle of the pitch. Kiko was a Titan in the Retama back line, defending every cross as, alongside him, Victor tidied up and blocked each hole with astute anticipation. On the flanks, Vasquez and Guido funnelled back to help their hard-pressed fullbacks against the incessant attacks. Adrián was strong and dependable as ever, offering a more than impressive leadership display reminiscent of the absent Sanz. On the other side, Felipe Blanco never put a foot wrong, disciplined and concentrated. In goal, the untapped talent of Torres was now being examined. He dealt with long-range shots with confidence and, on the rare occasions when the back line was penetrated, he was quick from his line to block out danger.

On the Retama bench, time was dragging like it was an anvil being pulled up a hill. Jon Moreton looked at his watch, again, again. Ten minutes passed, then twenty, thirty. The watch again. The players were working so hard, but the fatigue would be setting in. Forty minutes and now everything was flowing in one direction. Even Billy Swan was back helping. Five minutes remained.

'We could do this,' he confided to Sophia. The only reply was a nervous smile. Each clearance up field was received with applause from the bench, with the substitutes and injured players on their feet cheering on their team-mates.

Time was up. How much longer would the referee play? A minute passed, then two. Another cross into the box was headed clear by Kiko, but drifted behind for a corner. The last chance? In came the cross, and Kiko again dominated his kingdom, rising to head clear, as a San Esteban player stumbled in front of him. The referee's whistle blew, and the Retama players exploded in celebration. On the bench however, there was only despair. The official wasn't signalling the end of the game. Instead he stood rooted to a spot in the penalty arc, pointing to the spot twelve yards from goal, having deemed that the home player's stumble had been caused by a nudge from Billy Swan. It was the sort of blocking that happens so often in games without punishment, but on this occasion, Swan's stealthy manoeuvre had been spotted. With time up, Retama were facing imminent defeat.

The San Esteban left-back and captain placed the ball on the spot. Torres had a decision to make. Noticing that the San Esteban captain was left-footed, he guessed that he would have a natural tendency to drag the ball to the goalkeeper's left when he shot, especially as he was tired at the end of the game. His mind was made up. The Retama players stood on the edge of the penalty area hoping, rather than believing.

The shot was low, accurate and powerfully struck, arrowing towards the left-hand corner of the Retama net. Torres had guessed correctly, but could he reach the ball? Around one in ten people in the world favour the left sides of their bodies. The San Esteban player taking the penalty was one. The Retama goalkeeper was another. Reaching out a long, left arm, Torres's glove clipped the ball as it passed. The deflection was slight, but vital. The redirected ball cannoned into the post and bounced back towards the taker. Torres was now on the floor, helpless to recover his ground. A goal from the rebound looked certain, but alive to the scenario, Felipe Blanco raced into the area, and before the ball could reach the San Esteban player again, he hacked it clear. The referee blew for full time, and now all in Retama blue celebrated. After shaking hands with the San Esteban coaches, Jon Moreton ran onto the pitch. The celebrating throng of players and Sophia all mobbed the young goalkeeper. Moreton, however, made a bee line for the beaming figure of Felipe Blanco, grabbing and raising him up in the air, carrying him from the pitch as the others trailed along with Juan Torres on their shoulders.

Back in the dressing room, after the inevitable congratulations and back-slapping, Moreton called for quiet.

'Forget the wounds, the injuries, the cuts. Today is about this,' he said, firmly grabbing the Retama badge on his tracksuit top. 'This isn't a piece of cloth. This is a piece of Retama. A piece of our family.'

He looked around him, pausing for a second or two.

'Before we were a collection of players, of people, of individuals. We have faced defeats. We have faced ill fortune. We have faced intimidation and adversity. We have faced these things together, and we stood for each other. We stood together.'

He paused again.

'Now, we are a team.'

The coach journey from San Esteban, back to Retama was all downhill as they left the foothills of the mountains. For CD Retama and their English coach, however, the future was very much pointing in the opposite direction. The inevitable telephone call came from Charlie Broome, confused as to how another draw, and just two points from the opening six fixtures of the season, had resulted in the cheering and singing he could hear in the background.

The last sentence he heard from his friend though, would reverberate with him. Jon Moreton spoke with clarity, and a calmness born of conviction.

'Chaz. We can to do this.'

Charlie Broome flipped his phone closed, placing it on the table in front of him, stroking his chin pensively.

Lessons Learnt

As had become the normal way of things following the game on Sunday, Sophia spent the night in Moreton's apartment. The elation generated by the game had infected them both, and after eating an evening meal of salad sitting on the balcony, as the sun dropped towards the mountains in the distance, they retired to bed early. Fatigue was hardly the reason.

The following morning, the alarm clock said 6.15 when Moreton awoke. Although the sun rose on the opposite side of the apartment from the bedroom, its light filtered into the living area, and then to the bedroom, suggesting it was much later. Moreton looked across the bed to where Sophia was lying, sleeping. He wanted to reach out and touch her, hold her, draw her close to him. Whenever he saw her, he always had the same thoughts.

Suppressing the urge to feel his lover's soft, smooth flesh on his fingers again, instead he climbed out of the bed, reaching for a pair of shorts and a vest top, before quietly closing the bedroom door behind him. He made himself a cup of coffee, and strolled out onto the balcony, sitting down in the relative cool of the morning. He had some thinking to do.

An hour or so later, the sound of the bedroom door opening, and the bathroom one closing, before the shower kicked into life, told him that Sophia had now awoken. He walked back to the kitchen and made two fresh cups before returning to the balcony. A few minutes later Sophia appeared from the alcove that separated the bedrooms and bathroom from the living area. The old training top that he had loaned to her after their first night together had now become a permanent part of her wardrobe, and a favourite of his. Each time she wore it, and it alone, the sight would cause Morton to catch his breath. Standing in the living room, with the sleeves rolled up and the hem barely covering the curve of her buttocks, it looked like the shortest of short dresses, and the way it emphasised the beauty of her slender, silky smooth but taut legs never failed to enrapture him.

'Guapa,' he exclaimed, softly. Then: 'Coffee?'

'One moment, Jon,' she replied before disappearing back into the bedroom.

Five minutes later she reappeared wearing a denim skirt and blouse, buttoned demurely. It was not difficult for her to discern which image he preferred. She smiled as she sat down opposite him, picking up and sipping the coffee. 'This is for the outside world. The other look is just for you, Jon.' She mouthed a silent kiss in his direction.

'So,' he asked. 'What are your plans today?'

Sophia looked at her watch. 'I have to meet Elena in an hour. She has a first date with her new boyfriend tonight, and wants me to go shopping with her to buy a dress that will... you know, shall we say *impress* him.'

Moreton laughed.

'Well, you impressed me on our first date, so you probably know what works.'

'I do, don't I. But I'll see you this evening.' The glint in her eye was obvious. 'I'm thinking of cooking you something special for dinner. I have been talking with Mr Floyd.'

'Sounds great to me. But, before you go, I want you to do something for me.'

His thinking time and the coffee had produced a resolution.

'What's that?'

'I want to go and see Paco.'

'Paco? OK. But why?'

'Well, he hasn't been well, and I wanted to see how he is,' Moreton lied. He disliked deceiving Sophia but had decided that, for the moment, it was an unavoidable necessity.

'Torres has done really well while he's been away,' he continued hastily, trying to deploy misdirection to cover his mendacious tracks. 'It's not that I'm trying to rush him back. I'm just concerned about him.'

There was no reason for Sophia to suspect anything but the truth, and she accepted Moreton's words as precisely that.

Fifteen minutes later Sophia had called the office of Jiménez's electrical business and set things up. 'He's at the office,' Sophia announced with clear concern. 'But he sounded very strange when I told him that you wanted to go and see him, Jon. Are sure everything is OK?'

Moreton was faced with the dilemma of telling her everything, or hating himself for continuing to lie. 'Of course.' He could bear the burden of betrayal for a little longer. If his plan came to fruition, he could lay down that unbearable weight shortly. He needed to speak with Paco Jiménez first.

Sophia raised herself onto her toes and kissed Moreton, warmly, before heading out of the door and the complex to meet her friend. He watched her go, before showering to prepare himself for a meeting he didn't want, but needed to have.

Arriving at the electrical company's offices, Moreton was taken upstairs and offered a seat outside of a room where he could hear the voice of Paco Jiménez talking on the telephone. The conversation sounded very one-sided, with the company owner doing most of the talking. A few minutes later, the words: '*Vale. Vale. Claro, adios,*' suggested the call was over. Footsteps echoing across the wooden floor followed and the door swung open. Jiménez looked at Moreton, before sighing. 'Mister,' he said coldly, before turning back into the office and sitting down behind a desk full of paperwork. Moreton followed, closing the door behind him.

Twenty minutes later, Jon Moreton rose from his chair and reached across the desk, again offering his hand to the man with whom he now hoped he had reached at least a temporary truce.

On the other side of the desk, Paco Jiménez reciprocated the gesture, still unsure of the motives of the Englishman, concluding at least that there may now be less reason to distrust him.

They had agreed that neither had truly intended to deceive Sophia, and Moreton insisted that it was something he was prepared to do no longer. He had told Jiménez that he hated hiding the truth from her. He had made a promise to be honest with her, and he wouldn't break that. He also told Jiménez that he should speak to Alvaro and encourage him to tell Sophia about how he had contacted his uncle, and told him about her relationship with Moreton. He had said he would tell Sophia the truth that evening when they met again.

It had been a difficult conversation, but Moreton sensed that the man on the other side of the desk knew that these were the right things to do. In exchange, Moreton promised that he would encourage Sophia to continue with her studies, and tell her that no one knows how things can turn out. In his mind, in his soul, he had no doubt that the love they had between them would endure, but he wanted her to have options. There was one final thing. Moreton told the Retama goalkeeper that from the end of this day, he would not hide his relationship with Sophia, and that Jiménez should tell the other players what he knew. How he did that, and what he decided to say to them was up to him. He said that he trusted him to be honest and tell them the truth. He said that he expected him to return to training the following evening. Whatever his illness had been, it was cured now.

As Moreton descended the stairs from Jiménez's offices, the weight was beginning to rise from his shoulders. Back in the office, the owner of the electrical business was speaking on the telephone once more. '*Alvaro? Si, soy yo. Necesitas hacer algo...*'

He was in love with Dolores Sophia Isabella Medina Garrigues of that he was sure, and had resolved that he would never deceive her again, no matter how trivial the occasion may seem. It was a commitment he held true to, even when, much later, so many others believed that to be so very far from the truth.

That same afternoon, Moreton was sitting on his balcony formulating plans for the upcoming game on Sunday. The sun had now climbed over the roof of his apartment, and only the lowered sunshade mitigated its effect on where Moreton sat, at least making the temperature tolerable. After returning from his meeting with Jiménez, he had swum for a while, enjoying the pleasant sensation of freedom offered by the water, and the feeling of having done the right thing, before showering and preparing a light lunch of a panino with tomato, cheese and two slices of the Jamón Serrano that he was becoming increasingly enamoured of. Now, sitting at the table in one of the big, comfortable wicker chairs on the balcony, he noticed Sophia, walking up the short street towards the apartment.

He was tempted to wave to her, but not knowing how much of the agreed plan with Jiménez had been enacted, he opted instead for caution, and waited for her to arrive at the door. She disappeared from his view as she headed towards the gate leading into the complex. He heard it open and close behind her, and waited for her to open the door. Ten seconds passed, then another ten. Ten more, and no approach to his door. Concerned, Moreton rose from the chair and walked across the apartment to look out of the kitchen window. Had she stopped to speak to someone? There was no sign of her. Then he noticed that there was a light on in the apartment opposite, perhaps she was dropping some shopping off in her own apartment before returning to his. He decided to wait.

He had glanced at his watch on eight occasions, each brief interval comprising of no more than three minutes. The time for waiting has passed. Collecting his notes into a tidy pile and placing them on the living room table, he grabbed his keys and left the apartment for the short journey to Sophia's door. He knocked gently, once. Then again. A few seconds later, a clearly tearful Sophia opened the door.

'Oh, Jon,' she exclaimed through the tears as she threw her arms around him, holding him tightly to her, and burying her head in his chest.

Wrapping his arms around her in response, he spoke softly. 'Hey, it's OK. Don't cry.'

'I'm so sorry,' she said between sobs.

Moreton guided her back into the apartment and, closing the door behind him, eased her from the embrace as he placed her on the sofa, sitting down next to her. He took her hands in his.

'What's all this for?'

He suspected, but wasn't sure.

Sophia looked up at him, and tried to smile. 'I'm sorry, Jon. I'm sorry to have put you through all of that.' There was a moment's pause. 'Alvaro called me.'

'That's OK. Everything's fine.'

He reached up to her face, and brushed away a few tears.

She smiled at him, holding his hand and kissing it softly.

'Alvaro called me. He told me everything, about how he had told Paco about us, about how Paco had confronted you, why he said he couldn't play.'

She paused and held his hand tightly. 'I'm sorry, Jon. He shouldn't have done that. It was my fault. Paco can be an angry person, sometimes.'

'Don't worry. I'm a big boy. I can look after myself.' He raised his hand, using it to lift her chin, allowing him to look directly into her dark, sad eyes. 'It wasn't your fault. You did nothing wrong. It wasn't Paco's fault. He was trying to protect you. And it wasn't Alvaro's fault. He just needed someone to talk to, and wasn't prepared to lie to his uncle.'

Sophia nodded in agreement, then laughed lightly.

Moreton was happy that she seemed to be reassured by his words, but surprised at her laughter.

'I'm sorry, Jon. I wasn't laughing at you, or your words.'

Moreton raised a finger and placed on her lips. 'Sophia. Stop apologising, or I'm leaving.' It was offered as a reassurance, a sympathetic but insistent way of easing any perceived guilt she may have felt.

Sophia understood, but the implication still caused concern.

'Don't ever do that, Jon. Don't ever leave me. Don't even joke about it.'

Jon Moreton's heart swelled. He couldn't help but love the woman in front of him.

'You could never make me.'

He reached across and drew her close to him.

'Never,' he repeated. '*Nunca*'

The embrace was balm to Sophia's troubled soul, and she was reluctant to let it end and draw away from him, but when Moreton spoke, it caused her to do so.

'So, what was funny?' he asked her.

Sophia sat back, and cleared her throat before speaking.

'Elena was with me when Alvaro called. We were having lunch, so I had to walk outside of the bar to speak with him. When I returned, she could see I was upset and I told her everything. About Alvaro, about you, about the call.'

Moreton's first emotion was one of relief that the relationship would no longer be secret, that was surely the case now.

'OK,' he said.

He was however, still more than a little intrigued.

'But what was funny?'

Sophia looked at him smiling.

He was happy to see her smile again.

'Well, when I told Elena, about you and me, she had just laughed, and asked me why I thought she had not realised already. She has known me for a long time, and we've shared so many secrets, thoughts, ideas. We've been really close. She asked me if I had really believed that I could have hidden something like that from her.'

New Beginnings

Moreton had explained to Sophia how he had also told Jiménez that he should tell the other players whatever he thought was the right thing to say. Sophia had been a little doubtful, but Moreton had insisted that it was for the best. 'These people are part of our Retama family. We need to be honest with them.' It was a compelling argument.

He had also told her how important it was that she should continue her studies with the same application as before. His insistence had caused Sophia concern. She was not going to Galicia any more. They were together now, so what was the point? She questioned whether he had any doubts about their commitments to each other. Explaining that he had no doubts whatsoever, he said that was the whole point. If he had, he would have wanted the extra security of knowing that she had burnt her bridges on that opportunity and her options for leaving Retama would have been reduced. He was so sure of things though, that he had no need for such assurances.

That evening, following the counsel of Keith Floyd, Sophia had prepared a dish of mussels, clams and prawns, purchased from the fish market in town when out with Elena earlier, cooked in a white wine and chilli sauce with rice and green beans.

When the plates were emptied, but for the remnants of shells, Sophia cocked her head to one side, confidently inviting comment.

'Very good,' Moreton nodded appreciatively. He raised his glass invitingly. 'Keith Floyd,' he said, as they clinked their glasses together. Sophia nodded, sipped her wine, before raising her glass again.

'To us, Jon Moreton.'

'To us, Dolores Sophia Isabella Medina Garrigues.'

Jon Moreton had never been happier. That day, heading towards the time when it becomes yesterday, had been difficult at times, but as he contemplated the outcome, looking across at the woman sitting opposite him, he had no doubt that it had all been worthwhile. The only thing missing to complete things now was to ensure Club Deportivo Retama achieved promotion, but that was for tomorrow. Tonight, was for him and Sophia. Ten minutes short of midnight, Moreton cleared the table, and quickly washed their plates and glasses. He returned to the balcony and took Sophia by the hand, lifting from her chair. He guided her through the patio door, locking it behind him, and led her into the bedroom.

The following day passed quickly. After breakfasting together, Sophia declared that she was returning to her apartment to study for a few hours, but they could then meet up to do some shopping and have lunch together. Later, they should go to training together. They should be unabashed about their relationship. Moreton readily agreed.

That evening they walked into the Estadio Antonio Núñez together. No one else had arrived, and Sophia sought out Esteban to open the dressing room, while Moreton set out cones and bibs for the sessions. A few minutes later, she returned to help as they waited for the players to arrive. Moreton noticed that she seemed a little distracted. 'What's the matter?' he asked.

Sophia hesitated before replying. 'Oh, it's nothing. It's just that Esteban seemed a little strange.'

'Strange? In what way?'

'I don't know really. I'm not sure. I hope he's not unwell.'

Time ticked by and 8 o'clock approached without any sign of the players arriving. Just then, Esteban appeared by the edge of the pitch, beckoning them to follow him. Moreton and Sophia jogged across towards where he had been standing, just in time to see him walk into the dressing room, closing the door behind him. Concerned, they hurriedly followed.

The entire Retama squad was already waiting in the dressing room, sitting on the benches that surrounded the room and, as Moreton and Sophia entered, they burst into a chorus of cheers and applause.

Paco Jiménez stood up, slicing his hand back and forth under his chin. He looked directly at Moreton. 'I told them,' he said.

Standing alongside Moreton, Sophia moved her hand slightly until it came into contact with his, gently gripping it, and squeezing slightly with restrained joy.

The cheering rang out again. This time, it was Moreton who called for silence a few seconds later, with a beaming smile betraying his happiness.

'Gracias. Muchas gracias.'

Sophia smiled up at him.

'Everyone outside,' he declared. 'Time for work!'

Moreton had always considered that the pace of Guido could be valuable to them, and with Santi out of action for at least two weeks, he was looking to spring the pacey wide man into space behind the opposition. The training session, and the one that followed were designed with that in mind. The ploy was to draw the opposition forward to create space, and then to deliver accurate passes that would release Retama's speedster. Those passes could best be hit by Revi or Billy Swan. So, whoever regained possession should look for either of those two players quickly. It required a lot of work by young José Palermo. He would need to drive into space towards the opposite flank, to try and draw defenders towards him and Vasquez, creating the required space. It was a plan that Moreton and Sophia had arrived at as had they chatted while she prepared the shellfish the previous evening.

Friday's training was less intense with regards to the tactics for the game on Sunday, and played at a much easier pace. The last thing that Retama needed now was any new injuries, to upset their plans. Fortunately, when Moreton announced the team at the end of Friday's session, aside from Santi's absence, there was a full squad to select from. Paco Jiménez had returned to training, but he had asked Moreton to retain Juan Torres in goal, as he deserved to keep hold of his starting position. It was something Moreton would have done anyway, but

Jiménez's comments had made the decision much easier.

In the early afternoon of the following Sunday, the coach carrying the Retama party arrived at the large industrial complex of Sobrolepeña Industrial, in the small town that bore the same name as the business. Clearly viewing the football club as an important part of the town, the company had spared little expense to ensure that the players, and the town itself, appreciated that they were valued. As the teams left the pristine dressing rooms, it was also clear that offering free admission to any and all who wanted to watch the club play, had been successful. Around five hundred or so fans, many decked in the green and yellow hooped shirts of the home team had gathered to watch, in expectation that the visitors, who had yet to win any of their first six games, may well provide their heroes with a comfortable victory.

Fired by the relative upswing in results following two games undefeated, it was clear that Retama were the more accomplished side. As Sophia had suggested would be the case when she and Moreton had discussed the opposing teams they would face, qualification for inclusion in the Sobrolepeña Industrial team was governed more by the location of employment, than by mere footballing ability. The Retama defence coped more than comfortably with the home team's probing, and ten minutes ahead of the break, they struck. His head now merely covered by a small adhesive bandage, Sanz comfortably secured possession, breaking down another fairly innocuous home attack, and quickly fed the ball to Revi midway in the Retama half. Setting off on his decoy run, the younger Palermo brother cut towards the right flank, drawing defenders to him. Seizing the moment, Revi arrowed a ball over the head of the home right-back. Guido kicked in the after-burners, quickly chasing down the ball and heading for goal. The defence recognised the source of danger and chased across field to try and cut out the threat. Released from his distraction duty, José Palermo now moved into the box. With defenders closing, Guido spotted his team-mate and crossed towards the leggy forward, who controlled with his chest and fired home. It was the sort of goal that delights all coaches. On the Retama bench, Moreton and Sophia were no different, hugging each other joyously, as the team celebrated on the field.

At the break, the lead was intact, and Jon Moreton delivered one of his briefest ever team talks. '*Perfecto*,' he beamed clapping his hands enthusiastically. '*Mismo otra vez, por favor*.' The same again was required. He turned and left a dressing room that was clearly buzzing. There would be more stings to follow.

Just three minutes after the restart, José Palermo challenged one of the home centre backs as he brought the ball out of defence. Unable to steal possession, the young forward merely diverted the ball towards Billy Swan inside the centre circle. Without hesitation, the veteran screamed out: 'Giddy!' and rolled the ball into the empty green space behind the home back line. Guido set off and was free on goal. Drawn to close the angle, the goalkeeper pre-emptively hurled himself at the forward's feet, just as Guido clipped the ball over him and into the empty net.

Two goals up, and with hardly a threat worthy of the name coming the other way, the game was over. There would be two more Retama goals, though. As the home team laboured fruitlessly to gain an elusive foothold in the game, gaps inevitably, and increasingly, appeared at the back. An over-hit pass was intercepted by Matías, who quickly fed Revi. A clipped pass over the top of a tiring and by now demoralised defence to the fleet-footed Guido, broke them down again. A shimmy, worthy of Billy Swan himself, defeated the goalkeeper and Retama were three goals clear. The goal of the game came with just four minutes remaining. Torres rolled the ball out to Victor who turned to look up field. Billy Swan was standing by the centre spot, closely marked by two defenders. 'Meldrew!' he yelled to his fellow Musketeer, and the defender drilled ball towards him.

Swan trotted towards the ball. Anxious to get a challenge in before the forward could inflict further damage, defenders closed down either side of him. Sensing the opportunity, instead of collecting the ball, Billy Swan merely stepped over it. Uninterrupted, it ran on into the totally unpopulated Sobrolepeña half of the field. Unpopulated that is until the blue blur of Guido emerged from the left flank, collecting the ball, around thirty-five yards from goal. Bursting with confidence, and with two goals already safely stored in his pocket, the young flyer looked up to see the goalkeeper advancing towards the edge of his area. Delicately, he clipped the ball into the air. The ground was silent as it gracefully arced over the home team's last line of defence and bounced into the net. Five minutes later, the referee blew for full-time.

Special attention was afforded to the hat trick hero, but Jon Moreton was also looking to have a word with his former team-mate, inevitably leaving the field with Victor and Kiko.

'Brilliant Billy,' he enthused to the veteran.

'What's that then, Jon?' The older man asked, feigning a lack of comprehension.

'That assist for Guido's last goal, Billy. Bloody genius, mate. A Billy Swan moment. A real Billy Swan moment.'

'Don't know what you mean, mate. That was Meldrew's assist. I missed the ball totally. I was knackered so thought: "cobblers, let Giddy chase it, he's younger than me".'

Moreton smiled.

'Yeah OK, Billy,' he said, wrapping an arm around Swan's shoulder.

As he did so, Billy Swan turned to him. 'Bloody brilliant though, ain't I Jon, eh?'

'You are, mate,' he replied. 'You are.'

Waking the following morning, was a pleasant sensation for Jon Moreton. Instantly, memories flooded back into mind. The win. The happy coach journey back to Retama. The evening meal he had shared with Sophia at Bella Cucina, and the time they had spent until the early hours of the new day, wrapped in each other's arms on the sofa, listening to music, with hardly a care in the world. He turned over in bed, towards Sophia.

Instead, though there was merely the indentation in the pillow where she had lain. He leant over and breathed in her scent, before looking up and seeing

Sophia standing in the doorway, donned in his old training top. 'Come on lazy boy,' she scolded playfully. 'I'm showered and have made breakfast. Get up. I have plans for today.' She turned and walked back into the living area of the apartment. With her back turned Sophia would not have noticed Moreton smiling appreciatively at her. He jumped out of bed grabbing shorts and a vest top, and headed into the shower. Fifteen minutes later they were sitting in the wonderfully cool morning air of the balcony.

'What plans?' Moreton asked as he jabbed his fork into another piece of melon from the bowl of fruit Sophia had prepared.

'Well, you've been here for a while now, and although you know this little area around here, the complex, the football ground and the local area, you know little of my town. In the next couple of days, I am going to introduce you to Retama.'

'So, we're going into the town are we?'

'Well,' Sophia replied. 'We'll do that tomorrow. Today, we're heading to the beach.'

She stood up and wiped her mouth with a napkin. 'I'm going back to my apartment to change. Get these things cleared up, sort out swimwear and towels and come over in fifteen minutes. Yes?'

'OK, boss.'

'And don't forget the sun cream, Jon. That's very important.'

She went into the bedroom and emerged in a pair of shorts underneath the training top, creating a more dignified look as she left the apartment.

'Don't be late,' she called back, closing the door behind her. 'It's not nice to keep a girl waiting.'

In swim shorts and a vest top, with a large towel rolled under his arm, Moreton rapped on Sophia's door thirty seconds ahead of schedule. 'Just about on time,' she remarked before reaching up and kissing Moreton. She was also wearing a vest top over a long, semi-sheer, skirt, elasticated at the waist, through which a pair of white bikini briefs were clearly visible. Leaning against the side of the door were two beach umbrellas in carrying cases. Sophia picked up a bag, and closed the door behind her, motioning to Moreton to bring the umbrellas.

A short stroll and bus journey later, they walked the twenty yards or so from the bus stop in Torre del Mar past a row of bars and cafes onto a beach of golden yellow sand with blue and white waves lapping at its edge. Following Sophia's lead, Moreton kicked off and picked up his sandals. Immediately, he could feel the heat of the sand under his feet, and shielding his eyes, despite his sunglasses, looked both ways. The beach lay in what seemed to be the crescent of a natural bay, and stretched away into the distance, for what must have been a mile or so in either direction. Although, the beach was hardly unpopulated, its size made it easy to find a spot to allow them plenty of space.

Moreton secured the stems of the umbrellas in the sand, before opening them up to create an area of shade where they each laid out their towels. Sophia slipped out of her skirt and peeled off the vest top, sitting on her towel, as Moreton removed his vest and dropped down beside her. For a couple of minutes, they sat in silence, drinking in the pleasant ambience. A gentle breeze offered solace against the heat, and the Mediterranean caressed the golden sand.

Raising himself on his elbows, Moreton sighed deeply, easing into the comfort of the moment.

'Why here?' he asked turning towards her.

'Why not?' she answered, knowing that it was hardly addressing the question. 'Don't you like it here?'

Moreton smiled at her tongue-in-cheek evasiveness.

'What's not to like. But seriously, why here? I thought you were going to show me Retama.'

'Three reasons,' Sophia replied, smiling. 'Firstly, this is a beautiful beach, isn't it?'

Moreton could only agree. 'And… ?'.

'Secondly, we start here, because this is where Retama started. And thirdly for the sardines.'

The initial point of Sophia's list was obvious enough, but the second two piqued Moreton's curiosity, much as she had intended it too. It showed.

'Torre del Mar was the original settlement in the area, hundreds of years ago. It was a community built on fishing and, as it grew, the military built a watchtower here, to keep an eye out for pirates or raiders from across the sea. You see Jon, in English, Torre del Mar, means Tower of the Sea –' Sophia broke off to sit up and point across the beach towards an area where a number of families were sitting above the sand. 'That is where the tower stood.'

'OK.'

'Then, as the community prospered and grew, it spread and, just around the headland, is another bigger bay with deeper water and better opportunities for the fishing boats. It became the growth area. That is how Retama came about.'

'And the fish they catch here are sardines?'

Moreton jumped in with both feet, and got wet.

'Well, yes, but also a little no, as well. There are sardines, but also other fish as well. Dorada, Lubina, Merluza and many other different types. The sardines though…'

She paused as if savouring the flavour of her words. Then adding, 'Do you like sardines?'

'Well, I can't say that I usually eat a lot of fish, I'm from the middle of England, very far from the sea and, to be honest, I'm not even sure what those others are that you just mentioned. I do have sardines on toast for breakfast occasionally though.'

Sophia laughed despite attempts not to do so.

'Oh, Jon,' she said between laughs. 'Tomorrow when we go into town, I'll take you to the Fish Market and introduce you to the fish. Those are just the Spanish names. You'll know what they are when I show you. And,' she laughed again, 'I'm not talking about sardines from a tin. I mean fresh from the sea, cleaned and freshly cooked on a barbecue. Have you eaten fish like that before?'

'No, not really,' Moreton replied, now feeling more than a little embarrassed to confess as much.

'Right,' Sophia declared jumping to her feet.

'Swim first, and then we'll go to a little restaurant over there.'

She pointed back to the row of similar establishments lining the beach. 'And you'll see what I mean.'

She reached out hand to pull Moreton to his feet.

He complied, and hand-in-hand, they walked into the waves of the gently lapping Mediterranean waters.

An hour later, refreshed and dried, with the sand washed from their feet, they were seated in a small restaurant, looking out over the beach towards the sea, with a shade sheltering them from the sun. After greeting the young waiter like an old friend, Sophia had ordered their food.

'This is really nice. I'm glad you brought me here.'

She smiled back and took his hand in hers as the waiter arrived with two large glasses of beer.

Moreton looked a little surprised. 'Not wine?'

'No, with barbecued sardines, we drink cold beer.'

She patted his hand as she picked up her glass with the other one. 'You'll see.'

A few minutes later, a scent of barbecued fish wafted across their table as the waiter returned with two empty plates, one of which he placed in front of each of them, and a tray loaded with sardines, in the middle of the table. Clearly detecting Moreton's hesitancy, Sophia scooped up one of the small fish with her fork, and transferred to her plate.

'Like this,' she said, scraping the flesh from one side of the sardine, lifting head and tail clear by flicking her fork under the exposed spine, and then eating the flesh followed by a swallow of beer. 'Wonderful,' she said, inviting Moreton to try.

Within minutes, the tray was left with merely the detritus of their lunch.

'Well?'

Moreton tilted his head slightly. 'Why have I never eaten this before?' He wiped his mouth with a napkin before draining the last of his beer. 'That was the perfect lunch, especially in this weather.'

Sophia smiled broadly. 'You are becoming more and more like a natural Spaniard, Jon Moreton. I like that.'

Moreton chuckled quietly to himself, acknowledging the flattering validity of her observation. His life had changed in so many ways since he had accepted Charlie Broome's invitation to visit Spain.

'Me too,' he said. 'I think I am beginning to.'

After lunch they returned to their umbrellas on the beach, and relaxed, dozing in the warm sunshine, replete from their meal. They headed back as the sun dipped below the buildings and the afternoon eased into early evening.

The following day they left the apartment early and headed into town, catching the bus only yards away from the offices with the large sign proclaiming *Broome Cerámica*. The bus weaved in and out of seemingly impossibly narrow streets before reaching the bus station. Exiting, Sophia led Moreton across the road, and began the tour, pointing out the various buildings and things she wanted him to see, the town hall, the churches, the harbour where the sardines they had eaten the day before had probably been landed.

Turning a corner, Moreton could hear a chorus of intermingling shouting from a large doorway to their left. Sophia guided him towards it and when inside, he realised this was the Fish Market. Units, each with large trays of ice in front of them, displaying all kinds of fish and seafood greeted his eyes. Sophia nodded to him, and they headed off down one of the aisles. Each of the fishmongers was calling out, marketing their wares, but much of it was lost to Moreton's untrained ears.

Stopping every few seconds, or so, Sophia pointed out various things.

'Dorada,' she said, pointing to a particularly glum looking fish that looked as if it had been flattened. 'In English, they are called Sea Bream.'

They moved on.

'And there.' She stopped again. A queue of people watched as one of the fishmongers hacked slices from a long fish with a mouth full of teeth that threatened to bite back, but never did. 'Hake' she said.

The name rang a bell with Moreton. 'Ah, yes. I've had that with chips,' he said, then wished he hadn't, as he realised how gauche it sounded.

'We call it Merluza,' she said, resisting the temptation to add that frying it in batter very much wasn't the Spanish way of celebrating the flavours of hake.

They passed fish labelled "lubina," and Sophia explained were known as sea bass in English, and then "pulpo," which Moreton recognised as octopus. 'Calamari – squid,' Sophia explained.

Towards the end of the line, Moreton flashed out a hand. 'Ah,' he said pointing to a pile of small silver fish, helpfully labelled as "Sardinas." 'Sardines,' he declared triumphantly, before realising that his moment of triumph was a little overstated. They both laughed and he wrapped an arm around Sophia.

That evening, using a small barbecue, Sophia cooked sardines on Moreton's balcony. The delicious aroma of the roasting fish swirled around them, undisturbed by the still night air, as they consumed the fish hungrily, washed down with cold beer. Afterwards, they cleared the table, and sat together watching as the sun disappeared and the sky melted from blue to grey and then black, before the stars appeared. Just after midnight, as the new day offered a new beginning, they left the balcony and headed for the bedroom and fell into a deep, untroubled, sleep.

Unexpected

Palermo was back from suspension and available, but Guido's performance blocked any quick return to his old position. Moreton considered playing the elder brother as the front man, instead of his younger sibling, but given the work that José had put into making his tactics play out so well, and the calm assurance with which he buried his only chance of the game, that too was out of the question. Palermo would need to await his chance. Moreton was all set to name the same team that evening, for Retama's third consecutive away game, when Sophia's phone rang as they sat eating lunch on Friday.

Immediately, although he could only discern a few words of the conversation, he knew it wasn't good news.

'Adrián,' she confirmed. 'His wife has gone into labour early. He won't be with us tonight and I can't see him being available on Sunday. Or for a while afterwards.'

'Is she OK?'

'I think so,' Sophia replied slowly, but hardly with conviction. 'Well, he thinks so... I hope so.'

The news dragged sad memories back into focus for Sophia. Moreton walked around the table to her, lifting her to her feet and holding her close.

'I know what you're thinking. But I'm sure it'll be fine. You have to believe that. We have to believe that. For Adrián and Ana.'

She nodded as she sobbed tears into his shirt. 'I know, but it's so cruel. They've suffered before. Why again?' Now the tears were flowing uncontrollably. 'Adrián even apologised. He apologised for letting everyone down.'

Later that evening at training, Sophia told the remainder of the players about the phone call. Some of them knew already. Having shared Adrián's pain two years previously, Jiménez and Sanz, in particular, had become very protective of the one so many considered the indestructible hard man of the team. They knew better.

It all meant that the session was subdued at best. No one had much thought for football, and Moreton had considered halting it early, but at least while they were working, it offered them a distraction. At the end of the session, Moreton was faced with one immediate issue. Who would fill the absent fullback's berth on the left side of the Retama defence?

It had been a difficult decision to make, not least because, for most of the session, both Moreton and Sophia had their minds on more important matters. There was an option to put the returning Juan Palermo in as a defender. He certainly had the build and strength to play there, but as with most positions on a football field, experience and knowledge of the role is important, and he was understandably lacking in that. The other option was Felipe Blanco. Coming on as a substitute for Sanz in the game against San Esteban, he had been impressive, dispelling the image of being too undisciplined and lacking in concentration. His last-minute clearance after Torres had saved the penalty was a strong recommendation and, in the end, it convinced them it was the right way to go.

There was one other change in the team. Matías had been the epitome of consistency and had hardly missed a minute of the season, but Samuel was now fit and available. Playing alongside the more creative Revi in the centre of midfield required not only an ability to read the game and shield the back line, but also the stamina to work almost relentlessly in order to allow Revi the freedom to play his role. It was a good opportunity to offer Matías a rest, and also give Samuel a game.

Later that evening, back at his apartment, Moreton was looking at the news on his laptop. Sophia had gone back to her apartment to study, and they had agreed she would stay there overnight. There was an assignment she wanted to finish, and Elena was calling to see her later. At around 10.30, however, there was a knock on his door. Opening it, he found Sophia standing there, laptop in hand. She walked into the apartment and placed the laptop down on the table.

Elena had just left, she explained, so, before going back to read through her assignment, she had quickly checked the league table ahead of the weekend's games. Unsurprisingly, Retama were near the bottom, but her attention was focused on the other end of the table. She asked Moreton if he remembered what she had told him about Costa Locos, and that the club from up the coast, had just been promoted. He nodded, commenting that as Retama had been two tiers higher than them, perhaps it was a good opportunity for another win. Sophia seemed less than convinced. 'I'm not so sure,' she said.

The league table displayed on her laptop, showed Costa Locos sitting in second place, behind Politanio B. Sophia suggested that, perhaps with confidence running high after promotion, the league's newcomers had surprised everyone. They had won five of their seven games and drawn with Politanio, away from home.

Moreton thought for a moment. There really wasn't much they could do now, other than ensure that the team was well aware of the task ahead of them before kick-off. He asked Sophia how her assignment was going. She said that she hadn't finished, but was determined to get it all done that night. She had wanted to keep Elena's visit short, but there had been problems with her new boyfriend and she needed someone to talk to. She kissed Moreton, and said goodnight, before disappearing back across the walkway and up the steps to her own apartment.

The forty-five-minute journey along the coast road to Costa Locos was subdued and quiet, and in the dressing room, the ebullient atmosphere after the victory the previous week, had been dispelled by concerns for absent friends. Suffering the same malaise, Moreton tried, and largely failed, to deliver a rousing team talk. The team that entered the field were physically ready, but emotionally already drained. The early consequence was almost inevitable.

A mere two minutes had passed when a long hopeful ball from the home defence fell between Sanz and Victor. Each of the Retama players left it to the other, and a home forward seized the opportunity to prod the ball past Torres. Retama were a goal down, and the young goalkeeper had conceded for the first time since being elevated to the number one position. For the remaining minutes of the first period, the confident home team swarmed over the clearly distracted players in blue. Torres was kept busy, but prevented the deficit increasing.

As the dejected players sat in the dressing room, Moreton tried to rouse them, shouting and clapping hands, but little seemed to be getting through. As he paused, Sanz stood up. He spoke quietly, but with a conviction that brooked no argument. Everyone listened, and Sophia translated for Moreton and Billy Swan.

'Adrián is one of us. Ana is part of this family too. We are sitting here feeling sad for them. We were feeling sad for them out there too,' he said pointing towards the pitch. 'But feeling sad is not helping them. If we want to help them, we should do something about it, not just feel sad. We have all told Adrián that we are all here for him. For him and Ana. He always gave everything for this team, for you, for me, for all of us. If we don't do the same, if we don't give everything for the team, we are letting him down. Do you understand?'

There were no answers. None were required. The players stood up and quietly walked out of the dressing room. As Sanz passed where the coach stood alongside Sophia, Moreton could see the tears running down the captain's face. At the referee's whistle, the game restarted. The home players began in similar style to the first half. Quick and incisive going forwards, and enthusiastically chasing back to regain possession when it was lost. This was a different Retama team from the first half, though. Instead of being hurried out of possession, being second to every loose ball and insipid going forwards, they had new resolve.

For all Retama's new-found ambition, Costa Locos retained the vigour fed by confidence and a string of outstanding results. The play was well-contested, but past the hour mark, there had been no further score. It would take something particularly explosive to get Retama level, and Billy Swan would deliver it. Receiving the ball in the centre circle from Revi, he adroitly turned his marker and strode clear before a despairing tackle brought him to the floor. Quickly grabbing the ball, he sprung to his feet seeing Antonio Vasquez in space on the right. He fired the ball out towards the tousle-haired wide man, ambled forward at the sort of leisurely pace his legs and age grudgingly permitted. Vasquez slipped past a defender and chased towards the by-line.

Seeing only José Palermo in the box, he looked back towards Swan, who had been passed by the quickly recovering defenders. Avoiding the penalty area, heavily populated by defenders, Vasquez cut the ball back towards the blue-shirted veteran around twenty-five yards from goal. There was never a doubt in Swan's mind as to what he going to do. His right foot detonated the ball on the volley and it exploded past the helpless home goalkeeper, ripping into the back of the net. It was a strike of rare genius, and Retama were level. Despite the exquisite nature of the goal, celebrations were brief and subdued. There was still work to do.

That was also the case for the home team. After their recent results, seeing a lead pegged back felt like an insult. They poured forward, eager to regain their advantage and, for the next dozen minutes or so, the game became ragged and open. Torres saved acrobatically on two occasions and, the one time he was beaten, the ball crashed against the crossbar and away. At the other end, José Palermo saw a header comfortably saved by the home goalkeeper, and when Guido threatened to break clear, a crude challenge brought his run to a halt. Revi struck the free kick but it drifted narrowly wide. A goal was surely inevitable. It came with fifteen minutes remaining.

Moreton had sent on the fresh legs of Sebastián for the tiring Guido and Matías for Samuel. The changes disjointed the Retama play slightly and before they had settled, Retama conceded. Revi lost possession in midfield, and a quick ball over the top caught the inexperienced Felipe Blanco slightly out of position. The home wide player gathered possession and, as Victor was compelled to come across and close the attacker down, a swift pass into the area found a team-mate who side-footed home. The young stand-in fullback fell to his knees, punching the ground in frustration at his perceived error.

Although the goal felt like a dagger to the heart of his team, Jon Moreton was perversely delighted to see the anger manifested in Felipe Blanco. Something else cheered him as well. As the celebrating home players trotted back into position, Sanz lifted the young defender to his feet, speaking quietly to him. It was not condemnation, but encouragement. Embracing the sentiment expressed by Sanz, Moreton turned to a concerned Sophia. 'We're not done yet,' he said. 'There's plenty of fight in our family.'

Moreton waved to the older Palermo brother to ready himself for action, and with less than ten minutes remaining, sent him on to replace his younger sibling. After missing games due to suspension, there was every chance that Juan Palermo would not be up to speed in terms of match fitness, but he offered a presence up front and the muscular awkwardness that can often cause problems. Would there be sufficient time though?

For the next few minutes it seemed unlikely. Time ticked by. Retama pressed, but the ever-present danger of getting caught by a counter-attack threatened to scupper any aspirations of an equaliser. Entering injury time, they forced a corner on the left. Vasquez flighted the ball towards the towering presence of Kiko inside the six-yard box, but the home goalkeeper punched clear. The ball fell back towards Vasquez. Fearing the same consequence if he repeated the earlier cross, he played the ball back towards Felipe Blanco. Kiko moved towards the near post inviting the ball. Instead though, the defender astutely crossed over the heads of Kiko and the defenders drawn towards him as planets to a star. On the far post, in space, Juan Palermo jumped and powered a header into the net. For the third game out of four, Retama had dragged a point from a game that had looked to be lost.

The coach journey back to Retama was as quiet as the one there, but an air of quiet satisfaction had replaced the earlier reflective melancholy. Twenty minutes into the journey, Sanz called out. Sophia whispered to Moreton that he was telephoning Adrián. After a few quiet words, the captain held aloft his phone and a chant went up from the players. 'Adrián, Ana! Adrián, Ana! Adrián, Ana!' Moreton and Sophia joined in for a minute or so, before Sanz again called for quiet. He spoke a few more words, then clicked his phone closed. It was the signal for applause from everyone. On the front seat, Moreton wrapped his arm around Sophia.

The following week, a comfortable home 3-1 home victory over Parque del Rey, as Retama returned to the Estadio Antonio Núñez, extended their unbeaten run to five games. A fit-again Santi was drafted in ahead of José Palermo, and his elder brother had a starting place on the left flank as Guido was rested. Vasquez opened the scoring, before the returning Santi and then Swan added further goals. Goals particularly enjoyed by an applauding Esteban in his blue shirt, who seemed to have adopted the veteran as his favourite player. It was something that Moreton teased Swan about, suggesting it was because they were about the same age. A late strike from the visitors had hardly put a stumble into the Retama stride.

Back on the road again the following week, the run continued. Visiting Torre del Olmos, a close and competitive first half preceded the breakthrough when a delightful free kick curled into the top corner by Revi put Retama ahead just after the restart. The defence then held firm against spirited home attacks until, inside the last ten minutes, a through-ball by Swan put Santi in the clear to confirm the victory.

Mirroring the way things were going on the pitch, the relationship between Moreton and Sophia was also developing at pace. On the evening following the win against Torre del Olmos, they went out to dinner with Elena and her new boyfriend, who turned out to be Nicolás, the manager of the team Retama had played in the pre-season games. Moreton had been concerned that, despite the progress made, his poor command of Spanish would leave him very much out of the conversation. With Nicolás keen to hear how Retama were faring in the league, and Sophia acting as translator, it was hardly the case. The conversation also revealed, that there was another link between Nicolás and Moreton. He had been a manager in charge of accounts at Retama Azulejos, and had stayed on when Charlie Broome took over the business.

The following Friday, at training, Moreton was surprised to notice that instead of Gonzalo chauffeuring Billy Swan to the ground, it was Charlie Broome. After setting up the usually light Friday session, Moreton strolled over to where his friend sat, perched on the wall surrounding the pitch, at the bottom of the concrete steps.

'Hi Chaz. How you doing?'

'Yeah, I'm fine thanks, Jon. How are you?'

'Pretty good. The team is really clicking now. Things are shaping up.'

'In more ways than one, I hear.' Broome nodded towards Sophia, overseeing the training session. 'It's OK, Jon. I don't have any spies, Billy told me.'

'Yeah,' came the hesitant reply. Suddenly Moreton felt uneasy about the situation, but didn't really know why. 'Yeah, yeah, of course. To be honest Chaz, I'm… well, I think we're very happy. It's funny how things happen sometimes isn't it?'

Charlie Broome nodded without taking his eyes from the players. 'It is, Jon. It is.'

'Anyway, what are you doing here? Where's Gonzalo?'

'It's his day off. I try to avoid him doing that when Swan needs ferrying about, but he asked if I could make an exception this once, and I said OK. It gave me a chance to have a chat with Swan anyway.' He paused. 'And with you, of course.'

'Yeah, Billy's doing really well now. I'm really surprised. Well, you know… happy of course, but still a bit surprised how quickly he's settled in with the lads. He seems really happy as well. You know, Chaz. For the first time in a good many years, I think he's actually enjoying playing football, you know.'

'Yeah, I think he is.' There was a pause. 'So the team is doing well now, Jon? How do you see things?'

Moreton rubbed his chin pensively. 'Well, we're about mid-table or so, but given the start we had, that's not bad. We're on a bit of a run at the moment, and if we can keep that going, who knows. Billy's been great, and he's fired some of the lads up too. He's become almost inseparable from Victor and Kiko. He reckons they're like the Three Musketeers.'

Jon Moreton was expecting a laugh, or at least a smile from his friend, but all he got was a slow nod. There was clearly something troubling him.

'You OK, Chaz? Business going well?'

'Yeah, sorry, Jon,' Broome snapped back to the present. 'Just a few things on my mind. Just work and business. Nothing for you to worry about. Anyway, get back over there to the players. That's what I'm paying you for.' He laughed. 'Not standing here chatting to me and spoiling my fun watching you lot work in the hot sun!'

Jon Moreton slapped his friend on the shoulder, and jogged back to the players.

He arrived back just as the players were taking a water break. Billy Swan walked over to him, thirstily gulping down the water as he did.

'How is he?' he asked Moreton.

'Ah, he's typical Charlie. Never says much. Got a few things on his mind. Business apparently.'

'Yeah,' Swan replied looking across to where CD Retama's benefactor sat. 'So, I hear.'

The next game was home to Desorio, the town was described as a highly developed holiday resort. Guido returned to his flank position in an otherwise unchanged team, and it was a confident set of Retama players that started the game. Ten minutes in, Swan opened the scoring. Collecting a pass from Revi, he slipped his marker on the edge of the penalty area, swayed inside another challenge and placed the ball into the corner of the net. Celebrations on the bench were echoed on the field as the veteran forward was mobbed by team-mates, and arguments broke out among the Desorio players. The defender that Swan had dismissed with a turn was being roundly blamed for his error, and Jon Moreton began to count on another three points going his way. The confidence was solidified ten minutes later.

Guido outpaced a labouring fullback burnt in the young flyer's slipstream as he tore into the box. The goalkeeper advanced to close down the space, and as Guido shot, the ball struck his knee, to send it ballooning up into the air. Billy

Swan's instinct had guided his movements towards the penalty spot and, as the ball dropped towards him, he nodded it into an unguarded net.

'Billy's on fire here.' Moreton grinned. 'He could get four or five in this mood.'

It wouldn't happen.

With halftime approaching, a ball was played into Swan with a Desorio player closing him down. Seemingly without provocation, the Retama player threw back an elbow and caught the defender across the nose. He fell to the floor as the other visiting players crowded around Swan demanding justice. The referee's red card delivered the inevitable, and Swan walked from the field, head bowed. Moreton couldn't comprehend what had caused his old team-mate to react in such an uncharacteristic way. In his career, Billy Swan had been kicked from pillar to post, but always took his revenge by scoring or humiliating his aggressor with impudent skill, never with violence. Asking Sophia to keep an eye on things for the last few minutes of the half, Moreton followed Swan into the dressing room, slamming the door behind him.

'I know, Jon!' Swan shouted before Moreton could even get a word in. 'Don't say it. I sodding know.'

Moreton shook his head, but couldn't merely stand there saying nothing.

'Why, Billy?' It was a question: a genuine lack of comprehension, rather than mere accusation.

'All game long. All poxy game, this twat's giving me the lip. "You're shit" this and "I'm going to break your leg" that. All sodding game. Then he says that, if I was a man, I'd fight back, but that I only break the legs of girls in nightclubs. Then he said, "What you got, old woman?" So, I showed him.'

'Christ, Billy. You let yourself get wound up by some loudmouth bloke who drinks ten pints a night and thinks he's fit to lace your boots. Stuff me, mate.'

Billy Swan had no answer. He sat there, head bowed, looking at the floor, before pulling off his boots and throwing them down, as the door opened and the players walked in for halftime. Victor and Kiko sat either side of their dejected fellow Musketeer, patting him on the back. Swan nodded and patted each of them on the thigh. 'Yeah, yeah, yeah,' he said quietly, accepting their sympathy, but knowing it changed nothing.

Regaining composure, Moreton had a brief, hushed conversation with Sophia, before announcing his plans.

'Right, we're down to ten, but we can still get this done. Revi, take a breather, I want to put Samuel into the midfield with Matías to give us some extra protection. They're going to see a lot more of the ball now and we need to be solid and organised. Santi, try and drop a little deeper to get involved. They'll be pushing forward. Look for an opportunity to release Guido over the top. One more and they'll be done. All OK?' A general grunting suggested in the affirmative and, after taking a drink, the players left for the second period.

As they walked out, the Desorio players were also leaving their dressing room. Identifying Swan's victim by the plaster across his nose, already turning a bloody scarlet in colour. Moreton called across to him.

'You all right, mate?'

The injured player looked surprised to be addressed in English.

'I've had worse. What's his sodding problem? Is he a bit loose up top?'

Moreton responded to defend his friend. 'If you don't want a reaction, don't provoke it, yeah?'

'What you on about. I never bloody touched him.'

'It's not what you did. It's what you said. A player like that. Someone who has played at the very top. An England international, who's out here playing at this level, at his age. Show a bit of bloody respect. Being a wind-up merchant isn't clever'

'What do you mean? Who is he? England international? I don't recognise him.'

Moreton threw his arm down in a gesture of dismissal. He'd had enough of the conversation and didn't want to be lied to. 'Yeah, whatever,' he said, turning and walking away.

Billy Swan stood in the doorway of the dressing room as the play took on the pattern that Moreton had predicted. Using the extra man, Desorio pressed, but the reinforced midfield and defence held out. Approaching the last fifteen minutes the lead was still intact, but the extra workload was beginning to tell. A ball down the Retama right flank into the penalty area offered Sanz a chance to intercept, but he was a fraction of a second late, and his challenge brought down the visiting forward. A yellow card and a spot kick followed. Striking the ball down the middle from twelve yards, with Torres diving to his left, the penalty taker cut the deficit in half.

The visitors now saw a chance to draw level, and perhaps even drive on for a win. It was all hands to the pump for Moreton's depleted team now. A late corner from the left led to a header on goal and the ball struck the hand of Santi. The effort may have been going wide, and the forward was quick to plead a denial of any intention, but the referee saw things differently. A second red card followed, and a second penalty kick. The same result from the spot meant that for the remaining minutes of the game, Retama would be down to nine men, and clinging on for a draw; fortunately for them, only three more were played, before the referee called a halt.

As his dejected players filed from the pitch, Jon Moreton stood on the sidelines, with his hands on his hips. A game that seemed to be won had slipped away, and now he had both his starting forward players suspended. Swan's punishment for violent conduct would bring three games out, but Santi's harsh handball dismissal, two. The unbeaten run had been preserved, but with six more games to play until the halfway point of the season, if Retama were to have any chance of hitting the promotion target, heroic draws against the odds would not get the job done.

Arrivals and Returns

The mood at training on the following Tuesday was flat, with players merely going through the motions, bereft of any real passion. Both Moreton and Sophia felt similarly, and the promotion required to keep the club alive seemed a distant prospect. The group needed a lift, and as Moreton was setting up some attacking drills with the Palermo brothers in tandem as the strike force to be used in the next game, it came as Sophia's phone rang. At first, Moreton was only vaguely aware that she had left his side, walking a dozen metres or so away, to take the call. Suddenly though, everyone's attention was drawn to her as she shouted in delight, jumping up and down, still holding the phone. The players and Moreton watched as she beamed while speaking. *'Claro. Vale,'* she said excitedly. *'Muy bien. Gracias. Vale! Estoy muy feliz por tus! Si. Adios.'* She closed off the call and rushed back to where Moreton and the players were waiting in anticipation.

'It was Adrián,' she explained in delight, first in Spanish and then in English for Moreton and Swan. 'Ana has had a beautiful healthy little boy. He is small but the doctors have told Adrián that he appears to be strong and healthy. Everything is looking good!'

Cheering and high fives broke out among the players and Sophia threw her arms around Moreton's neck as they hugged delightedly.

It took a few minutes before everyone had settled down again.

Paco Jiménez was the first to speak. *'Ellos han elegido un nombre?'*

Sophia smiled. 'Yes,' she replied. 'The name. I forgot to mention. His name is Javier, little Javi.'

Then, a different tone on Sophia's phone announced the arrival of a text message. Opening it, she smiled and then put her hand to her mouth as tears welled up in her eyes. She showed the screen to Moreton. On it was a picture of a new-born baby, wrapped in pristine white blankets. Moreton passed the phone around to the players as he put an arm around Sophia, sharing the moment of joy. A group of men training for football had transformed into a cooing collection of emotional fathers, brothers and sons as they took turns, and repeated opportunities, to celebrate the picture on the screen.

'I think we should wrap it up for this evening,' Moreton suggested.

Sophia nodded. 'Shall I tell them?'

'Sure.'

'Oh,' she said, quickly grabbing him by the arm. 'There's something else that I forgot to mention. Adrián said that if all goes as well as they expect, he could be back playing in two or three weeks.

'That's great. Only when Ana and Javi are ready for it though. Adrián's place is with them. They're more important than anything else.'

'He knows,' she whispered, reaching up and kissing him on the cheek.

She passed the additional information on to the players as the phone was eventually returned to her. She looked at the picture again, and smiled, whispering to herself, *'Muy guapo.'* Only Jon Moreton heard the hushed tones of her voice and, for a brief second, his mind raced to thoughts of the children he may have with the Spanish woman he had fallen in love with. Sophia clapping her hands and telling the players the session was over for the evening snapped him back to reality. The future that had seemed so flat just minutes ago was now brimming with opportunity and happiness.

Training on Wednesday evening had been as invigorating as the previous evening's had originally been uninspiring. The news had given everyone a lift, even the suspended Billy Swan. Despite both he and Santi being unavailable to play when Retama visited UD Palancio at the weekend, they worked with the Palermo brothers to both boost confidence and assist in transmitting Moreton's plans to them. Bereft of the subtle, beguiling skills of Swan, after discussing the options with Sophia, Moreton had decided to deploy the powerful Juan Palermo as a target man to lead the line. With the Musketeer's razor-sharp rapier temporarily unavailable, Moreton sought the bludgeoning power of the broadsword.

The previous evening, over dinner, Sophia had reminded Moreton of the conversation they had before the season started. She had told him that, although Palancio had only narrowly missed out on promotion the previous season, the team that they would now be facing would be very different. Now in charge of Politanio B, it had been Francisco who had guided the club the previous season. When he left in the summer to return to the club he had previously played for with such distinction, a number of the better Palancio players had seen the departure as a signal that the club was unlikely to challenge again in the new season and had followed him out of the door, with the majority of them joining Estrella Azul.

The league table ahead of the game suggested that Sophia's assessment was certainly on the mark. Palancio were a mere four places from the bottom, winning only twice in eleven games. They had however only conceded nine goals. It seemed that their defence remained efficient, but scoring goals was now more problematic. Sophia felt that, if the new forward line and Moreton's plans worked, there was a good chance of getting a decent result.

The Palancio team that faced Retama certainly had the air of one struggling for players. There was an obvious youthfulness about them, especially among the forwards. Any club losing a successful coach and then having five or six players also leaving were likely to go through a period of transition. Moreton considered that, so long as the younger players brought in to replace those that had left were not an exceptional crop, a team in a state of flux were vulnerable.

When the game got underway, although Retama held much of the possession, and the home team offered little threat in attack, breaking down a stubborn and well-drilled defence proved difficult. The Palermo brothers were working tirelessly, especially Juan who took a physical battering from the uncompromising play of the home defenders without complaint, but their efforts brought little reward. Halftime came and went without a breakthrough and, as the second half progressed in much the same way, Moreton couldn't see a breakthrough happening unless they got a lucky break. The Palancio defence was lying deep, negating much of Guido's pace, with little ground to run into behind them, and each time Vasquez received the ball he was double-banked by defenders.

There seemed little point in keeping four defenders at the back as the game entered the final twenty minutes, and Moreton withdrew Felipe Blanco and sent Samuel on to partner Matías in the midfield. He pushed Revi further forward, but to no great effect, the talented ball player suffering the same fate as the Palermo brothers engulfed by the massed ranks of Palancio defenders. Ten minutes remained when Sophia suggested to Moreton that they try something different, just to change things. Moreton saw scant reason to argue. He called Sebastián to come and sit next to him.

As the squad's youngest player spoke perfect English, it was easy for Moreton to explain what he had in mind. At the next break in play, he withdrew the exhausted Juan Palermo and sent Sebastián on in his place. Quickly advising his team-mates of the plan, he explained to Guido to move onto the other flank alongside Vasquez to overload on the right, and that he would then play on the left. Five minutes passed without much change, then Vasquez picked up the ball, exchanging sharp passes with Guido as defenders closed down the two attackers. He then threaded the ball through a gap and Guido hared after it.

Reaching the pass before it ran out of play, he squared the ball towards the near post. Both Revi and José Palermo raced towards the cross, tracked by three defenders. As it reached the posse of players, a series of ricochets saw the ball ping around, before running out the other side of the goal towards where Sebastián, heeding his coach's instructions had remained in a wide position. His marker had been drawn towards the melee of players but now tried to recover his ground. Nimbly skipping inside the onrushing challenge Sebastián found himself clear on the goal. A low shot through the legs of the advancing goalkeeper gave Retama the lead.

It was Sebastián's first goal for the club and, as he wheeled away in delight, he raised his shirt to reveal a vest with a scribbled message. In black marker pen it had an outline of a heart and the name "Javi." As the other players reached him, they too revealed vests with the same message. They ran towards where Moreton, Sophia and the other players were sitting on the bench. Sophia took out her phone and snapped the picture, before texting it to Adrián. Palancio had hardly threatened in the entire game, and that wouldn't change in the time that remained. Retama had won 0-1.

Back in the coach, Sanz was heard shouting for everyone to listen. He had his phone held in the air, and through the speaker, everyone could hear Adrián and Ana talking, saying thank you for the goal dedicated to their new son and the picture that they would treasure forever. Sophia explained what they were saying, as Jon Moreton eased back into his chair contentedly.

'You know,' he said quietly. 'That's the sort of win that makes all the difference.'

Sophia placed her hand on his thigh and squeezed gently.

'Yes. And that's the sort of gesture that makes a team.'

Moreton nodded in agreement. Just then his phone rang, and the name

"Chaz" appeared on the screen.

'Ah, I'm going to enjoy this.'

Training passed the following week without problem, and on Friday, there was anticipation about the team Moreton would select. Fourth in the league, Estrella Azul, complete with the four former Palancio players would be the next visitors to the Estadio Antonio Núñez. Facing a high-flying team was unlikely to mean another siege, and Moreton reverted back to the starting line-up he had deployed against Palancio.

As soon as the match began, the visitors quickly made it clear that anything Retama took from the game would be hard won. After a mere ten minutes, Estrella Azul were two goals clear. The first, a free kick immaculately curled into the top corner of the home goal with Torres helpless. Then, neat interplay in midfield saw Victor drawn forward out of position, a sidestep beat him, and a shot from the edge of the box did the same to Torres. Sensing the need to stay in the game, if anything was to be gained, he encouraged both Vasquez and Guido to drop deeper and help out the defence. It would mean the Palermo brothers being isolated, but for the moment, it was a price worth paying.

The plan at least it had staunched the flow of opposition goals. As halftime approached there had been no further concessions. Then, as Torres struck a goal kick long up field, he hobbled to the floor holding the back of his lower leg. The ball was scuttled out of play and the referee called Sophia onto the pitch to check the injury. Rotating fingers confirmed Moreton's fears. It was a calf muscle strain, and Jiménez was sent on to replace the stricken Torres. At least Moreton had the comfort of having the vastly experienced Jiménez to call on, but that would hardly be the sort of weapon required to turn the game around.

At the break, seeking to get a firmer grip in midfield, the younger Palermo brother was removed, with Samuel sent on and Revi pushed further forwards. The second half began encouragingly. The visitors had settled into a comfortable pattern and seemed to have convinced themselves that the game was won. The two holding midfielders for Retama worked to wrest control of the game, but the visitors appeared less than concerned as that happened, so long as they didn't threaten to score. Ten minutes after the restart, though, that's precisely what happened.

A long punt out of defence by Kiko saw Juan Palermo challenge for the ball in the air with two defenders around him, thirty-five yards from the visitors' goal. Chancing his arm, Revi ran towards the space behind the back line, just as Palermo's head managed to flick the ball towards him. Clear, and bearing down on the goalkeeper, Revi never looked like missing. A drop of the shoulder sent the goalkeeper to the floor and he rolled the ball into the empty net. If the Estrella Azul players required a wake-up call, it had been delivered, and a few yards from where Moreton and Sophia sat, the visiting coach bellowed at his players to ensure the message had been received. It had. Just three minutes later, the two-goal lead was restored as a corner from the left was firmly headed past Jiménez.

Moreton's players battled and pressed but, having been shaken from their lethargy once, Estrella players were unlikely to offer another way back into the game for the home team. A second home goal would come, but, with less than two minutes to play when Vasquez tapped home after a shot from Revi had been palmed out towards him, there was little chance of it affecting the result. It was the first game Retama had lost since the fractious defeat at Mostodra two months previously, but to Moreton it felt like another stumble on the road. Every fixture from here on in would be important, and every point vital. The next game had particular significance outside of football for Jon Moreton. On the following weekend, Retama would travel to a small village in the mountains to the north, and visit Árboles Altos, where Sophia's parents lived.

Moreton reinstated the returning Santi in place of the younger Palermo at the following Friday's training, and in the evening he and Sophia ate dinner at Bella Cucina. Both were aware of the potential importance of Moreton meeting Sophia's parents, but, for much of the week, the subject had been nervously avoided. As they awaited their meals to arrive, Sophia decided it was time.

'Jon,' she said sweetly but firmly. 'We need to talk about Sunday.'

Moreton pursed his lips pensively.

'Are you concerned about it?' she asked.

'Something tells me that you're not talking about the game, are you?' he replied.

Smiling, Sophia shook her head in reply. 'It'll be fine, Jon. They are really nice. Honestly.' She took his hand in hers. 'They're just like me. And you like me, don't you?'

Moreton couldn't help but laugh happily at the playfully endearing logic.

'Not really. I love you.'

He raised her hand and kissed it softly.

'And they will love you, Jon,' she replied, squeezing his hand. 'And do you know why?'

'Because I'm nice?' he offered with hopeful mock innocence.

'No, Jon. Well, you are nice. Of course, you are and they will like you because of that. But mainly they will like you because you love me, and I love you, and you make me happy.' She paused. 'OK?'

'Hmm. Yeah, OK. It's a fair cop I suppose.'

She slapped his hand playfully just as their meals arrived.

'How's it going to work?' Moreton asked, somewhat more seriously as they began to eat.

'I'm not sure what you mean.'

'Well, when are we meeting them? I mean, before the game, during or when?'

'No, Jon. I've told them that before the game and at halftime we are working, so they shouldn't distract you or me.'

'That makes sense.'

'So, I have said that after the game, we can meet for about ten minutes to say hello and chat, but then we have to go back on the coach with the players.'

Moreton nodded again. Ten minutes didn't sound too bad. He could do that he thought to himself. So long as he didn't fall over his own feet.

That night, as Sophia slept next to him, Moreton lay awake looking up at the ceiling unable to relax sufficiently to allow sleep to engulf him. He had never been comfortable with meeting people, outside of football anyway, but this was an entirely different matter. What if they had a similar feeling to Paco Jiménez about Sophia and Alvaro? Would they dislike him because he had been the cause of the split between them? At least they couldn't blame him for stopping Sophia studying. After they had discussed the matter, she had applied herself vigorously to the work and was doing well. His over-riding concern was what if they didn't like him, and the fact he and Sophia were, to all intents and purposes, living together? Would they resent him for that? Would they dislike him anyway? He turned to look at the clock. It told him that ninety minutes had passed since midnight. 'Enough for a game,' was the thought that rushed into his head. Football had always been his solace as well as his passion. Two minutes later he was asleep.

The journey to Árboles Altos took a couple of hours to complete, and for much of it, Moreton was preoccupied by the thought of meeting Sophia's parents. When they arrived at the village, it was easy for him to understand why Sophia had such fond memories of it as a child. The compact ground was set just off the town square, surrounded by trees that also lined the road as they entered the village. It seemed idyllic. Heading from the coach towards the dressing rooms, Moreton noticed Sophia giving a small wave towards a couple standing in the car park. Moreton recognised them from the picture he had seen in Sophia's apartment many weeks previously. He tried to smile at them too, feeling too self-conscious to wave, and was pleased that they seemed to smile back at him.

The game itself was disappointing for Retama and their two coaches. In a scrappy and undistinguished display, the team struggled for any coherence. Juan Palermo playing up front ahead of Santi was hardly successful and despite Moreton taking the elder Palermo brother off, putting Samuel on and dropping him into midfield to allow Revi to push forward in support of Santi, it seemed to make little difference. Following the loss against Estrella Azul, this result and performance merely confirmed to Moreton how much they had missed Billy Swan. As the full-time whistle went with the game remaining goalless, the Retama coach could at least console himself with the fact that he would have the veteran forward available for the next game.

After shaking hands with their opposite numbers from the home bench, Sophia grabbed Moreton's arm. He swallowed deeply as they reached Sophia's parents. Both were grey-haired, but looked young despite that. Her father was tall with a refined and confident air about him, her mother shorter with silver-grey cropped hair, that still had flecks of the deep black locks of Sophia, and a pair of sunglasses sitting atop her head. She had the air of a great beauty when younger that had now evolved into a mature charm, still clearly attractive. Despite himself, the smiles they offered towards him as they approached eased his mind.

'Jon. This is my father.' The elder man reached out his hand. Moreton took it and smiled.

'Please,' he said in perfect English. 'Call me Joaquín.'

Those three words were sufficient to break down the imaginary barriers that

Jon Moreton had constructed in his mind about the meeting. He relaxed.

'And this, is my mother.'

Unconsciously, Moreton bent down towards her, and they kissed on each cheek.

'Dolores,' she said.

'Thank you. I can see where Sophia gets her beauty from now, Señora Garrigues,' he said with a sincerity that he almost immediately realised may have sounded like mere casual flattery.

Dolores Garrigues, smiled and patted him playfully on the arm. Turning to Sophia, she spoke in English, clearly so that Moreton would understand, despite her putting her hand to the side of her mouth in mock conspiratorial secrecy: 'Ah, now I know why you said he was quite charming, Sophia.'

They all laughed and Joaquín Garrigues nodded to Moreton. 'I can see Jon,' he said. 'That we're all going to get along very well.'

He paused, then added: 'Of course, in a different world, you two could be working for me now, couldn't you?'

Moreton nodded and smiled, although unsure what Sophia's father had meant by that.

And that was it. Sophia insisted that they had to leave, otherwise they would be holding everyone up. Goodbyes were said.

'You were right,' Moreton said to Sophia softly. 'They are lovely. Just like you.'

As the pair walked away, Joaquín Garrigues called after them.

'When Árboles Altos visit Retama, we will come along and watch, and perhaps stay overnight. You will have dinner with us, yes?'

Moreton smiled and called back. 'Of course, that would be great. Thanks.'

The elder man nodded, as his wife added: 'Don't worry, Sophia. We will book a hotel. We understand how things are.'

Feeling slightly like errant schoolchildren caught bunking off class, both Moreton and Sophia blushed in embarrassment at the implication.

Twenty minutes later, on the journey back to Retama, Moreton asked Sophia what her father had meant when he said that they could have been working for him.

'At one stage, along with some friends, he was interested in buying CD Retama, when it was up for sale, but the deal that Señor Broome did was completed very quickly, without many people knowing, so it was all too late.'

'Ah, I see.'

He paused for a moment, clearly mulling something over in his mind.

'What, Jon?'

'Well, 'I guess if Joaquín had bought the club, he would never have sacked García would he?'

Sophia nodded slowly.

'And, in that case,' he continued. 'You and I wouldn't have ever met. You'd be working here with García, and I'd be back in England either coaching some non-league club in the Midlands, or filling shelves at a local supermarket.'

He laughed slightly. 'Or probably both.'

Sophia looked up at him and smiled. 'I'm glad Señor Broome bought the club,' she said looking into his eyes.

'Me too.'

Before the home game against UD Araganza, there was a particular buzz around training on the following Wednesday. On the previous day, Sophia had received a call from Adrián to say that he was ready to return, would be at training the following day – and that he would bringing Ana and a certain young boy along so that he could say hello. Inevitably, the visit caused an unavoidable disruption to the session, but Moreton recognised that it was a small price to pay for the boost in morale everyone got from having Adrián back and seeing the joy he had with Ana and their new baby. At the same time, though, he was aware of the implications.

Taking Sophia to one side, as Ana sat and watched training, pointing out to Javier and clapping every time Adrián had the ball, he outlined his thoughts. With Swan being out for three weeks, he was concerned about potential injury as occurred in the first game of the season, and he had similar concerns about drafting Adrián straight back into the starting eleven. Since UD Araganza weren't a particularly strong team he told her he was thinking of leaving both Swan and Adrián on the bench, together with Santi, and perhaps starting the Palermo brothers in attack.

Sophia nodded and understood the rationale of the move. She was less convinced about dropping Santi out though, especially as he had only just returned to the team. Moreton explained though that they were still short of halfway through the season, that Santi was still very young and his goals would be really important to them. She was convinced.

'I wanted you to be on board before I decided,' he told her. 'Your opinion is important, and I know you wouldn't just agree if you thought it was a bad idea.'

'No,' she said. 'It makes perfect sense. Let's do it.'

The team was announced on Friday after training as usual and Moreton was careful to explain the decisions. There were three games left before the midwinter break and the halfway point in the league. After the poor start, there had been a recovery of sorts, but still a few stumbles. If they were to have a serious chance of hitting the promotion play-offs at the end of the season, they would need to massively improve on results in the new year, but taking at least seven points from these last three games would be important, as each point gained now, was one less that they needed to accumulate after the break.

On the day of the game, Jon Moreton sat on the bench alongside Sophia and three players who would, in any normal game, have been part of the regular starting eleven. The visitors were hardly one of the most threatening teams that Retama had faced. For most of the first period, the home defence coped with relative ease, whilst the Palermo brothers worked to force an opening.

Ten minutes ahead of the break, Moreton's trigger finger was twitching on the substitution button when Retama went ahead. A dribble by Vasquez was ended at the expense of a corner and the cross was powerfully headed home by Kiko. As soon as the scorer's identity was clear, Billy Swan was on his feet calling Kiko and Victor towards him, so that the Musketeers could celebrate in time-honoured fashion. At halftime, Felipe Blanco was withdrawn and Adrián restored to the left flank of the defence.

The second period was much the same as the first, but a single goal lead is always fragile, and with thirty minutes to play, Moreton sought some insurance as the Palermo brothers were replaced by Santi and Billy Swan. The desired effect was not long in coming. Perhaps feeling he had a point to prove, Swan settled into the game and immediately fired it into action. Collecting the ball on the halfway line from Matías, he turned past the first defender and advanced towards the Araganza penalty area. Side-stepping another challenge, he exchanged a one-two with Santi before entering the area, collecting the return, strolling past the goalkeeper with nonchalant ease and rolling the ball into the net. A broad grin broke out on Moreton's face. As the Musketeers celebrated on the pitch, Sophia patted Moreton on the leg and returned the smile. Standing by the bench, Esteban, in his Retama shirt clapped enthusiastically, and even waved an imaginary sword for a moment.

The visiting players were now resigned to the defeat, and Billy Swan was in search of another goal. It came with ten minutes remaining. A pass from Adrián ran down the touchline with Guido in hot pursuit. Gathering control, he crossed towards Santi who had made a run towards the near post, taking defenders with him. Astutely though, as the ball reached him, he stepped over it allowing the pass to run on towards an unmarked Swan, sauntering casually in the penalty area. Calm control and a pass into the corner of the net closed out the game.

The following week, with Adrián, Santi and Swan restored to the starting eleven, the Retama team had more of the regular look about them when they travelled to San Vicente. Another three-goal haul without reply was more than sufficient to secure the points, thanks to a strike by Santi and a brace from Revi. Six of the seven points that Moreton had targeted were now in the bag, and only the visit of Torreaño CF remained before the mid-season break. Moreton selected the same team for the game.

After arriving in a luxury coach, liveried in the club colours of red with narrow white stripes, the players and officials of Torreaño CF, wearing club suits or tracksuits, walked around the pitch towards the dressing rooms. Sophia and Moreton went to greet them and exchange pleasantries. Walking behind and a little separate from the group of other players, talking to one of the coaches was a tall figure in the same red and white tracksuit. 'That's Montero,' Sophia confided to Moreton as they were passed by the last of the Torreaño party. 'He doesn't look anything special, does he?'

Moreton shook his head slowly. 'They never do until they're on the pitch,' he replied cautiously. 'Two straight promotions in two years, and he scored what? Thirty-eight goals last year in the division below? What's he got this term, so far?'

They both watched as the red clad party disappeared into the visitors' dressing room before Sophia replied. 'Eight, I think. Perhaps he's finding it a bit harder in this division.'

Moreton pursed his lips in contemplation. 'Let's go and get the guys ready,' he said in an unconvincingly upbeat way.

With the game under way, Moreton's comments about Montero only looking "special" on the pitch were borne out. Not only impressive in possession, linking up play as the visitors pressed confidently forwards, his movement without the ball impressed Moreton the most. Ahead of the game he had detailed Matías to sit deeper and provide cover if Montero dragged Kiko or Victor out of position. It was shown to be a prudent move as the rangy forward pulled the Retama back line about, driving into the corridors between central defender and fullback. It was also clear that, although Montero was without doubt the star player, Torreaño were hardly a one-man team and the club had supplied enough of a supporting cast to ensure their star could shine. Despite all the pressure the Retama back line held out and apart from a couple of comfortable saves from Jiménez, the half-time break was reached without too much trouble.

Moreton was in pensive mood as he walked back to the dressing room. The Retama forward line had been anonymous for much of the game with both Santi and Swan starved of possession as the visitors dominated the play. Despite keeping a clean sheet – the defence had not conceded a goal for more than three and a half games now – Moreton was aware that the pressure would increase as tired legs and minds took an inevitable toll. He needed to reinforce his back line, even if it meant sacrificing things further forwards. Turning to Sophia, he stopped them both just outside of the dressing room. 'I'm thinking of taking Billy off and putting Samuel to bolster the midfield in front of the defence,' he confided. 'What do you think?'

Sophia thought for a moment. 'I'm not sure, Jon. It would mean leaving Santi up front on his own, and he's been isolated enough already, and you'll just be inviting more pressure by leaving us without a way out.'

Moreton nodded slowly. It was a valid point. 'Yeah, I know. I just think that we need the extra legs at the back. I'd take a point now if offered it.'

Sophia was clearly not convinced. 'The problem is, that by doing this, you may just be inviting the very thing you're trying to avoid.' She paused. 'Thank you for consulting with me, Jon. But when you think one thing and I think another, you must decide. Whatever you do, I'll be standing beside you though.'

He reached down and kissed her gently on the lips. 'Thanks. I think it's the right thing.'

She smiled at him. 'Then, so do I.'

Billy Swan hardly seemed overjoyed at the changes when they were announced, but he just shrugged and slipped a top on over his Retama shirt. Samuel went out before the others to warm up, followed by Sophia and the remaining players. Moreton sat on one of the benches in the dressing room, still not totally convinced he had done the right thing. Only Billy Swan was left there with him. His old team-mate patted him on the shoulder as he got up to leave.

'Don't sweat it, Jon,' he said. 'I was hardly in the game, anyway.'

Moreton nodded slowly. 'Yeah, I know. Cheers Billy.'

The second half developed very much as Sophia had predicted. The visitors pressed hard, with Retama hardly enjoying any possession to speak of. Chasing the ball, almost consistently, was always going to be a drain on energy, and as time ticked by Moreton was keen to add fresh legs to his back-pedalling team.

Felipe Blanco was sent on for Vasquez with twenty minutes to play and then, five minutes later, Juan Palermo replaced Santi, with Moreton hoping that the muscular replacement may be able to hold possession up field and give the hard-pressed defence at least a little respite. Two minutes later though, the coach's plans were undone.

A cross into the Retama box was headed clear by Kiko, but a visiting player collected possession and fired in a powerful strike. Paco Jiménez threw himself to his left, deflecting the swerving shot onto the post. The ball bounced out towards the penalty spot, and as the goalkeeper tried to recover his ground, Montero illustrated why he was being paid so much money. A striker's instincts to the fore, he was first to the ball and crashed it into the net. The visitors' bench erupted with joy, as Moreton bowed his head. Sophia placed a hand on his shoulder. 'That could have happened at any time, Jon. At any time.' She paused. 'It had nothing to do with the changes you made. It nearly worked.'

Moreton smiled unconvincingly. 'Yeah, I know,' he said.

After the final whistle, the players sat in the dressing room with Moreton and Sophia. If the coach had any inner doubts, now wasn't the time to put them on display. He needed to lift his players.

'OK,' he said. 'That was tough, but we nearly came through it. Look, we've taken seven points from the last twelve, and only conceded one goal in four games. We're not a long way off being a squad that can deliver on what we all want.' He paused. 'We have twenty-three points on the board, after losing the first four games of the season. That's not too bad. Now we need to prove that we're a second-half team. It's halftime in the league, so we can all take a break for the holidays. When we come back though, we need to have a flying start. We need to improve our first-half points tally by at least fifty percent. If we do that – and we can, I know we can – we won't be far away at the end of the season. So, go away and enjoy your holidays. The work starts again when we return.'

Ascent

Jon Moreton had never experienced such a hiatus in mid-season when working in England. It was a novel experience for him, and one that he didn't really enjoy. Sophia was going to spend the holidays with her parents in Árboles Altos. She had invited, almost pleaded with him, to go with her. For two reasons, however, he had declined.

Firstly, he was a little uncomfortable about spending the holidays with people he hardly knew and, secondly, he wanted to go to England to visit his parents. Despite regular telephone conversations, it had been the best part of six months since he had seen them. Sophia was just as reluctant to travel with him to England, as he had been about the journey to Árboles Altos. They spent the break in separate countries.

When he returned to Retama, after meeting up with Sophia again and spending their first few hours wrapped in each other's arms, as the afternoon turned into evening, Moreton related how generous Charlie Broome had been, arranging and paying for his flights and even supplying him with a hire car while in England.

'That's really nice of him,' Sophia said, as they both stared up at the ceiling, lying side-by-side in the bed at his apartment.

'Yeah. But I guess he's employed me to do a job and wants to make sure I deliver for him.'

'Anyway, I'm worth looking after, aren't I?'

Sophia understood the implication in his voice. She rolled over until almost lying on top of him. Her warm body and soft, smooth skin pressed against him.

'Hmm,' she said softly. 'I'm not so sure.'

But she was. Twenty minutes later they both slept, weary but contented.

The heat of the Spanish sun, feeling so oppressive during his early days in the country, had eased, with the passing months, but it was still pleasant most days, if a little more inclined to the odd, brief, sometimes ferocious downpour. When they returned to the Estadio Antonio Núñez for the first training session of the second half of the season, there was no mid-January bite to the air, merely a feeling of something renewed. Moreton and Sophia had arrived early, so that they could greet each of the players as they arrived.

Each was greeted with a kiss on both cheeks from Sophia and a warm, '*Feliz año!*' Moreton shook each player's hand, and tried to repeat Sophia's greeting. Those that could, and it was an increasing number, replied to him in English, 'Happy New Year!' Only Adrián received an additional greeting from Sophia. '*Javi disfrutó su primera Navidad?*' she asked. The beaming smile on Adrián's face was answer enough.

Billy Swan was the last to arrive and after receiving the same greeting from Sophia, he went across to where Moreton was standing and shook his hand.

'Happy New Year, Billy.'

'Yeah, mate. Same to you.'

'Did you go back home for the holidays?'

'No point. Back there it's snow and cold and rain. And what have I got to go back to? No. I just stayed here in the hotel. I did meet up with Kiki Dee and Meldrew just after Christmas for a couple of drinks, but they didn't stay long. Neither of them drink, Jon. Just Coke and orange juice. So, I just watched a few videos and put my feet up.'

Jon Moreton was sad for his friend. 'Sorry, Billy,' he said.

'Nah, don't worry about it. Any other year, I'd have been out at parties, hooking up with a bit of skirt and then getting too plastered to be able to remember anything about what I'd done.'

It was an upbeat tone designed to convince the speaker as much as the listener, but Moreton dropped into line as required.

'Fair enough then, Billy. You ready to go?'

Billy Swan did a quick double shuffle of his feet.

'Ready? Are you bloody kidding? I've been bored out of my tree for a week. Show me a couple of trees, Jon boy. I'm ready to pull 'em up.'

Billy Swan trotted over to join the rest of the players singing: 'I've got the music in me,' as loud as it was off key.

Moreton turned to Sophia and shook his head in mock admonition.

It was Friday, and with no game that weekend this first session back would be very easy paced. There was plenty of time to settle into things the following week, before the first game of the second half of the season, away to Politanio B, the team that had crushed Retama 5-2 in the opening game of the season. The players were running through a gentle heading and passing drill when Sophia's phone rang. She walked a few paces away from the session to take the call, returning a couple of minutes later. 'Jon,' she said gathering his attention. 'I've got some news.'

The call had been from a friend of hers from university, who now worked in Madrid for a sports newspaper. She had told Sophia that there was a strong rumour going around that Francisco would shortly be promoted to take over the Politanio first team. The club had struggled in the Segunda in the early part of the season, and had dismissed their coach before the mid-season break. After Francisco's success both with Palancio and then the club's B team – they were top of the league – he was seen as the obvious candidate to take over. But there was more. It seemed that if he was given the job, he would be taking four or five players from the B team with him to play in the first team squad. If it were true, what had seemed like a very difficult first game after the break, was suddenly and unexpectedly taking on an entirely different perspective. Over the weekend, the news was confirmed. No replacement had been announced and it seemed likely that Retama's first opponents would not only be compelled to field a weakened team, they would also be in the hands of a caretaker coach. Fate had just presented CD Retama with a belated Christmas gift.

The following week, as training was ramped up, Moreton had to decide whether to restore the fit again Torres in goal, or stay with Jiménez. There was a natural inclination to bring back the younger man, if only to freshen up the competition for places in the team, but having conceded only a single goal across the previous four games, it would have been harsh on the veteran goalkeeper. Moreton decided to leave things as they were, and launch the second half of the season with the same starting eleven as had finished the previous one.

Politanio's B team, didn't play at the club's main stadium, but on a pitch used as part of their training complex nearby. Nevertheless, the towering stands, topped with floodlights, still dominated, a constant reminder perhaps of what players in the B team should aspire to. The team that faced Retama for the first match of the resumed league programme, though, seemed anything but inspired. Although wearing the same red shirts and white shorts as the team that had torn Retama asunder, the collection of players was unrecognisable in comparison. Perhaps it was the loss of their inspirational coach, or maybe the realisation that without four players promoted to the first team squad their chances of hitting that higher level were more distant than they had hoped. Whatever the reason, or combination of reasons, Retama were clearly the better team throughout the game and, when Santi netted goals either side of the half-time break, the first courtesy of a back heel through pass from Swan, the points were never in doubt. Jon Moreton had his team's flying start. It set a trend.

The next few games glided by as Retama struck a rich seam of form. Universidad San Juan visited the Estadio Antonio Núñez, and were sent packing to do extra homework after a 4-0 home victory. Goals from Santi, Guido, Swan and Vasquez were highlights, but just as satisfying to the coach was another clean sheet for the defence. Initially the visit to Independiente Lacitana looked as if it may trip up the Retama march, as they fell behind after only five minutes, but by now confidence was coursing through the blue-shirted players and second-half goals by each of the Palermo brothers – both coming on as substitutes after Swan and Guido had taken minor knocks – turned the game.

The early season game at CD Mostodra had been marred by bad feeling, but as the local rivals arrived at the Estadio Antonio Núñez stadium, it was clear that the tension had been lifted. Diego had been left at home, and both teams were on their best behaviour. Moreton had considered putting Juan Palermo into the starting eleven following his goal against Lacitana but, given the potential for rekindling any simmering ill feeling, had decided instead to let the younger Palermo brother carry the family honours as Santi was rested and Samuel took over in midfield from Matías for the same reason.

The decision was borne out when José put the home side ahead after ten minutes and a strike from Swan, volleying home at the back post after a cross by Vasquez, doubled the lead. Inevitably, as the visitors were forced to push further forward in forlorn pursuit of a comeback, the mercurial Guido raced clear to notch the third goal. Retama had started the second half of the season with four straight wins.

The following Monday morning, Jon Moreton was preparing breakfast when his phone rang. Picking it up, he saw the name "Chaz" displayed on the screen.

He offered a cheery '*Hola!*'

Charlie Broome, sounded very upbeat as well. 'Morning Jon. I hear things are no the up.'

'Yeah. I'm not getting carried away and there's still lots of work to do, but things are moving in the right direction.'

There was a moment's pause before Broome spoke again. 'That's good, Jon. How do you fancy coming round for a coffee and chat around ten?'

'Can you make it eleven? Sophia's going into town to meet up with some friends for lunch, so that would work better for me.'

'Sure. Eleven it is. I'm here all day anyway. There's no rest for the wicked, Jon.'

Two hours later, Jon Moreton walked into Charlie Broome's office, waving to Gonzalo who was serving behind one of the customer counters.

'Have a seat, Jon. I just wanted a bit of a catch up to see how things are. I keep meaning to get in touch to arrange dinner or something, but work here just eats up the time.'

Moreton settled himself into one of the smaller chairs facing his friend, as the door opened and Broome's secretary entered with two cups of coffee.

'Thanks,' Broome said as his was placed down.

'*Muchas gracias*,' offered Moreton, in turn.

'Right,' Broome said. 'So, how's it going?'

For the next fifteen minutes as they each took sips of their coffee, Moreton updated his friend on events: the games, the wins, how players were now looking inspired and growing in confidence. Goals were flowing and the defence was solid. Also, how he was filtering in other players, both to give them all a game, keep them involved, and also to rest other players at the same time. 'All in all. I have to say things are going well.'

Charlie Broome nodded slowly. 'Are we going to make promotion, Jon? Or have the first few games of the season cost us too much lost ground?'

'Chaz, I can't say. We've got a chance. Politanio losing Francisco will hurt them. They'll get over the shock, but I think the main dangers are Estrella Azul and Torreaño. That Montero of theirs is key for them.'

'Perhaps we should have bought him in instead of Billy Swan, Jon?'

'I don't know, Chaz. Billy's been great for us.'

Charlie Broome smiled. 'I was only kidding, Jon. I couldn't have afforded the money they're paying that other guy anyway.'

There was a moment's silence before Broome picked up again: 'So, that's the football. How are you, Jon?'

Moreton was taken aback for a moment. It seemed like a very "un-Charlie Broome" thing to ask.

'Yeah, I'm good,' he replied, regaining his composure. 'Yeah, really good to be fair. The team's doing well.'

'No, Jon,' Broome laughed a little. 'Not the team. Forget football for a moment. How are you? How's Sophia? Are you two still like lovebirds?'

Moreton was so unused to his friend asking about such aspects of his life. The questions sounded strange and made him feel a little uncomfortable.

'She's fine, Chaz,' he slightly stumbled. 'We're both fine. We're happy if that's what you mean.'

'That's great, Jon. I guess that I'm responsible for bringing you two together, so I just wanted to see how you were, both of you, together.'

'Thanks, Chaz. How's business?'

Jon Moreton really had little care for the explanation that Charlie Broome offered him about how he was improving things and making the business more profitable. It was merely a device to move the conversation onto less contentious grounds, somewhere where Moreton didn't feel the sands shifting beneath his feet. An hour later he was sitting on the balcony of his apartment, contemplating whether to go for a swim before lunch.

The following weekend's game was away to UD Callosa. If Retama could notch another win, they then had three home games in succession to keep the run going. It was the return fixture of the game where Jiménez had conceded a couple of goals, but that was settled and behind them now. If there had been any slight inclination to rest Jiménez for the game, Moreton quickly dismissed it. It appeared to be a wise decision, as the veteran again kept a clean sheet and Santi's second-half goal won the game.

Five wins in a row had been an outstanding start, since the league programme began again, but San Esteban had been a difficult game earlier in the season, when injuries had caused the team to fight out a goalless draw. With a run of success boosting confidence, however, Moreton was expecting a different sort of result in the game back at home, and decided to shuffle his players a little. Sanz had been outstanding but needed a rest and Moreton decided this was the right time. In came Felipe Blanco with the skipper's armband passing to Adrián. Young Sebastián came in for Revi and partnered Samuel in midfield. The younger Palermo came in for Swan, and the older sibling took his old place on the left flank instead of Guido.

For all Moreton's confidence, as the referee blew the final whistle the scoreline remained blank, despite attempts to turn the game by throwing on Swan, Santi and Revi as the second-half minutes drifted away. Retama's run of victories had stuttered to a halt. That evening as they sat eating dinner on Moreton's balcony, Sophia tried to assuage any feelings of guilt he may have been suffering from. 'This is football, Jon,' she said.

Moreton understood what she was saying, and knew there was more than a grain of truth in it. He still felt responsible, though.

'Look, Jon. Those players needed a rest. You did the right thing. If you hadn't, they could have suffered fatigue injuries, pulled muscles and sprains, and they would have been out for weeks. This way we only missed them for one game, and now, when they come back, they will be fresher and the team will be even more determined to start another run of wins.'

Moreton smiled, this time with more conviction. 'I love you,' he said.

He hoped she was right.

The next four games would show that she was.

With Retama's first-choice players restored to the starting line-up, Sobrolepeña Industrial's visit was never going to be enjoyable for them. A hat trick from Santi and a brace from Swan handed out a five-goal mauling with a late consolation goal for the visitors only serving to irritate the Retama defenders and coach.

When they had visited Costa Locos earlier in the season, the newly promoted club had been surfing a wave of confidence, sitting near the top of the league. Now, however, the tide had turned as defeats gnawed away at optimism and a string of games without victory left them looking like easy prey for the rapacious Retama forwards. Plundering from the right flank, Vasquez had netted twice before the break and Guido added another just after the restart, all set up by astute play from Swan. The veteran then capped an outstanding display by beating two players in a couple of yards, advancing into the penalty box to draw the goalkeeper, before squaring to substitute José to score the fourth goal.

It had been a sublime performance, and a delighted Moreton congratulated each of his players as they left the pitch. Turning to Sophia, he smiled broadly and nodded with satisfaction, but her attention seemed to be elsewhere.

'Jon,' she said quietly. 'Look around you.'

He did so, but noticed nothing unusual.

'What?'

'Look around you. Look at the people. All of the people.'

Following her instruction, he looked around at the fans still standing and applauding the players as they disappeared into the dressing room.

Moreton hardly ever noticed the crowd watching any of the games he had coached or played in, a mere off-stage buzzing in his ears serving as a backdrop to the real focus of his attention. Now, however, as he scanned the concrete-stepped sides of the Estadio Antonio Núñez, he could appreciate Sophia's comment. The early games of the season had hardly garnered sufficient numbers for the assembled people to justify the epithet of a "crowd." The scene now was very different. With the improving results, supporters who had deserted the team through the bad times over recent years, had begun to return. After the dispiriting start to the season, the recoveries, setbacks and rich form after the mid-winter break, Retama were now improbably top of the league, and had a following worthy of that lofty position.

A visit to Parque del Rey leant further evidence to a growing conviction. The home club was now struggling at the foot of the table and the result never seemed in doubt. A rare strike by Matías gave Moreton's team a lead that they never looked like losing and when Swan scored the second, nodding home a cross from Guido with a dozen minutes remaining it merely confirmed something had hardly ever been in doubt.

Retama were six points clear at the top of the league. The next game would see Árboles Altos visit, together with Sophia's parents. The result of the game would go well for the club and, after Estrella Azul and Politanio B played out a draw on the same day, their lead at the top of the table would stretch to eight points. By the end of that same evening though, the prospects of CD Retama achieving promotion looked to be in severe peril.

Fall

The following Sunday morning, Sophia was out of bed and showered before Moreton had awoken. With a towel wrapped around her, she returned to the bedroom with a cup of coffee, placing it down on the cupboard by the side of the sleeping Moreton before gently kissing him on the cheek to rouse him from slumber. '*Hola*,' she whispered softly, kissing him again, this time on the lips. '*Hola*,' he replied, smiling after their lips had reluctantly parted.

'I have to go and meet my parents this morning,' she reminded him, returning to the bathroom to dress. 'I've made coffee,' she added pointing to the cup of steaming liquid by his side. '*Te quiero*,' he mouthed softly as she walked away. Ten minutes later, Jon Moreton was sitting up in bed draining the last of his coffee when Sophia returned from the bathroom, dressed and ready to leave. 'Right. I've cut up some fruit for you and there are croissants and yoghurt in the fridge. Sleep for a little longer if you like, then go and have swim, shower and eat breakfast. I'll be back by around 10.30.' It sounded like an itinerary that allowed little room for discussion.

Placing his coffee down, Moreton raised his right hand to the side of his head in an exaggerated salute. 'Yes, Ma'am!'

'*Hasta luego*,' she called, closing the apartment door behind her.

Two hours later, after swimming and showering, he was sitting on the balcony looking out to the mountains in the distance as he finished breakfast, when he heard a car slow to a stop outside. Peering down, he saw a black Ranger Rover drawn up in front of the gate to the complex. Sophia climbed out of the passenger door, waving to the driver as the car pulled away. A minute later, the apartment door opened and Sophia walked in.

'Ah. I see you have followed my orders then. Very good!'

She cocked her index finger at him beckoning him towards her, with a flirtatious smile. It was an instruction he was happy to obey.

He took her in his arms and held her close.

'Did you miss me?' she asked.

'Missed you? Have you been somewhere? I hadn't noticed.'

Sophia explained how she had met her parents and travelled with them into Retama as they registered at the hotel owned by Sebastián's family. When she had told them that it was the same hotel where both Billy Swan and Charlie Broome were staying, they had insisted that, after the game, they should all meet up for dinner there. At first, Moreton was a little unsure, but Sophia reassured him that it would be very informal, and besides, with Broome and Swan there, it wouldn't be like he didn't know anyone. 'And I'll be there as well. It'll be fine.'

For the game against Árboles Altos, Moreton decided to give the newly returned Adrián a rest after consecutive games following his absence. Felipe Blanco was drafted in as cover. Vasquez was also given a break from the right flank, with Juan Palermo taking his place. The result was never in doubt after the elder Palermo brother had nodded in at the far post from Guido's deep cross with just three minutes played. From then on, it became the "Billy Swan Show." A goal either side of the half-time break sealed the game. First, a lazy, mazy dribble through the middle, a one-two with Santi, and a right-footed clip finish over the visitors' goalkeeper doubled the lead and then a nonchalant inside-of the-back-heel, left-footed flick through his own legs from a low cross left the same custodian transfixed as the ball rolled into the net. The best, however, was yet to come.

With fifteen minutes remaining, and the game clearly won, Moreton decided to throw a few substitutes on. He signalled to Swan, asking if he wanted to come off, but the veteran's response, drawing a ring around the top of his head, indicated he had his mind set on a hat trick. Instead, the two Palermo brothers swapped positions, Samuel replaced Matías and Sebastián was sent on to replace Guido.

Five minutes later, all three substitutes were to combine to deliver Billy Swan's third: the outstanding goal of the game. With time ticking away, the Árboles Altos players had clearly realised that there was precious little chance of redeeming the game and had ceased to press forwards, being more intent on limiting the damage at the other end. It allowed the Retama defenders a freedom to press forward, almost at will, and when Jiménez rolled the ball out to Felipe Blanco, the substitute decided to take advantage of the space in front of him.

Fresh and enthusiastic he drove forwards with Sebastián outside of him, and crossed the halfway line before any of the visiting defenders sought to close him down. Skipping past the first half-hearted challenge, he then slipped the ball wide to Sebastián. With defenders packed into the penalty area there seemed little point in flighting in an aimless cross. Instead, Sebastián hit a cross-field pass to José Palermo on the opposite flank, switching the point of attack. The younger Palermo brother approached the penalty area, drawing two defenders towards him, but there seemed little prospect of further advancement. Looking up, he saw Swan drop out of the penalty area, moving closer towards him, and played the ball to him. Throughout his career, Billy Swan had dared to dazzle and dismally disappoint in roughly equal measure. It was time to adopt the former of those two opposing characteristics. Advancing with a shuffling jog, he glided past the first challenge, before putting the second defender onto his backside with a step-over move that left his opponent befuddled.

Now into the penalty area, again he dipped his shoulder feigning to go left before flicking the ball to the right evading the third attempted tackle. He had beaten three defenders in little more than five metres and now, arriving by the penalty spot, only one more stood between him and the goalkeeper he had deceived twice already. Rolling his foot over the ball as his challenger closed in, he flicked it through his legs in a perfect nutmeg, dancing around the fallen opponent and collecting the ball on the other side with just the goalkeeper to beat. This time however, the clipped finish was expected, and the goalkeeper managed to get a touch on the ball, sending it spiralling into the air. Calmly, Swan walked past his fallen opponent, towards the goal line, never taking his eye from the ball as it dropped towards the empty net. It reached his forehead as he stood, less than a metre from the goal and, offering a mere "good morning" nod to welcome its arrival, headed it into the net.

Turning away, he jogged towards the Retama bench as if nothing had happened. Catching up to him before he got there, he saw the excited figures of Victor and Kiko drawing the rapiers from their scabbards and waving them in the air. Responding in kind, he waved them to follow towards the bench. Despite a loping jog that appeared anything but brisk, he arrived there first. Moreton, Sophia and the withdrawn Retama players were stood applauding the extravagant display of skill, with Esteban standing alongside, as animated as anyone.

Noticing the elderly man wearing the ubiquitous cap and the blue number eight Retama shirt, Swan headed for him. Arriving, he stood beside Esteban, motionless and seemingly emotionless, with his arm around the older man's shoulders and a nonchalant expression, as if questioning what all of the commotion was about. Seconds later, the veteran footballer and his new fan were engulfed by the other players. It took Moreton a while to pull the players back off the pair, directing them onto the field.

Finally, there was just Swan and Esteban standing there. The elderly man beaming with joy. He took off the cap that hardly ever seemed to leave his head, and placed on top of Swan's unruly locks. The veteran footballer who had seen and done so much on a football field without ever suggesting it was anything but labour offered in exchange for money, laughed out loud as he ceremonially doffed the cap to his coach before returning it to Esteban. 'Now, Jon boy,' he declared. 'There's a hat trick, for you.'

Moreton patted him on the back as Swan walked back onto the field. 'It was a perfect hat trick, Billy,' he called after him. 'Right foot, left foot and a header.'

Suddenly Swan stopped in his tracks. Turning back towards Moreton, he appeared unexpectedly irritated. Looking down at the ground first, and then back up at Moreton, Swan shook his head slowly, as if in regret. 'Jon,' he said slowly. 'You should know better than that.'

Moreton was unsure of what was happening, but when Swan spoke again, all quickly became clear: 'All of my hat tricks are bloody perfect, mate. All of them.'

Jon Moreton turned to Sophia and whispered in her ear. 'I've never seen Billy so happy. I think we can do this,' he said, with quiet conviction.

That evening, as they prepared to leave for the dinner appointment, Sophia already dressed in a long two-toned blue dress that hugged her body, was looking up the results of the other games on her laptop. 'Wow, Jon,' she exclaimed, calling Moreton into the living room from the bedroom where he was dressing. Wearing in only a buttoned-up shirt, underpants and socks, Sophia looked him up and down, giggling girlishly to herself, as he entered the room.

'What?' he said with a hint of annoyance.

'I don't care what people say. I think British men have a lot of style.'

Moreton offered her a crooked smile in reply. 'OK. What's the "Wow" for?'

Sophia pointed to the screen of her laptop, displaying the results and updated league table following the day's games. Retama's win had put them on fifty-one points, and their lead at the top of the table had increased to eight, with just seven games remaining. Estrella Azul were second, with Politanio B two points further back followed by Torreaño on thirty-nine.

Moreton pursed his lips and nodded in satisfaction. 'That looks good, really good.'

'It does, doesn't it, but there's still lots to do. Torreaño have struggled a bit since the break. Montero has been injured and they've hardly picked up any points with him missing, but he's back now and they're winning almost all of their games.'

Moreton nodded slowly. 'Yeah, OK, but we're twelve points clear of them, and it doesn't matter if he rattles in a dozen goals. So long as we keep winning our games, or at least don't fall apart, we should be safe from them. Politanio aren't doing well since they lost Francisco and their best players, so they'll struggle to catch us. Estrella could be the danger, but it all depends on what fixtures they have left. We have to play them in a couple of weeks. Go there and avoid defeat at worst, and it could put them out of the picture as well.'

Sophia seemed unconvinced. 'You may be right, Jon, but football can be hard sometimes. Anyway,' she said, closing the lid of the laptop, 'let's not worry about that now. The taxi will be here to take us to the hotel in ten minutes, so let's be ready.'

Moreton turned to walk back to the bedroom.

'And Jon. Please don't forget your trousers. People may stare.'

Exiting the taxi at the hotel, Sophia and Moreton walked into the reception area to be greeted by Sebastián. Standing behind the desk, in a dark suit and tie, he looked so much more mature than when playing football. He smiled broadly at them, pointing towards the door of the bar. They followed the suggested direction, and walked into a large, well-lit bar area, with a staircase off it curling around a corner away and up, to be greeted warmly by Sophia's parents.

After exchanging hugs and polite kisses, Moreton looked around, checking for a sight of Charlie Broome or Billy Swan, but neither were present. Detecting Moreton's curiosity, Joaquín Garrigues spoke. 'We have just received an apology from your friend Señor Broome. He and Señor Swan will be a few minutes late. Would you like a drink with us while we wait?' Ten minutes later, they were chatting pleasantly about the game.

Sophia's parents explained that despite the fact they now lived in Árboles Altos, Retama would always be their home town, and how excited they were that the football club was doing so well.

'Perhaps,' Garrigues suggested. 'It is for the best that Señor Broome bought the club instead of me and my friends. After all, otherwise, you two would never have met.'

Dolores Garrigues reached out a hand and patted Moreton warmly on the arm as Sophia took hold of his hand.

'*El amor siempre encuentra su propio camino*,' Sophia said softly, smiling at Moreton.

A loud tumbling noise arising from the unseen section the staircase startled the group. Both men jumped to their feet, hurrying to investigate. As they rounded the corner of the stairs, they found Billy Swan lying on his back, with Charlie Broome crouched beside him.

'Billy, are you OK?'

'He slipped at the top,' Charlie Broome shot in. 'I think he missed the step and then he slid down here all the way on his back.'

The veteran footballer offered a low groan in confirmation.

'Sophia,' Moreton shouted down to the two female members of the Garrigues family, and Sebastián, who had come running after hearing the noise. 'Call an ambulance.'

'No, Jon,' Swan said, wincing. 'No ambulances. I hate them things and hospitals. I'll be all right.'

Jon Moreton was clearly not convinced. 'Billy, you've fell down the stairs. You'll need to see a doctor.'

Swan shook his head insistently. 'No, Jon. No ambulances. Please.'

Charlie Broome spoke. 'Look, Jon. I've got a friend staying here who's an orthopaedic surgeon. We went to school together.' Then, turning to Swan: 'Can you move Billy? Move your legs and arms.'

Swan waved his limbs about slowly indicating to the positive.

'Jon,' Broome suggested, 'you and me help get Billy back to his room and I'll ask Simon to come and look at him. If he thinks Billy should go to hospital then that's what's going to happen.'

Then to Swan: 'Right, Billy. No arguments.'

Swan nodded. 'Yeah, OK.'

Fifteen minutes had passed since Jon Moreton had returned to the Garrigues family in the bar after getting Swan onto his bed when Charlie Broome descended the same stairway into the bar. He raised his hands in calming motion.

'Simon's examined Billy, and he's certain there's nothing broken. He said it's probably just going to be bruising, although it could be pretty extensive. He also said it was fortunate that Billy was an athlete used to tumbling around, and that probably helped him to avoid any serious damage. He's given him some painkillers to help him sleep and is going to check on him again in the morning. He has a few contacts over here, and if it looks anything near serious, he'll know what to do.'

The news lifted the mood and when Broome added: 'Jon, it's likely he won't be able to play for a while,' it seemed the most trivial of additions.

'Don't worry about that, Chaz. So long as he's going to be OK, and there's no real damage. That's the only thing that matters.'

Charlie Broome looked down at the floor. 'I blame myself,' he said slowly.

'Why? It wasn't your fault. He slipped.'

Broome looked at his friend and frowned. 'Yeah, but it's why that matters. Since Billy's been here, he's been as good as gold. Behaved well and, to the best of my knowledge, has avoided alcohol almost totally.' He looked at Moreton and half smiled. 'He keeps telling me how happy he's been and how he's enjoying playing football with you and the team. The problem is that when he got back this evening and told me about the game, I insisted that we open a bottle of champagne to celebrate. It's why we were a bit late.' He looked intently at

Moreton, then the others in turn. 'It was just one bottle, Jon. Truthfully, and I think I drank most of it. I just think that as he hadn't been drinking for a while, it may have affected him more than normal and that's why he slipped.'

Moreton patted his friend on the leg. 'Chaz, stop blaming yourself. I'm sure that's not the reason. Lots of people slip when they haven't been drinking. It's just one of those things. It happens.'

'Cheers, Jon,' he said.

Sophia asked whether they should just call it a night now. It seemed the only thing to do.

Charlie Broome excused himself, saying he was going to check up on Swan and then would probably work for a while before ordering some room service and eat in his room. Moreton said that it really didn't feel right to stay and enjoy a meal with their friend lying injured upstairs, and Sophia nodded. Her parents agreed and, after saying goodbye as they were returning to Árboles Altos in the morning, Sebastián arranged a taxi to take Moreton and Sophia back to the complex.

When they arrived, Sophia prepared a few sandwiches as they hadn't eaten anything since lunch. They sat out on the balcony as the night closed in around them.

'Jon,' she said, breaking the silence, lost in their own thoughts and concerns. 'I'm sure he's going to be OK.'

Moreton stroked his chin slowly, and tried to smile in acknowledgement. It was a task deemed impossible by his emotions though. All he could muster was a sad sigh.

'Jon. He'll be fine, and it's not helping matters if we sit here feeling sorry for ourselves, instead of sorry for him.'

He knew that she was right, but at such times, the weight of emotional gravity outweighs logic and common sense.

'Come to bed,' she insisted. 'Come to bed and we'll fall asleep holding each other. It'll seem better in the morning.'

Moreton wanted to be convinced, but wasn't.

'I promise,' she affirmed. It broke the barrier and he smiled softly.

'OK,' he said.

Early the following morning, Jon Moreton called Broome on the mobile his friend had given him, enquiring about Swan.

'Jon, you know all about timing don't you. I've just spoken with Simon. He went in to see Billy this morning and he seems much better. Well... when I say *better*, it's a lot better than we feared last night. All limbs and body movements are working fine, but he's still in a fair bit of pain from the bruising to his back. Simon said that it's best he stays where he is for the time being – not that he can get up and move anywhere, anyway.' It seemed an inappropriately flippant remark at the time, but Moreton just passed it off as Charlie Broome, being Charlie Broome. 'Simon's going to be staying with me for a couple of weeks, and then he's off to a conference in Valencia, so Billy's in the best of hands and if he needs to pass him on to someone else when he leaves, he can do that.'

Moreton felt better. 'Thanks, Chaz. That's good news. Pass on regards from

Sophia and me to the patient, will you?'

At training the following evening, it quickly became clear that the players all knew of Swan's situation, courtesy of Sebastián. Kiko and Victor seemed especially concerned, enquiring with Sophia for any latest news, brightening up slightly with the information she could pass on. For the remainder of the week, there was still a subdued note to the training and when it came to naming the side on Friday for the visit down the coast to Desorio, Moreton was keen to put out as strong a team as possible in the hope that a win would lift everyone's mood. Adrián returned to the left back role, with Antonio Vasquez reinstalled on the right flank. Revi was pushed forward to be the creative force behind Santi in the absence of Swan, and Samuel slotted in alongside Matías in the centre of midfield.

There was clearly a measure of bad feeling remaining with the Desorio players after what they perceived as Swan's unprovoked assault on their player, and they were quick to let the Retama players know it. Ten minutes in, Desorio were awarded a corner and, in support of his forwards, the home defender who had had his nose restructured by Swan's elbow, had plenty to say to each of the players near him. Sounding off to Victor he shouted into his face. 'Where's your superstar now then eh? Too scared to face us, is he? Or is in jail or something. That's where he should…' The sentence remained unfinished as Kiko stepped between them, cautiously easing the home defender away from his team-mate. Unwisely, and perhaps hyped up by his own words, a punch was then swung at the Retama defender, who merely swayed back to avoid the blow and gently pushed the assailant away. Tumbling to the floor, the Desorio player held a place on his face in an entirely different location to where Kiko's gentle push had contacted his chest. The provocation had served its purpose, though.

The referee had missed the first offence, but by the time Kiko's contact had apparently sent his opponent to the floor, his observation was fixed. A red card was inevitable and Retama were not only facing the remaining eighty minutes of this game without a key defender, but the following three games as well. To cap matters, before Moreton had an opportunity to make a substitution and plug the gaping hole in the Retama defence, the corner was swung in and headed powerfully home. Retama were both a man down and a goal down. Deprived of their most creative player and now also of Kiko, Retama's self-belief was punctured. Moreton sent on Juan Palermo to drop into the back line, sacrificing the talents of Revi to do so.

At the break, there had been no further score, but although Palermo was working hard to cover for the missing Kiko, he had neither the positional knowledge nor experience of playing alongside Victor to be more than a stopgap replacement. Retama needed a goal, but the only chances to score were all at the other end of the field. Moreton and Sophia faced a dilemma, and decided that their best chance was to try and keep things as tight as possible, avoid conceding again, and look to grab an equaliser late on. It meant that for the next thirty-five minutes or so a performance of resilience and concentration was required.

In front of the back line, Samuel and Matías offered cover and support, blocking out attacks before they had developed. Both Vasquez and Guido dropped back to support their fullbacks, and, up front, Santi cut a lonely figure. The experienced Jiménez was cool under pressure and agile when needed, though, and Sanz twice cleared from the line when the ball eluded the veteran goalkeeper. With a dozen minutes left to play, Retama were still just a single goal astray. Moreton decided it was time to play his card.

Removing Santi, he sent on Felipe Blanco in his place. Guido was instructed to move into the central striking role, and wait just inside his own half of the field, hoping that the home defenders would push up close to him, with Felipe Blanco taking his place on the flank to help support Adrián in defence. The ploy was basic, but hopefully would lead to at least one opportunity to level the game. Each time a Retama player had the ball, they should look to deliver a long ball up the field and over the heads of the Desorio back line hopefully exploiting Guido's pace and, waiting in his own half of the field, should eliminate any offside decisions.

For the next ten minutes, nothing seemed to change, the home side still pressed for what would be a killer second goal, but the overworked Retama defence held out. Jon Moreton wrung his hands in frustration on the sidelines as the minutes ticked by towards full time. 'One chance,' he said to himself. 'Just one chance.' Ninety minutes passed and then Sanz won a tackle on the right side of the Retama defence as the home winger tried, and failed, to dance his way past the visitors' skipper.

He tried to drive the ball long, as instructed. With fatigue gnawing at his muscles, however, he shanked the clearance, and the ball drifted into midfield. As two Desorio players casually sauntered to gather possession, Samuel saw his chance. Sprinting to get to the ball first, he clipped it between them and into the vacant Desorio half of the field. Seeing his chance, Guido turned and sprinted after it, easily outpacing the defenders as one grabbed at his shirt. Impeded, he half-stopped, but as the defender pulled at it again, the shirt ripped on his back. He was free again. Shifting through the gears, with his torn short flying behind him like a superhero's cape, he collected the ball and drove onwards. No defender would catch him now, by fair means or foul. It was a one-on-one with the goalkeeper. Choosing his moment, he feigned to lift the ball, but then stabbed it low to the goalkeeper's right, past his despairing reach and into the net. There was barely time to restart the game before it was ended. Retama had stolen a point from the game. It solved the problem for that day, but there were more games to come and the lead in the league table that looked secure seven days ago, was now far less so.

With Kiko absent and health updates on Swan only suggesting a gradual improvement, the next two games, at home to UD Palancio and then the visit to Estrella Azul looked increasingly difficult. Seeking to find a solution to the problem of losing the dominating presence of the suspended Kiko, Moreton slid the skipper inside from his usual right back role to partner Victor in the centre of the back line, with Felipe Blanco drafted in to defend the flank. It seemed the least bad option.

For all his rugged and inspirational determination, Alejandro Sanz was no centre back and struggled badly, with Victor constantly scurrying to cover. Twice

Retama had gone ahead against Palancio, only to be drawn back each time. After fifteen minutes, Guido, wearing the vacant number nine shirt after his was deemed beyond repair following his breakaway strike against Desorio, crossed for Santi to head home. The lead had lasted just a few minutes before a through ball eluded Sanz's lunging attempt at an interception and a visiting forward coolly stroked the ball beyond Jiménez's reach. Then, early in the second period, Revi curled a free kick home after he had been upended on the edge of the box. The gap in the centre of the Retama defence was exposed again with ten minutes remaining. A cross from the right saw Sanz out-jumped, and a header flashed into the net.

It could have been worse. More confusion in the home defence saw a visiting forward through on goal. A desperate challenge from Victor halted his progress, but at the cost of a spot-kick. It brought the defender a yellow card, and an automatic one game suspension for his troubles, thanks to the accumulation of cautions throughout the season. The penalty struck against the upright, however, and bounced clear. Moreton was relieved to come away with a point, and confided to Sophia that he was glad Palancio didn't have Billy Swan in their team for that penalty, or Retama would have ended up empty handed.

Back at the apartment in the evening, Sophia looked up the other results from the games that day and the updated league table. It made for worrying reading. Torreaño CF had continued their winning run, crushing San Vicente 7-0, and wins for both Politanio B and Estrella Azul had seen what had once appeared to be a solid lead at the top of the table for Retama, melt away like ice in the hot Spanish sun.

The next game would see Retama travel to the increasingly dangerous Estrella Azul. Following the game against Árboles Altos, Moreton had suggested to Sophia that if they could return from that fixture without defeat, it would probably remove their opponents from the list of challengers for the title. That was hardly the case now. On Thursday evening before the announcing the team for the fixture, Moreton and Sophia had spent long hours considering how they could best deploy their players without any of the Musketeers being available. Billy Swan was still laid up in the hotel and, despite making progress, was unlikely to be fit again until the end of the season. Kiko was serving the second match of his ban, and Victor was also suspended thanks to his late yellow card against Palancio. They needed to shuffle their cards, but were playing with a vastly denuded deck.

The following evening, the decision was announced. Sanz was returned to his normal berth at right back with Juan Palermo and Samuel now the "make do and mend" pairing in the centre of defence. Guido was brought inside to replace Samuel, with Sebastián drafted in on the left flank. Moreton was far from convinced that they could hold out against an Estrella Azul team that had, by now, eaten chunks out of their lead. His pessimism was entirely appropriate. By halftime, the home side were five goals clear, and a further two were added by the end of the game. The coach could see the dejection on the faces of his players. Everyone knew that even the seven-goal mauling could have been much worse.

What had looked like a title-winning position had now all but deteriorated into a dogfight. Retama had 53 points, and their lead had been cut to just five points by Politanio B. The bigger dangers though were Torreaño and the rampant Estrella Azul, both of whom were enjoying winning runs at the right time. With just four games to play in the league programme, any one of the top four clubs could still prevail, and increasingly, Retama were looking to be the outside bet; the club that had peaked too soon.

Jon Moreton had never experienced such a morale-shattering defeat in his coaching career and that night, lying in bed, waves of inadequacy came over him time and again. He blinked his eyes shut again, trying to block out the negativity, and failed. Turning on his side, he saw the slender shoulders and back of his lover. Needing the comfort of contact, but not wanting to wake her, he reached out a hand a gently ran it through her hair. Seeing his hands lost in the blackness of the locks told him that, no matter what happened, he could always lose himself in her. '*Siempre te querré,*' he mouthed silently. '*Siempre te querré,*' came the unspoken reply from Sophia's heart as she slept. Reassured, he closed his eyes and joined her.

Run-in

The following morning, Jon Moreton woke early. Sophia was still sleeping as he quietly grabbed a pair of shorts and vest, and slipped out of the bedroom. An hour or so later, Sophia's eyes flicked open and noticed the vacant space next to her in the bed. Throwing on that same old training shirt of Moreton's, she left the bedroom to find him sitting on the balcony.

'*Hola*,' she said softly, kissing him on the top of his head.

He looked up and smiled.

'How long have you been awake?'

'I'm not really sure. An hour or so, I guess.'

'Couldn't you sleep?'

'Well, not for a while, but I was OK later. Too much to think about.'

A moment passed. 'You helped though.'

'Did I? How? I think I was asleep most of the night, I felt worn out.'

'You were asleep. But even when you're asleep, your heart talks to mine.' Immediately as the words left his lips, he realised how crass the sentiment sounded spoken out loud, whilst it made perfect sense in his mind.

Sophia had heard his heart though. Still standing, by his chair, she reached out an arm, and drew him to her, until his head rested against her breasts.

'*Siempre te querré*,' she whispered.

'*Siempre te querré*,' he replied, completing the circle.

Thirty minutes later as they ate a breakfast of croissants and fruit, Moreton confessed the reason for his early rising. 'We need something to lift the players. Something to get the positivity back into the team. To be honest, we need something to lift us as well.' A pause. 'You and me. Not here and now, but when we're at work. We need to do something. Arrange something. Get the spirit back again. That's what I was thinking about. I'm just not sure what though.'

Sophia raised the coffee cup to her lips, and then stopped, as if transfixed.

'I've got an idea,' she said.

A couple of hours later, after many telephone calls and discussions, the plan was laid out. In three days it would be Esteban's eightieth birthday, and the club would hold a party for him at Sebastián's family's hotel. All of the players would be invited, and Sophia had managed to find five former Retama players who had been in the same team with the old man. Moreton had spoken to Charlie Broome, who had agreed to cover the costs of the event, which Sebastián's father had been happy to offer at a discounted rate anyway.

Broome had also agreed to have some banners made for the event. One saying: '*Por siempre nuestro número ocho!*' and the other wishing the now octogenarian: '*Feliz cumpleaños!*' To cap things off, Broome had promised that Billy Swan would make it down to the party – on crutches if necessary. He hadn't mentioned that the banners would be produced in Broome Cerámica colours of white letters on a green background, rather than the club's blue, and that they'd carry the text "Sponsored by Broome Cerámica" but no one seemed to either notice or mind.

At training, on Friday, it seemed that the plan was bearing fruit: having the group together, where getting a result from the next game wasn't the main topic of conversation had put people at ease. Esteban had even given a short speech saying how good it was to see the club flourishing again, and how important it was for the team to stay resolute and confident. Moreton whispered into Sophia's ear: 'Wow, that was ideal! If I had written the speech, that's what I would have said.'

She whispered back: '*I wrote the speech for him, Jon.*'

The air of positivity was also enhanced by Victor being available for selection and Kiko just a single game from his own return; Moreton was keenly aware that with the mood of the squad now lifted, it was important to ensure that it was maintained. Whatever happened in the home game against Torre del Olmos, another defeat must be avoided. With this in mind, he decided to switch tactics at the back to reinforce the defence. Their opponents were only mid-table, and, had Kiko and Swan both been available, Retama would surely have fancied their chances of victory. These were different times, though, and different circumstances call for different priorities. The team Moreton announced reflected that caution.

Despite conceding seven goals, Jiménez was retained in goal. The defence, however, took on a different look. Sanz and Adrián defended the flanks, but inside of them, instead of the usual two centre backs, Moreton had added an extra body. Victor would be added to the pairing that had suffered so badly against Estrella Azul. They had the same midfield four, and Santi as the lone striker. Revi was rested.

The game was as tight as Moreton had hoped it would be. The visitors had little to play for, and seemed content to take the point on offer and return home with a draw against the league leaders. The resulting goalless draw was almost inevitable. The league table now showed Retama on 54 points, with another victory for Torreaño CF seeing them into second place on 50, thanks to a hat trick from Montero against Desorio in a 4-0 victory. Politanio B were in third, a point behind, and Estrella Azul were still closing the gap after their seventh successive win. The lead was now down to four points, but Moreton was prepared to write off the Torre del Olmos game as a "job done" situation. The team for the visit to UD Araganza, took on a more regular appearance, and with his ban completed, Kiko was back in the starting eleven. It was a clear boost for the team, but another development, a minor issue at the time, would later take on a much larger significance.

Paco Jiménez had performed more than adequately against Torre del Olmos, displaying the sort of game experience that allowed a seasoned professional to dismiss any lingering doubts following a seven-goal hammering from his mind. With that accomplished, Moreton had toyed with the idea of reintroducing Juan Torres for the upcoming game, but the young goalkeeper had been struggling with illness for the past few days and was the only member of the squad not to make it to Esteban's party. He wouldn't be available to travel to Araganza.

The game began encouragingly. Retama took early control and, after a dozen minutes, Vasquez played in a cross from the right, Santi headed the ball down, and Revi fired the visitors ahead. Araganza tried to press for the equaliser, but with Kiko and Victor now back in tandem at the heart of the defence, they coped with most things adequately, and Jiménez seemed in control of his area. The half-time break came and went without any further goals, but approaching the hour mark, Retama doubled their lead when Santi controlled a pass from Guido, before sidestepping his marker to fire home.

The game looked to have been won, but just two minutes later things swung dramatically the other way. Leaping to catch a hopeful cross into the Retama box, Jiménez collided in mid-air with an Araganza forward, landed awkwardly and twisted his ankle. Sophia went on to look at the injury and, had Torres been available to step in, the veteran goalkeeper would have been substituted. With that option not being available, Jiménez insisted on carrying on, despite his movements being palpably limited.

The home team quickly sought to capitalise, firing shots in from any distance, sensing the goalkeeper's discomfort. The tactic took a mere three minutes to bring tangible reward as a limping Jiménez failed to gain any height from a jump, and a shot from thirty-five metres sailed, uninterrupted, over his hands into the net. With twenty-five minutes still to play, Retama were now facing an uphill task to stay in front.

Moreton sent Felipe Blanco on in place of Vasquez, with instructions to help out the back line, but the momentum of the game had irreversibly swung against the visitors. Moreton and Sophia debated whether a fit stand-in goalkeeper was a better option than an injured specialist. Five minutes after the first goal, the answer became clear as another speculative shot found the goalkeeper unable to make ground on what would ordinarily be a routine save. The scores were level.

Jiménez limped from the field, and Juan Palermo was sent on to lead the line as Santi dropped back into goal. Although clearly less than ideal, the young forward was at least competent to keep out the long-range efforts that had been peppering Paco Jiménez's goal. The defence seemed more assured and things settled down. Another draw for Retama looked increasingly likely. Entering the final five minutes though, a tussle between Adrián and a home forward resulted in the latter hitting the floor in the penalty area, and the referee awarded the spot-kick. Gambling, and plunging to his right, Santi looked back forlornly across the goal to see the ball rolling into the opposite corner. From two goals up, Retama had lost 3-2.

That evening back at the apartment, when Sophia pensively opened up the laptop to review the results elsewhere in the league. Torreaño had won again, this time defeating Costa Locos 2-0, with Montero scoring both goals. Politanio B had lost, however, going down to a single goal defeat at Árboles Altos. 'I must ring up my parents and thank them,' she confided to Moreton as she changed the screen to move to the league table. Still stuck on 54 points, Retama's lead was now down to a single point from Torreaño and the rampant goal scoring exploits of Montero, who they would visit for the final fixture of the season.

The league's nouveau riche club were now in striking range of Retama, with their fate in their own hands, albeit their next game would see them visit Estrella Azul, who trailed them by three points. Whoever came out on top in that one, would now surely be favourites for the title.

The following week would see San Vicente visit Retama for the club's final home game of the league programme. Simply put, two victories would ensure Retama were league champions, and qualify for a straight play-off game for promotion. With the other clubs baying at their heels like a pack of slavering hounds in pursuit of their quarry, any other result was borderline unthinkable.

Before training on the following Tuesday, Moreton met up with Billy Swan for lunch and was delighted to see his friend sitting in the hotel bar waiting for him.

'Hey Billy. You look better. Feeling any better?'

Giving an exaggerated wince as he raised his arm to shake hands with the newcomer, Swan nodded slowly. 'I'm getting there, Jon. I can walk about now, and get down the stairs if I don't rush. Playing is a different matter though. I'm not sure I'm going to be any help to you and the guys.'

'I'm not so sure about that, Billy,' he said with a glint in his eye.

That evening, as the players gathered for training, a familiar figure, with a less familiar gait, appeared above the concrete steps at the gate side of the ground. Assisted by a helper with a newspaper tucked under his arm, he slowly descended the steps, sat on the boundary walls, eased his legs over and walked across to where Moreton, Sophia and the squad were standing.

With the hint of a hobble in his walk, Billy Swan left Gonzalo with his newspaper sitting in his usual position and was immediately mobbed by his team-mates, led of course, by Victor and Kiko, drawing rapiers as they ran. Struggling to reply in kind with the kind of effort that would hardly have struck fear into the hearts of Cardinal Richelieu's henchmen, Swan appeared more concerned that his welcoming committee did him no harm in their enthusiasm, holding his hands up to plead for restraint. Moreton had seen the need for the players to receive a lift in spirits and calculated that having Billy Swan back amongst their number, even as a spectator, could be that very tonic. It seemed to work, and across the next sessions before the game on Sunday, the mood became much more upbeat.

With Jiménez still struggling, but insisting on being kept on the bench in case of emergencies, the team for Retama's penultimate challenge of the season virtually selected itself. Juan Torres came in to replace the injured veteran, with the regular back four of Sanz, Kiko, Victor and Adrián in place. The midfield had Vasquez and Guido on the flanks with the steady and reliable Matías and Samuel in the middle. Revi would play behind Santi, with the forward restored to the sharp end of the team. Retama's visit to San Vicente, just before the mid-season break had produced a comfortable three goal victory, and the same club's apparent meltdown in conceding seven goals in the recent match against Torreaño merely reinforced the impression of a set of players seeing out the season without exerting too much effort. A victory surely wasn't beyond Retama's reach, even without Swan.

On Sunday afternoon, as Moreton and Sophia took their places on the bench alongside the outfield substitutes and two injured players, the Retama coach noticed the dark clouds gathering overhead, with the threat of rain. Sophia noticed his concerned look to the skies.

'If it rains. It will be heavy, but probably brief. It will probably affect the pitch though.'

Moreton nodded solemnly.

Then she smiled, adding: 'The song wasn't correct, you know?'

Moreton looked puzzled, precisely as Sophia had intended.

She laughed a little and pulled him close to her, whispering in his ear: 'The rain in Spain doesn't really stay mainly on the plain.'

The quip broke the tension nicely, but Jon Moreton kept a studied eye on the skies above and the threat of precipitation.

As the game got under way, the tension felt by their coach was also affecting the Retama players. Passes were mishit, control of the ball was poor and shots seemed to be hit aimlessly, all of which saw confidence slowly drain away from the home team. Conversely, the San Vicente players appeared carefree and eager to express themselves. There was little doubt that Retama had the better team, but by the break the score remained goalless.

Back in the dressing room, together with Sophia, Swan and Jiménez, Moreton spoke to each of the players in turn, reassuring and encouraging, before taking the last two minutes of the break to deliver an impassioned drive forward. Amid much handclapping and shouts of *'Somos Retama!'* the players exited the dressing room – to be faced by torrential rain. It was precisely as Sophia had predicted: heavy, but brief. Ten minutes later, the clouds had passed and the sun beamed out once more. By this time, however, players, officials and the assembled huddled groups on the benches were all soaked, and many of the supporters had decided to head for their cars.

Unlike a grass pitch, the synthetic playing surface of the Estadio Antonio Núñez was unable to soak up the excess water, and much of it settled, forming a series of small puddles. Retama's control of the game evaporated much more quickly than the surface water as the game degenerated into a series of long punts downfield that either skipped on rapidly after contact with the dampened surface or stopped, if the ball landed in one of the puddles. With players losing their footing repeatedly the game was becoming a lottery, and, with ten minutes of the second period gone, San Vicente revealed a winning ticket.

Another long ball down field cleared the heads of Kiko and Victor, initially skipping on towards Juan Torres after bouncing, but then plunging into a puddle and stopping midway into the Retama half. Sensing an opportunity, a visiting forward sprinted after it as Victor turned, before slipping to the floor, sliding into Kiko and also taking him to ground. Hurdling over the fallen pair of home defenders, the San Vicente forward was clear on goal with just Torres to beat. Disdaining any thoughts of dribbling around the goalkeeper on the now treacherous surface, he hit the ball as firmly as the conditions allowed. It fizzed along the surface, as Torres threw himself to his right to block the effort. Inevitably, the ball slithered from his grasp and trickled towards the now unguarded goal some ten metres behind him. In his anxiety to regain his feet,

Torres then suffered the same fate as Victor, slipping to the floor. The gleeful San Vicente forward trotted past him and walked the ball into the net. Moreton's head sank onto his chest.

The next ten minutes of the game suggested that the Retama players had shared their coach's despondency as a feeling of sad inevitability washed over them, dampening their ambition, much as the rain had drenched their shirts. On the bench, though, Moreton and Sophia were hatching a plan. Playing their normal game on this pitch simply wouldn't work. Plan B was required.

The last fifteen minutes were approaching when Moreton made his changes. Antonio Vasquez, his silky skills now made rendered redundant by the surface, was removed, with the bustling, muscular Juan Palermo sent on in his place. On the other flank, the speedster, Guido was also removed, and the younger Palermo brother joined his sibling. Finally, Sebastián was placed into the centre of midfield alongside Matías. Samuel was sent into the back line, with Kiko also thrown forward. Moreton had planned an all-out aerial assault on the San Vicente goal. It wasn't going to be pretty, and it was hardly the sort of football he approved of, but Moreton accepted that the rain had changed the game, and he had to respond accordingly.

The San Vicente coach was quick to respond, also increasing the average height of his team with substitutions. The remaining portion of the game would be more thud and blunder than *Jogo Bonito*. Moreton slumped down alongside Sophia, shaking his head slowly as he did so.

'I hate this sort of thing,' he conceded, confessing his sins, without seeking absolution. 'This isn't the way to score goals.'

He received it anyway. 'It's the right thing to do, Jon.'

The next five minutes saw a series of high balls pumped into the San Vicente area with the reinforced Retama front line battling for them, largely without success. Defenders headed clear, and the goalkeeper came out to gather on occasions. Even when it was a home player's head getting the all-important contact on the ball it ran away out of play or towards the goalkeeper, or a free kick was awarded for some over enthusiastic endeavour. Revi, Retama's most skilled player on the pitch took on the guise of a mortar, lobbing the ball forward, but his time was about to come.

Another punt forward saw Kiko battling on the edge of the penalty area with two visiting defenders. Again, the shrill whistle of the referee halted play, but this time, the infraction was deemed to have been caused by a defender. Retama had a free kick, a metre or so outside of the area. A relative Pygmy, lost in a land of giants, Revi placed the ball, intent on stating his case for the little man. He peered with obvious intent over the heads of the towering San Vicente wall, assembled to prevent a direct shot on goal. A curled shot into the top corner was clearly the plan as he jumped up and down a couple of times to establish the position of the goalkeeper: it would require an immense piece of skill to pull that one off. The Retama forwards stood either side of the wall, with others stationed wider, in the hope of gathering any shot deflected by the barrier erected in front of Revi. They wouldn't be needed.

With one final look over the wall as the referee blew his whistle, Revi fired in his shot. The wall jumped to close out any increasingly narrow route to goal that the Retama playmaker had to aim at. As they did so, however, the ball skipped beneath them, zipping across the damp surface as Revi aimed his shot low and hard. Completely taken in by Revi's antics, the goalkeeper stood transfixed as the ball skidded into the corner of the net supposedly guarded by the wall.

For a moment, everything was quiet and still, as recognition of Revi's cunning ploy drilled into their senses. Then came the explosion of joy. With arms spread wide, the little playmaker ran towards the bench in celebration, chased by his team-mates. They caught him as Moreton, Sophia and anyone uninjured on the bench joined in. After they had settled down, and Revi was climbing to his feet to walk back for the restart, Paco Jiménez, hobbled towards the goal scorer, took him by the shoulders and turned Revi around to face him. The frown on the veteran goalkeeper's face quickly melted to a smile, and then a grin. '*Guapo!*' He declared. '*Muy, muy guapo!*' He hugged the younger man, before sending him back onto the pitch and returning to the bench, still smiling.

Sophia looked at Moreton with an impish smile. 'Is that the way to score goals?'

By the time the referee had blown for full-time, for Jon Moreton the elation of the strike had been overtaken by the reality of merely having gained one more point, and now being vulnerable to losing their top spot in the league had Torreaño overcome Estrella Azul. Even a win for the home team would merely be stacking up the challengers behind Retama with the final game to come.

In the dressing room, Sophia and a number of players were using their mobile phones to try and track down the result of the other game, but with little success. Calls to friends proved to be equally fruitless. Whilst the result was of massive importance to Retama and the clubs involved, in the great scheme of things, it was hardly headline news for anyone else. Even a call to Charlie Broome brought no further information as Moreton relayed the events of the day. As he was about to hang up, however, a cheer broke out. It spread rapidly as the news was passed on. Moreton stopped for a moment as Sophia thrust the screen of her phone into his eye line.

'They drew, Chaz,' Moreton yelled down the phone to his friend, unable to contain his elation. 'They bloody drew, mate. We're still in with a chance.'

On the other end of the call Charlie Broome was calm, hardly copying Moreton's frenzied joy. 'That's great, Jon. That's great. So, where are we now?'

Moreton gathered his composure. 'OK, Chaz,' he said almost breathless. 'If I'm right, it means that we're on 55 points, Torreaño have 54 and Estrella Azul are on 51, along with Politanio B.'

Unseen by Charlie Broome, Moreton was looking at Sophia for confirmation, and when it was given by rapid nods and a beaming smile, he passed it on.

'Yeah, that's it, Chaz. It's down to us and Torreaño now. The others can't catch up, whatever happens in the final round of games. They're out of it. It's all on the last game now, Chaz.'

All Moreton could hear was silence, though.

'Chaz? Chaz, you still there?'

The reply was slow and measured. 'Yeah, I'm still here, Jon. I was just thinking of what we need to do now if we're going to make this all work. Do we need to beat them?'

'No, mate. A draw will do it. They need a win. We just need a draw.'

Again, a brief silence before the answer. 'OK, Jon. What about Swan? I think we should get him to play.'

It seemed like a strange suggestion, but Moreton realised that perhaps his friend hadn't spoken with the injured player recently. 'No. It would be great if he was fit enough. We could certainly use him, but it's too soon. He's walking better, but probably still weeks away from being able to play.'

'I could talk to him. See if he could make it.'

Moreton dismissed the idea. 'We can't do that, Chaz. He's not ready. I tried playing with an injured player when Paco got crocked, and that cost us. I'm not doing that again. Anyway, if we get the point, we'll need him for the play-offs if he can make it.'

It seemed a convincing argument. 'Yeah, the play-offs. Yeah, you're right, Jon. It's your call anyway.'

Moreton closed the call, and turned to Sophia. 'Tell you what. We've got a big game coming up!'

End of the Day

It seemed increasingly likely that Paco Jiménez's injury would have cleared up in time for the visit to Torreaño. Moreton spoke briefly with Sophia about restoring the veteran to the starting line-up for what would probably be Retama's most important fixture for many years. His experience could be a calming influence on the squad, but replacing Torres would be harsh, especially considering that the goal conceded against San Vicente had hardly been his fault. In the end both agreed to stay with the younger man. It was a call that Jiménez endorsed.

Aside from Billy Swan, Moreton and Sophia had a virtually full squad to select from. At this stage of the season, it is hardly unusual for stress injuries and the collective effort of more than thirty games to mean some enforced absences, but the careful deployment of the assets at his disposal were now delivering its rewards. There was even a slight thought in the back of his mind that perhaps he should put Swan on the bench, just in case he was needed for a last throw of the dice. Sophia quickly dismissed the folly though, and Moreton needed little convincing. It was more the recollection of Charlie Broome's seductive suggestion rolling around in his mind, than the result of his own consideration that opened up the thought.

Following a fairly light session on Tuesday evening ahead of Wednesday's training, Moreton and Sophia sat on the sunlit balcony of his apartment, discussing how they could nullify, or at least reduce, the Torreaño goal threat of Montero. They came to the conclusion that in an ideal world, if they could man mark him effectively, playing ten against ten would give them a much better chance of success. But who would they give such an onerous task to?

Sophia suggested Kiko. He certainly had the physical presence, pace and youthful energy for the task, but taking him out of the back line, and breaking up the effective partnership he had established with Victor, would inevitably weaken the defence. Moreton's inclination was to draft Samuel into the role, and then bring in either Sebastián or Felipe Blanco alongside Matías. That would mean a weakened central midfield unit and, although Samuel had played important games through the season and regularly since Swan's injury, his game time had been limited. There was even a brief discussion about using Juan Palermo. He had the physical attributes necessary, but it would be asking a lot of someone who, despite fully committed effort, had struggled when dropped into the defence previously. Eventually the decision was reached, not because it was the best option, but probably because it was the one with the least negative consequences.

On Wednesday evening, after Sophia had run the players through a warm-up exercise, with increased involvement from Billy Swan, Moreton broke with convention and announced the team to face Torreaño. Juan Torres was retained in goal, with a defence comprising of Sanz, Kiko, Victor, Adrián, and Felipe Blanco. In midfield were Vasquez, Matías, Revi and Guido, with Santi as the lone striker. He went on to explain that Sanz would man mark Montero throughout the game. As the club's most experienced defender, Moreton continued, he was the obvious choice for the role and Felipe Blanco would play as right back in place of the captain, adding that, for this session, and the one on Friday evening, they would concentrate on attack v defence scenarios with Sanz marking Santi. The new back four and Sanz would be attacked by the remainder of the players to practise the system.

As the session progressed, Sophia confided in Moreton: 'The problem with this of course, is that Santi isn't Montero. He's very good of course, but Montero is exceptional. Having Alejandro stop Santi from scoring doesn't mean he can stop Montero as well.'

Moreton turned to her as the practice continued. 'I know. But it's not about that really. We need to give the players confidence that the system can work and Alejandro confidence that he can do the job. It's not about practising stopping Montero. It's about practising the formation and understanding how it works. If we can get that sorted over today and Friday it'll give us a chance.'

All through that session and again on Friday, the Retama players practised and, as time went on, Sanz became increasingly in tune with his role, following Santi like a dutiful hound, tracking his master's steps. But this hound had a bite to deliver. At the end of Friday's session, Moreton was satisfied not only that Sanz had been the right choice for the role, but also that they had prepared as best as they could.

As she and Moreton headed home, Sophia suggested that they stop at Carlito's bar for a glass of wine. Moreton was already feeling tense about the upcoming game and what it meant to the club and took little persuading. Waving to Elena as they entered, they found a table near to the window and sat down. Sophia signalled to Elena and she brought them each a glass of white wine.

'*Salud*,' they echoed in unison, raising their glasses to each other, sipping the wine.

'Jon, can I ask you a question?'

Unsure what was coming, Moreton agreed nervously. 'OK,' he said.

'What happens next?'

Moreton was still unsure of her intent. 'Next?'

'Yes, what happens next? What happens next if we get a result on Sunday? What happens next if we don't? What happens next if we get promotion?' She paused. 'What happens next…What happens next… with us?'

Sophia picked up her glass and took another sip of wine, unconsciously offering Moreton a moment's thinking time, before speaking again. 'I don't expect a fully detailed plan, Jon.'

Moreton's brain raced frantically looking for answers to a question he had never even considered: But what happens next?

Jon Moreton surprised himself with the honesty of his answer. He picked up his glass, then placed it down again, reaching instead for Sophia's hand. Taking it in his, he squeezed it gently.

'There are two answers to that, I guess,' he said, intently staring into her dark eyes. 'One of them depends on circumstances. The other does not.'

She opened her mouth to speak, but he raised his hand slightly: 'Firstly, circumstances will depend what I'm doing. Chaz has plans for the club, and what happens in the next couple of weeks will shape how that plays out. I may still have a job here, I may not. And,' he said smiling at her, 'I guess that's true for you too.'

She nodded, accepting the implicit consequence.

'Then,' Moreton continued. 'There's the thing that doesn't depend on circumstances.'

He released her hand, picked up the glass and, this time, sipped from it before placing it down, and again taking her hand in his.

'And that's you. Wherever I am, whatever I'm doing, I want it to be with you.'

Reluctantly, he felt a tear welling up in his eye. Sophia's somewhat crooked smile suggested she was experiencing a similar problem.

Although in a bar, with other people having conversations of their own, as words, thoughts, hopes and fears mingled with each other in the ether of myriad human interaction, to Moreton and Sophia they were alone. At that moment, no one else, nothing else, existed, only them.

'Do you remember what you said to me on our first night together?' Moreton asked.

Sophia nodded slowly, as that tear finally escaped and ran down her left cheek. 'I asked you if we were going to try to love each other.'

'There was more though. You told me that we must be honest and kind because hearts are precious and so fragile. You told me never to deceive you and promised that you would never deceive me. You asked me to make you happy and consider you important. You told me that I was important to you, and that you wanted to make me happy. You said that you didn't need money, but needed commitment, and that I would always have your commitment. Do you remember?'

Sophia hadn't stopped smiling since he began.

Moreton spoke again. '*Te quiero*,' he mouthed quietly to her. 'For me, all those things, all those promises, are still true.'

Jon Moreton looked down at the table for a moment, then back up at the woman he had assured of his devotion. 'You too must be sure though. After we spoke of Alvaro, we agreed you must finish your studies and then you would know what you wanted to do.'

This time it was Sophia's turn to look down at the table, thinking for a moment about her now faded affection for an old love, before smiling and speaking. 'You told me that you would love me for ever, Jon,' she said tearfully. 'Do you remember what I said then?'

Moreton smiled and laughed a little. 'You told me you would love me for longer than that.'

'Well,' she said. 'There you are then.'

They drained the wine from their glasses and left the bar, walking hand-in-hand for the five minutes or so back to Moreton's apartment. Closing the door behind them, they hugged, holding each other closely. Ten minutes later, exhausted by the emotional truths revealed, they lay asleep in each other's arms. The coming weeks would submit those pledges to a test, the ferocity of which, neither of the now peacefully dormant souls, could contemplate.

Saturday lasted forever. The hours dragged by as Moreton and Sophia found it difficult to concentrate their minds on anything other than the game that would define Retama's season. They walked into town and strolled along the beachfront as the waves of the Mediterranean lapped gently onto the golden sands. They stopped for coffee, but hardly spoke and then headed home.

Moreton read on his own whilst Sophia broke her normal habit and decided to study in the afternoon, returning to her own apartment. The solitude of earnest endeavour offered a place to hide for a brief while. As afternoon melted slowly into early evening, they decided to go for a stroll.

They had no destination in mind but, fifteen minutes later, neither was surprised as they stood outside the gates of the Estadio Antonio Núñez. Moreton reflected briefly that although the scene was almost the same as when he had first arrived in the town and left the air-conditioned comfort of Charlie Broome's Mercedes, in his mind it had changed so much. The faded and flaking paint no longer looked like the entrance to a bedraggled and unloved piece of ground. Now it was the gateway to a life he had come to treasure, and a group of people he had come to respect and love. He knew that he never wanted to leave.

Turning, he smiled to Sophia. 'Sorry, I was just… '

Sophia smiled back indulgently. 'I know. Don't worry. I understand.'

They hugged briefly and Sophia whispered in his ear. 'Do you remember when I said: welcome to Retama, after you had given the shirt to Esteban?'

'Sure,' he whispered. 'Are going to say it again?'

Sophia shook her head slightly. 'No,' she whispered. She looked him in the eye. 'Now I say, welcome home.'

Bolts from the Blue

The coach journey into the hills and the town of San Julio del Rio took a slightly more than an hour, and, when the first sign announced their arrival, Moreton was a little mystified. Sophia had described it as a small and quiet town, but he had expected more than what appeared to be a single road with a few score small houses, local businesses and a school, with other dwellings dotted around on the one or two side roads that led off left and right. As the coach continued along the narrow road, and taking a sharp turn to climb a little further, all became clear.

Climbing clear of what passed as the main area of the town, the land to the right fell away into a picturesque valley, framing the river from which the town took its name, and beyond to the sea on the horizon. Ahead, instead of the small neat whitewashed houses of San Julio, larger villas appeared, clinging to the side of the hills. Although the two areas were only separated by a hundred metres or so, the distance in economic terms was of an entirely different proportion.

A few minutes later, the coach carrying the Retama players and coaches to their day of destiny pulled up outside a small, but clearly new, stadium. It was the home of Torreaño CF, and clearly identified a club on the way up, with their local benefactor apparently happy to subsidise its hunger for success – and the *Menu del Dia* was promotion at Retama's expense.

Entering the dressing room to offer last advice and guidance, Moreton sensed the tension among his players. He decided to tap into their concentration. 'This is your day. This is your day. Don't let anyone take your day away from you.' With that he turned and walked out, taking Sophia by the hand and leading her out of the dressing room as well before closing the door behind them. A few paces away he stopped and they both listened to the mumble of words coming from the players, before in Alejandro Sanz's distinctive and authoritative tones, came the shout, '*Somos Retama!*' It was answered with an echoing call that almost shook the room.

As the two teams lined up, Torreaño in red shirts with narrow white stripes and red shorts, Retama all in blue, it looked and felt like another episode of an eternal battle. Red against blue. Princes against paupers. Stars against underdogs. It was all of that and more. The early phase of the game was very much as Moreton and Sophia had expected. The Torreaño players buzzed busily, retaining possession and seeking out opportunities for Montero. With Retama's back four less inclined to track the forward's runs though, the defence retained their positional discipline as Sanz hassled and harried the home team's star player with dogged application.

It was hardly a new experience for Montero, his reputation had earned him the dubious honour of a man marker on any number of occasions and, almost without exception, he had found a way to release himself from even the tightest grip of his attendant sentinel. As the first fifteen, then twenty, then twenty-five minutes passed without Torreaño breaking through, their preponderance of possession without any tangible reward worked in Retama's favour whose confidence grew in measure with the home team's frustration.

Retama's goal was threatened with a few efforts that Juan Torres dealt with comfortably, and, with ten minutes to go to the break, the blue defence was holding out with an unexpected measure of ease. Montero shielded a ball that was played forward, as Sanz closed in to block any progress. A swift turn, however, caught out the Retama skipper and the forward was clear running towards the Retama defence. Laying off the ball, as Kiko closed to challenge, Montero raced passed the defender to receive the return pass exactly where he wanted it, taking the defender out of the game. As he shaped to strike, however, Victor, having astutely read the play, slid in to challenge and funnelled the ball back into the welcoming arms of Juan Torres. Montero's first escape from the clutches of Alejandro Sanz had come to nought.

The half-time break came and went. With the benefit of both a rest for legs wearied by persistently chasing the ball and the comforting knowledge that the job was half done, the first quarter hour of the second-half held no major dangers. Again, the home team dominated but, apart from his one break, Sanz's task was being accomplished, and, whilst hardly a peripheral figure, Montero's contribution was stunted by Retama's captain. Such was the suffocating presence of the defender that Montero began to sink further and further back to gain a foothold in the action.

The move caused a moment's confusion for Sanz. Should he follow the forward all the way back into the other half of the field, or wait until he ventured forward again? The defender chose the latter option and fatefully gave Montero a little breathing space and room to operate. Collecting possession in his own half, he charged forward evading a couple of tackles. The distance between himself and the Retama defender allowed him to have picked up sufficient space to run past rather than round his marker and, again, he was free. He wouldn't let this opportunity slip. With team-mates left and right, he ignored their calls for a pass and, when still twenty-five metres from goal, hit a fearsome rising shot that beat the despairing dive of Torres and rifled into the top corner of the net. Montero had put Torreaño ahead.

Moreton's heart sank. His team had hardly crossed the halfway line with any conviction, and now they were a goal behind. There was still half an hour to play, but Retama needed to score a goal or accept that their opponents would end up top of the league. Moreton's mind was scurrying in frantic search for a solution, but next to him, on the other side from Sophia, Billy Swan decided on more immediate action. Jumping to his feet in a way that belied a troublesome back, he shouted to the players on the pitch in an Estuary-inspired version of Spanish. '*Somos Retama! Somos Retama!*' Then he reached down, waving the substitutes to join him. First it was Paco Jiménez, then Samuel, the Palermo brothers and Sebastián. The players on the pitch responded. Sanz shouted, as did Adrián and soon the bellowing belligerence of the team that had conceded, dominated the cheers of the team that had scored.

As the game restarted with an enlivened Retama team now bent on going forward, Swan sat back down. Jon Moreton put his arm around his former team-mate's shoulders.

'Thanks, Billy.'

'Don't worry about it. What was I saying anyway? I always thought that shout was saying the coach is a right pain or something. Ain't that right?'

'Yeah, Billy, that's right.'

'Thought so. This coaching malarkey is bloody easy, ain't it?'

Whilst none of the players on the pitch had changed, the mood of the game had shifted perceptively. Now it was more a match of equals, and Retama's more determined forward play had the added bonus of keeping the home forwards, and particularly, Montero from having the ball. For all that, the improvement in Retama's scoring potential had shifted only slightly, if at all. The next fifteen minutes passed and the league title was remorselessly slipping away. Moreton had to gamble. Felipe Blanco was taken off with Sanz dropping back to his normal position. It released the shackles on Montero, but unless Retama could score, it mattered little. Juan Palermo was sent on with instructions to support Santi to try and force a breakthrough. Samuel went on to replace a tiring Matías.

In almost a reversal of the early minutes of the game, it was now Torreaño who were defending in depth, anxious to preserve that invaluable one goal lead. Even the striker was pulled back deeper as both possession and territorial advantage was conceded in order to keep the back door locked, barred and bolted. Ninety minutes had now passed. Retama pressed but it seemed a forlorn task. Two more minutes passed and, as the seconds slipped away, so did Retama's hopes. Sanz ventured forward and exchanged passes with Revi before firing in a speculative shot, but the Torreaño goalkeeper plunged to his right to push the ball wide.

All the red shirted players defended their box, and Retama threw all the blue-shirted ones forward. The only exceptions were Vasquez, charged with delivering perhaps the most important corner kick in Retama's recent history, and Victor who was left just inside the Torreaño half as the last sentinel, crossing the halfway line for one of the very few occasions in his career. Even Juan Torres was waved forward by Moreton to enter the fray.

The corner was floated in and, despite challenges from the visiting players, the Torreaño goalkeeper rose to punch clear. The ball dropped midway inside the home team's half of the field and, seizing the moment, Montero sprinted after it. The scent of glory and a goal to close out the game flared in his nostrils. Compelled to make a last-ditch challenge, Victor sprinted forward to deny him. It was a race as to who got there first, and one that the Retama defender won.

Reaching the ball, and with little other option, Victor struck it with all the power he could muster. From some thirty metres away from goal, and with twenty-one other players between him and the Torreaño goal, the fair-haired defender watched as the ball threaded the eye of a needle, evading all contact, until it crashed against the Torreaño crossbar and down into the back of the net.

For a moment everything was quiet, but only for a moment. As the realisation struck home, the Retama camp exploded. The players threw themselves to the floor, on their knees or in piles and, on the bench, coaches and players hugged as they jumped up and down. Alone and unnoticed by anyone, the slight figure in the blue shirt, with the white number six on his back, ran around the pitch, swimming through waves of delirium. He fulfilled the pledge to his fellow Musketeer, shouting out in a faux English accent, heavily tinted by his native Spanish tongue, the words he had been taught.

'I don't believe it!' he screamed. 'I don't believe it! I don't believe it! I don't believe it!'

As the celebrations eased a little and the other players sought out their unlikely saviour, Victor reached where Billy Swan was standing, his face an expression of both ecstasy and disbelief. Now eerily quiet but equally firmly, he yelled forth the mantra once more.

'Nor me, mate,' answered Swan. 'What have you bloody gone and done.' He hoisted the young defender into the air as the others swarmed around him. Despite the euphoria, Jon Moreton couldn't help but shout out: 'Billy, be careful. Your back,' but the alarm was engulfed by the waves of joy.

It took minutes for the referee to restore order to break up what was descending, or perhaps more appositely ascending, into a league title winning party. The game was restarted and now it was Torreaño's turn to launch hopeful punts downfield, but they amounted to nothing. As the final whistle went, Moreton and Sophia hugged.

'You did it,' she shouted to him.

'No, I didn't,' he replied, kissing her. 'We did it.'

The Torreaño coaches and players were clearly despondent at seeing the prize dashed from their hands at the very last moment, but accepted the result with grace and warmly shook hands with their opposite numbers. Perhaps a third successive promotion via a league title was reaching a step too far, too quickly, but there was still a route open for them, albeit more complicated than that now available to Club Deportivo Retama.

Returning to the coach after prolonged celebrations in the dressing room, Moreton settled into his usual seat next to Sophia. 'I'll tell you something,' he said softly. 'I can't wait until Chaz rings to ask how we got on.' They both laughed and as if by some celestial connection his phone than rang. Happily taking the call, Jon Moreton spoke before the owner of Broome Cerámica and Club Deportivo Retama could even ask the question.

In deliberate overly calm tones, he simply said: 'Hi Chaz. Yeah, mate. Job done.'

From Moreton's reaction to the reply he was hearing, Sophia could tell that the statement had been met with some surprise.

'Chaz, I'm telling you mate. We did it. We got a draw.' He was now speaking with an emotion that both betrayed his joy and confirmed the credibility of the statement. 'The guys were magnificent. All of them. We equalized in the last minute. And the goal, mate: bloody hell, you should have seen it. Forget Goal of the Month. This was Goal of the Century. It must have been from 40 yards, a bloody screamer.'

A pause then followed as the other person was clearly speaking.

'Yes, 1-1. A draw. It was Victor. Victor of all people. What a goal.'

Another pause.

'No, mate. I don't know the other scores, but it doesn't matter. We've got 56 points. Torreaño have 55, and the most Estrella Azul can get, even if they win is 55, and Politanio are well behind. We just need to wait until later tonight to find out who we've got in the promotion play-off.'

Charlie Broome already had the answer though. Jon Moreton nodded slowly, as his friend passed on the information.

'OK, Chaz. I'll pass that info on. What? Yeah, cheers mate. Thanks. Speak soon.'

He hung up on the call as Sophia looked at him expectantly. 'What Jon? Who have we got?'

At first Moreton seemed reluctant to answer. 'I think I remember you saying something about them to me. It's Atlético Santa Kristina.'

The smile on Sophia's face melted slowly. 'Fouad,' she said softly.

An hour or so later, back in Moreton's apartment, Sophia confirmed the news as she reviewed the results, final table, and play-off pairings on her laptop. Retama had topped the table much as Moreton had insisted during his phone conversation with Charlie Broome. Torreaño CF were runners-up, one point behind with Estrella Azul in third and Politanio B in fourth. She also confirmed that Retama's future would now be decided in a two-legged play-off against Atlético Santa Kristina. The team that Fouad had joined after leaving Retama. They had won their league by no less than twelve points, having lost only twice all season.

As she was relating the facts to him, a thought was running around Jon Moreton's brain. He knew the name of that club for some other reason as well. There was something that Sophia had told him, but he couldn't quite remember.

'Did you tell me something else about Atlético Santa Kristina before?' he asked. 'Something other than about Fouad?'

Sophia thought for a moment. 'Well, they're a very wealthy club now. A couple of years ago, they were taken over by a big corporation. That's how they got the money to persuade Fouad to join them.'

There was something more. Then it landed with him. 'Cerámica Internacional?' he asked.

'Yes, that's right,' she replied. 'They're very famous in Spain. You know them, then?' Moreton apparently did, but didn't remember why. 'I guess I must. Perhaps I've seen an advertisement on TV for them or similar.'

Two days later, as he and Sophia were eating lunch on the balcony of his apartment, Moreton received a phone call from Charlie Broome. 'Are you doing training this evening as usual?' he asked.

'Sure. Got three sessions to work with the players before Sunday, so we'll be giving it all we've got, mate. Don't worry.'

'No, Jon. I wasn't checking up on you. I was asking because Billy tells me that he's ready to play again, and wants to join in the training.'

'Yeah, that's great, Chaz…'

'Is there a problem, Jon? Don't you want him to play? Christ, Jon. It was you that persuaded me to spend the money to get him here in the first place.'

'No Chaz. It's not that. Here's the situation. Our first leg is away in Santa Kristina. They're a really good side and it'll be a bit of a backs to the wall job for us there. Then, in the second leg, we can try and get the result we need. Billy will be much more important in that game than in a muck and nettles away game where we'll be spending most of the time defending. Do you see what I mean, Chaz?'

'Yeah, OK, Jon. I understand. It's your decision of course, but why not just stick him on the bench, just in case. Who knows?'

The idea made sense.

'Yeah, we could do that. Send him over this evening and we'll see how he gets on with the training over the week, and take it from there.'

A few hours later, as Moreton and Sophia arrived at the ground for the evening's training session, the regular sight of the green-liveried Broome Cerámica van parked outside announced that Billy Swan had beaten them to it. Much as Charlie Broome had suggested, Billy Swan certainly seemed fit again. He looked both sharp in training and eager to be back with the squad. The improvement from the last weekend, when there had been an occasional, but clearly discernible, hint of a limp was impressive. Even lifting the goalscoring hero into the air, after the last gasp equaliser, seemed to have had little adverse effect.

Moreton kept the session deliberately low-key, but as Sophia completed the warm-down exercises and the players trooped back to the dressing room, he walked over to her with a pensive expression betraying his thoughts.

'Billy?'

Sophia had been expecting the question. She shook her head slightly. 'Look, Jon, if he was ten years younger, it might be worth the risk – *might* be. He hasn't played for weeks, and has had one really gentle training session. Do you remember what happened in the first game of the season?'

Moreton nodded.

'It's not the injury,' Sophia continued, 'It's the lack of recovery time and opportunity to regain fitness. Real fitness. Match fitness.'

He already knew the truth, but hoped to be persuaded otherwise. 'Yeah, I know. You're right. Of course, you're right.'

He looked across as Swan, Kiko and Victor entered the dressing room together, with the latter again apparently shaping a shot and recalling his moment of glory. Swan draped an arm around his friend's shoulder, with an unseen smile. Musketeers United.

Turning back to Sophia, Moreton asked a question he knew to be forlorn. 'What about putting him on the sub's bench?'

'That's fine. So long as you leave him there,' she said with her head slightly cocked to one side, inviting an inevitable agreement. 'Throwing him on with ten minutes left after a few training sessions could be even worse. Jon, you know this, don't you? It's a bad idea.'

'I'm sorry,' he said, drawing her close to him.

He kissed her gently on the head. Sophia rested her head on his chest.

'I'm sorry,' he repeated.

'Another week's training and then put him on the bench for the home game. It's worth the risk then.'

Training the following day followed a similar pattern. Again, Billy Swan buzzed around during the drills, clearly out to impress. The apparent new-found vigour on display would have confounded so many of the coaches who had endured lacklustre attention to such matters during his professional times. The Retama effect had given the jaded, cynical veteran a new lease of life.

Although Moreton knew that Sophia's assessment was right, he feared that leaving Swan out of the squad may just deflate him totally, and the apparently boundless and widely infectious enthusiasm he was displaying may well have been dissipated, at the same time. After speaking with Sophia, Moreton decided to take up Sophia's idea of putting Swan on the bench, and then leaving him there. As he had explained to Charlie Broome, the away game at Santa Kristina would hardly be the sort of game where a talent like Billy Swan would be most effective, but giving him a place on the bench would keep him involved and, hopefully, maintain the bubbling zest he was creating among the squad.

Before lunch on Friday, Moreton and Sophia were sitting on the side of the pool, as Sophia's phone trilled out and, after closing out the call, she jumped to her feet. 'I have to go. That was Elena. She said that she wanted to talk to me about something.'

'OK.'

'I'm meeting her for lunch. Carry on and enjoy your swim. We'll catch up later.'

'No problem. See you later.'

'I hope it's not boyfriend trouble,' Sophia added, as she turned.

Jon Moreton held his nose and, folding his legs beneath him, dropped into the cooling water until it covered his head. The eerie quiet of the underwater world paused all thoughts, and when he lifted his head clear of the surface again, Sophia was gone.

Three hours later, Moreton was sitting on his balcony reading, when the apartment door opened, heralding Sophia's return. Walking through the living area onto the balcony, she kissed him tenderly, before sitting down opposite him. It was not difficult detect that there was clearly something on her mind. Offering an empathetic ear, Moreton mused. 'Boyfriend trouble?'

Sophia thought for a moment before replying.

'Not really. Well, yes. Perhaps. I'm not really sure.'

Unsurprisingly, the reply left Moreton confused – and it showed.

'Give me a moment to get a glass of water, and I'll explain,' Sophia said, rising from her chair.

Returning with the water, and thoughts now more coherently organised, she sat down. 'OK,' she said after a while. 'I met up with Elena. She wanted to tell me something. It's about Nicolás, and about Señor Broome.' She paused. 'And perhaps about the club.'

Now the information was new, but Moreton felt that the mists were deepening rather than clearing. He sought a resolution.

'I'm not sure what you mean.'

'You remember that Nicolás works at Broome Cerámica, don't you?'

Moreton nodded slowly in reply, recalling the conversation they had had with Elena and her boyfriend some months ago.

'He works in the accounts there, managing a team dealing with invoices, payments, all that sort of things – including all of the club's finances.'

She paused, inviting Moreton to acknowledge the information.

'A few days ago, Nicolás told Elena that there was a rumour in the office that some of his team were going to lose their jobs. One of the team asked him if the rumour was true, but he knew nothing about it, and told them so.'

Moreton had never worked in an office, but in any business involving a group of people, there are always rumours. Football clubs were no different. He thought it a strange thing to be causing concern.

'Later that day, Nicolás decided to ask Señor Broome whether the rumours were true, so he went to see him.'

She paused again, almost as if for dramatic effect.

'He told Nicolás that it was true. Three people would be leaving in a month or so.'

'So Nicolás is going to lose his job?'

Sophia shook her head. 'No. Nicolás isn't losing his job, but three people in his team are.'

Sophia could tell that Moreton wasn't following the trail of breadcrumbs she had left.

'They are the part of the team that deals with the club, Jon.'

She waited for a moment, expecting a reaction from Moreton.

'Jon, if these people are leaving, what's happening to the club?'

Moreton now understood her concern, but wanted to reassure her that things probably weren't as Nicolás, Elena, and indeed she, had thought.

He reached out his hand, and took hers in it. 'Look. You don't know Chaz like I know him, Sophia.' He smiled. 'He's taken over that business to make it more efficient and more profitable. If he's cutting back on some staff, it's because he feels there's enough people there to cover all the work required. He's out to make money. I know he's got plans for the club, for its future. We're doing what we have to do, and when the time comes, he'll do what he has to do to make things work.'

Moreton was convinced that the understandable concern that Nicolás had for his colleagues losing their jobs had, in Elena's mind, become translated into something with adverse consequences for the club and she had wanted to appraise her friend.

Sophia seemed reassured.

He continued. 'I'm sure it's nothing we should be worried about. We'll take care of the football side of the club. It's what we're good at, and Chaz will deal with the finances. That's his end. He knows what he's doing. I trust him.'

The last three words chased away the final lingering doubts in Sophia's mind. She squeezed Moreton's hand, happily accepting his reassurance.

'I'm sorry, Jon. It's just that we've come so far, all of us: you, me, the players, all of us. And now we're so close. I don't want it to fall apart.'

Moreton smiled at Sophia with affection. As well as loving her more than anyone in his life, he realised that he liked her so much as well. She was so caring and passionate about things.

'Look, we need to get ready for training. Not sure if you know, but there's a bit of a game coming up.'

The Games People Play

After Friday night's training session, Moreton announced the team that would face Santa Kristina two days later. There had been lingering thoughts in Moreton's mind, whether to retain Sanz's role as a man-marker and deploy him against Fouad who, if Sophia's assessment was accurate, would be the opposition's most potent weapon. Deciding to revert to the usual formation, however, and with no injury concerns – aside from Billy Swan – the first eleven virtually selected itself.

Juan Torres was in goal with Sanz, Kiko, Victor and Adrián in front of him. Swan's continuing absence allowed Moreton to partner Matías and Samuel in the centre of a solid-looking midfield, with Guido and Vasquez on the flanks. Pushed forward into the number ten role, Revi was there to provide ammunition for Santi. When the substitutes were read out, there was a small but noticeable cheer when the last name was "Swan." The Musketeer was back into the action and, sitting either side of the veteran, as always, Kiko and Victor both patted him on the back.

Now away from their regional group, Retama would need to travel for almost three hours to get to Santa Kristina for the first leg of the play-off. It meant an earlier than usual start, but the mood on the coach was anything but sleepy. A mixture of expectation and tension ensured that everyone was wide-awake and ready for action. The journey passed quickly with excited talk, shouts and even the occasional song burst out – often led by the lilting tones of Kiko: everyone had the music in them.

A little short of the active time it would take the participating clubs to play out both legs of their promotion play-offs, the coach delivering the CD Retama party to Santa Kristina drew up outside a pristine looking stadium, a hundred metres or so from the gleaming glass-fronted regional offices of Cerámica Internacional. The name of the club owners on the hoardings around the pitch and emblazoned in white on the otherwise all green kit of the home team players let everyone know who was calling the shots.

As the players left the coach and walked towards the dressing room, a buzz of excitement erupted as one of the Santa Kristina players, jogged across from his team-mates to meet the arriving group. Watching from just inside the gates of the stadium, the many hugs, pats on the back and handshakes, quickly told Moreton that the African player with the number nine on the back of his green shirt was Fouad. After greeting his former team-mates, Fouad made a direct line for Sophia and the hug between them illustrated the deep affection of a brother and sister separated for so long. After exchanging a few words, and another hug, Fouad then jogged back to his team-mates.

Moreton walked over to where Sophia was standing. He had purposely stood away from the others, feeling like an uninvited guest at a reunion party.

'Fouad?'

Sophia nodded.

'He doesn't look like much'

'I know. Not big, not fast particularly, not a great dribbler, but he scores goals.'

Moreton shook his head a little. 'How?'

'I don't know. But he does. All types of goals too. Long range, tap-ins, headers, whatever. He just has that ability. If we can stop him scoring across these two games, we'll have a great chance to clinch promotion, but it won't be easy. He just told me that he'd only failed to score in eight games all season, and he was out injured for four of those. Of those four games, two were the only games that they had lost during the season, and the other two were both draws.'

An hour or so later, with the two teams lined up, the referee's whistle set the game in motion. The neat ground was filled with around three thousand fans, mainly in the green and white colours of the home team. Behind one goal was a large green banner with Fouad's face on it, and the word '*Gol!*' emblazoned across it in bold white letters. It was clear that the former Retama player was now the local hero in Santa Kristina.

The Retama coach had told his players to ensure a solid start. If the instruction was intended to ensure his players spent little time attacking the home team, it had almost been superfluous. The Santa Kristina players were insisting on that requirement themselves. Intent on taking an early lead, they played neat, passing through the blue Retama lines, with Fouad's clever runs keeping Kiko and Victor particularly busy. Revi was guided back into a midfield five by his coach's prompting, to try and stem the flow of the game, but the home team were dominating both possession and position.

Danger seemed to have been averted when a cross into the Retama penalty area from the left drifted over Fouad's head. With instinctive reactions, however, he pivoted acrobatically, and fired in a scissor-kick shot. An alert Torres was compelled to gratefully turn the effort over the bar. It marked the end of the opening quarter-hour of the game, and Retama's goal was still to be breached. By this stage, Moreton had hoped that his team, having weathered the early attacks, would grow both in confidence, and into the game. The general direction of play showed little change, though, as the home team continued to press and Fouad's uncanny knack for being in the right place at the right time offered a relentless threat.

A last-ditch block from Kiko diverted the striker's goal bound shot after he had wriggled past Victor. Then, from a corner, a Fouad header struck the outside of a post before bouncing clear. Torres handled a couple of long-range efforts confidently, before having to plunge low and left to divert another shot around the post. With less than ten minutes to the break, the defence was still holding out, but another move saw Fouad glide past Matías, before a despairing challenge from Samuel brought him down just outside of the penalty area.

Fouad lined up to take the kick, firing high with top spin to attempt to bring the ball down behind the wall and below the bar. Torres had read his intention, and was already moving across to cover, but the shot was deflected by the head of Guido, standing in the wall, and flew across to the side of the goal now vacated by Retama's last line of defence. The goalkeeper could only stand and watch as the arcing flight of the ball drifted towards the gaping net, before striking crossbar, then post, and bouncing into his grateful arms. On the Retama bench, Moreton threw up his arms in relief. A few metres away, the Santa Kristina bench did the same in anguish.

Without any further great alarm, the break was reached and, back in the dressing room, with half of the required job done, Moreton and Sophia congratulated the team on their efforts. Looking around him it was clear that the effort of keeping the rampaging Fouad out, and chasing his team-mates around the pitch as they guarded possession like a spoilt child unwilling to share his candy, had taken a physical toll. Choosing the right time, and personnel, for substitutions in the second-half would be key.

The pattern of the game was hardly interrupted by the fifteen or so minutes the players spent in the dressing rooms, except for the general direction of play now moving in the opposite direction. Even Santi was being funnelled back into a midfield role to help out his beleaguered team-mates. In the first ten minutes, Fouad had seen another two attempts on goal thwarted at the last. Covering behind his goalkeeper and guarding the post, Sanz had headed one from the line after another header from a corner, and then a cross-shot from an acute angle had Torres scrambling back to tip the ball around the far post.

Fifteen minutes passed, and Moreton decided to make the first change. Withdrawing Santi, he sent Felipe Blanco on instead. Reprising a previous ploy, he positioned Guido as the central striker and Blanco replaced him on the flank. The pace of the young Guido may turn any vague opportunity to break into a real chance but, even if that opportunity never arose. At least the threat he carried would ensure some measure of defensive cover was required by the home team, keeping players occupied at the back, rather than having them run free further forwards.

The change made little difference and although a couple of chances came to hoist a long ball over the heads of the home back four for the speedster to chase, both were squandered as the passes were hurried, and carried too far in front of the chasing Guido. At the other end, the play was intensifying as the home team pressed for that all-important first goal. Torres made a further two saves, as shots flew in from distance.

It was clear that more Retama legs were in need of assistance as fatigue and lactic acid tugged and burnt at their tiring muscles. With twenty minutes to play, Moreton withdrew Revi. Instead, Moreton sent on the rugged Juan Palermo with instructions to work in the midfield, support Matías and Samuel, and compete in the aerial battles, helping Kiko. Just two minutes later, it seemed like an inspired decision, gifted from the gods of football.

Running onto a pass from the right, Fouad cut into the gap between Adrián and Victor, bearing down in a one-on-one with Torres. Fouad shaped to drive the ball low to the left-handed goalkeeper's right side, before checking and lifting it, as Torres appeared to fall for the feint. Reading the ruse at the last second however, the young goalkeeper threw up an arm and his fingers caressed the ball as it slipped past them on its way into the net. Fouad turned in celebration but, as the ball rolled unerringly towards its appointed destination, a muscular figure in blue, sprinting back, slid in desperately to divert it around the post for a corner, before careering into the net via collision with the post, a leg either side of the upright. For a moment, Juan Palermo lay motionless as his team-mates rushed to his aid.

On the Retama bench, Sophia reached for her bag, but as she was about to enter the field, the rugged elder Palermo brother pulled himself to his feet, to be mobbed by his team-mates. A thumbs up to the bench confirmed he was fit to carry on and, as if to underscore the fact, he climbed to reach the resulting corner, and head it powerfully away. Jon Moreton jumped to his feet and clapped his hands above his head in acclaim and thanks to a player who, for the most part had lost his regular starting berth in the team, but had still offered full commitment to the Retama cause. As he lowered his hands, he noticed Juan's young brother stranding beside him punching the air with tears in his eyes.

The heroic rescue had given new vigour to the visiting team, but adrenalin rushes can only be temporary and now with a dozen minutes remaining, Moreton played his last card. He had intended to send young Sebastián on to replace Antonio Vasquez who had laboured hard to help Sanz defend the right flank of the Retama defence, but the emotional display of the younger Palermo brother caused a change of mind.

Withdrawing the right-winger, he sent on José Palermo, asking Sophia to tell him that his brother needed his help. The younger sibling raced onto the pitch, clenching his fist at his brother as he ran past him and screaming at the other players. Jon Moreton knew that in many games that season, his team had been second best, but had overcome the odds thanks to their spirit and togetherness. He'd played that card again.

Time ticked on, and Moreton began to console himself with the fact that whatever happened now, surely, they couldn't concede more than an odd goal, and even that would still mean they were still alive in the tie, with the home leg to come. As the seconds slipped by, it began to look like the home team were losing heart. Fouad continued making runs into space, but the passes to him were now over-hit, intercepted by the massed Retama defensive ranks, or not seen, as possession was wasted with shots from distance that sailed high and wide of the Retama goal.

In the dying seconds of the game, as another wave of attack broke on the rock of the blue defensive line, a quick interchange of passes saw the ball played to Samuel who hit it long over the halfway line. Guido turned to give chase, outrunning the Santa Kristina defenders deployed to guard him. He collected the ball and, closing in on the goalkeeper, threaded it past his right hand. A goal for the visitors would have constituted the ultimate smash-and-grab raid, but the ball trickled wide and the whistle went to end the game.

Jon Moreton rose from the bench and together with Sophia shook hands with the Santa Kristina coaches. Returning to his players, he felt a little disappointed that the late chance hadn't drifted the other side of the post, but overall the sense of pride and respect for his players quickly dispelled such thoughts.

Entering the dressing room to be greeted by a group of players that had clearly given their all, Moreton made a beeline for Juan Palermo. The rugged hard man of the Retama forward line was drinking heavily from a water bottle, but lowered it as his coach approached. Moreton picked up another bottle and raised it to his player. They banged the bottles together and Moreton shouted *'Salud!'* as they each took long draughts of the cold liquid. *'Héroe!'* acclaimed the coach, as they all cheered. Then quietly to the player: *'Que t'al?'* Juan Palermo puffed out his cheeks, before pulling the waistband of his shorts forward and peering inside. *'Uno. Dos.'* He counted methodically, before looking up and smiling at his coach. *'Todo es bueno!'* He declared wiping his brow in exaggerated relief.

If the journey from Retama had been marked by the hubbub and noise of nervous anticipation, the return was far more subdued. Satisfaction at what they had achieved settled over the group like a comforting blanket and, combined with the physical and emotional exertions of the day, many slept. At the front of the coach, Sophia dozed, leaning on Jon Moreton's shoulder as he watched the fields pass by, reflecting on the changes to his life since he had arrived in Spain. Now, the club were on the verge of achieving something that he had never, up to that day, allowed himself to even seriously contemplate. One game from promotion and salvation.

Most importantly though, he could remain in Spain with the woman who had become an indispensable part of his life; and then, what next? He realised he had now arrived at the same crossroads that Sophia had asked for directions from a few days ago. Just then, his phone rang. Sophia was startled from her doze by the insistent tone of Moreton's mobile, and she sat up as he related the story of the game to Charlie Broome.

There was a lot of pride in his voice as he talked, but also recognition of the efforts of the players, and indeed her. She smiled at him broadly as he spoke, and he winked at her in return. Having closed out the call, he placed the phone in his pocket, and turned to Sophia.

'Guess what he asked me?'

Sophia thought for a moment, and then her eyes lit up, convinced of the answer. 'He wanted to know if Billy had played?'

'Yep. I think Chaz has a crush on our Billy, you know.'

Two days later, at training on Tuesday evening, it was a group of still tired, but largely happy coaches and players that assembled at the Estadio Antonio Núñez for what would be little more than a gentle warm-down and strolled session to relieve fatigued muscles. As they gathered in the centre of the pitch, a small figure appeared on the concrete wall beside the coaches' bench, wearing the blue Retama shirt, the ever-present, faded cloth cap on his head. Esteban held his hands in the air, and clapped the players in appreciation of their efforts. Moreton beamed a huge smile at Sophia.

'In a few days,' she said. 'The crowd watching will be much bigger than that.'

The training sessions across the following day and then on Friday were also low key, with the exception of Billy Swan, as Sophia took him apart from the remaining squad, working through a series of exercises and routines, designed to build up fitness after his absence.

Moreton knew that the task for the coming Sunday would be even more demanding than the away leg. Another dogged defensive display would be required but, on top of that, Retama would also need to score a goal. Friday's session was therefore structured with that in mind and, after discussing plans with Sophia, he had decided on his tactics, and selected a starting eleven that would best serve the plan.

In front of Torres, the back four remained in place. Ahead of them the changes were significant. The Palermo brothers were both given starting places, replacing Vasquez and Guido on the flanks, whilst the reliable mechanics Matías and Samuel remained in the team's engine room. Felipe Blanco was also drafted in as an extra man in the centre of midfield, with Santi again required to be the loneliest of lone forwards. Moreton and Sophia had rationalised that if this artisan team could restrict the Santa Kristina forwards for an hour or so, they could then deploy the artistry stacked on the substitutes' bench when they could be most effective, against tiring opposition. The visitors would be keen to secure an early lead; ensuring that they were denied this would be key. Given the success of Moreton's tactics over the past months, the players had come to accept his ideas almost without question. Few disputed the logic he used to explain this selection. Well, not exactly few – in fact, just one.

After the session had broken up, Billy Swan took Moreton by the arm, and as the players and Sophia headed in the opposite direction towards the dressing room, the veteran guided his former team-mate towards the centre circle.

'Jon. Why not give me a game. I'm fit. I told you already. You should play me.'

Moreton started to speak, but Swan cut him short.

'Stuff that, Jon. You have to play me. I *have* to play.'

It was a tone of voice that seemed alien to Moreton. He'd never seen such a reaction from Billy Swan to not being selected. Had the experience and season playing with Retama affected him so much? Moreton was unsure, but one thing he was determined to underscore was that it was he who selected the team, not Billy Swan, and in the few words he used to reply to the apparently sulking player, he made that situation abundantly clear.

The following day, Moreton sat on the balcony of his apartment, enjoying a light lunch and coffee, as Sophia had gone into town to meet Elena for lunch. Just then, a powder blue Mercedes drew up on the road below, and the tanned Charlie Broome stepped out. Ten minutes earlier, Moreton had received a call from his friend, asking if he could call round "for a chat." It seemed an innocent enough request, especially with such an important game the following day, but there was a hint of something in his tone that unsettled Moreton.

Rising from his chair, he waved at Broome who was heading towards the gate of the complex. Moreton was on his way to let him in, when the door opened. Charlie Broome clearly still had keys to the apartment. Moreton invited his visitor to sit on the balcony while he made him a cup of coffee. He returned to his chair on the balcony as Charlie Broome was tapping on his phone, and placed the cup down in front of his guest. Broome briefly looked up in acknowledgement.

'Yeah, Jon,' he said absently. 'Thanks.' And then he slotted the phone into his jacket pocket.

'So. What can I do for you, Chaz?'

'Billy tells me that he's on the bench again tomorrow. Jon, you persuaded me to lay out the money to get him here.'

There was a clear irritation, now percolating through, and Moreton lifted his cup of coffee to his lips to give him an opportunity to contemplate how he should respond to the implied accusation. Opting to try and reclaim a calmness that he felt was quickly disappearing from the conversation, he replied in studiously measured candour. 'I did. And has it worked out well, or not?'

'Yes, Jon. He's been a great asset for the team.' A short pause. 'Our best player.'

Moreton nodded, accepting what he felt was everything but an apology.

His friend continued. 'So, in this massive game tomorrow, play him, Jon. If this is going to turn out right, he needs to play. He's the best chance of getting the right result. I understood why you didn't want to risk him in the away leg, but this is the big game: the last game. Everything hinges on it.'

Despite knowing Charlie Broome for many years, and often being as close to him as apparently anyone ever got, Jon Moreton readily accepted that, even to him, it was always difficult to read the intentions of his friend. Now however, the passion he was displaying regarding the future of CD Retama, seemed to lay his soul bare. Jon Moreton smiled easily at the figure across the table from him.

'Chaz, I've never really known you care so much about a football club, let alone a single match.'

Broome smiled back. 'Of course, I care, Jon. More than you think. It matters to me, Jon. Tomorrow's game can make such a massive difference here, to me, to the town, to the business. Everything.'

'Look, Chaz, unless we're winning well and cruising to victory – and despite how much I'd like that, I can't see it happening – Billy is going to get on the pitch. He'll be there at the end of the game, hopefully when it'll matter most. If everything goes to plan. He'll probably be the one that makes the difference.'

He paused a little, discerning his friend's softening demeanour. 'He's our ace. The wild card we have. I'm not going to go down still holding that card, mate. When the big hand is played, it'll be on the table, face up.'

Moreton's words appeared to have the desired effect.

Across the table, Charlie Broome seemed much more assured.

'OK, Jon. I understand. It's just that so much hinges on this game, and we need Billy out there.'

Moreton nodded.

'I know Chaz. Don't worry. When it matters most, he will be.'

Charlie Broome got to his feet, and glanced at his watch. 'I've got to go.'

'OK, mate,' Moreton replied, rising as well, and walking towards the door as his guest made to leave.

'You won't believe it, Jon,' Broome, as he paused by the door. 'Billy's even been doing some extra training to make sure he's fit and ready.'

Jon Moreton's expression unwittingly revealed surprise, bordering on disbelief at Broome's words.

'Really?'

'Yeah. He's working through the exercises that Sophia had him doing at training and running up and down the stairs as well.'

'Christ, Chaz. Tell him to be careful on those bloody stairs, mate.'

Charlie Broome was around halfway down the steps when he stopped and turned back, looking up at Moreton with apparent confusion, inviting explanation.

'The stairs? The fall? Billy?'

'Oh, yeah.' The penny dropped. 'Yes, I'll tell him. Oh, by the way, there'll be one more spectator there tomorrow. I'll take a couple of hours off from Sunday overtime at the office. Put on a good show for me.'

Standing at the door of his apartment, Moreton shook his head slowly. How could his friend not have understood the reference to the stairs? Head's too wrapped up in other things, he concluded.

As he was about to close the door, he heard Sophia's voice. She was talking to Broome. Perhaps it was merely exchanging pleasantries, but Moreton smiled that the animosity between her and his friend had now apparently disappeared. He stood waiting in the doorway until she opened the gate, and walked up the stairs to greet him with a kiss.

'What did he want to talk to you about?' she asked, walking into the apartment. 'Not about Billy, again?'

'Yeah. A little bit. But, also about his plans for the club. We need to make sure Billy's out there at the end of the game tomorrow. He's going to be important.'

Sleep was elusive that night for Jon Moreton. He tried to turn his thoughts away from the events of the following afternoon, but without much success. It was a strange phenomenon for him. Many of the games he'd been involved in, either as a player or coach, were more prestigious, in terms of the relative standard of league or competition, but this game meant more than merely the result of a football match, more than a trophy and promotion, more than success or failure. This outcome of this game would shape his life.

He was unsure how many hours he had searched for that elusive haven of sleep. In the half-light of the early hours of a Spanish summer Sunday morning, Moreton lay there staring at the ceiling. Next to him, Sophia slept soundly. The gentle rhythm of her breathing and the hypnotic hum of the air conditioner were the only sounds he could hear. He sat up, swinging his legs over the side of the bed, rubbing his over-tired eyes and quietly opened one of the drawers in the cupboards. Grabbing a pair of tracksuit bottoms and a vest, he padded silently out of the bedroom. He walked to the kitchen and took a bottle of cold water from the fridge, tipping the liquid into a glass, before moving back into the living room and opening the curtains a little to look out over the rooftops of the houses and towards the mountains in the distance.

The myriad lights twinkled at him, as the pre-dawn stillness of the night wrapped itself over the scene. He took a sip of cold water and, convincing himself of a clarity of vision forbidden by the darkness, looked in the direction of the Estadio Antonio Núñez. Could he discern the unlit floodlights peeping above the surrounding rooftops, like sleeping eyes lifted high on an antenna, above the mundane reality of everyday life, able to look down on the world below and discern otherwise hidden secrets?

He pondered for a moment. If those eyes were open now, what dark deeds would they see? He yawned widely and, taking a final sip of water before closing the curtains again, he returned to his bed and his vigil, staring at the ceiling. Sleep must have eventually wrapped its arms around him, though: a few hours later, he awoke to a bright sunny sky. It was game day.

The hours passed slowly. Both he and Sophia were tense and excited in equal measures. They tried to make breakfast and lunch last a long time, merely to eat into the hours before they could leave the apartment and head towards the ground. Normally, they would arrive around a couple of hours or so before kick-off, but on this day, normality seemed ill-fitted. Immediately after lunch, they left the apartment and walked the fifteen minutes or so towards the ground.

By the time Moreton and Sophia were standing in the home dressing room, giving last minute instructions to the players, a crowd bordering on two thousand had found seats among the dusty concrete steps of the Estadio Antonio Núñez, hoping, daring to believe, that their local club could achieve promotion, although perhaps not realising how crucial such success, or its alternative, would be.

If the players had not already appreciated the size of the crowd awaiting their appearance, the cheer that sounded out as they exited the dressing room and walked onto the pitch, dispelled any such doubts. Moreton and Sophia took their places on the bench, after shaking hands and renewing acquaintances with their opposite numbers from Santa Kristina.

Sophia looked around at the crowd, beaming. 'Wow. 'This town has a football club again.'

Moreton smiled back at her but shook his head. 'Not really. This football club has a town again.'

'And we mustn't let it lose them again.'

Above the pitch, above the watching fans and above the players, the eyes of the floodlights peered down. The night had now passed. There was no escape, and all things would now be open to the full glaring spotlight of day.

As the referee blew to start the game, it was as if the intervening seven days had hardly happened at all. Aside from being in a different location, nothing very much else had changed from the game played on the previous Sunday. Again, it was the team wearing green that dominated. As they monopolised possession, moving the ball quickly around the pitch probing for an opening that Fouad could exploit, the Retama players chased and harried. On the flanks, the Palermo brothers justified their inclusions, energetically chasing back to assist the defence with Felipe Blanco also working to limit space for the visiting midfield.

A dozen minutes had passed with the home team hardly enjoying any possession, and certainly none in the other half of the field. As Moreton had thought would be the case, the visitors pressed energetically for an early goal.

A cross found Fouad in the box, but alert to the danger, Kiko moved swiftly to clear the ball. On fifteen minutes, a slip by Sanz allowed the visiting left winger to cut into the area, bearing down on Torres at a narrow angle. Kiko was drawn across to try and block, but Blanco, seeing had Fouad drawn back towards the penalty spot for a pass to be pulled back from the bye line, headed to mark him instead. His intuition was rewarded when the inevitable pass came Fouad's way and the Retama player was able to step in and intercept.

After twenty minutes, the energetic threat of an early goal from Fouad or one of his team-mates eased, and the game settled into a battle of attrition, with the Retama players diligently applying themselves, spending their energy grinding down the attacking forwards. Fouad was now dropping deeper, in search of more possession. Conversely, while it kept him away from the penalty area, it also gave him a greater opportunity to influence the game. Two shots hit from distance went narrowly wide, but midway through the first period another effort from outside of the penalty area required a flying save from Torres to turn the ball away for a corner.

With the Palermo brothers and Kiko, plus Santi dropping back to assist in any aerial attacks, Retama were well served with height, and from the corner, the Santa Kristina players eschewed the normal cross into the box. Instead the ball was driven low into the goalmouth. The younger Palermo brother jabbed out a foot to block, but the attempt merely diverted it towards the edge of the area, and a shot was fired in that struck the crossbar before bouncing clear.

On the Retama bench, the tension was clearly building. The thirty-minute mark was passed as Adrián slid in a tackle to deny Fouad's run from the right, conceding another corner.

'I'm not sure how much longer we can keep them out,' Moreton whispered quietly to Sophia by his side. The concern etched onto her face required no spoken confirmation. Five minutes later, Moreton kicked at the ground as Torres clutched another cross to his chest. Now with just minutes to the break, Retama eventually found Santi up field, and a neat turn inside of his marker saw him into space. Galloping away like some stallion offered an unexpected chance of freedom from the yoke of bridle and saddle, he left the defenders trailing as he headed towards goal. Moreton was on his feet, roaring his young forward on, but, at the vital moment, he overplayed the ball and the visiting goalkeeper plunged to collect as Santi hurdled over him. At least the effort had eaten up a few seconds, and without any further major problems, the referee ended the first half of the game.

Back in the Retama dressing room, Moreton and Sophia discussed using their substitutes, but decided it was too early. They needed to take more time off the clock with the "artisan" team they had put out. Every minute they kept the Santa Kristina players out, would eat into both their confidence and reserves of energy. This was a team used to winning games, and relying on Fouad's goals. For three halves of football, so far, Retama had denied them both of those comforts, and the longer they continued to do so, the more the potential for the home team to strike would increase.

A similar thought may have been eating into the thoughts of the Santa Kristina coach. His team certainly began the second period with a renewed vigour and intent. The first ten minutes of the half saw no less than six attempts on target for the visitors. Fortunately, three were blocked and Torres dealt competently with the others, avoiding any spill of the ball with Fouad prowling hungrily in pursuit as each effort was hit in. Ten more minutes passed with further attempts. Fouad hit one post with a header, and the other one with a shot on the turn after receiving the ball on the edge of the penalty area, swivelling clear of Victor. On both occasions, Torres was a hugely concerned, but impotent, spectator.

The halfway point of the second half was reached when Moreton made his first change. Felipe Blanco was removed with Revi sent on. As the floppy haired playmaker trotted onto the pitch and a weary Felipe Blanco dropped onto the bench, Moreton heard an urgent call from behind him.

'Jon!' The shout rang out clearly.

Moreton turned to see the face of Charlie Broome standing behind the bench. 'What about Billy? Put Billy on for Christ's sake!'

Jon Moreton had two choices. He could either stand and argue with his employer or merely acknowledge his presence and carry on. He chose the former, raising his thumb, and eyebrows, nodding as if agreeing. The ploy worked as Broome disappeared, apparently returning to his seat, in an unseen part of the ground.

As in the first game, the Santa Kristina players began to look increasingly frustrated at the failure to break through and their game deteriorated with passes mishit and control of the ball diminishing. They were still the dominant force, but their threat on Torres had noticeably receded. Entering the last fifteen minutes of the final game of CD Retama's season, another substitution was played. A weary and forlorn Santi was taken off and Guido sent on. Moreton placed the wide man in his normal position, moving Juan Palermo into the central striker role.

Jon Moreton sat on the bench, staring steadfastly ahead as he heard that voice again; however, the noise from the crowd as Retama came more into the game offered the option of pretending he hadn't heard anything. Despite the voice increasing in both volume and intensity, Moreton refused to acknowledge it, as one more minute ticked by. Then, jumping to his feet, he waved down the touchline to where the remaining Retama substitutes had been warming up, beckoning Billy Swan. As the veteran trotted back towards his coach, Moreton sneaked a masked smile to Sophia as the urgent noises in his head suddenly disappeared. With the thirteen minutes remaining, Retama were playing their card.

Billy Swan stripped off his training top and stood beside his coach receiving last minute instructions, before trotting onto the field, replacing Matías, with Revi now moving into midfield alongside Samuel. As he did so, something shouted from the crowd, clearly caught the veteran's attention. He paused momentarily, glancing towards the source of the voice, before looking down at the ground and then back to where Jon Moreton was standing. Turning back towards the pitch, Swan clenched his right hand into a fist and smacked it hard into the palm of his left hand. Whether it was a gesture of determination or angry frustration was unclear. Either way, Jon Moreton's had now played all his cards; all of the season, all of his future, now depended on the dozen or so minutes remaining.

A couple of those minutes passed without much significant action, then came the moment that the Retama players had so patiently awaited. Revi gained possession inside his own half and, turning past his marker, spread the ball out to the left and the waiting Guido. With energy undimmed, contrasting with the depletion of his marker, he confidently played the ball into space beyond the fullback and tore after it, easily outpacing the flailing attentions of the defender. Reaching the bye-line, he clipped the ball into the Santa Kristina penalty area, hoping for a blue shirt to be awaiting the delivery.

Juan Palermo had been the home team's lone front man since Santi had been withdrawn, but, he'd had the opportunity to recharge his energy whilst standing forlornly on the halfway line awaiting a chance of possession. Invigorated by the sight of Guido's advance, he had forced his body into a forward run towards the penalty area. As the ball arced in and flighted towards the forehead of the elder Palermo sibling it seemed that fate had smiled on CD Retama.

Some fifty or so metres away, Moreton, Sophia and the remaining Retama players on the bench each slowly climbed to their feet in expectation. Had the ball been laser-guided it could hardly have married up with Palermo's run any better as they met by the penalty spot. Palermo jumped, confident in targeting his header just inside the far post, but the ball sailed mysteriously past him and away to safety. At first, he couldn't understand how he had missed his appointment with what seemed to be destiny, in the guise of a football. The shrill demands of the referee's whistle, however, offered an indication.

As he had jumped, a trailing defending, realising he could not prevent the attempt on goal legitimately, had taken hold of Palermo's shirt, impeding the height of his jump and allowing the ball to escape his eager attentions. It was a desperate attempt to deny the goalscoring chance and brought both a red card for the perpetrator and a penalty kick for the home team. On the bench, although Moreton's anger and frustration fumed at seeing the chance denied by foul means, there was at least the comfort of having the penalty to follow. Swan would convert and there'd be less than ten minutes for the remaining same number of Santa Kristina players to achieve something that a full side had failed to do in the best part of three hours.

On the pitch though, there seemed to be some confusion among the Retama players. Instead of Billy Swan confidently strolling forward to convert the spot-kick, it was Revi with the ball in his hand walking forwards.

Jon Moreton shouted furiously from the touchline: 'Billy. Billy.' Then more insistently, holding on to the middle of the word for a few seconds, demanding compliance: 'Billy!'

Revi put the ball down and turned to the bench with arms outstretched, hunching his shoulders, indicating that him taking the penalty had hardly been his idea.

'Billy,' Moreton shouted again. With apparent reluctance, the player in the number fourteen Retama shirt drank from the poisoned chalice, looking across towards Moreton, and a little beyond him, slowly shaking his head. Standing next to Moreton, Sophia appeared both concerned and confused.

'Is he nervous?'

Moreton shook his head slowly. 'Nerves? Not Billy,' he replied without feeling fully reassured. 'Perhaps he's tweaked his back again or something.'

Billy Swan placed the ball on the ground, twelve yards from the Santa Kristina goal.

'His back seems fine,' Sophia commented.

'Don't worry. Back problem or not. It's a penalty. It's Billy Swan. He's never missed one.'

Moreton was unconsciously repeating the words that had been drilled into him by Swan over the years.

'I'd bet everything on him scoring,' he added, without realising that this was precisely what he was doing.

The referee blew for the kick to be taken and, in his usual style, Swan ambled forward, feinting before kicking the ball, compelling the deceived goalkeeper to commit to his left, as the ball was sent in the opposite direction. Seeing the goalkeeper plunge the wrong way, Jon Moreton was already celebrating, acclaiming the goal that would now surely propel his club towards promotion as the ball clipped the upright and rolled out of play for a goal kick. What happened? For a moment or two, Jon Moreton was in shock. His arms, already raised to celebrate the goal, sank slowly to his sides as, a few yards away, the Santa Kristina bench acclaimed their escape with relief. Billy Swan walked back from the penalty area, head bowed, to be greeted by the consoling attentions of his team-mates. The floodlights peered down, observing, without comment.

'Oh, Jon,' Sophia exclaimed.

'I know. I can't believe it. Billy never misses a penalty. It's something he always bangs on about. Billy takes a penalty, it's a goal.'

He shook his head as the play resumed, and the Santa Kristina goalkeeper punted the ball long downfield from the goal kick. It took a full two minutes before Moreton could push the impossible scenario to the back of his mind, and refocus his attentions on the game. Despite the missed spot kick, with a man advantage, surely things would still favour his team. Out on the field though, it looked like a ten against ten game as Billy Swan walked around in the centre of the field, hardly looking for a pass.

Minutes passed, and now it seemed like both sets of players had settled for a period of extra-time to settle the game. With any goal now surely deciding the issue, nobody wanted to make a mistake. Time was almost up when the visitors won a corner. Sensing a last chance of a break, Moreton funnelled all of his players back to defend except for Guido. A quick clearance and perhaps the game could still be won. Moreton waved his arms frantically encouraging everyone to fall back, bar the fair-haired flyer. Even Swan was shaken from his torpor to defend.

As so often is the case however, when so much depends on a last throw of the dice, the set piece was mishit. Scuffed by the Santa Kristina player trusted with what surely the last roll of the dice, the ball scuttled low into the Retama penalty area, bouncing twice on its journey. Billy Swan had lost himself among the plethora of players but, as the ball apologetically bounced towards the edge of the six-yard box, he ran forward, swinging a right boot at it. Instead, of clearing downfield however, the ball skewed from the side of Swan's boot, and arrowed inside the near post of the home goal, past a startled Juan Torres.

For the second time in the space of less than a dozen minutes, there was a brief silence. Then, for the second time in the space of less than a dozen minutes, the Santa Kristina bench jumped up in celebration. Finally, for the second time in the space of less than a dozen minutes, Billy Swan bowed his head. The Retama players stood in silence as the celebrating visiting players jumped on top of an ever-growing pile of green in the corner, submerging the player who, a few brief seconds earlier, believed that he had cast his club's last chance of victory into the abyss.

There was barely sufficient time for the game to be restarted, before the final whistle was sounded. Retama had been beaten, and it would be the club owned and sponsored by Cerámica Internacional that would take the prize of promotion, while the one owned and sponsored by Broome Cerámica would now face an elongated process in pursuit of the same prize. As the eyes of the floodlights looked down on the disparate emotions of exuberant celebration and a fatigue induced by despair, all deeds were done.

Green shirts celebrated. Blue shirts trudged to the dressing room in twos and threes. Moreton rose to his feet, and hugged Sophia seeking the warmth of her body and the generosity of her spirit to raise him. They smiled weakly at each other. At that moment the voice that had been urging the inclusion of the unfortunate Swan, called out again.

'Jon!' called Charlie Broome from that same position behind the bench.

Broome cocked his head to one side, blowing out his cheeks. 'Hard luck, Jon. So close.'

'I'll catch you up,' Moreton said to Sophia.

She nodded and walked away as Moreton flipped his legs over the wall and walked towards his friend.

'I'm sorry, Chaz. I thought we'd done it. I can't believe Billy missed that penalty.'

'I know, Jon. These things happen. It's not your fault. Sometimes the cards are stacked against you.'

'Thanks, mate. I'm really gutted. Gutted for the guys, the town, and you of course. So many people put their trust in me and... I've come up short.'

Charlie Broome placed a hand on his friend's shoulder. 'Not really, Jon. You've let nobody down. You did all that you could: everything in your power.'

'Yeah,' Moreton replied

At that moment, the Santa Kristina coaches were leaving the field, the celebrations with the players at least put on hold for a while. Moreton looked across with unavoidable envy at the three men in green tracksuits arms around each other, laughing. 'I should go and congratulate them.'

'Sure, Jon.' He said turning to leave. 'I'm going back to the office to catch up on a few things. I think you'll want to find me later, to talk. So that's where I'll be. OK?'

'Sure, Chaz,' Moreton replied, before scrambling back over the wall and walking across to the Santa Kristina coaches.

It was a further fifteen minutes before Jon Moreton shuffled towards the Retama dressing room. Two of the Santa Kristina coaches spoke perfect English and were full of admiration about the job he had done with Retama. One had even remarked about the possibility of working together in the future. Moreton was more than a little surprised that they knew so much about his club, and indeed him. Although it was surely a mere polite comment, he was also flattered by the allusion to potentially be working with them in the future. The conversation had taken much longer than the regulation handshake and exchanging of pleasantries, but at least it had delayed the inevitable return to his players and Sophia, for what would surely be a painfully emotional time.

As Moreton opened the dressing room door, however, the first thing that struck him was the expanse of blue wall behind the benches encircling the room. The walls were visible, as all of the benches were empty. Save for, in the corner, the hunched figure of Billy Swan, surrounded by discarded shirts and shorts, scattered on the floor.

'Where is everybody?' Moreton asked.

The figure in the corner was unmoved.

'Billy? Where is everybody?'

Billy Swan, now appearing a decade older than his years, slowly raised his head, revealing red eyes, puffed up by wiping tears away.

'It's over,' mumbled the figure that was once Billy Swan, the professional footballer, bon-viveur, full of swaggering arrogance.

'What's over, Billy? Where is everybody?'

Billy Swan dragged the sleeve of his blue shirt across his eyes, mopping away both sweat and tears, but not the dark anguish gnawing at his soul.

'They've gone, Jon. It's done. It's over.'

There was little doubt in Moreton's mind that the answers he was seeking would be anything but reassuring. Despite that, it hardly dimmed the incessantly urgent need to know.

'I don't understand, Billy. Christ, have they all just decided to piss off, because we lost.' Then he shook his head slowly. 'No. It's not that. I know them. It's not that. What is it?'

Billy Swan yanked the boot from his right foot, and hurled it against the wall on the other side of the room, before it fell at Jon Moreton's feet.

'I did it, Jon,' he said, his voice trembling with emotion. 'I did it. That's why they've gone.'

Moreton bent down and picked up the boot.

'No way, Billy. There's no way they'd just clear off because you missed a penalty and then sliced that clearance.' He threw the boot down again. 'No sodding way, Billy.'

Swan looked up at him, and now there was almost a hint of anger in his eyes.

'Miss a penalty? Do you think I'd miss a penalty, unless I meant to? You don't even know me, do you? Can't you work it out?'

The look on Jon Moreton's face clearly illustrated that he couldn't.

'Look,' Swan said, waving at the bench opposite him. 'You'd better sit down, Jon. I meant to miss the penalty. I scored the own goal on purpose, didn't I?'

'What? Why?'

'Why do you, think, Jon, huh? Charlie, soddin' Broome. He never wanted to get the cub promoted, Jon. Never. He wanted it to fail. He needed it to fail.

'It's all about money, Jon,' he continued. 'Did he ever tell you that, when he bought that business up the road, another company was after it as well?'

Almost without realising it, Moreton nodded slowly as the memory of the conversation with Charlie Broome echoed in his head.

'Wait a minute... that's why I knew the name: Cerámica Internacional were the people that Charlie outbid to buy the business. And they own Atlético Santa Kristina.'

'No,' Swan said. 'He didn't outbid them. They brought him in to buy it. They wanted it, the location was good, but it was too small for them to develop properly and with the housing being built on the other side, the only possible place to expand the land was...'

'The football club.'

Swan nodded.

'The problem was that they already owned this other club, and couldn't own two. Otherwise, they'd have bought the business and the club, knocked down the club and expanded the business. So, they needed someone, and heard that your *mate*—' He spat out the word '—was looking for business opportunities. They approached him and set up a deal. He'd buy the business, somehow kill off the club, and then sell the business and premises of the club to them for a big profit.'

'That can't be true...' Deep down though, he knew it was. 'But why would he bring me in? Why would he bring you in? That cost him money, I know, and it made the team better. It doesn't make sense.'

Swan replied after another wipe of his sleeve across the face.

'He brought you in because he thought you'd fail. After though, he brought me in case you didn't: Billy Swan – plan B. He'd already got shot of the last coach. Giving him the elbow after the club was relegated, even though it was Broome who flogged off all the best players. He knew though that if the deal was to go through, he needed it to at least look like he was trying to save the club.'

The words were slowly sinking in, and Jon Moreton began to feel physically ill.

'Remember I told you I was in big trouble? I owed money to people who would break your legs if they were bored and wanted something to do to pass an hour or two. You don't owe these guys brass, unless you want to find out what hospital food is like, Jon. Then Broome turns up and offers to pay off the debts if I come and play in Spain and guarantee to screw you over and make sure the club fails.'

Rage was growing inside Moreton

'Jon, I tried to tell you, but...'

Moreton jumped in as Swan hesitated. 'But what, Billy? But you wanted to carry on being a prat and pissing your money up the wall, so you pissed on me instead?'

'Yeah, something like that. I guess that's how it looks. You know me. I'm a right prick. It ain't about the football, it's about the dosh. That's me. Shaft my mates for a tenner.'

'I don't believe you, Billy. It looked to me like you were enjoying your football again. What about the three musketeers? The laughs we've had? I saw something in your desire to play.'

'You carry on believing that, if it makes you feel better about it.'

'Christ, Billy,' Moreton said, regaining a little composure. 'Do you know what you've done?'

Billy Swan raised his hand and rubbed his forehead. 'Yeah, I know. I've screwed everybody. You, the lads. Christ, even Meldrew and Kiki Dee. They liked me, Jon. They liked me. Me? This total tosser. Me. They liked me. Now they hate my sodding guts. I screwed it up.'

He lifted his head again.

'You've got to understand though, Jon. Those guys would have maimed, me. Bad. I needed that dosh. I had no choice. I had to do Broome's bidding. That's why I got myself sent off. Why I had to say I had a bad back. Things were going too well.'

Each second was bringing a new and increasingly unpleasant fact into the daylight.

'You mean when you fell down the stairs? Christ, did he push you?' To Jon Moreton, anything now seemed possible.

Swan shook his head. 'I didn't fall down the stairs, Jon. It was a con. He made sure that you were there to witness it so that it would be convincing. I was already sitting on the stairs, and we just kicked the ground a few times to make it sound like I'd slipped.'

Moreton was confused.

'But what about that doctor? What about Simon? Was he involved as well?'

Swan shook his head once more. 'There was no fall, Jon. There was no Simon. He didn't exist. It was all bullshit. He just lied to you. Then when it looked like you might still get promoted, he had to get me back into the team so that I could make sure it was all screwed up.'

The last five minutes or so had, without question, been the worst of Jon Moreton's life. Things he had held dear, were suddenly ripped mercilessly from him, thrown into the gutter and stamped on. Then a thought struck him.

'No. It's not over. There's still the play-off. We can still make it. We can still get promotion and fuck that twat's plans up.'

He reached for the mobile in his pocket. 'I'll ring Sophia. She can get the guys back. We can still do it. You though,' he said angrily, pointing at Swan. 'You are fucked. Why don't you just piss off and collect your blood money.'

Moreton tapped in the number and herd the ringing tone. Billy Swan hadn't heeded the advice, though. He sat there. Head bowed. Unmoved.

A minute or so passed, before Moreton closed the phone down. 'She's not answering.'

'She won't,' Swan muttered.

Moreton looked at the man still dressed in the blue colours of Club Deportivo Retama. Someone he thought he knew. Someone he looked upon as a friend, but now someone who appeared to be a total stranger.

'What? Why wouldn't she answer?'

Swan couldn't look at the man, who now loathed his very presence. 'She won't answer, 'cos that's all screwed up as well.' He spoke to the floor. His self-respect and mood were at precisely the same level.

Jon Moreton feared there was even worse to come. He was right.

Still speaking to the floor, Swan explained: 'This was all part of it. He wanted nothing left to chance. After this game he wanted to ensure that there was no way back. No recovery. That promotion was stuffed. The club was dead and buried.'

Swan rose to his feet slowly. Turning to the wall behind, he banged his head against the blue painted concrete. Once. Twice. Then turning back to Moreton, with blood oozing from wounds above his right eye and across the bridge of his nose, he delivered the worst of it.

'I had to tell them you were involved. You were all part of the plan. He'd bought you as well, and you were always going to stuff the club. You putting me on in the last minutes of the game made it look so real as well. You shouldn't have made me take that pen. I've fucked everything up, Jon.'

He looked down at the floor and then up again at the devastated Jon Moreton. 'They hate you even more than they hate me.'

A sharp pain shot through Moreton's mind.

'Sophia…'

'They wouldn't even hit me, the lads. I wanted them to. They hated me. Shit, I hated myself. I still do. But none of them would hit me. They shouted and threatened, but never hit me. I wish they'd have killed me.'

He stopped for a moment. Jon Moreton looked on, stunned by it all, but apparently still lost in thought.

Then once more, Swan banged his against the wall, leaving trickles of blood dripping down the blue paint.

'If they won't do it. I will,' he said, hitting the wall for the fourth time.

'Sophia! What about Sophia? Was she there? What did she say?'

New wounds had opened up on Swan's face, but the emotional hurt he was about to deliver would sting much more deeply.

'At first, she called me a liar. She defended you, Jon. Said it couldn't be true, but then Paco and the others started talking to her in Spanish. I don't know what they were saying, but she shouted and they shouted. Then she didn't say anything. She just cried, and Paco took her away.'

Moreton grabbed his phone again and tapped in the number. The ringing tone merely mocked his anxiety though. Constant, unchanging.

'Sophia!' He shouted at the emotionless phone. The ringtone merely continued. 'Shit,' he said, closing down the phone.

Billy Swan slumped back down on the bench. He'd unburdened himself of the secret that he'd carried for so long, and that had played out over the last hour or so, but there was no relief for him in that. Jon Moreton thrust the phone into his pocket and, after one further condemning look at his former friend, he raced out of the dressing room, sprinting across the pitch and towards the gates of the Estadio Antonio Núñez. His journey would take less than five minutes.

After hearing a few heated voices outside of the door, Charlie Broome took a deep breath, and sat back in his chair behind the desk as the door of his office burst open.

'You shit! What are you fucking on, Charlie? You've screwed everyone over, just for a bit of extra money.'

Walking with determined purpose towards where Charlie Broome was sitting, he threw the chair placed for him in front of Broome's desk to one side, placing both hands on the wooden surface, with red face, and eyes streaming with rage and tears.

'You screwed me. You've pissed all over my life.'

On the other side of the desk, Charlie Broome leaned back in his chair. It was more intended to keep a safe distance between himself and the out of control Moreton than any act of nonchalance, but unsurprisingly, it didn't seem that way to the furious interloper.

'Got your deal, have you? Got your twenty pieces of silver?'

Charlie Broome had been preparing himself for this moment for many months. He'd prefer for it not to have happened, but if it was the price to pay for seeing his plans come to fruition, he would willingly settle the bill.

'Jon, I know how it looks, but these things happen in business. It's just the way it goes.'

The calm demeanour of another former friend of Jon Moreton was intended to pour oil on violently troubled water, but it was received like petrol poured on flames instead.

'No, these things don't just "happen" – not with normal people. Just with twats like you who sell people for money and betray their friends.'

'Betrayal?' Broome said with unsuppressed, but largely affected, anger. 'Let's talk about betraying friends, shall we? You soon pissed off and left me with those twats at Ridgeway when a chance came along didn't you? What about me? It was a nightmare there after you'd gone. Why do you think I packed it in, Jon? Eh?'

'That's bullshit. I'm not your sodding dad. That was a chance to chase my dream. You'd have done the same thing.'

Broome had been expecting such a reply to his accusation.

'Yeah, well. Perhaps I needed a dad. My own wasn't much use. Never there. Tried to buy me off. I needed someone – a big brother – but you pissed off as well. And, let's be clear,' he said tapping the desk pointedly. 'You had your dream. This was mine. Yours was screwed up, but that's not happening to mine. Remember you said you owed me big time when I got you that coaching job with the old man's club and then the job over here? Well, I called the marker in.'

'How many lives have you screwed over just so that another company can step in and earn you a few grand? How many lives, for how much, in this town?'

'You think all this, all of what I've done, was about this little deal here?' There was clear contempt in his voice. He slumped down in his chair, clasping his hands together, and putting them on top of the desk.

'This,' he said, separating his hands and waving his arm in the air. 'Is just the hors d'oeuvre. The main course is back in England.'

Detecting a clear lack of comprehension in Moreton's demeanour, the final pieces of Charlie Broome's elaborate deception were about to be revealed.

'Yeah, I set up a deal with Cerámica Internacional to buy this place and CD Retama, kill off the club, then sell both to them for a nice profit so that they can build the big complex they want, but that's not my plan. That involves a bit of pay back.'

Jon Moreton detected a selfish pride in the scheme that Charlie Broome had hatched, and he detested him even more for it.

'You see,' Broome continued. 'They also want to expand outside of Spain, if they could find something ready-made to buy that would continue to earn profit as they developed it. And I knew just the place. Remember what I told you about my deal with the old man?' He didn't wait for an answer. 'Well, now this is all sorted, I can take the brass from Cerámica Internacional, use that to make him honour the deal, sell me the shares, and make me an equal partner. Then, that leaves the accountant holding the balance, and free to make any decision, no longer obligated to support the majority shareholder, because there isn't one. Got it?'

Sat in his chair, boasting to someone of his plans, and wallowing in his own perceived genius was now becoming almost perverse fun for Charlie Broome.

'So,' he continued. 'The CI guys are going to come in with a bid to buy Broome Interiors.' The last two words were delivered with a flourish, as some conjurer revelling in his magical powers, displaying the girl now apparently sawn in half.

'Of course,' he continued. 'The old man will say no, but I'll be in favour and, seeing as the accountant has been promised that he'll be retained for the new company, and assured that it will remain so as the business develops across the UK, it'll go through.'

He opened his palms upwards inviting Moreton to accept the overwhelming case for his business acumen, then added: 'Oh yeah, plus I'm getting a directorship in the new firm, but won't be expected to do too much. Just pop in and show my face occasionally, to keep the Broome name linked, and then spend the money they're giving me for my shares. And that's a nice tidy sum.'

Jon Moreton was beginning to face the reality that two people he had considered friends had each betrayed him, albeit one because of malign design and the other due to weakness. Inevitably, he was drawn to the clear conclusion that he knew very little about people.

'I can't believe how many people have you screwed up?' He paused. 'Even your dad!'

'Your dad is supposed to be there for you, to help you, guide you. He was never there to do any of those things. It killed my mother as well. I never knew her. Do you know what it's like never to have known your mother? He screwed us both over for his business, so this is a bit of a pay back.'

For all his anger and resentment, Moreton recognised that the losses, and perceived betrayals in Broome's life had been a big factor in bringing him to this point. He felt like collateral damage in a family feud. The melancholy that had swept over Broome also seemed to have brought some recognition of the harm he had caused to Jon Moreton.

'Look, Jon,' he said. 'To be honest, I never meant to hurt you. I thought that you'd come over here, give it your best shot, but... ,' he hesitated.

'But fail?' Moreton finished the sentence.

Broome nodded slowly, with hot pangs of remorse at last penetrating the frozen wastelands of his conscience.

'Yes, you were supposed to fail! I had to bring in someone who looked good on paper – to make it look like I was serious – but I'd already made the job impossible – it was a zombie club: I'd binned their experienced manager, left them with only a handful of kids and a couple of has-beens. It was supposed to be impossible even for Saint Jon Morton with his Protestant work ethic. But can't you see, despite that, I was doing a favour to an old mate, too? Failing to save the club wouldn't be your fault, you'd have some foreign coaching experience on your CV and you'd still have had some fun along the way.

'Then when you came to me with the idea of Swan, it was an opportunity too good to miss. An insurance policy just in case you did pull off some sort of saintly bloody miracle. The man's a wastrel and always will be, but he served his purpose. I bought him out of trouble for now, but he'll scuttle back to England with his tail between his legs, blow all the money I gave him and be back wallowing in shit in a few months' time.'

As Broome spoke, the validity of his prediction appeared all too accurate for Moreton, and the anger he had felt at the betrayal by the bloodied figure of the broken man probably still sitting in the CD Retama dressing room wiping blood and tears from his face, began to dissipate.

'What about me, Charlie?' Moreton said as the image of Billy Swan merely reignited his anger. 'Am I supposed to scuttle back to England as well. Battered, but better prepared for a world where your supposed friends queue up to stab you in the back and then leave you lying in the gutter?'

Surprisingly, Charlie Broome seemed a little insulted by the accusation.

'No, Jon. Not at all. You were also part of the plan. I'd spoken with some of the guys at CI, and set it up for you to get a job with Atlético Santa Kristina, no matter how it went. To be honest, when they saw what a job you were doing with that shower down the road, they were really keen to get you into the club anyway. They'll pay you good money, find you an apartment near the ground and, with their money backing the club, they're on the up and up. You could do really well there. Plus, I've put a bit of a bonus into your pay this month. I'm sorry about Sophia. That was never meant to happen. I thought you might indulge in a bit of fun there for a while, but I never thought you'd end up seriously involved. I can try and get her a post at the club as well if you like.'

He paused, as Moreton simply stared at him.

'Would that help?'

There was no reply.

'Jon,' he repeated. 'Would that help?'

'Help? Are you joking? She's gone. I've lost her. That bollocks you made Billy say after the game has convinced her that I'm the kind of shit that would take handouts from twats like you.'

He paused for a moment, looking down at the floor with a thousand thoughts running through his head. 'You know what, Charlie? I ought to chin you right here and now. It wouldn't solve this unholy mess, but it would be something of a payback for all the people you've pissed on.'

As he had been practising this conversation in his mind, Charlie Broome had always considered that it may come to this. He'd made his peace with what seemed highly likely to happen. A punch would cause pain, but it would pass in a couple of hours, and he would still be immensely rich. Again, he'd willingly settle the bill. The invoice was never delivered though.

'Stuff your blood money and your job, you piece of shit. I wouldn't touch them.'

On that, Jon Moreton turned and left Charlie Broome's office, slamming the door behind him.

Even before reaching the foot of the stairs, he was calling Sophia's number again. Still no answer. Before he had reached the apartment, he had tried five more times. Still the ringing tone was the only response he received. Reaching the complex, instead of climbing the stairs to his own apartment to the left, he'd turned right instead. Reaching the door where he had so often seen Sophia standing, he thumped on it urgently, but to no avail. With knuckles bleeding from the insistent question that was never answered, he returned to his own apartment. Closing the door behind him, he sank onto the sofa, putting his head in his hands, and sobbed.

Just then, a text message arrived on his phone. It was from Sophia. Any initial elation quickly turned to despair though. *I've spoken to Alvaro and am going to him in the morning. I can be happy with him. Never try to contact me again.* The words were cold, and chilled Moreton to the very soul.

Fifteen minutes later, he closed down his iPad after completing the necessary transaction. It was the only bit of Charlie Broome's money that he would take. It was now well into the evening and he decided to make one more call to Sophia. He tapped in the number, reluctant to hit the final key that would invite the inevitable return of the ringtone that would never be answered. After a pause, he hit the key and the tone duly arrived. This time though he waited until the answerphone kicked in. He had to tell her the truth.

He spoke in a voice quivering with emotion. 'Sophia,' he said softly. 'I know what Billy told you. What he told you all. It isn't true. I knew nothing about it. Billy was being blackmailed by Charlie Broome. I wasn't involved at all. Sophia, you have to believe me.'

He'd planned what to say, but quickly drifted off script, as desperate emotion guided the way instead.

'Sophia, please. Please. Please believe me. If you ever loved me, you'd know it wasn't true. I couldn't do anything like that. Please call me. Let's talk. Please.'

He closed the phone and put it down by his side on the sofa, but decided that there was one more thing he could say. If there was any chance of him convincing of the truth, any chance of seeing her again, any chance of speaking to her, he had to try.

He picked up the phone again, tapped in the number and waited while his unlamented friend, the ringtone, engaged with him once more. Waiting for the answerphone, he spoke to the woman he had fallen in love with, who had now been torn from his life.

'Look Sophia. I can only tell the truth. If you believe me. If only a small part of you believes me, then please call. I have to know that there's a chance for us. I can't stand being here in Spain, so close to you, but so far away. If you don't call, I'll have my answer. Please don't give me that answer. I have a flight to England booked for lunch time. I can't be here in Retama without you. If you want to call me. I'll be here until ten tomorrow morning. Please call me. I can't bear not holding you, not seeing you, not knowing about you. By ten please, Sophia. *Te quiero.*'

He closed the phone and, having little else to do, went to bed. The night was full of restless sleep interrupted by disturbing dreams. Each time Moreton awoke the dawning reality appeared far worse than the places that his unconscious mind had taken him to. The place next to him, so recently so occupied by the woman who had taken his heart remained empty; cold and empty.

The following morning, unsure how many hours he had slept, if at all, he woke, immediately reaching for the phone he had placed on the chest of drawers by the side of his bed. It told of the story he had dreaded. No incoming calls. He showered, dressed, and placed a few things in the bag he had brought with him all those months ago. He wanted nothing that had been tainted with Charlie Broome's supposed largesse. As he sat down for a light breakfast, the clock had already ticked round to 9.15. Another glance at the phone. Still no calls. He cleared the breakfast things and tidied the apartment as best he could, leaving all of the clothes that he had bought with the money paid to him by Broome sitting in a neatly folded pile on the bed.

When the clock cruelly moved its hands round to ten o'clock, Jon Moreton let out a deep sigh that spread into a sob, before wiping a tear away from his eyes. He put the uncooperative phone back down on the table he had picked it up from, when first entering the apartment. He closed the shutters damning it into a cold darkness very much reflective of his soul, collected his bag and left, walking the hundred metres or so to where a couple of white taxis sat in the rank, awaiting custom.

Walking over to the first one, he opened the door. '*Aeropuerto, por favor?*' He asked. '*Vale,*' came the reply. He climbed in as the driver threw his bag into the boot, before returning to the driver's seat. The car pulled out, drove forwards to the island where workers were already replacing the name on the building that had formerly, albeit briefly, been Broome Cerámica. Checking his watch, he saw it was five minutes past ten.

Back in the dark apartment, bereft of sunlight, a mobile phone sitting on a table, burst into life. The name illuminated on the screen said 'Sophia' but all the caller could hear was the unforgiving, uncaring, unsympathetic ringtone.

Acknowledgements

As my first somewhat naive journey into fiction, this work has been particularly challenging. At such times, the experienced guidance of a publisher is invaluable. I'd like to acknowledge my sincere thanks to Steven Kay of 1889 Books for his tireless work, infinite patience and professionalism in assisting in the production this novel. Without his help and diligent attention, I'm not sure it would have got to this stage.